PALINGENESIS

PHOENIX DIARIES: BOOK ONE

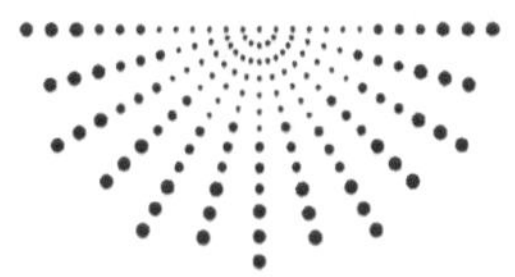

TYERONE M JOHNSON

Cover design by Rocko Spigolon

ISBN: 978-1-952972-00-3 (paperback)

ISBN: 978-1-952972-01-0 (hardback)

This book is dedicated to my father, William Johnson, who instilled in me a love of reading and storytelling; to my mother, Michelle Johnson, who fiercely advocated for me and my health; to my Composition teacher, Mr. Dull, who believed in me when I didn't; and to every geeky, LGBTQ+ person of color who thinks their narratives and lives don't matter.

This one's for you.

Who looks outsides, dreams; who looks inside, awakens.

— CARL JUNG

CONTENTS

Hey   ix
Trigger Warnings   xi

Chapter 1   1
Chapter 2   12
Chapter 3   19
Chapter 4   26
Chapter 5   33
Chapter 6   38
Chapter 7   45
Chapter 8   49
Chapter 9   53
Chapter 10   60
Chapter 11   67
Chapter 12   72
Chapter 13   77
Chapter 14   83
Chapter 15   89
Chapter 16   99
Chapter 17   109
Chapter 18   116
Chapter 19   121
Chapter 20   128
Chapter 21   133
Chapter 22   143
Chapter 23   150
Chapter 24   162
Chapter 25   173
Chapter 26   184
Chapter 27   191
Chapter 28   203
Chapter 29   211

Chapter 30   222
Chapter 31   234
Chapter 32   239
Chapter 33   248
Chapter 34   256
Chapter 35   259
Chapter 36   266
Chapter 37   272
Chapter 38   278
Chapter 39   283
Chapter 40   295
Chapter 41   305
Chapter 42   313
Chapter 43   323
Epilogue   326

It Gets Better   331
Acknowledgments   333
Afterword   335
About the Author   337

HEY

For updates on this series and other books join my mailing list at tyeronejohnson.com/mailinglist

TRIGGER WARNINGS

Content / Trigger Warnings:
This book does contain language and references to events and subjects that may be triggering to some readers. I will list those here so that readers may protect themselves from these subjects by preparing as best they can or even choosing not to read. None of these is included in a gratuitous manner, everything is plot-relevant, but I mention them anyway out of respect for my reader.
Suicidal ideation; Self-harm (ideation & action); Police brutality (including reference to real events), Racial slurs including n-word; Homophobic slurs and homophobic language; Intellectual disability slurs; Sexist slurs; Reference to school shootings (no reference to real events); Sexual assault

CHAPTER ONE

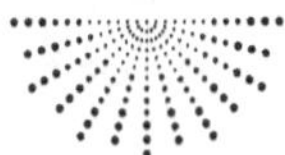

Intelligence, strength, loyalty, generosity, heroism. The name Travis Turner is synonymous with them all. But to understand the man, we must venture back to when he was a boy who'd yet to learn that heroes aren't born; they're forged in the crucible of adversity. And that the greatest force in the multiverse is hope.

The year was 2017, and children in khakis and red blazers embroidered with the crest of Azure Plains Preparatory Academy (a shield with a large fleur-de-lis, inscribed with "children are our future" in Latin underneath) laughed and hurled soggy snowballs at each while upperclassmen had their faces buried in their phones, occasionally looking up to shoot the younger students dirty looks when they got too close.

But our would-be hero wasn't a fan of such plebeian sport. Instead, Travis was ensconced in his native habitat, Ms. Martin's English class, eating lunch as they tried stumping each other.

"All right, smartass, define perspicacity for me." She folded her arms, a smug smile splitting her wrinkled face wide.

Travis licked the mayo off his lips. "It means having shrewdness or insight into things. For example, used-car salesmen are a cunning lot and demonstrate ample perspicacity. From the Latin *perspicere*, meaning—"

"Cut the crap. We both know you could teach my twelfth grade Honors English class easily."

He paused eating and cocked his head to the side, worry bubbling up in his stomach. "I'm sensing a 'but' coming."

She steepled her fingers. "While I enjoy your company, I think you should spend lunch in the cafeteria or playing in the quad. Otherwise, how will you make friends?"

He rose, throwing his half-eaten turkey sandwich in the trash on the way out.

"Hold up. I didn't—"

He shot her a cold look. "No. You've made it clear you don't want me around."

I'll leave, and we'll return to our normal pedagogue-pupil rela-tionship.

Before she had a chance to reply, he was out the door, heading to the bleachers where he'd eaten his lunch before he was stupid enough to befriend her.

"Beep, beep. Wide load coming through," Keith Maxwell barked as Travis passed him. He ignored Maxwell until the older boy yanked on his arm, twisting it behind Travis's back.

"When I talk to you, you reply. Comprende, shit head?" He yanked Travis's arm again, almost dislocating it.

Travis pictured Maxwell lying at his feet, begging for mercy, and smiled.

"What's got you so happy, freak boy?" Maxwell said, loosening his grip.

"Nothing." He pulled his arm free and walked on to the athletics wing.

"Kid, you need to stand up for yourself," his headmate said.

Right. News at seven: Travis Turner gunned down by cops. No thanks. He scoffed at the voice in his head and carried on until he spotted JJ Giovanni with his sycophants.

His stomach twisted in knots.

What will it be today?

"Hey, Turner," Giovanni said in the grating tone Travis had come to hate. "Settle our argument. I say you got acid poured on your face, while Mitchells here says you're like a mutant. So, which is it?"

He shoved past them. "Neither!"

"Someone's on her period," Giovanni called after him. Their laughter echoed off the walls, trailing him as he strode down the hall, rage and shame warring inside him as he willed his tears not to fall.

Stop it. Crying solves nothing.

He spent the rest of his lunch hour under the bleachers. When he entered Ms. Martin's class, he didn't return her greeting or answer any questions about last night's reading assignment unless she called on him.

The rest of the day passed uneventfully, and when he got home, he did his homework, ignoring the raucous noise the twins (Bobby and Amber) and their friends made. By dinnertime, he'd finished most of his homework.

After setting the table, he slumped in his seat as his mother said grace.

"How was your day?" she said.

And it begins. "Fine, Mother," he said, forcing himself not to scream.

She stuck her nose in the air, her lips curling back into a grimace. "Don't get snippy with me, or I'll ground your ass."

"Sorry, Mother. It was fine. And no. I didn't make any friends."

"Course ya didn't, jerkwad," Bobby said, sticking out his tongue, "with a face like that, who'd want to hang with ya?"

He kicked Bobby under the table, and Bobby whined to their mom.

"Travis, you know better. Apologize."

"But he—"

"I said apologize, or you'll go without dinner."

He gave Amber a look that said, 'Can you believe this ish?' but she was too busy on her phone, her fingers a blur.

"I'm sorry." *That you're such a weakling, you can't fight your own battles.*

After suffering through his mother's interrogation (she ought to have gone into law enforcement), Travis excused himself to his room and finished his homework. When he was done, he locked the door and put a chair under the handle so he wouldn't be disturbed.

He removed the loose floorboard under his bed and retrieved his grandfather's pocketknife. As the worn handle settled in his hand, his breath hitched. Travis lifted his right sleeve and looked from his arm to the bloodstained blade.

He hesitated a moment, the blade catching the overhead light, twinkling like a star.

No, I promised Jenny I would do this anymore.

He put the pocketknife in his dresser and then opened the Harry Potter wand coding kit he'd been meaning to try out. After two hours off troubleshooting, he got it working and then grew bored. Opening his junk drawer, he removed his tool kit and a few spare parts, setting to work.

Ninety minutes later, he swished his wand, and a laser beam emitted from the tip.

"Whoot!"

He swished the wand again, and it exploded, singeing his eyebrows.

Well, I know not to try that again. He smiled until his mother banged on his door. After he explained what happened, she banned him from "tinkering" for two weeks.

So, he played video games a while before turning to his copy of Mary Shelly's *Frankenstein*, which Ms. Martin had assigned two weeks prior. After reading a few chapters, he tossed the book aside and went over the incident with her.

I was a fool to let her in.

He looked toward his dresser but shook his head. To occupy himself, Travis went to his lab in the garage and worked on Cha, the robot he'd built and had been trying to program to do the Cha-Cha slide. Cha had fully functioning hydraulic arms, a camera, and mecanum wheels that allowed it to move in any direction. The parts had cost him five months' allowance, but it was so worth it.

He typed in the last line of code, hit execute, and it jerked to life, getting halfway through its routine when it stopped.

"Ugh," he growled. "Not again. What am I doing wrong?"

By the time he'd found the bug, it was too late to try again, so he called it a night, vowing to get it right tomorrow.

The weekend passed without much incident, and soon it was Sunday night. Travis tossed and turned, but every time he drifted off to sleep, he dreamt about The Fire. The pain like being stung with a million hornets at once, the heat like bathing in a volcano, but the worst was the smell of burnt hair and flesh. He'd never forget that. He'd been having the dream for the last month, and each time it felt more intense, more real, like his skin were on fire again.

Around midnight he abandoned all hopes of getting any sleep, dressed, and went for a walk, taking his pocketknife with him. For safety, he rationalized.

His thoughts turned to school the next day.

Everyone walks around so jubilant, taunting me with their stupid smiles. Nice to your face, then stab you in the heart the first chance they get. They don't know what it's like to just want to be normal. God, I just want to bash their stupid happy faces in. And Giovanni's the worst ever, walking around with all his friends, laughing and smiling. But what do I have to be happy about?

"Nothing!" Travis's voice rang out through the deserted cul-de-sac. A wind picked up, and he wrapped his arms around himself, shivering until it passed.

As he walked the rain-soaked street, his thoughts drifted back to the last time he was happy: the night he died. Clutching his chest, he remembered the paddles slamming into him over and over again.

"Do you know how annoying listening to you wangst is?" said his headmate.

Travis groaned. *What do you want?*

"For you to shut up and nut up."

What?

"Don't what me, asshole. You don't know how sucky it is being stuck inside such a weakling. You're a freak? Oh, boo-hoo. Grow a pair already," it said and then was gone.

Memories of life before the accident rushed back to Travis, when the least of his worries were getting to go out and play or avoiding the crazy nuns during Mass at St. Peter's. Try as he might, the tears wouldn't be denied their due this time.

As if in response to him, the wind picked up again, and the April drizzle became a deluge. Travis knew it would probably land him in the hospital, but then what didn't? Head tilted forward, he removed the hood of his favorite gray hoodie.

For the longest time, he stood there, the storm bearing witness to his pain.

Enough!

He tossed the hair out of his eyes and then clenched his fists so tight his stubby nails dug into his palms, drawing blood.

The tears stopped.

He put his soaked hood back on, shivering, and then berated himself for giving into such weakness. He knew better. Emotions, especially love, were pointless. They diverted time and energy that could be better spent elsewhere.

He ripped the pocketknife from his pants, rolled up his sleeve, and savaged the tan flesh of his arm. He replayed the scene between him and Ms. Martin again, berating himself for being so stupid.

The pale moonlight reflected off the edge of the blade as he slashed the back of his forearm from wrist to elbow. The metallic scent of blood filled the night air, and the warmth of inflammation overtook him once more. Although a pale comparison, it reminded him of the abyss he found himself in the night he died.

And at last, he was at peace.

He knew he should have felt pain, and on some level, he supposed he did. Yet only a dead emptiness filled him as he calculated how much gauze and disinfectant would be needed. The cold sensation of congealed blood intertwining with his searing skin intrigued him.

God, I'm such a freak. And no matter how hard I try, that's all I'll ever be.

Then he wondered . . . *Should I end it all?*

No!

He couldn't do that, wouldn't do that. He'd come too far, been through too much to allow *them* to win. He was better than that, better than them, stronger than that.

"Earth to Travis, done with your period yet?"

Self-mutilation? Menses? Ha, good one.

"Thank you, thank you very much. Now, if you're done being all extra, can we go home?"

Fine.

Before Travis could take a step, like a crack of thunder, another voice boomed in his ears, chilling him to the core:

"Blood will rain from the heavens."

In the next instant, Travis was transported to a nightmare world. The sky was pitch-black, the only light from a sea of flames that stretched out as far as he could see. All around him, islands of bones and corpses were piled high into the sky. The stench of rotting flesh and death choked him, and he swallowed back vomit, disgusted but curious more than anything else.

In the distance stood a massive throne that he felt pulled to. Travis shook his head. He must be dreaming. But if this was a dream, then he might as well make the most of it and explore.

As he ventured closer, he spotted a figure upon the throne that rooted him to the spot. The figure was him, only pure white, as though drained of all his color.

"Blood will rain from the heavens," it said again. *"Ash will fill the air. The dark prince will reign on a throne of despair, and all will know his pain. Corpses will cover the land, and none will he spare. As water turns to fire, the sleeper will awaken and herald the end of everything. From my desire—"*

"Hey, I'm happy for you, and Imma let ya finish. But everybody knows Macbeth had one of the best prophecies of all time, man. All-time," he quipped.

The ground shuddered and cracked wide open under him. White tentacles burst forth toward him.

Travis ran, his legs pumping as he struggled to put distance between them. Every fiber of his being screamed for him to flee, his heart doing flip flops, terror unlike anything he'd experienced flooding through him. Goosebumps covered his arms as he swung them in time with his pistoning feet. His chest tightened, his breaths coming in shallows fits as he fought to fill his lungs.

Running proved futile as the tentacles overcame him and wrapped him in their vice-like grip. Travis struggled to free himself yet only succeeded in worsening his imprisonment.

Strolling toward him, the demonic doppelganger exuded smugness and triumph as he spoke. *"Insolent whelp. You speak of matters far beyond your station. The war between good and evil has raged throughout countless eons but always ends in a stalemate."* It paused, coming face-to-face with Travis. *"You could change that. Join me, and you will have untold power."*

Travis looked up at the creature looming above him. "What kind . . . of power?"

"The kind to make your bullies wish they were never born."

Travis pondered this a moment. "What would I have to do?"

It smiled. *"Allow me into your heart, and it is done."*

"Oh no, kid. You don't want none of what this guy's offering. He's major bad news. Stick with me."

"No one asked you," the creature said, and Travis paused.

They can hear each other? Yup, I've finally gone crazy.

"Crazier, you mean. And as for you," his headmate said, addressing the creature. *"Keep playing and see if I don't kick yo punk ass back to whatever rock you crawled out from under."*

"I will not be spoken to in such a familiar way."

The creature and his headmate continued arguing, each trying to convince him not to accept the other until Travis shouted, "Shut up!"

A cataclysmic explosion rocked the landscape as an ever-expanding blue inferno obliterated everything in Travis's wake. The tentacles retreated to their master, and the discombobulated look on its face made Travis smile.

Travis looked at the devastation he wrought and let loose a maniacal laugh. Face set in a determined grimace, nostrils flaring, jaw clenched tight, veins bulging on his forehead, Travis charged forward, determined to defeat it.

A yard separated them, but then it flung Travis backward, and he lost his balance. Catching himself, Travis rolled forward and had the sudden urge to flung out his hand. A wall of fire erupted from his hand and blasted the creature.

"Cool," he said, even as he winced, his hand burning and the air filling with the scent of charred flesh.

It dropped to one knee. Then erected a white shield around itself.

"I take it back. You are strong. But then you are my vessel. No matter. You will comply."

Spurred on by the creature's challenge, Travis unleashed every ounce of power he had in a torrent of fire and fists. But the shield remained. The creature laughed and tossed him aside like a ragdoll.

Every part of him aching, Travis struggled to regain his footing. Just drawing breath was an exercise. Then Travis collapsed onto the scorched earth, convulsing.

The creature lowered its shield and impaled Travis with its tentacles.

Unbelievable pain flooded Travis's body, and he knew this was the end. With every second, he felt the life flowing out of him and the monster taking over his body. The bitter taste of blood filled his mouth, and the coldness in his chest spread ever wider. He groaned in agony.

"Yield and your suffering will end. Resist, and it will be legendary," it said.

No, I can't let it end like this.

I don't care whether this is a dream or a hallucination. I didn't care how long it takes or how painful it is. I will reign victorious.

All my life, I've been a victim. Never once have I stood up for myself. If I die here, it will not be on my knees.

He stood, head held high.

"Aw, is baby about to cry?"

"Shut up. You don't know the first thing about me. You think I will bow down because you say so? Hell no!"

Searing tears streamed down Travis's cheeks as he ripped himself free. The creature's tentacles evaporated into plumes of smoke, and Travis lumbered forward, fueled by an ever-rising fury born of a lifetime of repressed emotions.

He no longer saw the creature but all those who ever made him feel weak. Everyone who ever picked on him or made him feel left out, like he was a freak. He saw their mocking faces, and something inside him broke.

The cry of a great bird issued forth.

Then he saw an infinite horde crying out for justice, for retribution. And at last, Travis would answer them.

As a scream bellowed from him, the creature's domain was ripped asunder, its throne crumbling as Travis's blue inferno consumed it. It attacked him again. But this time, Travis would not fall. The creature's tentacles weren't enough to satisfy his flames; he hungered for all of it.

Eyes narrowed to slits, face set in a grim expression, the creature raised its shield, but one blast from Travis shattered it into a thousand shards, sending the creature to its knees.

Travis laughed, his body turning into a sea of black flames, the conflagration pouring from him as he hurled it toward the creature.

It pushed back the wall of flames with a beam of white energy. *"Fool! You haven't won anything. I am that which is ageless, the darkness which dwells in the hearts of all; that great dragon, the progenitor of the eternal sea of evil. I am Oblivion."*

"My name is Travis Turner, and I am done being anyone's victim." He poured everything he had into the wall of flames, and it enveloped Oblivion.

"You are mine through and through. Even now, I feel your hatred

growing, hear your soul calling out to maim and murder. We will meet again, and you will yield," Oblivion said and then faded away.

"I'll be ready."

"Correction: we'll be ready. What now, genius?"

Before Travis could reply, his legs went weak, and his vision darkened.

The last thing he was conscious of was the sensation of weightlessness as though he were being carried along a wave of liquid energy.

Then it stopped. Why or how, he didn't know, and he slipped into a deep sleep.

But how can you dream in a dream?

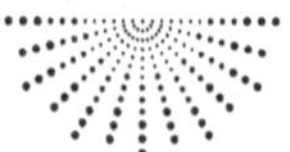

CHAPTER TWO

*T*ravis awoke to his body aching all over, especially his face, limbs feeling like they weighed a ton. His head pounded like the percussion section of MSU's marching band. Through his groggy fog, Travis heard his alarm, rolled over, and shut it off.

He felt as though he hadn't slept in days. But what caught his attention were the bandages on his left arm.

He didn't remember doing that, but he must have. Shrugging, he rolled out of bed, flipped on the bedside lamp, and checked the aftermath of last night's little mishap. Though the gauze was covered in blood, there were no scars.

Okay, cue the Twilight Zone music.

Travis laid out his uniform, then gathered his undergarments for his morning ablution, praying to whatever gods may be that he was the first one up. He could *not* deal with a cold shower that morning on top of everything else.

Halfway to the bathroom, he spotted Bobby coming down the hall. They looked at each other a second before Bobby broke into a run. Travis hauled ass, but though Bobby was almost two years younger, he beat Travis, stopping at the door to do a victory dance.

"Beat you again, loser. Hope you like having shriveled nuts if you have any." He did another victory dance, wiggling his butt in Travis's face.

More than anything, Travis wanted in the bathroom right then.

To his amazement, the next instant he was standing behind Bobby, Travis's clothes slightly singed around the edges.

"Hey, where'd you go?"

He tapped Bobby on the shoulder, and the eleven-year-old whirled around, shock all over his face. "What the . . . You were there, but now you're here. How?"

"Don't know. Don't care. Scram!" He shoved Bobby out the door and locked it before setting his clothes out, only for severe nausea and stomach pains to wrack him. Doubled over, he fell to his knees and crawled to the toilet in time to coat the bowl with brownish-yellow bile.

What's going on?

When the strange sickness passed, Travis washed his mouth out. Heart racing, he checked his burn-scar-covered face out in the mirror. The skin around his right eye, a bright red, popped against his normal golden-brown complexion. So, he removed the burn ointment from the medicine cabinet and set it aside.

Once he got in the shower, no matter how hot he turned up the water, it felt as though he were bathing in the Arctic Sea. He soldiered through it, but when he got out, the mirror was foggy, as you'd expect after a hot shower.

This day keeps getting curiouser and curiouser.

When Travis dabbed the ointment on his face, he dropped some on his chest, and as he was cleaning it, he saw something that made his heart skip a beat.

On his chest were a set of fresh scars in the exact place Oblivion's tentacles had pierced him in the dream. And when he ran his finger across them, it was like touching a block of ice.

"Travis Marshall Turner, get your high-yellow behind out that bathroom this instance, or you're grounded."

He swore under his breath, rolling his eyes. It was too early to deal with her high-strung theatrics. Especially when he either might be going crazy or was the devil's vessel.

Swell options.

Shaking his head, he slipped on his underclothes and then high-tailed it to his room to iron his school blazer, dress shirt, and khakis. When he was done, he gave his loafers a quick shine, finished dressing, and grabbed his messenger bag.

God, why can't I go to Thurgood Marshall Middle School like everyone else in my neighborhood? At least then, I'd have a better chance at having friends. Stupid Opa and his will.

This was the umpteenth time in as many days he'd had this thought, but then he corrected himself.

"Rule Zero: People come into and out of our lives without reason, so we can only depend on ourselves. Say it again," he told himself until he was ready to face another day at AP Prep.

After eating a breakfast of Pop-Tarts and brushing his teeth, he asked his mother to drive him to the bus stop. She looked up from a stack of papers, expression grim, staring right through him.

"You pay any bills?"

He furrowed his brow. "Huh?"

"Don't *huh* me, boy. Since you think you can run up the gas bill by using up all the hot water, you can walk your tail to the bus stop."

He checked the time. "Even if I run full stop, I'll be five minutes late."

"Then you should have thought about that before, huh? Have a nice day, dear. And if I find out you skipped school, not only will you be grounded, but you can kiss going to your grandmother's this summer goodbye."

Sweat rolling down his cheeks, gasping for breath, calves on fire, Travis made it to the bus stop seven minutes late. Luckily, the bus driver was late herself, and students were still milling about. He took a few puffs from his inhaler.

Joy of joys.

"What's got you in such a rush, Turner? Lost track of time spanking it?" Giovanni said, walking toward him, sneering all the while as his idiotic friends brayed like donkeys.

And once more into the breach.

Giovanni and his crew thought they were so cool because they lived on the east side of Azure Plains in homes that made the ones in Travis's neighborhood look like hovels.

Normally he would have ignored Giovanni, but Travis wasn't in the mood to take crap from anyone that day. He puffed out his chest. "Nah, I was busy fucking ya mom."

Giovanni's pale face went red as his friends whistled and chortled at him. He clenched his fists and narrowed his eyes. "Funny, I wasn't aware your balls had dropped."

"My testes descended a year and a half ago. Not that it's any of your business, ya troglodyte. Why don't you go back to your friends? God knows they're more your speed, what with them having a collective IQ smaller than your shrimp dick."

At his remark, the crowd jeered.

Giovanni got in Travis's face, his ears red, fists white-knuckle tight. "What'd you say to me?"

Travis put on a brave face, ready to take his beating, when he had a vision: Giovanni crumpled at his feet, skin turning blue as he choked on his own blood.

The vision left Travis torn between horror and glee. He grinned darkly.

Giovanni's eyes went wide, and he flinched.

"JJ, you gonna let Turner clown you like that?" Henry Huntington said, his uniform straining to contain his muscles.

Giovanni looked between Travis and his friends, then shook his head. He raised his fists, drawing back the right one when Travis spoke up. "Go ahead, tough guy. I can take it."

Giovanni looked at Travis a second, mouth hanging open, before lowering his fists. "Dude's not right in the head. Besides, I don't wanna ugly up his face any more. He could legit play Deadpool without any makeup."

Giovanni's friends laughed and clapped, reminding Travis of howler monkeys. How banal. He'd heard better insults from toddlers. Flipping him off, Travis paid Giovanni no further mind, and Giovanni and his friends left him alone."

That was a close call," he said to himself as he drifted into the world of his imagination.

~

Today on Wide World of Douches, we've stumbled upon a pack of Midwestern Dumb Asses. Distinguishable from the southern variety by their love of lifted trucks, SUVs, and all things edgy, they rove in packs, catcalling the female of the species, trying to impress them with talk about how hardcore they are.

"Dude, I got so much ass at my birthday party."

What's this? By Jove, it's the rare and elusive Rubeus Parvus Ignarus. Identified by his short stature and reddish-orange hair, Rubeus is prone to fits of prolix and extreme braggadocio, squawking to all about his sexual prowess.

"JJ, you're so full of shit."

It seems Rubeus's claims have been challenged. Not the strongest or brightest, he gets by on his jokes and appeals to stronger dumb asses to fight in his stead. With his protectors nowhere in sight, how will Rubeus face this challenge to his dominance?

"Oh, you can fuck right off, Mitchells. You weren't even there. Probably too busy at home screwing your sister. BT dubs, tell her to watch the teeth next time I come through. I hate toothy blow jobs, yo."

Mitchells lunged at Giovanni, taking him to the ground.

David Green and Jason Miller showed up then, gasping and covered in sweat.

"There a problem here, Mitchells?" David said, putting some bass in his voice.

Mitchells got off Giovanni and dusted himself off. "Nope. JJ was just telling me about his birthday bash, right?"

Damn it, and here I was hoping to see Giovanni get his imbecilic ass kicked. But the day is young.

Travis's vibrating phone drew his attention, and he smiled when he saw the caller ID. "Hey, Grams!"

"How's my caramel cowboy this morning?"

Stifling a laugh, cheeks hot, and looking around to see if anyone had heard her, he said, "I told you not to call me that."

"Right. You turn the big one-three this year and think you're grown now. So, I'm getting everything in before you forget about your old Grams."

"Never in a million years. You're too weird."

"Right back at you, kiddo. What's my favorite grandbaby up to this morning?"

"Mm, waiting on the bus, hoping a fight breaks out, plotting world domination . . . you know, the usual."

"That's nice, dear. While I have you on the horn, what do you say to joining me for the winter holidays this year?"

"Wish I could, but you know how—"

Mitchells grabbed Travis's phone, holding it just out of reach. "Who ya talking to?"

"My grandmother. Now, give it back!" He charged the bigger boy, but Mitchells side steeped him and tossed the phone to Henry Huntington, a ninth-grader, who tossed the phone to Giovanni.

He looked at Travis a moment, then sneered. "Keep away!"

Miller caught the phone and laughed. "Jesus, Turner, this phone's older than my grandma. Get with the times, kid."

Travis stuck out his hand, shouting, "Give me my phone."

A wind picked up out of nowhere, knocking everyone but Travis off their feet. Travis stared at them, mouth agape.

Did I do that?

Everyone froze, staring at Travis. He looked at his hand. *What the hell . . .*

"Travis, are you still there?" Grams said, breaking the spell that had fallen over them. While everyone was getting up, he retrieved his phone and told Grams he'd call her back.

And the weird-o-meter jumps up another notch.

Travis's palms were slick, and his heart pounded in his ear, his breaths coming in jagged fits as he processed what happened.

No one looked at him after that, and by the time he'd calmed down, the bus arrived. He began the gallows march to his seat, slipping on his over-the-ear headphones and drifting off to sleep.

"Rest up, big dog. You're gonna need it."

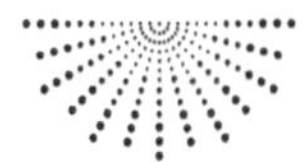

CHAPTER THREE

J Giovanni ducked, avoiding a spitball to the face. He reloaded his straw and returned fire, catching Mitchells between the eyes, and they called a truce. He sank into his seat smiling to himself.

For the twenty-five-minute ride to school, he didn't have to worry about the politics of popularity or being a Giovanni. He could fade into the background and just be. Sometimes he wondered why he bothered fronting so much. Then he remembered what it was like before David and Jason let him hang with them, before he met Brianna, Rachel, Mitchells, Lance, and Henry: his squad. He couldn't, wouldn't, go back to that.

He was laughing with one of his many friends on the bus when they jerked to a stop in front of Azure Plains Preparatory Academy, AP Prep for short, or APPA, as he and the cool kids called it.

"Josh, sweetie, do me a favor and wake up Travis," the bus driver said.

He cringed at the use of his first name but kept his voice cheery. "Okay."

As he passed David and Jason, he stopped to shoot the shit. "How are my favorite cum dumpsters this morning?"

David flexed his muscled. "Nice to see you too, squirt."

David stood and bearhugged JJ, giving him fourteen noogies, then planted a wet kiss on his cheek. "Happy birthday, dude. Love ya."

JJ wiped his face, fighting back the blush he felt creeping up his neck. "Remind me to get a restraining order against ya."

He turned to leave when Jason called to him. "What, don't I get some love?" He puckered up his lips.

JJ reared back. "Yeah, no. God only knows where your lips have been."

David and several others nearby laughed, causing Jason to dive over David, pull JJ over his knee, and give him fourteen spankings with his worn Detroit Tigers cap.

"That'll learn ya, fucker. Happy birthday, short stuff."

"All right, boys, that's enough. Josh, you go ahead and wake Travis way in the back like I asked ya. And the rest of you need to head inside," the bus driver said in the tone she used when she meant business.

JJ screamed internally when he realized she was talking about the *other* Travis on the bus.

He must have let his horror show because Jason adjusted his hat and said, "What's a matter, Joshy boy? Ya scared of mean old Turner?"

Thinking fast, he replied, "Bitch please. I ain't scared of shit," then flipped off Jason, strutting to the back of the bus. He exchanged hive fives and fist bumps with various people, stopping to tell a few jokes which he admitted were weak-sauce.

However, the fun ended when he got to Travis's seat.

JJ hesitated, then took a deep breath and shook him. Getting no response, he shook Travis harder and got the shock of his life when the sleeping boy shifted, latching onto his arm.

"God, let go, would ya? The bus driver just wanted me to wake you up. Anybody got a crowbar I can barrow 'cuz this kid has mad retard strength, yo." His comment drew a few rounds of laughter while he tried to contain himself, shifting from one leg to the next.

Jason and David catcalled JJ, then at Jason's insistence, they went to the back of the bus to troll him.

Jason adopted a falsetto voice, saying, "Isn't that cute? Our little Joshykins has a boyfriend. My, they grow up so fast."

Looking from Travis to Jason, JJ rolled his eyes. "Please. I wouldn't hit that with yours." Smiling wide, tongue hanging out, he flipped Jason off.

David doubled over in laughter. "Ooh, burn man."

Jason made a sour face. "Fuck you."

"We've been through this before, numbnuts. I'm exit only, and you're so not my type."

"We both know you want this dick. Ouch," Jason said when David elbowed him in the ribs.

JJ shook his head. "If you're done busting my balls, Andale." He waved them off.

Combing back his hair and putting on his Ray-Bans, David ruffled JJ's hair, then ran away. "Later, squirt."

"Let me know how this turns out," Jason said, laughing his head off as he followed David to the exit.

The moment Travis had grabbed JJ's arm, his palms became wetter than Niagara Falls, and he tried not to pass out. Looking everywhere but at Travis, he could hardly believe he was this close to him.

Damn it! I should have bailed or made up an excuse not to wake him, but that would have been too sus. And that's the last thing I want.

He put up a good front, hoping no one noticed his damp palms or the blush he knew was creeping across his cheeks. But if this continued much longer, he was going to lose it from sensory overload. Forcing a laugh as people passed and stared at them, he hazarded a look at Travis and wondered if he was ever going to budge.

Once the others left, his eyes drank in Travis, honing in on his gaping mouth, drool dripping on his messenger bag, and those thick, kissable lips. JJ's breath hitched, and he averted his eyes, willing away his semi-erection.

No, he couldn't think like that about Travis. Not here, not now; it was too dangerous. Okay, yeah, so Travis wasn't buff like David or hunky like Jason. And maybe he was on the chunky side. But damn it if Travis wasn't top billing in JJ's spank bank.

Come on, dude. Stop perving. But ... maybe I could get a quick whiff of his hair?

He leaned in but then stopped himself.

What the hell's wrong with me? Why is this so hard? Why can't I talk to him like he's any other dude? Instead, I pick on him like ... like a bully.

JJ couldn't stop thinking about him, but Travis probably thought JJ was the lowest form of scum. He kept saying today was the day he'd finally go up to him and say hi, but he just couldn't do it. He was such a coward.

And while he didn't know if Travis even liked guys, JJ had high hopes since he never saw Travis with girls. Then again, he never saw Travis with anyone. But maybe if JJ confessed his love for Travis, they would become boyfriends just like he always dreamed of?

But maybe Travis wasn't even into him like that. Hell, Travis probably hated his guts.

Ugh, I can't keep doing this to myself. If I don't talk to him today, Imma go crazy.

The chime for homeroom rang out over the loudspeakers, breaking JJ's train of thoughts. However, Travis was still sleeping with his vice grip on JJ's poor wrist. The awkward situation ended when Travis let out a huge yawn, woke, and released him.

JJ jerked back. For a second, he could have sworn Travis's eyes had a red glow to them, like back at the bus stop, giving him a legit Sith Lord vibe.

"What are you looking at?" Travis demanded, then pushed JJ out of the way, not sparing him a parting glance.

JJ flexed his arm, trying to get the circulation going again. He watched Travis head inside, then followed him.

What an asshole.

Travis turned and stared at him as if he'd heard JJ's thoughts. Caught off guard, JJ mumbled, "Um, you know if we don't hurry, we're gonna be late to homeroom, and you know what a dick Mr. Rosh is. So, um . . . yeah, let's hoof it. Bye."

∾

JJ watched Travis sleep through homeroom, taking in his messy curls and that dopey smile. He ignored the general chaos around him as his friends vied for his attention.

"I'll catch ya later," he told them and hung back. Seeing his chance, he kissed his St. Jude pendant for luck and woke Travis.

He smiled wide. "We gotta stop meeting like this."

Travis yawned, glared daggers at him, then blew JJ off. This only strengthened JJ's resolve.

He stood in the doorway of an empty classroom, watching as Travis made his way through the sea of students to his locker. Then he followed him. He'd need to get his things at some point, but this was more important.

As Travis keyed in the last number and reached to open his locker, Keith Maxwell slammed it shut, towering over him. JJ knew of the brain-dead jock from going to parties with David and Jason and thought he was a huge douche. Seeing his opportunity, he made his way over to them. Then he stopped.

What am I doing? Keith would crush me like a bug. But maybe I'd get in a few shots, and Travis would think I was brave for defending him?

JJ inhaled, exhaling slowly through his nose, working up his courage. He willed his heart not to burst from his chest.

The things I do for love.

Keith, leering, said, "How's my favorite freak today? Oh, can't wait to blow me, you say? Okay, just this once since I'm such a nice guy."

JJ puffed out his chest. "Leave Travis alone."

Keith turned. "Or what, Giovanni? You gonna kick my ass?"

"Move it," came Travis's cold reply.

Keith whirled around. "It speaks. I'm shocked."

"I can talk. I just tend not to engage people less intelligent than me. Ergo, I don't talk that often. Now move."

"You heard him, Maxwell."

Travis glared at him, and JJ could have sworn the edges of Travis's eyes turned red for a split second.

"I don't need or want your help. And who said you could call me by my first name? Now both of you move so I can get into my locker."

Keith got in Travis's face and poked his chest. "Make me, tough guy."

Travis shoved Keith, sending him flying a meter down the hallway, much to everyone's surprise. A small crowd gathered to watch the potential fight, but before things escalated, their principal came around the corner.

"There a problem here, boys?"

Keith shook his head. "I slipped. Right, Turner?"

"Yeah."

Mr. Malo gave them a skeptical look before saying, "Move along. First period is about to begin."

When Mr. Malo was out of earshot, Keith punched his hand, glaring a hole through Travis. "You're dead."

Travis smirked, a bit of red creeping into his irises again. "Any time you feel froggy, leap." He laughed and then walked away.

One thought ran through JJ's mind: *Da fuq?*

JJ and Travis shared many classes, such as art, which was a free period that day. Once Ms. Molly arrived, JJ asked for a pass for the bathroom and instead got his supplies from his locker.

He loved free period art classes because they were perfect for napping, doing homework he should have done earlier, talking with his friends, and … Travis watching.

By now, the rumor was Travis had put Keith in the hospital. JJ dispelled this the best he could, but people believe what they want. So, he turned toward Travis, who was sleeping again and not very well as he kept shifting in his seat, head on the desk. The noise of the students must have gotten to him because Travis yawned, stretched his arms, and began doodling on a piece of sketch paper.

Their teacher walked through the room, offering a compliment here and constructive criticism there, but always with a positive attitude. When she came to Travis, she stopped, saying she'd never seen him produce anything above crude contour line drawings and how impressed she was with the level of detail in his current sketch.

JJ had to agree. Though, it looked like something out of a nightmare, what with the bodies strewn everywhere. And was that a lake of fire?

"Travis, dear, this is an interesting piece. I suggest you use a larger medium to capture more of the fine details. And when did you start drawing with your left hand?"

"Joy, I get to use the canvas like a big boy."

JJ laughed at this, but Travis scowled at him. "Something funny?"

"Just what you said about using the canvass like a big boy and all. Totes hilar, bro."

Travis's eyes widened. "I didn't say anything."

JJ's jaw dropped. *WTF? This day's getting freakier by the minute.*

They stared at each other for a moment, neither of them saying anything. Confusion all over his face, Travis turned away and continued working, stopping every now and then to massage his forehead. He finished before the end of the period, running out before giving Ms. Molly a title for his work.

"Joshua, be a dear and ask Travis what he wants to title his piece."

"Will do, Ms. M."

CHAPTER FOUR

When Travis finished his sketch, a familiar scene stared back at him: Oblivion's domain. His insides churned as he remembered the dream, echoes of pain washing over his hand and chest. Swallowing back breakfast, he told himself to calm down. It was only a dream. Right?

As he packed his things, his head pounded as though someone was smashing his brain with a sledgehammer. Halfway down the hall, Giovanni called to him.

What does he want now? He'd better have a good reason for talking to me, or I'll castrate him with my bare hands. Then I'll force-feed the stupid redhead his balls.

"Wait up, Travis. Ms. Molly wanted me to ask you the title of your drawing and where the idea came from. Oh, and Coach Campbell's subbing for Ms. Martin's English class today." Redness splashed across Giovanni's face, painting his neck, his ears, and finally, his face scarlet.

"Tell her it's called 'A Midwinter Night's Scream.'" He scowled at Giovanni. "Anything else you need?"

"Um, and like, that fight you had with Maxwell was hella sweet. The look on his face when you pushed him was legit priceless. I'm so glad someone finally put that ass muncher in his place," Giovanni continued, his words slurring together in a squeaky tone.

"One, it was from a dream. Two, if you saw it, then you know it wasn't a fight. Three, I can handle myself without you butting into my affairs." He stomped away, wishing he were at home right then playing a few rounds of *Mortal Kombat.*

"Oh, okay. See you in the gym."

Travis stopped and turned. "Don't remind me."

"Green and Miler will be there too, so it should be tons of fun."

Lovely.

~

French class passed without incident until a spider landed on Travis's desk, making his skin crawl. He raised his textbook, ready to smash it when he had another vision.

A giant spider with bloody legs and foot-long fangs covered in saliva stood over him, its onyx eyes boring through him. Then it lowered its head.

As quickly as it had come, the vision left him, and he sat there dumbfounded, his stomach queasy with terror.

What's happening to me?

The chime ending class sounded, breaking his stupor. He shook his head, gathered his things, and made his way toward the gym. Along the way, Giovanni joined him, and Travis struggled to contain his annoyance.

As they jogged to the athletic wing of the school, Giovanni chatted away as if they were acquaintances or something. Travis ignored him for the most part but occasionally suppressed a laugh when he said something genuinely funny, though he didn't think Giovanni meant to.

Class with Mr. Campbell subbing meant a trip to the gym and a one-way ticket to the bleachers for Travis. He glared at his inhaler and then plopped down, retrieving his sticky-note-laden copy of *Franken-stein* and began reading.

AP Prep was technically a charter school, which meant anyone could attend, although they charged the students fees for everything, including gym outfits and lockers, even if you never used them. This made it cost-prohibitive for most of the kids on Travis's side of town to attend. Travis would have attended Thurgood Marshall Middle School, but his paternal grandfather's will stipulated he had to go to a prep school or the equivalent to access his trust fund. Bobby and Amber had no such stipulation. The lucky bastards.

He looked up when he heard someone calling his name. Just his luck; Keith Maxwell and his cronies were also there, shooting him dirty looks and making obscene gestures when Mr. Campbell wasn't looking.

"You're toast," Maxwell mouthed, then made a throat-slitting gesture.

Travis mouthed, "Bring it," and then stuck his nose in his book.

Once the kids who were late had finished running laps, Mr. Campbell told those from Ms. Martin's class that she'd assigned them a group project of no more than three people. They were to write a twenty-page report on *Frankenstein*, due at the end of the year, worth fifty percent of their final grade.

He passed out the assignment packets, telling those who wanted to that they could form groups now or dress out and join the activities in the gym. Then he dismissed them while he went to look after his gym class. There was much groaning all around.

Slackers. What did they expect from Honors English?

Since he had no social life, and that's the way he liked it, Travis was on his third read. The only problem was the group part of the equation. He shrugged and figured he could talk Ms. Martin into letting him work alone if his paper were twice the length. He dug back into the book. A few minutes passed when Giovanni saddled up next to him, all smiles.

"Hey, you wanna do the project together?"

He didn't look up from the book. "Yeah. No. You've spent years tormenting me and now wanna act like we're bosom buddies? I don't think so."

"Um, yeah. I've been meaning to formally introduce myself and apologize. JJ Giovanni, resident smartass and the dude you had a kung-fu action grip on this morning." He stuck out his petite hand. Travis looked at the proffered appendage a moment, then continued reading.

"Way to leave me hanging, dude." He pulled his hand back. "Anyway, you um, want to do the paper together or what?"

Travis glanced at Giovanni over the brim of his book, his annoyance rising. "No, thanks."

"Come on, bro. I see you're almost done, and I'll be finished in like a week, giving us more than enough time to—"

"Nein, nyet, no."

"Alas! It seems I must level up my charisma if I'm to get Travis the Moody to join my party."

Travis snorted. "That was pretty funny. Not like the scatological humor you usually trade in."

Giovanni's face light up in a smile. "Seriously? No one likes my geeky shtick. And what's with the ten-dollar words?"

"I wouldn't say I liked it. And it's not my fault you have the vocabulary of protozoa. Now, will you leave me alone? I'm sure your friends are starting to wonder about us. And we wouldn't want that, right?" He quirked an eyebrow, the corner of his mouth turned up in a half-smirk.

Giovanni wiggled his bushy eyebrows. "Or would we?"

"You're quite droll, you know that? However, much like a dog humping one's leg, the novelty has worn off."

"But I was just trying to be friendly. I just thought maybe—"

"That you'd say a few kind words to the freak you've bullied for years, and he'd be duped into doing your work for you? That you'd flash that cocky smile of yours, and I'd bow down to you like everyone else does?" Travis replied, dropping his book and getting to his feet. "Leave!"

"Why are you so mad at me? I just thought you could use someone to talk to. You're not who I thought you were," Giovanni said, taking a step back, his lips trembling and eyes wet.

Travis stared him down, his rage at Giovanni's presumption of knowing him spilling over. "Fuck you. Don't ever in your life try to holler at me like that again! You don't know the first thing about me and don't have the right to speak on me. Until you do, you'd best keep my name out yo' mouth or you finna catch these hands."

"Dude, mood whiplash much? What did I ever do to make you hate me so much, huh? All I did was treat you nice today."

"But what about all the other times you and your friends clowned me, huh?"

He took a step toward Giovanni, delighting in the fear he saw in the smaller boy's eyes.

Giovanni stepped back, and barely loud enough for Travis to hear, said, "You don't know how hard it was just to say hi to you today." Giovanni then straightened his spine, his head held high, and clenched his jaw. "You don't know the first thing about *me*!"

Giovani's fist slammed into Travis's jaw, disorienting him, and for a moment, he heard alarms blaring.

He made to hit him again, but Travis dodged as if his body were moving of its own accord. He caught Giovanni in the stomach with a knee, doubling him over.

Well, all those years spent playing fighting games weren't a waste after all.

Travis followed up with an uppercut, and blood gushed from Giovani's nose. When it looked like Travis was going to hand Giovanni his ass, several of his friends piled onto Travis, kicking and punching him all over.

He crawled into a ball, trying to protect himself, but there were too many. As darkness encroached on the edges of his vision, a tingling sensation ran up his spine, and his vision blurred. And then Travis was on a plateau overlooking a forest.

Before he had a chance to process things, it was as if he were watching events through a camera high above the room, as though he were out of his body, asleep but awake at the same time. Travis watched himself roll out of the clutches of those hooligans and kick their asses like no one's business.

"Enjoy the show, kid," said his headmate.

Watching Giovanni get his face bashed in was such a joy, but then Travis saw Maxwell coming up from the side.

"Look out!" he cried too late as Maxwell bashed in the back of his head. And for a moment, Travis saw stars.

"Next time, be faster."

He watched their body stumble, but his headmate righted theirself and charged Maxwell. The two collided, pushing them backward by the force of the impact, while Maxwell remained upright, smiling.

They lost their footing, and Maxwell laughed.

But not for long.

They caught theirself, got on their feet, and charged Maxwell again. This time when they approached him, they kicked him in the chest with both feet, bringing Maxwell to the ground with a *boom*.

Maxwell's eyes rolled up in his head and then closed.

"One down," Travis said.

Then David Green's massive frame crashed into Travis, sending them head-first into the bleachers. Their forehead split open, blood cascading down their face as pain jolted through Travis. His headmate, however, showed no signs of being hurt and got up, smiled, then wiped the blood out of their eyes.

Green made to strike them, but they caught his wrist and tossed the musclebound teen over their shoulder. Straddling Green's hips, they rained down blows as if they were a UFC fighter, Green's Star of David pendant becoming covered in blood.

Travis spotted Jason Miller barreling toward them, his lanky frame a human missile.

"Look out."

The view of his body somersaulting in the air and then landing on Miller's back wasn't graceful, but he'd be damned if it didn't fill him with glee seeing that bastard get his comeuppance.

Miler went down as if an anvil had hit him, the breath and fight going out of him in one big whoosh. He lay still, his eyes glassy and mouth frozen in a grimace.

They turned back to Green, who'd recovered and was in a defensive stance that reminded Travis of the old kung-fu movies he loved to watch.

"Give it up, Turner. I've been taking karate since I was four."

"Then this should be all the more fun . . . for me."

"Everyone on the ground now," shouted a school resource officer as she reached for her stun gun.

"Hey, pretty lady. You wanna get freaky with me?" his headmate said.

"Okay, things have gotten way out of hand."

Travis floated down from his perch near the ceiling, but as he neared his body, he hit an invisible wall, sending him backward.

"Naw, kid. The show's just starting."

"What are you doing? In case you haven't noticed, that's a cop you're talking about hurting."

"She don't start nothing, won't be nothing."

Travis tried entering his body again but met the same fate. How could his body turn on him like this? The one place he had to himself, the place no one could enter but him, was no longer safe. How dare his headmate take that from him. How dare it violate his inner sanctum. Waves of rage washed over him, and in the distance, he heard the cry of a great bird again.

"This isn't a joke. It's time you let me back in control."

"Nope."

"I said on the ground now. Kid. Or I'm going to tase you."

Travis tried again, this time getting closer to his body, feeling the invisible barrier give a little.

"I ain't going back in there. If you don't want this cop to pull a Michael Brown on us, then I suggest you calm yo' ass down and . . ."

The resource officer shot her taser at them, and as 10,000 volts coursed through their body, the invisible wall fell, and Travis slid back inside his body.

Whether he would live was another matter.

CHAPTER FIVE

$\mathcal{J}$enny Adams nibbled her thumbnail to the quick as she checked the readout on the EEG machine, shaking her head. A week had passed, and still no change.

It didn't make sense. When they'd brought Travis into ER, he had several lacerations, many broken or bruised ribs, and a fractured skull. Yet, most of his wounds had healed in a matter of hours, save two broken ribs. While she had seen some strange cases in her time at St Michael's, none were as *Outer Limits* worthy.

So far, she and the others who'd treated Travis since he was a child had managed to keep things quiet by fudging his records, so it appeared he was still seriously injured. But the rest of the staff were starting to get suspicious. Moreover, two men in suits had just entered the room, and something told her they would be trouble.

"Miss Adams, I'm Agent Smith," he said, all scowls and glares, flashing his badge. It didn't say what agency he was with. "And this is my partner, Agent Anderson. We would like to have a word with you about Travis Turner."

Agent Anderson stepped forward, wearing an Aquaman tie and Green Lantern cufflinks. "We've come across some interesting information about him, and it would be in the boy's and your best interest to come with us."

Jenny squared her shoulders and placed her hands on her hips, resolute in protecting her sweet boy. "I haven't the foggiest idea what you're talking about. Who did you say were with again?"

"We didn't. Suffice to say, we are with a branch of the government that deals with these situations," deadpanned Agent Smith.

She glanced at the still form of Travis, his chest rising and falling in sync with the beeping of the heart monitor.

"I don't care if you're the president of the United States. We aren't going anywhere with you. Now kindly leave before you disturb him."

Agent Anderson smiled, showing off a set of blinding-white teeth. "I apologize for my partner's rude behavior. We're trying to help the boy." His cheeks reddened. "Ma'am, could we grab a cup of coffee and maybe talk a bit?"

She glanced at Travis, nibbling her nail. "I don't know."

"Please," he said in a whiny voice. "Promise it'll be quick." He flashed that dazzling smile of his again, and her heart melted a bit.

Jenny thought it over a moment.

What could it hurt? Besides, he's kinda cute.

"Um, okay. Just let me check in with the nurses' station, and we can go." She looked again at Travis and couldn't help wondering what he'd gotten himself into.

Jenny locked eyes with Agent Anderson, the silence stretching out before them as she glared with unblinking eyes, willing him to be the first to cave. But finally, Jenny's pale blues eyes teared up, and she unloaded on him.

"I won't let you take him to Area 51. You have no idea the world of pain he's suffered, and I'll be damned if you put him through more!"

"Melodramatic, aren't we, ma'am? The boy is all of what, thirteen? What's so gosh-darn special about him, anyway? And for the record, Area 51 doesn't exist."

Smack. Jenny's hand connected with Agent Anderson's face. She balled up her fist, prepared to strike again, but regained control of herself. Once composed, she recounted how she met the Turners.

Fresh out of medical school, working in an army hospital over in Bayreuth, Germany at the time, she'd been on duty when they'd rushed in Travis. He was whisper-thin, covered in third and fourth-degree burns.

Though she'd read about burn victims, none of her classes prepared her for what lay ahead. She still had nightmares about Travis screaming when she changed his dressings.

His parents, while present, seemed to care more about how his prolonged stay would inconvenience them.

Agent Anderson, coffee in hand, leaned in. "What happened to him?"

"Oh, you give a damn now? He was in a fire, and the trauma caused him to go into shock, and he flat-lined. After about an hour, we brought him back, and he spent the next eighteen months in the ICU. The fire was so intense it melted the skin from his bones."

Agent Anderson stared at her, slack-jawed. "Wow."

"At first, he was a good little soldier. Didn't complain about all the skin grafts and reconstructive surgeries on his face. But kids can be such monsters. Though he didn't let on how their teasing affected him, I watched as the light in his eyes died, replaced by hate. Maybe had I stepped up to the plate, he'd be a lot better off. I don't know. But, I'll tell you this much." A wild glint came into her eyes. "You'll have to pry my cold dead fingers from him!"

"Whoa, back Simba, back." He laughed, a nervous tone to his voice. "I have no intentions of handing Travis over to my bosses. If even half of what you've said is true, then we're beyond boned here."

"Why the change of heart? Did my feminine wiles beguile you?" she said, sarcasm dripping from her words as she batted her eyelashes.

"Ha, no. Even if you are quite the hottie. But let's just say it's better to keep on his good side because . . . I shouldn't be telling you this, but he's basically an omega class mutant."

"What?"

"Oh, sorry, huge X-Men fan here. The omegas are uber-powerful mutants that can basically end the universe. We don't know what Travis is capable of now. But, based on what he could do as a five-year-old, we do *not* want to piss him off."

Standing, Jenny shoved him into a wall, his coffee cup splattering to the ground. "What are you talking about? I've known him all his life."

"Jesus, you're stronger than you look. I *really* shouldn't be telling you this, but there was an incident when Travis was around two. He developed pyrokinetic abilities, and the government experimented on him until he escaped at age five. The details are fuzzy, but afterward, children around the world developed superhuman abilities which set off an arms race, so to speak."

"I don't believe you."

"Whatever," he said, shrugging off her hand and straightening his collar, "but Travis is a bomb waiting to go off. And I'd rather be his friend than his enemy. Here's what happens now."

He told her to get Travis and make a run for it while he distracted Agent Smith. She was to take Travis north to a small town called Otter Lake, where his friend, Dr. Richard Hu, lived. "Make a right at the gas station, and you'll come to a cabin. Stay there, and when the coast is clear, I'll join you. Tell Doc that Tommy sent you about Project Hellfire. He'll know what it means. Go."

"Why should I trust you?"

"I've been straight with you from the get-go, haven't I? We were sent here to bring in Travis but . . ."

"But what?"

His face reddened. Then alarms sounded, and a message came over the speakers saying they were locking down the hospital. "Never mind. Change of plans. Get your car ready, and I'll get Travis."

She thought a moment. *I don't know if I should trust him. Maybe if I pretend to like him, he won't betray us. It's worth a shot. Besides, he's a snack and a half.*

Then she said, "Fine. You know I could definitely see myself falling for you if things were different, hun."

"Well, aren't I the lucky one?"

"Yes, you are." Jenny leaned in to kiss him, then pulled back smiling. "Later," she said and left to get her Explorer, saying a silent prayer as she went.

CHAPTER SIX

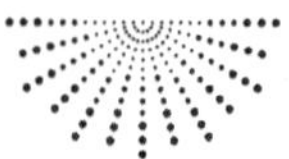

JJ, nose taped-up, lip-busted, face bruised, visited David in the hospital and couldn't help laughing at the sight.

David flipped him off. "Shut up. It's not that bad."

"Right, I hear the eggplant look is so in right now," JJ said, dodging David's incoming spitball. "Real mature, Green. What are you, five?" he said, launching a spitball of his own.

"Aw, you shrimp. You got me right in my eye."

JJ loaded his straw with another spitball. "That's what your mom said."

They burst out laughing.

David pressed the button to start his morphine drip. "JJ, seriously, don't make me laugh. It hurts too much."

"Sucks to be you, dude. I only got a broken nose and a few bruised ribs out the deal." He shot another spitball, catching David on the nose.

"You're lucky my leg and ribs are broken, or I'd come over there and teabag your punk ass." He launched a spitball at JJ, missing him. "I'd rather be all jacked up like this than be an albino four-foot-nothing stick with no dick."

JJ really wished his growth spurt would come, as it had last summer for David. "Well, excuse me for not being a sasquatch like you. And for your information, I'm four-foot-eight . . . and a quarter inch."

Laughing, David clutched his ribs. "That's still short as hell. Tell me, do ya still shop in the toddlers' section?"

"Screw you! I'm big where it counts."

"Dude, you crack me up. You prolly don't even know how to use it. I've seen you talk to the ladies, but have you hit it?"

He remained quiet, hoping David would move on to another topic, but he didn't, and the lull in the conversation engulfed them. JJ hazarded a look at David, and their eyes met. "I mean . . . no."

David looked at him askew. "What's up with that?"

JJ paused, looking at the floor as he thought, his heart ready to rocket into outer space. *I'm sick of hiding, but what if David and Jason don't want to hang with me anymore? Could I live with the loneliness? And what if they tell everyone at school and my parents find out?*

But I can't keep bottling this stuff inside. Like Nana Giovanni says, 'Que sera sera.'

Taking in a deep breath, JJ steeled himself, ready to bolt for the door. "H—has it ever occurred to you that I might not like girls?"

"Come again? You're joking, right?"

JJ shook his head. "This isn't a joke. I like dudes."

"Shit, man. You're not secretly in love with me now, are ya? 'Cuz The David don't swing that way, bro."

JJ's nose and chest ached from the fit of laughter that wracked him. When it passed, he said, "No offense, but you are so not my type. I'm not big on the whole 'roided-out look. Seriously, man, there's such a thing as too much muscle."

David gestured at himself. "How could you not like all of this?"

"Conceited much? Just cuz I'm gay doesn't mean I drool over every guy I see. I'm not a man-ho like you and Jason."

"Ha, good one, squirt. So, you like got a boyfriend?"

"You're being pretty meh about this, but no. I'm single."

"Well, that's 'cuz Jason's bi, and we're like total bros, ya know?

Yeah, it's kinda weird when he talks about hooking up with guys, but otherwise, dude's hella chill. There someone you got your eye on?"

"Hold up. Jason is bi? Since when? I legit didn't suspect that. Man, my gaydar must be broke or something. And if you must know . . . I liked Travis until I found out what a complete douche nozzle he was."

"Turner or Smith?"

"Turner," he mumbled.

"No offense, JJ, but your taste in guys stinks."

"Says the breeder." He scowled. "It's frustrating. I hate him, but I love him. Like I'm the only one who sees the pain he hides behind his walls, and I just want to take it all away. But he hates me and is so screwed in the head. FML."

JJ's sobs filled the room.

"Listen to me. Everything's gonna work out, okay?"

JJ sniffed and wiped his eyes. "Really?"

"Yeah. I love you, man. No homo."

JJ chucked his soda can at David, and it clunked his forehead. "That'll teach ya, fucker."

"That's assault."

"You earned it."

"Meh. We cool?"

"Yeah. So . . . Jason's bi?"

"Mmhmm. Say, if you like Turner, then why have you been picking on him?"

Before JJ could reply, the unmistakable sound of an explosion from the floor above them caught his attention.

Out of the darkness that covered him, Travis found himself back on the plateau overlooking a river with trees and plants of all colors.

"Beautiful, ain't it?"

He turned, and seeing himself, he got in a defensive stance.

"Yo, chill cuzo. I'm not Oblivion."

Travis focused on his hand and gathered a ball of black flames. "Why should I believe you?"

"Wouldn't I have attacked you by now?"

Pursing his lips, Travis thought it over. "Then who are you?"

"Your headmate, silly."

If this were a Tex Avery cartoon, Travis's eyeballs would have popped out of his head. "I'm crazy."

"The verdict's still out on that, but this is for real for real."

Travis inclined his head, not believing what he was hearing. *How is this possible?*

"Hey, I'm just as confused about this as you are."

Travis stared at him dumbfounded. "You can hear my thoughts?"

"Duh. We share a body . . . among other things."

"What's that supposed to mean?"

"Never mind."

Travis scrunched up his face. "Whatever. Where are we?"

His headmate scratched its head. *"Well, I don't exactly know how to describe it, but we're in your head. Or rather our heads. I think."*

Nodding slowly, Travis said, "Right. You have a name or what?"

"'Course I got a name. It's Prometheus, but you can call me Pro, bro."

Like an itch in the back of Travis's mind, the name seemed familiar, but he couldn't quite place it.

"Don't strain yourself, kid. When the time's right, all will be revealed."

Scoffing, Travis folded his arms. "Way to be vague. I'd say it was a pleasure meeting you, but then I'd be a liar. Now, if you don't mind, I'd like to go home."

He turned away, but Prometheus grabbed his shoulder, turning him, so they were facing each other.

"No can-do partner. I saved yo' ass, and now you owe me. So, how's about you start by saying thank you?"

Travis shrugged off Prometheus's hand. "Didn't ask for your help."

Prometheus grimaced and sucked in his lip. *"I knew it was too soon to meet your stingy ole bitch ass self."*

How dare this usurper speak to him like that. He gritted his teeth, his vision going red as he balled up his fist and focused all his anger on forming a ball of blue flames. After blasting him with fire, Travis turned to leave, but Prometheus appeared in front of him, murder in his eyes.

"Nice try, dumb ass. But we were born of fire and ash."

He socked Travis in the jaw, and they exchanged blows. Travis dodged the best he could, but Prometheus was faster than him and played dirty, teleporting behind him and getting in cheap shots.

When Travis tried teleporting, he felt as though being torn into a million pieces.

"Ha, kid. You ain't ready for that yet. Now sit yo' hyper self down and listen up while your boy Pro schools ya for a minute."

"Yeah, no. I'm going home."

Prometheus laughed. *"I'd liked to see you try. I got that ass on lock, son."*

He snapped his fingers, and Travis found himself wrapped in chains.

"What the—"

"You in Pro's house now, nigga. And you ain't going nowheres till we had a little chat. See, that dream you had weren't no dream."

"Then I—"

"You fought the devil and won. Course not before we underwent a little change."

He pointed into the distance and told Travis to look. Following Prometheus's hand, a creeping gray mist was coming toward them, draining everything it touched of color; it was fast enough for Travis to notice but nothing that concerned him.

"So?"

"So, numbnuts, that grayness is . . . well, I don't know what it is. But I know it's bad news."

Travis laughed. *They must have hit me harder than I thought to hallucinate this—or given me some primo pain killers.*

Groaning, Prometheus wiped his hand across his mouth. *"Look, we got powers, okay, and one of them is like ESP."*

Rolling his eyes, Travis tried to hide his mounting fear. "We can see the future? Yeah, right."

"I ain't say all that, but we get hunches and can see bits of what might happen. That's how I knew Oblivion was no good. You'll get them, too, once you stop being so uptight."

Screaming internally, Travis said, "Whatever you're smoking, stop."

"A'ight. I'll prove it. You know JJ?"

"What of the paramecium-brained dunderhead?"

"He likes you, and you likes him."

"What did you just say to me?" Black energy arced from Travis's body.

"Still in denial?"

Travis growled. "Giovanni is the last person I'd ever be with."

Laughing, Prometheus shook his head. *"Oh, boy. You just don't know. But that's all Imma say about that. While I have you here, let's get a few ground rules out the way. First, no mo' being a punk-ass nig—"*

White tentacles sprouted from Travis. "Use that word again, and I will eviscerate you."

Prometheus backed up. *"Chill!"*

Travis looked down and the chains binding him were gone.

"Kid, ya have to watch yourself. Every time you get angry, Oblivion's. . . shit I don't what's it called. But if you don't chill with all this wanting to kill folk, it's game over, nig—negro."

Travis thought over the day's events. "Say I believe you about Oblivion and the other stuff. Why is this happening now?"

"Hell if I know. Maybe it has something to do with us hitting puberty. Anyways, rule two: any time you require my help, asked for or not, I get to take the old body for a spin. Starting now."

Prometheus disappeared, leaving Travis standing there beyond perplexed and pissed. It was bad enough having Prometheus in his ear 24/7 ragging on him, but to be trapped in his own body? Hell to the fuck naw. "Next time we meet, Imma bust my foot off in your ass!"

~

Sometime later, Travis ventured out from his spot on the plateau and tried teleporting and the flame attack he used on Prometheus. He didn't know how long he'd be there, so he made the most of his time training. "You won't beat me again."

In the distance, a faint bird cry reached him. Again, he felt as though there were something he should remember but couldn't, and for reasons unknown to him then, Travis cried.

CHAPTER SEVEN

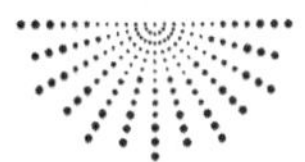

William Smith had been a DMRC agent for nearly 30 years, and he showed it. The balding, pudgy man had long since stopped caring about being gregarious. In his work, good manners were a luxury he couldn't afford.

The Department for Metahuman Research and Control, commissioned by DARPA to investigate unusual incidents, had the goal of finding candidates for their super-soldier program. Most of the time, it turned out to be false alarms caused by over-panicky people, but sometimes they hit pay dirt.

There was Kyle from Ohio, who could crush cars with his mind, currently deployed in Somalia. Then there was Marie from New Orleans, who could paralyze people with her touch, and Rosalita from Florida, who could become invisible. Both were in Afghanistan running black ops together.

Of all the cases Agent Smith had been on, this was the first time he had a personal interest in the subject. Although the face had become more angular and the nose broader, there was no mistaking it: Travis Turner was Subject Prometheus from Project Hellfire.

Agent Smith reached down to get his cuffs when the EEG machine exploded.

The boy opened his eyes. "Long time no see, Billy. Consider this payback for all the times you experimented on us."

Agent Smith screamed, then crumpled to the ground, blood gushing from his shattered nose. Another man in a suit entered the room and gasped; he introduced himself as Agent Anderson, Agent Smith's partner.

Pro glared at him, a softball-sized fireball in his hand as he trembled with fear mixed with adrenaline.

Agent Anderson backed up, holding out his hands. "I'm not going to hurt you. Follow me, and we'll get you out here," he said in a soothing voice, his hands shaking and eyes wide.

"As if you could hurt us. Let's get one thing straight. I'll ice anyone who tries to make us a guinea pig again. Understand?"

Agent Anderson's hand hovered over his gun. "If anything happens to me, you can kiss your freedom goodbye."

Pro laughed. "Try me. I'd done melted that pea shooter before you even got a shot off."

Outwardly he was cocky, but inside, Pro was scared shitless. But he had to keep up the act.

Agent Anderson broke out in a sweat. Then the fluid in Travis's IV bag boiled before bursting. Pro smirked as the bedding and furniture smoldered, then burst into flames. More alarms blared, and people screamed as the hospital went into lockdown.

Agent Anderson drew his gun, hands shaking. "What the hell? You just turned a simple extraction into a cluster fuck."

Pro sized up the baby-faced man in front of him. Why should I care?"

Sighing, Agent Anderson ran his hand through his sweaty hair. "I'm trying to be nice here, but if you'd rather I call my superiors and deal with them, be my guest."

Pro's veins filled with ice, but he inclined his head, rose from the bed, and in a fluid movement, grabbed Agent Anderson by the neck and lifted him off the ground. "Why shouldn't I kill you?"

"Jenny's waiting to drive you to my friend's house. He holds Ph.D.'s in molecular chemistry and genetics and has experience with cases like yours," he said, his voice hoarse and high-pitched.

He paused a moment. "I bet' not find out you lying, or it's that ass."

Agent Anderson nodded, and Pro released him.

He took in a big, gulping breath. "Was that called for?"

Pro ripped the IV from his arm and removed the EEG and heart monitor leads from his body. "Like I said, I ain't going back there."

"Thanks to that little stunt of yours, we have five-ten minutes max —before the police swarm this place. Not to mention Homeland Security will be sniffing around come tomorrow. Come on!" Agent Anderson yelled over the chaos and pulled Pro with him. They ran into Jenny on the stairs and filled her in on the way to the car.

As the trio exited the garage, The Michigan State Police stopped them.

"Great. How are we going to get away now?" Jenny whined.

Pro smiled. "I'll handle it."

Agent Anderson shook his head. "You've done enough."

"You got any better ideas?"

"No."

"Then either make with the planning or STFU," he said, hopping out of the car. He cracked his knuckles and neck.

The lead officer approached Pro. "Something the matter, son?"

"Depends," he said.

Jenny stuck her head out her window. "Don't mind him, officer. He's just stretching his legs. We'll be moving along as soon as he gets back in the car." She shot him a dirty look.

The officer stared at her hard. "I'm afraid I can't allow that, miss. Everyone's to stay put until we determine the cause of the explosion at the hospital."

Agent Anderson flashed his badge. "Officer Davison, is it? There's no need for you to keep us here. This is official government business, and if you'd like, I can call my superiors and have them—"

"Bored," Pro said, melting the cop's gun and flinging him into his car with a telekinetic blast.

However, before they could escape, two black hawk helicopters landed, and soldiers surrounded them.

"How about you save yourself some trouble and come along nice and easy?" the commanding officer said.

"How 'bout you suck deez nuts?" Pro unleashed a shockwave that left a three-foot-deep hole in the street, knocking most of the soldiers unconscious. The few still battle-ready prepared to open fire. However, shrapnel impaled them when Pro exploded their helicopters.

Not satisfied, he exploded things around him at random, reveling in the pandemonium. For so long, he'd been trapped, and now that he was free, he was going to do it up big. Screw the consequences. Travis could deal with them.

Jenny shielded her eyes from the smoke and crept toward Pro. "Stop this, sweetie. We're safe. You're safe."

"I finally have a bit of fun, and you want me to stop? Hell naw!"

Pro continued his rampage until he felt a prick in his neck and turned. Jenny was holding a hypodermic needle.

"You suck."

His vision blurred, and the world went black.

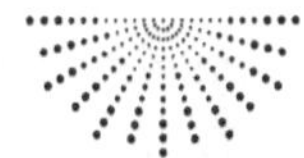

CHAPTER EIGHT

*W*hen Travis awoke, he was in a sparsely decorated room with two windows and a table. Someone had hooked him up to an IV bag full of a clear liquid. His head throbbed, his body aching in places he didn't know he could ache. The last thing he remembered was the fight with Giovanni. *That pipsqueak probably has something to do with this.*

He sat up only to discover he was handcuffed to the bed. *"Giovanni, if you let me go, I promise you a death quick."* When no one replied, he pulled at the cuffs but only succeeded in chafing his skin.

A pit of fear formed in his stomach. *"This isn't funny anymore,"* he said, raising his voice, *"Let me go right now, or—"*

The pitcher of water by his bedside exploded, showering him with porcelain debris. The sound must have alerted Jenny because she came into the room, red-eyed and haggard. "Oh, you're up," she said, a nervous lilt to her voice, her medical bag clutched tight in hand.

"Mind telling me what happened?"

"Sure, sweetie. But can you stop shouting in my head like that and talk normally?"

He did a double-take. *"What are you talking about?"*

She worried her lips. "This whole time, you've been communicating telepathically.

"Come again?"

She set her bag on the table and approached him, her hands trembling. "Travis, you have powers. No, I'm not punking you or whatever you kids say today. I watched you blow up helicopters and shoot fireballs at the police like you were a character out of those video games you love so much."

"This isn't happening. Any second now, I'll wake up."

Jenny rubbed his shoulder. "This is for real."

Mouth agape, eyes wide, he stared at her in shock, not knowing what to say. She let him take things in a bit before telling him how things would proceed. "Once we know you're not a threat to us, Dr. Hu and I—"

"Who?"

"Dr. Hu is Agent Anderson's friend. You remember him, right?"

He shook his head.

"What's the last thing you remember?"

"The fight."

Pursing her lips, she filled him in on what happened.

"That bastard!"

"Who, sweetie?"

Growling, Travis told her to leave, so he could think without anyone overhearing him. She nodded but checked his vitals first. Once he was alone, he tried talking normally, but it was harder than he expected. He checked his pockets and retrieved his phone, and opened the voice memo app. "This is not happening," he spoke into the microphone. Hitting play, he heard: "is pen ing."

Gritting his teeth, he tried again until he managed to speak the whole sentence and then moved on to a longer one. And by the time he was able to say a full paragraph, Jenny had returned with a new pitcher of water and some sandwiches.

Eating with one hand proved difficult, so he asked Jenny to release him.

"Let's see how you do these next few days, okay?"

"Fine, but at least give me something to read."

Nodding, she took the plate and returned with a stack of books, most of which he'd either read already or wasn't interested in. Though, there was a book on meditation and Zen Buddhism that piqued his curiosity. He skimmed over the introduction and first chapter before digging into the chapter on breathing and finding your center.

With nothing better to do, he closed his eyes and took in a deep breath. He pictured a pinprick of light that grew with each breath, and when it was as big as the sun, he sent it into every corner of his body. A liquid warmth like being wrapped in an electric blanket enveloped him.

Just when he was getting used to the sensation, Oblivion butted in.

"Having fun, are we, boy?"

Travis's eyes shot open, his face a mask of fear. *But I defeated you!*

"Let us not speak of our first encounter."

What do you want?

"To talk and strike a bargain, perchance?"

About what?

"There are certain facts about your powers and past that people close to you are hiding."

And how do you know that?

Oblivion laughed. *"I've been watching you for years."*

Yeah. That's not helping your case at all.

"Ask your Jenny, your parents, your Grams."

Why should I believe you?

"Don't. Either way, I'll be in touch. Can't wait to see what you're capable of, especially after Project Hellfire. . . ."

Oblivion's voice faded away, leaving Travis with more questions than answers. If people were hiding things from him, they would spill it, or he'd make them.

Jenny entered the room with dinner, breaking his train of thought. "Time to chow down."

"Yeah . . . but first tell me about Project Hellfire."

Her eyes went wide. "How do you kno—"

"Don't try to change the subject."

She set down a tray of tomato soup and grilled cheese sandwiches. "I'll get Agent Anderson and Dr. Hu. They know more about it than me."

While he waited for them, he dug into his meal, glad that he would finally get some answers. But why had Oblivion helped him? He was evil incarnate, so what was his angle?

Travis would later learn that even the devil has his good days.

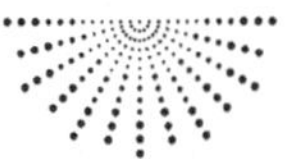

balding man with a rotund body and beady eyes entered the room and introduced himself as Dr. Richard Hu. "Travis, I'm sure you have questions, but—"

"Doc, I thought we agreed not to tell him about you know what?" The suited man that Travis assumed was Agent Anderson asked.

Oblivion was right. What else are they hiding from me?

A cobra of anger reared up inside him. "No! I want to know what's going on." The windows rattled, and the adults turned to him with concerned expressions.

Jenny approached him, speaking in a babyish voice. "Travis, calm down, or we'll have to sedate you again."

Glaring, he balled his fists. "Tell me about Project Hellfire, or I'll burn this place to the ground." As he spoke, his clothes smoldered. The adults looked at each other before nodding their heads.

Agent Anderson took the lead. "Project Hellfire was a clandestine operation that studied your abilities after they manifested when you were two years old."

Travis's mind reeled. "You mean to tell me I had powers as a baby?"

Agent Anderson shook his head. "From what I've gathered, your powers activated following a traumatic event of which I'm not sure. But afterward, the military got involved and . . . experimented on you, for lack of a better term."

How can this be true? I would have remembered it.

Travis wracked his brain, recalling his earliest memories, but everything before The Fire was hazy. He remembered the first time he met his grandparents and going to Sunday School, but not much else.

Could this be true? And if so, how could my parents have allowed this? No. They have to be gaslighting me.

However, part of him knew that was a lie.

"What did they do to me?" he said, a tinge of fear creeping into his voice.

Agent Anderson scratched his head. "Doc knows more about that than me."

Dr, Hu, face red and eyes watery, stepped forward and sighed. "We tested your abilities by having you incinerate various materials . . ."

Travis saw a flash of woodchips bursting into flames. He shook his head. "What else did you do to me?"

"We . . ." Dr. Hu cleared his throat. "We tested your healing powers, first by shocking you with cattle prods. Next, we stabbed you. Then we shot you with rubber bullets before graduating to regular ammunition."

Jenny whacked Dr. Hu. "You monster. He was just a child!"

"I was only following orders."

An argument broke out between Jenny and Dr. Hu that stopped when Travis asked them about The Fire. "Did that happen the way I remember it or . . ." He let his unspoken question hang in the air.

"I think Travis has had enough excitement for one day. How 'bout we let him rest?" Agent Anderson said. Dr. Hu concurred, but Jenny insisted they uncuff Travis first. Agent Anderson looked at her sideways a moment before handing her the keys.

Once he was free, Travis worked the kinks out of his arms and legs. "By the way, what's that clear crud you got me hooked up to?"

Jenny hesitated a moment before saying, "It's something to calm you down."

"Does it have a name?" he said, rolling his eyes.

"Ketamine."

"You put me on horse tranquilizer?"

Worrying her bottom lip, she nodded. "It was the fastest way to keep you calm while we figured out what to do with you."

He side-eyed her hard. "And what are you going to do with me?" He'd be damned if he let them turn him into some science project again.

"We're still working out the details. Why don't you go explore outside while we talk?"

He folded his arms, scowling as his anger threatened to boil over. "Don't you think I should get a say in what happens to me?"

Jenny ran her hand through her messy brunette hair, sighing. "Just do what I said, okay?"

"Fine."

She capped off his IV and showed him the way out.

The outside of Dr. Hu's cabin was decorated with topiary shrubs shaped like bears and other circus animals, along with a rock garden with black, white, and silver stones. The cabin sat on twenty acres and had a pier that led right onto Otter Lake. Travis walked to the edge of the pier, took off his shoes and socks, and dangled his feet in the water, cringing at the shock of the cold.

As he acclimated to the water, He thought back to his conversation with Oblivion. He'd been straight with Travis, but could Travis trust him? Then again, could he trust his parents or Grams? What else might they be hiding from him? And for that matter, what was Prometheus hiding from him?

He nearly jumped out of his skin when Jenny called him in for dinner. After washing up, he joined them at the dinner table, where they had grilled burgers and bratwursts. As he ate, Travis noticed Jenny and Agent Anderson sneaking glances at him.

"You decide what you're going to do with me?" he said, and all eyes turned to him.

"We'll discuss that after dinner. Pass the ketchup," she said.

Travis grumbled under his breath. *Why do adults treat me like a kid when I'm smarter than eighty percent of them?*

He finished dinner in silence, not letting on how shocked he was at picking up snippets of their thoughts. Jenny was nervous and scared for and of him while Agent Anderson thought Travis would be his ticket to a corner office. As for Dr. Hu, his mind was abuzz with fears of something called "Day Zero" and the location of guns he'd cached around the cabin.

Initially, it was cool being able to read people's thoughts, but then things turned awkward when he picked up on Agent Anderson's salacious thoughts toward Jenny, and when he attempted to shut out those thoughts, he found himself trapped in Agent Anderson's mind.

"Something the matter, sweetie?" Jenny said to him.

"Just a little tired. I think I'll go have a nap," he said, rushing back to his room. Distance helped, but he still had Agent Anderson's thoughts in his head. As quickly as his fingers would go, he grabbed the book on meditation and looked up how to shut out thoughts.

He skimmed the section, ready to hurl at Agent Anderson's thoughts, and paused when he came to a bit about warding your mind to others. It was a lot of New Age word salad, but he had nothing to lose. Closing his eyes, he saw through Agent Anderson's eyes. Before he was carried deeper into Agent Anderson's mind, he pictured a door leading back to his own mind and walked through it, locking it behind himself.

While he could still hear Agent Anderson's thoughts, they weren't as loud. Travis next imagined walls surrounding his mind from others, and bit by bit, the voices in his head disappeared. When he was done, he could barely keep his eyes open, so he crawled into bed and fell asleep.

Travis awoke the next morning to Jenny and Dr. Hu standing over him. They spent the next several hours drawing blood samples and running tests on him. Dr. Hu said his colleagues at a lab he used for cases like Travis's were discrete and would keep the results secret. Meanwhile, Jenny told him they'd come to a decision.

Agent Anderson would feed his superiors false information to buy them time while they worked out a long-term solution. The preliminary test results revealed several anomalies, such as the lack of key amino acids and enzymes, and the presence of an unknown substance in his blood, prompting further testing. While they waited for the results, Jenny and Dr. Hu monitored his condition and give him injections for the enzymes and amino acids he lacked.

No stranger to injections and hospitals in general, Travis took in this information with detached interest. He did ask them what they would tell the police and his parents.

"The incident at St. Michael's will be treated as a terrorist attack. This way, no one knows the real reason, and the police can save face. As for your parents, Jenny suggested we tell them you have a novel genetic disorder, and Dr. Hu, being the world's foremost expert on such disorders, has agreed to treat you pro bono."

He nodded, not paying attention until Agent Anderson mentioned his hair and eyes. "What about them?"

"Apparently, when you get mad or excited, your hair turns red and gray, and your eyes turn red and green. We'll try getting you colored contacts to hide them and dying your hair. But you gotta be careful. Just to be on the safe side, you should start wearing these." He handed Travis a pair of Ray-Ban sunglasses. "One slipup, and it's game over for all of us."

Letting out a big sigh through his nose, Travis said, "Why are you helping me? I get you're sprung over Jenny, but still—"

"How do you know about that?" he whispered.

Rolling his eyes, Travis tapped his head. "Duh. I'm telepathic."

"Stay out of my head."

Travis gave him a dirty look. "It wasn't by choice."

They parted ways, and Travis sat on the pier meditating. Then he tried to use his powers until Dr. Hu called him in for breakfast. After he ate and did the dishes, it was time for another round of tests, starting with his vitals followed by testing his reflexes, recall, and other mental faculties, then his stamina and strength by timing his laps around the cabin and how many times he could lift a three-gallon jug of water over his head.

This continued for a week until they sat him down and told him they had something serious to discuss with him.

The way they're acting, you'd think I was dying or something.

Dr. Hu breathed on his glasses and cleaned them. "There's no easy way to same this, so I'll just dive right in. Your latest test results arrived today, and after speaking with my colleagues, we all agree you have a severe case of genetic instability. What this means in layman's terms is, if you don't develop several forms of cancer first, your body will shut down due to being unable to produce the enzymes and amino acids it needs to function. Furthermore, we were unable to identify the substance in your blood, though we think it might have something to do with the extra DNA we found in your genome . . ."

The rest of Dr. Hu's words were lost as Travis shut down. *I'm dying? Why me? What did I do to deserve this? I haven't even lost my virginity—hell, I've never kissed anyone. Ugh. Fuck my life!*

Glass shattering broke him out of his pity party. In his angst, he'd inadvertently broken one of the windows with a telekinetic blast.

"I know now it's the best time for this, but that's coming out of your pocket," Dr. Hu said.

"Yeah. Whatever," he said, trudging away to the pier, where he sat watching the water until the sunset, and Jenny called him in for dinner.

He picked at his plate, moving around the food until he asked to be excused.

The next morning, he returned home and sulked in his room for two weeks, only leaving to use the restroom and shower. It rained every day those two weeks, adding to the malaise that hung over Travis. He barely ate or slept, and when his parents asked what the problem was, he told them it was his genetic disorder acting up.

He would've stayed brooding in his fortress of depression had

Jenny not shipped him off to Dr. Hu's cabin. He humored her, going through the motions as she and Dr. Hu ran more tests on him.

They were moving into May, and warm weather was on the horizon. Though, he didn't see much cause for celebration. He was dying and knew it may well be his last summer.

Little did he know that summer would change his life forever.

CHAPTER TEN

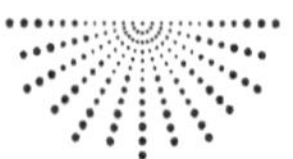

JJ huffed as his mother applied rouge to his cheeks. "I look like a fifth-grader."

"That's the point," she said. "Studies show that the younger a person looks, the more likely they are to receive a lenient sentence."

He straightened his tie, brushing the hair out of his eyes. "Ugh, let's get this over with."

Mrs. Giovanni gave his cheeks a final brush and deemed him ready for court. In the weeks since his fight with Travis, JJ had been to court multiple times as the district attorney and the parents of the others involved in the fight negotiated plea deals; as the instigator of the fight, JJ was looking at felony assault charges until his parents pulled some strings and had his charges dropped to misdemeanors.

Travis's parents were livid until JJ's parents agreed to pay them an undisclosed amount to cover medical bills and court fees since Travis was facing multiple assault charges himself. When JJ had testified before the grand jury regarding his role in the fight, he made sure to keep his answers short and to the point, and the grand jury decided there was enough evidence to proceed with a trial. As the Giovannis and Turners wanted the matter settled fast, they agreed to bench trials.

The judge officiating JJ's case was in her late fifties and had a reputation for being a hardass. JJ's nerves were shot; he didn't get much sleep the night before and threw up the toast he had for breakfast. Meanwhile, all his parents talked about was how much shame he'd brought upon their family and how they had to miss work because of his stupidity. Sometimes he wondered why he loved them when they couldn't care less about him.

He sighed and dabbed his sweaty forehead, praying his makeup didn't run.

On the ride to the 50th District Courthouse, his parents acted like he wasn't there, on their cells like always. The chauffeur seemed to hit every pothole along Woodward Avenue. When they arrived at the courthouse, JJ headed to the bathroom to pee and checked himself over before joining his parents outside their assigned courtroom. He checked his social media feeds while he waited, tapping his right foot as he did so. Twenty minutes later, the bailiff called them inside.

A million thoughts ran through his head as he stood before the judge, her owlish eyes boring into him. He took a deep breath to calm himself and prayed to St Jude.

He opened his eyes when the judge cleared her throat.

"In the matter of docket number 17-AP-12345-MI, I find Joshua Giovanni guilty of all charges."

JJ felt faint as his heart dropped to his feet, and the room spun. He gripped the lectern to balance himself until it passed.

"Are you all right, son?" the judge said.

"Just a little dizzy, Your Honor."

"Very well. Moving along, taking into consideration your age, ties to the community, and this being your first brush with the law, I'm leaning toward going easy on you."

JJ smiled, but the judge wasn't finished.

"That being said, your actions directly contributed to Mr. Turner's injuries, and I'd be remiss if I let you off with just a warning. Which is why I'm sentencing you to serve 300 hours of community service, mandatory anger management classes, and placing you on probation for three months. You are to report to your probation officer once a week, return all their calls, and submit to random drug tests. Let this be the last time I see you or next time, I won't go easy on you. Am I understood?"

JJ's mouth went dry, and he took a swig of water before answering her. "Yes, Your Honor. Thank you."

"If there's nothing else to discuss, the bailiff will show you to my clerk, who will give you the information on your probation officer and anger management courses and the timesheets for your community service hours."

As they exited the courthouse, JJ's only thought was, *There goes my whole summer.*

At school the next day, he broke the news to the Squad.

"That sucks, dude," Lance said in between bites of lasagna at their table in the cafeteria. "See ya when you get off lockdown."

"Yeah," Henry said and then downed his bottle of Red Bull, burping loudly.

Rachel shook her head, her box braids getting in her face. "Don't mind those assholes. Me and Bri got your back. Assuming we don't have anything else planned," she said, laughing.

He shot her major side-eye. "With friends like you, who needs nemeses."

Rachel bopped him on the head. "JJ, you my boy and all, but you can't expect us to be holed up at your place all summer. A girl needs to get her party on. Ya feel me?"

He held back the curse words on his tongue and instead said, "Promise you'll text and party up for me?"

Mitchells laughed. "Deal, bro."

After that, everyone talked about their plans for the summer while JJ scanned the room for Travis, who'd been absent going on a month now. The paper on *Frankenstein* was due in a few weeks, and he still hadn't heard back from Travis about it. To keep his mind off his court case, he'd dug into the book and wrote a fifteen-page first draft. He doubted Travis would want to work with him after their fight, but every other group he asked was either full or had turned in their paper already, so he was pretty much stuck.

Maybe if I give him a peace offering, he'll agree to be my partner? It's worth a shot.

He checked his phone. There were still twenty-five minutes left of his lunch period, so he went to the office and asked for Travis's schedule and locker code so he could bring him the work he missed. The secretary refused, citing privacy issues, but caved when he gave her his kawaii eyes.

Textbooks and assignments in his backpack, he lugged it onto the seat next to him and rode the SMART bus to Travis's side of town, walked the familiar path to the Turner house, then rang the doorbell. As he waited for the door to open, JJ's insides squirmed with eels of nervousness and excitement at finally being inside Travis's house. He'd imagined this moment countless times, and now it was—

"What do you want?" Travis said, his voice nasally as if he'd been crying. He was wearing Ray-Bans and a raggedy gray hoodie with matching sweatpants.

JJ commanded his mouth to make with the words. "Um, since you've been absent a while, I've brought the assignments you missed."

Travis grunted. "Where are they?"

JJ's face warmed with embarrassment. "Sorry. One second." He opened his backpack and handed Travis his books one by one, then the worksheets. "If you want, I could help you?"

Glaring, Travis said, "I don't. But thanks for the assignments and getting my textbooks. How did you get them and know where my house is?"

"The secretary in the office told me," he said, not missing a beat. "Maybe we could do that *Frankenstein* paper together? I have a first draft done."

JJ rummaged in his backpack and pulled out the paper, handing it to Travis with shaky hands. He prayed Travis found the paper worthy.

"Well?" he said when three minutes had passed.

With a pensive look on his face, Travis said, "Not bad, Giovanni. And here I thought you were an idiot like the rest of the kids at AP Prep."

"Hey, I resemble that remark," JJ said, doing his best Groucho Marx impersonation. Travis's lips quirked up in a smile before changing to a frown.

"Goodbye, Giovanni," he said, closing the door.

"Wait! The *Frankenstein* paper is due in three weeks, and no one else wants to be my partner."

Travis opened the door. "Then I guess we can be partners. Leave your paper with me. I'll combine it with mine, and we can workshop it together over Google Docs."

JJ smiled. "Whoot! And Travis?"

"What, Giovanni? And I told you, it's Turner to you."

Sweaty and cheeks flushed from being this close to his crush, JJ swallowed the lump in his throat. "Sorry for the fight and always teasing you."

"It's a little late for that." Travis slammed the door shut, and when he didn't open it after JJ banged for two minutes straight, JJ walked away, head low and a pit of anger building in his chest. *Screw Travis in the cute ass.*

On the ride home, JJ called up his friends, starting with David.

"Sorry, dude, but unlike you, The David is getting laid tonight."

"Bastard," JJ said to himself as he dialed Jason's number. He, too, was busy, and it was the same story when he called the Squad.

Assholes! When I throw a party, they can't get over here fast enough, but ask them to watch kaiju movies or anime, and they act like I'm contagious or something.

He went to his walk-in closet, selected his battered copy of *Stand by Me* from his DVD collection, then called Mariana on the intercom and told her to bring him a bottle of vodka and orange juice.

She set the tray down, brow furrowed, grimacing. "JJ, I don't like it when you drink."

He removed a wad of fifty-dollar bills from his pocket and handed her a few. "It'll be our secret."

She looked at the money, tutted, and then took the bills. "Don't drink too much, Mijo. It's not good for growing boys."

He smiled. "I promise."

She left, telling him dinner would be ready in a few hours.

He settled in, singing along and laughing at his favorite parts, wishing that he had friends like the boys from Castle Rock.

Sure, I'm popular. But no one knows the real me, and I'm sick of hiding who I am. I wish I could go so far away no one knows me or my family. But I can't. I'm just a kid.

He fought back the tears. *Would anyone even notice if I were gone? Would anyone care if I didn't show up to school tomorrow? I thought Travis was different, but he hates me!*

JJ let the tears out. It wasn't like Marianna hadn't seen him cry before, and as usual, his parents were gone.

After he cried himself out, he dried his eyes and watched the rest of the movie.

At dinner that night, his parents actually showed up, but they were so busy on their phones, they might as well have not been there. He asked them about getting a dog or maybe an iguana, but they shot him down, saying he was too irresponsible.

After a torturous half hour, he excused himself to his room and spent the rest of the night listening to his *Lonely Boy* playlist. It was filled with his all-time favorite songs by Simple Plan, My Chemical Romance, Dashboard Confessional, Paramore, My Darkest Days, Skillet, Linkin Park, and Trading Yesterday.

The good thing about having the second floor to himself is no one could hear him scream-cry his lungs out. When he was done, JJ's thoughts turned again to Travis.

After the explosion, St. Michael's transferred David and the other patients to nearby hospitals, telling them a patient on oxygen had been smoking. However, JJ didn't believe that at all, especially given the supposed terrorist attack that happened mere feet from the hospital.

No, his gut told him Travis had something to do with both incidents. He couldn't prove it yet, but he'd keep an eye on Travis, whether the other boy liked it or not.

CHAPTER ELEVEN

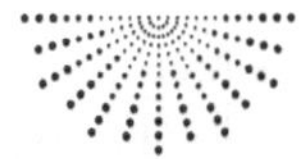

Over the next few days, Travis and Giovanni went back and forth on edits for their paper. Travis wanted to stick to the themes of alienation and societal norms, while Giovanni wanted to go with the theme of identity and how that related to marginalized groups. They compromised and combined their themes for a paper on how the monster represented the other, while the townspeople represented society and the systems of institutional racism and other forms of discrimination inherent within it.

Working with Giovanni proved migraine-inducing, though, as he was prone to flights of fancy, and Travis had to rein him in when he got off course. It wasn't all bad, though. Away from school, Giovanni was kind of funny. Almost nice, even.

"So, when ya coming back to skool?" he messaged Travis one night.

Honestly, he didn't see the point since there were only three weeks left of the term, and there was the little matter of his death. However, after two weeks cooped up at home, his parents said it was time to go back.

~

He was getting his books out of his locker when he heard Giovanni call his name.

"Hey," he said, looking around.

Frowning, Travis gave an anemic, "Hi."

Giovanni tugged at his right ear, his face going red. "BTW, nice shades."

"Thanks. Later."

"Wait."

Turning, Travis gritted his teeth, annoyed beyond belief. "What?"

Giovanni fumbled his words before saying, "Wanna hang this summer?"

Travis shook his head. "What makes you think I'd want to do that?"

Shoulders slumped, Giovanni's face fell. "From our conversations, I thought—"

"Let's keep it one hundo. You've been looking around this whole time; why would I want to socialize with someone who's embarrassed to be seen with me?" Travis slammed his locker shut and walked away, ignoring Giovanni's pleas to let him explain. He avoided Giovanni the rest of the day and ignored his messages on Google Hangout, all of which were variations of: "I'm sorry, let's talk."

The week passed without incident, save his waking up tired with scars he didn't remember having. He attributed both to his genetic disorder and shrugged it off.

On Wednesday, he got a call from the 50th District Court stating his bench trial would begin next Monday. For the rest of the week, Travis's mind came up with a million apocalyptic scenarios. He tried blocking them out, first by focusing on his schoolwork, then by working on Cha, but that didn't take the edge off his anxiety. So, he tried meditating.

~

Closing his eyes and taking three deep breaths, he centered and found himself back on the plateau . . . only he wasn't alone. Oblivion was there in the guise of Travis.

"What do you want?"

"To talk. Do you know what evil is?"

Travis shrugged. "The opposite of good?"

"Yes and No. Good and evil are like day and night; one can't exist without the other."

Travis furrowed his brow, thinking hard. "Then you're saying they're like yin and yang, two parts of a perfect whole?"

Nodding, Oblivion continued, *"Have you ever stopped to wonder why it's good to be good and bad to be bad?"*

"Because it just is."

"But what if I were to tell you everything you've been told your whole life is wrong—no, not just wrong but a lie?"

"First, I'd wonder what you were on. Second, I'd tell ya to cut back on it. Third, I'd ask how you knew such a thing."

Oblivion chuckled. *"I see you're still clinging to sarcasm as a defense mechanism. To answer your last question: I've been watching you since the moment you were born."*

"Again with the creepiness. You going somewhere with this or what?"

"My point, if you'll let me make it, is that you are an extraordinary boy."

"Yeah, no. I don't wanna be evil's chosen one or whatever that prophecy of yours says I am."

"My boy, some are born great, some achieve greatness, some have greatness thrust upon them. You are all three, and I can help you become stronger."

Scrunching up his face in thought, Travis said, "And what do you get out of the deal?"

"The chance to see you live up to your full potential and fulfill your destiny."

"Uh-huh. And how do I know I can trust you?"

"I've been upfront with you from the start, haven't I?"

Travis nodded.

"Here's a tip. Check out the animated series Avatar: The Last Airbender. I think you'll find it most helpful. Farewell, Travis."

"Wait, what are you exactly?"

"That's a conversation for another time," he said and disappeared.

Prometheus appeared before Travis, pale and sweaty. *"Kid, don't listen to him."*

"And I should listen to you? Last I checked, he hasn't been lying to me about having powers before and Project Hellfire."

Prometheus wiped his nose and sniffed. *"A'ight, so maybe I haven't been telling you the gospel truth. But I got my reasons."*

"Screw your reasons!" Travis shoved Prometheus, knocking him flat on his butt. He stood, and they tussled, the rage inside Travis building until it exploded out of him in a tornado of white flames. Prometheus raised his arms, and an earthen shield surrounded him.

"Was that called for? Calm your dingy self down before I put my foot all the way up yo' ass."

"Bring it, chump."

They squared off, but before they could fight, Travis's mother shook him, bringing him back to the real world. "Dear, I've been calling you for the last five minutes. Dinner's ready. I made meatloaf, mashed potatoes with gravy, and green beans."

He rubbed his eyes and went to wash up.

"This ain't over," Prometheus said from the reflection in the mirror. Travis flipped him off and left.

Perhaps I should see a therapist or something? Naw, I'm fine. Like they say, if you think you're crazy, you're not.

He dried his hands and forgot all about Prometheus and Oblivion.

Looking back, Travis marked this as the point a small part of him became seduced by Oblivion.

Any time Travis wasn't at school, he was preparing for his bench trial with his lawyer. Abigail Kurtzman was fresh out of law school, barely twenty-seven, but she'd come on good recommendation from Gram's lawyer.

"When the judge asks you a question, what do you do?" she asked, sipping her iced coffee.

"I answer their question. But don't give more information than I must."

"Good. And what happens if you're asked a question you don't know how to answer?"

He straightened his collar, adjusting his tie. "I ask them to either rephrase the question or ask for clarification."

She nodded, twirling her curly blonde hair. "And what's the number one rule?"

"Don't let them fluster me."

"Right-o, kiddo. I think you're ready. We have a good shot at beating the charges since this is your first offense, and you didn't start it, though Judge Williamson has a reputation for being hard on minorities. If convicted, you're looking at a maximum of one year in juvie and a fine of $4,000. I'll argue you were acting in self-defense but got caught up in the moment. Anything you want to ask me?"

"No," he said, his stomach gurgling as fear and nervousness threatened to make him lose his lunch. His trial was in three days, and though a year wasn't much time, given his condition, it might as well have been a life sentence.

At that thought, it started raining again. It seemed to be doing that a lot lately. He called a taxi, and as he waited for it to arrive, his thoughts turned to his birthday. *Will I make it till then?*

On the ride home, he promised to take full advantage of what time he had left, however long that was.

CHAPTER TWELVE

While Travis slept, Pro took control of his body, using it to teleport to his favorite hangout, a seedy bar on the east side of Detroit called Booker's. It was located in what used to be a warehouse, and you could only get in with a password.

"Roughriders," he said at the door, and the bulky bouncer nodded, then patted him down before letting him in. He'd heard about the place from an online message board about underground fights, and his first trip to Booker's almost cost him his ass.

The bouncer at the door had taken one look at him and told him to scram. Pro persisted, flashing him a wad of twenties, which the bouncer snatched. When he went to grab it back, the bouncer pulled a 9mm.

Pro left but came back the next week and cold-cocked the bouncer. Patrons came out to see what the commotion was, and when Pro told them what happened, they balked.

"Let me fight, and I'll prove it."

"Let the kid fight," Booker, the owner, had said, his belly quivering from his laughter. When he won his match and the next one, Booker let him continue fighting if he cut him in on forty percent of his winnings. "An allowance," he said.

After that, Pro became a fixture at the bar, shooting dice, playing spades, and sneaking drinks when Booker wasn't looking,

Tonight, Booker was behind the bar and smiled when he saw Pro; he stopped pouring a drink and waved Pro over. "Where ya been, kid?"

"Around. Any action tonight?"

Booker lowered his voice. "Fights start at midnight. Entry fee's $200."

Pro whistled. "You're breaking my balls." He pulled out a wad of twenties and laid ten of them in Booker's grubby hand.

Booker nodded and finished making the drink he'd started. "You want anything?"

"Hennessy, straight up."

"Not on your life, kid," Booker said, handing him a can of Mountain Dew instead.

Pro grimaced, but took the can, guzzled it, then ordered some hot wings and a bacon triple cheeseburger. He wolfed down both in record time, then patted his belly. He burped, earning him sideways looks.

The bar was packed with the usual scrubs just off work or getting ready to go there; they smoked cigars and blunts, if they had them, while they drank and shot dice or played spades until Ivy got their attention and began her routine. She worked the pole like nobody's business, and Pro was right in front, making it rain. Smiling, she planted a big kiss on his cheek and giggled when he stared stupefied.

"How's about a little VIP treatment?" He wiggled his eyebrows.

She laughed. "Boy, like I be telling ya, you're too young for me."

"Age ain't nothing but a number. Besides, I'm old enough to give ya a good time."

She punched him in the shoulder, laughing. "Pro, you a trip-and-a-half. Come see me in ten years, and I'll rock your world."

Big dopey grin on his face, Pro promised he'd hold her to that.

Drumming his fingers on the grimy counter and sighing, he willed time to move faster. After a while, he rose and took part in a dice game, using his powers to make the dice land as he pleased, careful to lose a few hands, so they didn't catch on.

At ten to midnight, Booker announced the festivities would begin shortly and introduced the fighters. The first person could pass for a Sumo wrestler he was so big. The next was a thin but jacked man who wore a red bandanna around his right leg. The next two sported crew cuts and globe and anchor tattoos. Last was a woman who Pro suspected could bench press him.

Pro stepped up, and Booker said they would draw lots to determine the fight order. As the reigning champion, he would face whoever won the third round of fights. The marines faced off first, and he took note of them, analyzing how they moved before attacking and filed that away.

The first fight ended in a draw, so it was left to the audience to decide who won by show of applause. The shorter of the two won, leaving his friend to bitch at the bar.

In the second fight, Summon Guy fought the Bandana Guy and lost. Next, Buff Chick faced the winner of the first round. She beat him and soundly. Finally, it was Pro's turn to fight.

Pro downed the shot of vodka he'd snuck and strutted to the fighting area, which was little more than a duct tape ring on the dusty floor.

"I'm not fighting a kid," the woman said.

"Afraid I'll whoop that ass?"

She grimaced. "Have it your way."

He shook hands with her, and she made it a point to crush his hand in her grip.

"Just so ya know, I don't like hitting women. Especially not ones as fine as you."

She laughed in his face, showing off her chipped front teeth. "Don't worry. I'll be doing all the hitting."

The bell rang, and he was off, sidestepping her until he'd gotten a feel for her style.

"Fight me, coward!"

"Okay."

He feinted to the left, and she threw a right cross. He blocked, throwing her over his shoulder. Leaning over her, he whispered into her ear, "Give up, sweetie."

She butted her head into him, busting his lip, and stood.

Wiping his mouth, he cocked his head to the side and cracked his knuckles. "I see we doing this the hard way."

Juking around her, he took her to the ground and put her in a sleeper hold.

She elbowed him in the ribs, and he wheezed, struggling to catch his breath.

"Bitch," he said, releasing her.

She stood, fire in her eyes. "What did you call me?"

"You heard me, bitch."

Glaring daggers at him, she charged. He sidestepped at the last second, and her momentum carried her right out of the ring. The audience booed, but a win was a win.

He saddled up to the bar and ordered a Jack and Coke. Booker slid the glass toward him, though it was just Coke, with a napkin under it. He lifted up the glass and saw a note on the napkin: "Take a dive, and we'll split the pot fifty-fifty."

He thought it over. I'm *sitting on $500, and between what I stand to make betting on myself and winning, I'm looking at four, maybe five grand. I don't trust Booker not to screw me.*

"No deal," he said to Booker.

He put on a good show with Bandana Guy, then knocked the guy out cold.

The audience cheered, and when it looked like things would pop off, Booker pulled his Uzi and foghorn from under the bar, triggering the latter.

"Now that I got yo' attention, you ignorant niggas best listen up. The next motherfucker I catch acting a fool will get lit up. Settle up and bounce."

Booker counted out the money and handed it to Pro.

"Where's the rest of it?"

"My fee for letting your mulatto ass in here week after week."

Pro looked at him sideways, ready to bust him in the head until the white meat showed. "You foul as hell for this."

"You want the money or not?"

He snatched the money and counted it out: $3500. Combined with what he won, gambling and betting on himself, he took home $5500. When he got back to Travis's house, that total, minus $200, went into his emergency fund, which he hid in an old shoebox at the back of Travis's closet.

He counted the stacks of bills in the box, and they totaled $12,000. That should be enough to get him an apartment. Now he just needed to find a landlord shady enough to rent to a kid. He put the money away, tended to his injuries, and crawled into bed, drifting off just as the sun peaked through the window.

One of the few good things about sharing a body was he could party it up and not have to deal with the consequences.

He did have a major problem, though. The blocks he'd placed in Travis's mind were weakening, and eventually, Pro wouldn't be able to contain those memories and the powers that went with them.

But if he could keep Travis focused on Giovanni, maybe that would buy him more time?

God, keeping dingus from going all antichrist is a full-time job. I swear, I should be getting hazard pay for this crap.

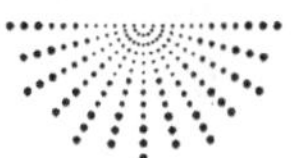

CHAPTER THIRTEEN

Travis took Oblivion's advice and binge-watched *Avatar: The Last Airbender*, taking notes. It helped keep his mind off his impending trial, but between that and everything else, it was like he was drowning. And the only thing that made him feel right was cutting himself. He knew it was wrong, but at the moment, it felt right.

And he would have gone on mutilating himself like that had Jenny not spotted the dried blood on his basketball shorts one weekend at Dr. Hu's cabin. He was beyond ashamed when she asked him if she needed to have a talk with his parents about it.

"No, don't. Please?" he begged her.

"On three conditions. You stop self-harming, give me your cutting tools, and start therapy."

"Deal, but no therapy."

"Travis, you need help. Otherwise, you wouldn't be doing this."

"No. Rule One: Dependency on anyone for anything is a weakness I will not abide."

She groaned. "I thought you were over those stupid rules of yours?"

"One, they aren't stupid. Two, I'm not going to waste what time I have left sitting in front of some quack talking about my feelings like this is the Dr. Phil Show."

He dug in his pocket and handed her his Swiss Army knife. "If you'll excuse me, I have work to do." He stomped away to the lake, where he toed off his shoes and removed his socks and shorts. He wadded in up to his knees, shivering as the water soaked through his boxer-briefs, but he had a purpose.

He squatted, lowering his hands, and then brought them up slowly, picturing the water rising up. Tendrils of water followed his hands. Smiling, he repeated the motion, this time causing water to raise up to his chest. Teeth chattering, he commanded it to lower, but instead, it rose, covering his mouth and nose.

I can't breathe!

As water poured down his throat, he beseeched it to lower.

Please, stop. I don't wanna drown.

Clawing at the water, he screamed for help, but the water muffled his voice. *Please, please, stop. This isn't fun anymore.*

The edges of his vision darkened as he fought to get air, but the water remained in place. Fear coursing through every atom of his body, Travis ran from the lake, but the water followed him. Over a minute since his last breath, his eyelids became heavy; he struggled to stay conscious. One eye shut, and the other was on its way.

He'd all but given up when the image of a multicolored bird appeared before him. At once, he felt at home. Blue flames poured from him, evaporating the water, and he took great gulps of air. The fire died down, leaving his clothes dried but singed.

Note to self: next time, try that with less water.

Thankful to be alive, the shock of what happened didn't hit him until he was curled in bed trying to fall asleep.

These powers aren't toys. I could have hurt myself or Jenny. I could have died today. And for these reasons, I must master them.

He drifted off to sleep, but his day was far from done.

~

Once more, Travis found himself in the hellscape where Oblivion luxuriated on his throne, in the bleached guise of Travis. *"Nice of you to join me again."*

"What do you want?"

Oblivion wagged his finger. *"Is that any way to talk to your elders?"*

"Can we skip to the part where we fight?"

"Actually, I wanted to commend you on your training today."

"The part where I almost drowned? Or when I scorched my clothes?"

"We can't all be wunderkinder, but you did well for your first attempt."

"Something tells me you know more than you're letting on. Where do these powers come from?"

"From me, silly."

Travis frowned, his face scrunched up in thought. *"How so?"*

"Our first encounter changed you; you now contain a portion of my Essence."

"Your what?"

"Think of it as my soul. And along with it comes certain . . . abilities."

Travis looked around, his stomach turning at the sight. *"You're saying my powers are because of you?"*

"Correct."

"I want nothing to do with you!"

"If that's the case, then why did you take my advice?"

He didn't answer.

"Could it be part of you enjoys your newfound strength and wants more?" Oblivion smirked. *"Perhaps we are more alike than you think."*

"I'm nothing like you!"

Oblivion laughed. *"Calm yourself. We wouldn't want you setting fire to Dr. Hu's cabin in your sleep?"*

"I . . . can do that?"

"That and more, but we can talk about that another time. Do you know who I am?"

"The devil?"

"Yes and no. I am the primordial force of destruction in the multiverse. Your kind calls me evil, yet I serve a function: balance."

"But why do you want me to be your vessel or whatever?"

"As I've said before, you are special. After the fire that scarred you, you died and spent an eternity in the Abyss."

"The what?"

"The void from whence all life springs and returns to."

"This is madness. Heaven, hell, they don't exist."

"Not as you understand them. The nature of reality is far too complex for you to comprehend. What I am, what we are, is too strong to be contained in one dimension."

"That makes no sense. There's only this universe."

"Sit a spell and listen."

A chair appeared next to Travis, and he sat as Oblivion told him his tale.

Eons ago, before the multiverse existed, there was only Oblivion and the Void. For countless millennia, Oblivion floated in the sea of nothingness, content to drift along. Then came the great schism. In a whirlwind of fire and light, an entity called Pantheos expelled him from his paradise, telling him he must uphold the cosmic balance by destroying that which He created.

And so, he took the name Oblivion in remembrance of the Void from whence he came and longed to return. As time passed, his duties expanded from causing star systems to implode and creating blackholes to running Pandemonium, the realm of darkness set aside to punish those who disobeyed Pantheos.

At first, he didn't want to punish anyone, but epoch after epoch of hearing the crimes of his prisoners hardened his heart.

Overseeing Pandemonium was a brutal and lonely job, so he decided to create children in his own image like Pantheos did. From fire and ash, he molded them, breathing life into them with his Essence.

His first children, the Prima, were deformed but loyal to him. However, their children, the Supremes, weren't content to follow his orders and rebelled. In a cataclysmic war, the Supremes and the prisoners of Pandemonium pushed back against Oblivion and the Prima. Weakened from prolonged battle, Oblivion and the Prima fell to the forces of the Supremes.

As punishment, the Supremes killed the Prima and absorbed their Essence. Using their new power, they bound Oblivion's powers and exiled him to the Nullverse, a hell worse than Pandemonium.

But Oblivion vowed he'd return one day to exact his revenge. He prophesied the coming of his vessel: a being of immense power who would free him and bring on the End of Everything. And he waited, ever-patient, until the day he sensed Travis.

∾

"You know the rest."

Travis scratched his head. "But why me, and why did The Supremes rebel?"

"Why did Cronos castrate Uranus only to be usurped himself by his sons?"

Thinking for a moment, he replied, "Because it is the nature of the young to supplant the old?"

"Correct. But my children and their children's children have thrown off the balance. And the only way to correct this is—"

"By my releasing you and bringing on the apocalypse?"

"Bingo."

The thought of it reviled Travis. There was no way he'd ever release Oblivion. Prophecy smoffecy.

"Then you'll be waiting another lifetime."

Oblivion pursed his lips. *"I respect your choice, but in time, you'll see I'm right and accept your destiny. Until then . . . pleasant dreams, my child."*

Oblivion disappeared, and Travis drifted off.

That night, his dreams were a jumble of faces that seemed familiar, but he couldn't place them. Some of them were men in lab coats that took his blood and made him melt metal slabs.

Only later did he realize these weren't dreams.

CHAPTER FOURTEEN

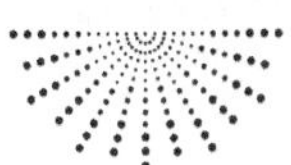

Dr. Hu roused Travis from his sleep. "Come on. I have news to share," he said smiling. Travis grumbled about it being too early but followed him to the kitchen, where Jenny was making coffee while Agent Anderson fried up bacon and eggs.

Once they'd eaten, Dr. Hu called their attention. "I have news about Travis's condition."

Travis swallowed the lump in his throat, trying not to let his nerves get the better of him.

"My colleagues and I have been analyzing your blood samples, and we think we've come up with a treatment. In addition to replacing the amino acids and enzymes you lack, you'll receive regular injections of polypeptides and an experimental compound we've been working on called Agent X. There are, of course, risks . . . which I'll get to in a second. But we're confident that if this treatment works, it could extend your life up to a year."

It's not much, but it's better than nothing. "What are the risks?"

Dr. Hu licked his bottom lip. A nervous glint in his eyes. "Headaches, nausea, vomiting, diarrhea, partial paralysis, temporary blindness, and sudden cardiac arrest."

"But I'll live longer?"

"We think so, yes."

He sighed. "Then I think you should call my parents."

They agreed to downplay the severity of the situation, and Jenny made the conference call and put them on speakerphone. As the adults argued, Travis listened to them, shaking his head. He knew this would happen.

They act like I'm not even here. I'm old enough to make this decision about what to put in my own body.

"I think we should hear from Travis," Jenny said, breaking his train of thought.

He looked around as if she were talking about another Travis until catching on. "Given all the side effects weighed against the other options, I think we should wait until after my bench trial to start the treatment. And if the side effects are too much for me to handle, we stop it."

It was quite a moment. Then Travis's mother said, "That . . . sounds reasonable."

The call lasted several more minutes as they hammered out the finer details, such as transportation to and from Dr. Hu's cabin and logs charting Travis's vitals and reaction to the treatment. Travis's parents and Jenny would alternate taking him to the cabin each weekend. And he would be responsible for keeping track of his own medical logs.

He agreed and went back to bed.

When Travis awoke, he headed to the pier to think. He'd yet to tell his parents about his powers, and he'd been toying with the idea of keeping them secret. After all, they'd kept secret that he was a government experiment for years. The thought of it was enough to make his blood boil. The edge of the pier smoldered before catching fire.

Shit!

He looked at the water and tried 'water bending' it, but nothing happened. As the fire crept toward him, he shook with fear. Trying and failing again to water bend, he screamed at the lake, "Why won't you obey me and come here?"

This time the water complied, soaking the pier and dousing the fire.

"That was close," he said. "I guess I need to be assertive." He laughed, but when Dr. Hu told Travis he'd be paying for the repairs, he didn't find that funny.

There goes my allowance for the whole year. Why does my life suck so hard?

With mutinous thoughts, Travis stalked away to mediate before he caught another case.

The night before he was due for court, he tossed and turned, struggling to fall asleep as his mind went over everything that could go wrong. Ultimately, he wound up sleeping maybe three hours and had blood-shot eyes with bags under them to prove it. The twins caught rides with their friends that morning, and his mother took him to court. Travis felt like he was at sea during a tsunami, so he only had dry toast for break-fast and barely kept that down.

The ride to the courthouse was silent, and his mother kept shooting him reproachful looks.

Not my fault Giovanni decided to throw hands, and I had to open a can of whoop-ass.

She turned to him, "You say something?"

A jolt of fear shot through him. "Nothing, Mother."

"Okay. We're here."

Scheisse! I have to be more careful.

As they exited the car, he raised his mental barriers, praying that would be enough to keep him from projecting his thoughts.

Travis's nerves were so frayed, he couldn't stop sweating, and soon he'd soaked through his suit, a low-rent outfit his mom bought him last Easter. His face flushed with heat when the security guard patted him down and complained about his hands getting wet.

Abigail greeted them at the elevators. "How are you doing today, Travis?"

"Could be better. I just want to get this over with."

She nodded and told him to follow her to the bathroom, where she had him splash cold water on his face. Once his face dried, she applied concealer to his eyes. "There. Now you don't look like day-old crap. Come on."

As they rode the elevator to the fifth floor, Abigail reassured Travis that they had a good shot at winning the case. That did little to stop him from worrying. When they got to the courtroom, Abigail told them there were two cases before theirs, but they shouldn't take too long since they were a DUI and a speeding ticket case.

Travis watched the clock. Each second ticking by was another drop in the growing ocean of his rage. *Why should I be punished for defending myself? Hell, I wasn't in control of my body. And it's not as if Giovanni and his pugnacious, philistine friends didn't deserve a taste of my pugilistic prowess. This situation is ludicrous, especially given I'm dying.*

"It's our turn," his mother said. She grabbed his hand but then pulled away. "You're burning up."

Abigail leaned over and said she could ask for a continuance if he was sick.

"No," he said, "let's do this."

Abigail elected to have District Attorney Waterson go first.

"Your Honor, Travis Turner is a timebomb waiting to go off, and if you fail to convict him now and get him the help he needs, he could go on to commit a school shooting or act of terrorism."

He riffled through a file and handed a stack of papers to the bailiff, who passed them to the judge. "Before you are exhibits A-D: photos of Mr. Turner's electronics and robotics lab in his parents' garage. It is our contention that using his technical expertise, he could create an improvised explosive device that he could remotely detonate, potentially killing hundreds at his school if left unchecked. Which is why we are asking you to sentence him to the maximum of one year in juvenile prison and a fine of $4,000. Thank you, Your Honor."

While Mr. Waterson was talking, Abigail had been scribbling on her legal pad, and once it was her turn, she read the Prosecution to filth. "Your Honor, not only has DA Waterson argued facts not in evidence, but his opening argument is built upon prejudicial evidence that should be excluded."

"Overruled. I'm a big girl and can sort out the truth for myself, Counsellor. Carry on," the judge said with a bored expression.

"At no point in the investigation of the brawl at AP Prep did the police find evidence of any such terroristic attack that DA Waterson alluded to in his opening. Does my client like to tinker with electronics and build robots in his spare time? Yes. And did he take part in said brawl at AP Prep? Yes. But what DA Waterson has conveniently left out is that my client was defending himself from Mr. Giovanni, who started the fight, and his friends. He sustained several injuries, including a fractured skull and broken ribs. I now point to exhibits E-G for your attention." She handed the bailiff photocopies of the x-rays of Travis's skull and chest.

The judge glanced at them before placing them aside. "Carry on."

"Thank you, Your Honor. It is the defense's contention that Mr. Turner has been the victim of bullying for years from Mr. Giovanni and his friends and that the fight in question was the latest in a long pattern of abusive behavior."

"Counsellor, do you intend to call Joshua Giovanni to the stand?"

"I would, but he cut a plea deal with DA Waterson, and his record has been sealed."

"Then you may only make reference to Mr. Giovanni's action in relation to this singular event. Understood?"

Abigail looked down, flipping through her notes. "Yes, Your Honor. On the day in question, Mr. Giovanni threw the first blow, starting the fight, as evidenced in a video taken of the fight. If you'd allow me to play it for you—"

"That won't be necessary. I've already watched it."

"Moving along, it is the defense's contention that Mr. Turner defended himself against many assailants, and fearing for his life, he used the force he felt necessary to protect himself. Therefore, Your Honor should find him not guilty on all counts."

"Duly noted. My bladder is about to burst. Ten-minute recess? Then Mr. Turner can take the stand?"

DA Waterson and Abigail nodded, and the judge called the hearing to recess.

Travis took the break to go to the bathroom and calm down. He centered himself, taking a series of slow deep breaths. Then he returned to the courtroom, ready to tell his side of the story: the truth.

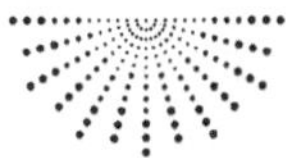

CHAPTER FIFTEEN

Though Abigail had prepared him for this moment, Travis's stomach gurgled as the bailiff swore him in. The water pitcher next to him trembled. "Calm down," he told himself, taking a series of deep breaths. The water pitcher stilled, and he heaved a sigh of relief until DA Waterson started in on him.

"Travis—is it okay if I call you that?"

"Yes, sir."

"As I was saying, Travis, would you say you have an anger problem?"

He nibbled at his thumbnail as he thought about how to respond. "No more than anyone else."

DA Waterson smiled. "And does everyone get involved in brawls that lead to the hospitalization of . . ." He paused, flipping through his legal pad. "Ten people?"

"I don't suppose they do, but—"

"And do they have a lab where they can cook up all manner of explosives?"

Abigail shot from her seat. "Objection. Prejudicial and arguing facts not in evidence."

The judge looked at her but shook her head. "I'd like to hear his answer."

"One, it's not the mad-scientist lab you're making it out to be. Two, I've never created anything more harmful than a laser. Three, were I to carry out an attack on AP Prep, hypotactically speaking, I wouldn't use explosives. They're unreliable and would require access to the school after hours, which I don't have."

The DA stroked his chin. "You've given this a lot of thought, then?"

Abigail sighed. "Objection. Irrelevant. Mr. Watterson's whole line of questioning has no bearing on this case."

Travis looked to the judge, whose face was pinched. "Overruled. However, Mr. Waterson, get to the point or move on."

"Yes, Your Honor. Travis, is it true Joshua Giovanni and his friends have bullied you for years?"

He scowled. "Yes."

"Then would it be correct to say you've held a grudge against them and on the day in question had enough and struck back at them?"

Fists balled white-knuckle tight, Travis fought back his anger. "Giovanni started the fight, and when his friends joined in, I had no choice but defend myself."

Abigail smiled at him and mouthed, "You're doing great."

Mr. Waterson smirked, a glint in his eyes that Travis didn't like. "Were you defending yourself when you broke the ribs and leg of one David Green, or when you attacked a school resource officer? But perhaps, given the neighborhood you come from, violence is to be expected."

Travis didn't need to read Mr. Waterson's mind to catch what he was implying. His whole life, people made assumptions about him because of the color of his skin and where he lived. And now this asshole was trying to paint him as some thug? He wasn't having it.

"You weren't there. You didn't have fifteen savages surrounding you, stomping and punching every inch of you. I did what anyone in my situation would: I fought for my life. Did I go overboard? Maybe.

But I dare you to say you wouldn't have done the same thing in my situation."

"Permission to treat the witness as hostile?"

"Permission denied. Mr. Turner, I instruct you to stick to the questions asked of you and not digress."

Mr. Waterson nodded. "Travis, do you regret your actions?"

"I regret injuring people more than I'd intended to, but no. I don't regret my actions."

"Tell me, Travis, do you know who Helena Aurum is?"

Travis sat up in his seat, eyes narrowed to slits, his anger threatening to boil over; the water in the pitcher next to him steamed. "What does Grams have to do with this?"

"Then you admit Helena Aurum, the richest person in the world, is your grandmother?"

"Of course. But what does that—"

Then it hit him. Mr. Waterson was laying the groundwork for stiffer sentencing due to Travis having affluenza. Abigail had warned him the DA might go this route.

"Then, as the grandson of the heiress to the Cadmus Fortune, you have ample resources to flee the country if you so choose?"

"First off, I'm the heir to the Cadmus Fortune as of Grams' latest will. Second, I'm not like the rich kids that got to AP Prep. I don't have Mumsy and Daddy make a donation every time my grades slip because I'm too busy getting intoxicated every night to study. I never even wanted to matriculate that school and only do so because Grandfather's trust dictates it. Anything else you want to ask me, or are you done trying to pigeonhole me as some disaffected youth waiting for the right time to rain vengeance upon my tormentors?"

The water pitcher next to Travis sailed off the stand, shattering on impact with the floor. Everyone stared at Travis, not saying a word until Abigail asked for a five-minute recess.

Travis wandered to the restroom in a daze, his head spinning with a million thoughts.

Did I just screw myself royally? Did I move that pitcher? And if so, how? Stupid powers; they never work when I need them to and always work when I don't want them to. I'm probably missing some Freudian subtext here, but meh. Hopefully, Abigail can turn things around.

He urinated, washed his hands, and checked his eyes. The concealer ran, and with his sweating, it was useless to apply more, so he washed it off. He was drying his face when Oblivion spoke to him.

"Why do you endure this farce of a trial when you hold the power to bring nations to their knees?"

Sure, I could do that, but then I'd be no better than the rest of those scat-brained trilobites at AP Prep.

"You vex me. Why drag this out? You are stronger than them; therefore, you make the rules."

Power isn't everything. A wise man once said: 'Power tends to corrupt, and absolute power corrupts absolutely.'

"Trust me when I say this. Power is the only thing that matters. The strong always prey upon the weak. You've experienced this yourself, and now you have the means to reverse the roles."

Perhaps you're right, but I was always taught that an eye for an eye makes the whole world blind.

"And how well has that worked for you?"

Travis didn't reply.

"That's what I thought. We will talk more another time. Farewell, my child."

That was weird. But maybe he's right. Why should certain rules apply to me and not others? Why should I get followed at every store I go to when I've never stolen a thing in my life? Why should I be held to a higher standard than my white peers? Why should I fear for my life every time a cop car passes? With these powers, I could . . .

"Travis, are you in there?" Abigail said, sounding exasperated. "The recess ends in two minutes."

Taking a deep breath to steady himself, he exited the restroom and headed to the courtroom with Abigail in tow.

After being sworn in again, Travis retook the witness stand.

"Travis, let me ask you a question: you don't like me very much, do you?"

"No, but then you've spent this entire day besmirching me. So, do you expect me to wash your feet and throw you a banquet?"

Mr. Waterson leaned in so close Travis could smell his toothpaste. He flinched back, and Mr. Waterson leaned in closer. "You want to punch me right now, don't you?"

"Yes, but there are many things I think about doing and never do."

"Any how's that?"

"I control my thoughts and emotions, not the other way around."

Tutting, Mr. Waterson said," Then you admit you intentionally injured those boys?"

Travis rolled his eyes. "No. As stated earlier, I feared for my life and acted with the force I deemed appropriate. Or does that defense only work for white cops who shoot unarmed Black people?"

The judge banged her gavel. "Mr. Turner, I will not have my courtroom become a battleground for your identity politics. I've already warned you once to stick to the questions asked of you. Disregard this warning, and I'll find you in contempt of court and fine you $300. Is that clear?"

"Yes, Your Honor."

"You may continue, Mr. Waterson."

"Nothing further, Your Honor. But I reserve the right to re-examine the witness at a later time."

"So granted. Ms. Kurtzman, you're up."

She stood, her hair frazzled. "Travis, why don't we start by having you tell us about the real you."

Like they practice, he said, "My name's Travis Turner; I'm 12 years old and am the oldest child of Sara and Sampson Turner. I like video games, computers and other electronics, and reading. I go to AP prep, where I'm one of forty students of color and have been bullied by Joshua Giovanni and others since I started there five years ago."

Abigail mmhmmed. "Let me stop you right there. Did you tell anyone you were being bullied?"

"No."

"Why?"

"Many reasons. Chief among them, I wanted to handle it myself, and I'm no snitch."

"Right. Can you walk me through the events of the day in as much detail as possible, please?"

"Objection. Relevance," Mr. Waterson said.

"Overruled. I gave you some leeway, and now I'm giving Ms. Kurtzman some. You may answer the question."

Travis went over the day of the fight, leaving out the strange events.

"Good. Now remind me again, who instigated the fight?"

"Joshua Giovanni. I was minding my business, reading the book Ms. Martin assigned us when he came over, acting overly-familiar like he hadn't antagonized me at the bus that morning and every day at school."

She cupped her hand over her mouth. "Right, and you told him to go away, but he wouldn't leave you alone, correct?"

"Yes, ma'am. I told him I didn't want to be his partner, and he persisted until I told him off, and that's when he hit me."

"I want you to tell me about the fight. Do you remember who was involved?"

"Besides Giovanni, four: Jason Miller, David Green, Keith Maxwell, and Lance Hollister. The rest are a blank."

"What's the last thing you remember?"

"Taking down Green, and then the resource officer rushing in and tasering me."

"Right, and how did that make you feel?"

"I was afraid, more afraid than I'd been since The Fire. So many people hitting me, hurting in so many places."

"And you would have done anything to make that pain stop, right?"

"Objection. Leading the witness."

"Objection sustained. Either rephrase the question or move on."

"Travis, what would you have done to stop that pain?"

"Anything."

"Even if that meant hurting people?"

"I didn't mean to—" He looked to the judge who had cleared her throat and was giving him a dirty look. "What I meant to say is yes. It was me or them."

Abigail next questioned him about his injuries and the genetic disorder he was diagnosed with. He told her all he knew, emphasizing the novelty of the disorder and his impending death due to it. "Thank you, Travis. I have no further questions, Your Honor."

The judge looked to Mr. Watterson. "Any more questions?"

"No, Your Honor. The Prosecution rests."

"What say you, Ms. Kurtzman?"

"No more questions."

The judge adjourned the trial and told them closing arguments would begin tomorrow. Travis dreaded the ride home as his mother had been glaring at him since he mentioned being bullied.

"Why didn't you tell us you were being bullied?" she asked as they pulled onto their cul-de-sac. "And what's this about you dying?"

"Later," he said, going straight to his room to change and then play his favorite game, *Street Fighter II.* He was halfway through a perfect match against M. Bison when Bobby barged into his room. "Family meeting in the kitchen. Something about you dying a bully."

Travis groaned and shut off his Xbox. *I'll whoop that ass another day.* Upon entering the dining room, Travis suppressed the urge to scream. *Get it over with quickly and only give as much information as needed.*

"Something you need to tell us, son?" Mr. Turner said in his gruff voice.

"Joshua Giovanni and his friends, the boys I got in a fight with several weeks back, have been bullying me basically since I started AP Prep. Also, I might have left out that my genetic disorder is slowly killing me. That's it, bye."

He turned to leave, but his mother called him back to the table.

"When Jenny called us, she made it sound like you'd be fine with treatment. Come to find out you're dying? Your father and I want to know why you hid this from us."

Because I knew you'd overreact and play nice like you cared about me. "I didn't want to worry you."

His mother cut him a scathing look. "Right, and is there anything else you're hiding from us?"

Being the devil's vessel and having powers. You know, nothing major. "Nope," he said. "Can I go now?"

His mother looked at his father, who nodded. "Yes, you may. And you won't be going to court again until the judge renders her verdict. You've missed enough school this year."

"But there's only like a week left in the term."

His mother scoffed. "All the more reason you should go."

"What's the point? I'm dying, remember?"

"We don't know that for sure," his dad said. "Best to stick to routines. Now go to your room while we talk with the twins in private."

He stalked away, beyond pissed.

Stupid parents. Why bother going when all the teachers will do is show us movies or have us write idiotic essays on what we plan to do this summer. It's not as if my answer has changed since first grade: read, stay up late playing video games and watching cheesy horror and sci-fi movies, and visit Grams. But thanks to Giovanni, I might be spending my last summer ever in juvy.

He threw himself on his bed, booted up his laptop, popped on his headphones, and listened to music on YouTube for the rest of the night. And when he finally drifted off, Prometheus visited him in his dreams.

They were on the plateau overlooking the river and forest.

"What's up with you and Devil McDevilson being tight all of a sudden?"

"One, the phrase is 'all of a sudden.' Two, we're not tight. And three, he's been straight with me from the beginning, unlike some people."

Prometheus sucked in his bottom lip and wiped his nose. *"What's that supposed to mean?"*

"Don't BS me. I know you're hiding things from me, like why I can't remember certain things or why I wake up feeling tired even when I get over ten hours of sleep."

"A'ight, maybe I have been keeping things from you."

"I knew it!"

"Hold up, cuzo. I'm just tryna help ya."

"Did I ask for your help?" The ground around Travis quaked then cracked as white energy radiated from him. "I'm sick of people thinking they know what's best for me."

Prometheus backed up. *"Chill, before I have to put a hurting on ya."*

Travis, angrier than ever, pumped all his rage into a ball of flames and blasted Prometheus with it, knocking him off the plateau and into the water below.

Then the scene changed to Oblivion's domain. He rose from his throne, clapping. *"Well done, Travis. You're learning fast. But may I make one suggestion: If you could somehow find a way to separate yourself from your emotions, it could grant you the control you want."*

"That makes sense, but how do I go about doing that?"

"Something tells me you'll figure it out with time and practice. Sweet dreams."

"Wait, how are you able to visit me in my dreams *and* when I'm awake?"

Oblivion's laughter echoed throughout the land. *"Darkness exists in the hearts of all, and through it, I can enter their dreams and influence them. As for my visiting you in your waking hours, our souls and fates intertwined. Goodnight, my child."*

~

Travis had a dreamless sleep that night and awoke feeling better than he had in a while. At school, Giovanni tried approaching him several times throughout the day, but Travis turned around and walked away each time, as Abigail had advised him, and the week passed without event. On the final day of school, Ms. Martin returned the grades for their papers on *Frankenstein*. They'd gotten an A+, and in a postscript, she'd written to him:

"Your and Josh's ideas worked well together. I also loved your use of the quotation, 'The child who is not embraced by the village will burn it down to feel its warmth.' Have a great summer."

He shoved the slip in his messenger bag and carried on to his next class. In their last class, their teacher left them out thirty minutes early so they could clean out their lockers if they hadn't already done so. He was in the process of tossing candy wrappers and chip bags into a trash can when Giovanni approached him.

"Hey," he said, "you wanna hang this summer?"

"Under advisement from my lawyer, I've been told not to interact with you, so please leave me alone."

"Fine, but can I help you with your locker?"

Travis thought a moment. "If you're quiet."

Giovanni nodded, and they set to work.

"Thanks," Travis said when they were done. As he walked to the bus, he turned back to look at the school. A wave of melancholia hit him. This could be the last time he'd ever be here, and he was both happy that he'd never have to deal with Giovanni or Keith Maxwell again and sad that he might never graduate to high school.

The honking of a horn drew his attention, and Travis continued to his bus, looking out the windows as they hurtled toward summer and the unknown.

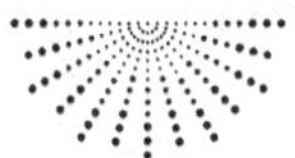

CHAPTER SIXTEEN

"All rise," the bailiff said, and the judge called the courtroom to order. Travis was half asleep, thanks to insomnia caused by a combination of his nervousness and the side effects of Dr. Hu's treatment. It had been a week since school ended, and he'd had his first dose. The first two days after the injection, he had little energy and slept most of the time. Then he couldn't sleep more than two hours at a time due to the migraines and nausea.

"Mr. Turner, I asked you a question," the judge said. "Do you have anything you'd like to say before I render my verdict?"

"Sorry, Your Honor. I'm on a new medication that makes me drowsy. I would like to reiterate that I didn't set out to hurt anyone that day, but I thought my life was in danger and used appropriate force to defend myself."

"Very well then. I find you guilty on all counts. Given the severity of your crimes coupled with your health issues and this being your first offense, I'm inclined to go easy on you. But I feel you should be punished to deter you from further criminal offenses.

"Thus, I'm sentencing you to serve 1,000 hours of community service, placing you on two years' probation, and requiring you to attend anger management classes. Let this be the last time I see you in this court, Mr. Turner, or next time I won't be so sympathetic. If you'll follow my secretary, she'll give you the information regarding your probation officer, local anger management classes, and timesheets for your community service. Good day." She banged her gavel, and Travis's father led him out by the arm.

Travis couldn't believe this was happening. His whole summer was gone, and it was all Giovanni's fault. Damn him and his red-orange rat's nest. He cursed the day they ever met.

On a muggy Monday, Travis found himself in Dr. Douglas Dull's Class for the Aggressively Challenged. The class wasn't scheduled to start for another ten minutes, but his mother had to work a double shift at the hospital, and the twins' babysitter was running late, so she'd elected to drop him off early. As they were saying goodbye, Giovanni and his mother arrived.

"What are you doing here?" they all said in unison.

"It was part of Joshua's—" Mrs. Giovanni began.

"Sentencing?" his mother said. "Same with my Travis, but I refuse to let him be in the same room with your ruffian of a son."

Mrs. Giovanni balled up her fists and cut his mother a dirty look. "The feeling's more than mutual." She stalked toward the other woman, and an argument ensued. Travis's face flushed as others arrived for the class.

"God, this is so embarrassing," he said to no one in particular.

"I know," Giovanni said. "Talk about the battle of the Beckys."

Travis turned to him, glaring. "Hey, your mom started it."

"Did not." Giovanni got in Travis's face. "I wouldn't even be here if it weren't for you!"

Travis, rage on the verge of exploding outward, clenched his jaw. "Me? You're the one who started the fight that landed me here, and now my summer's ruined." He shoved Giovanni back and was about to punch him in that cocky little face of his when someone whistled.

"That's enough. Ladies, is this any example to set for your children?" said a man who introduced himself as Dr. Dull. "And boys, I'm sensing some animosity between you. What say we talk things out before you do something you'll regret?"

Travis sneered at Giovanni. "Too late. This supercilious simpleton is the reason I'm in this class."

"Oh, you think you're so smart using big words. Compensating for something else, eh? Maybe that face of yours?"

Travis lunged at him, and they tussled on the ground before Dr. Dull separated them.

"What are your names, boys?"

They gave him their names, and the man checked his stack of papers. "It would seem you're in my course. As class hasn't officially started yet, I'll let this incident slide, but one more outburst, and I'll contact your probation officers. Understood?"

Travis's mom sneered. "My son isn't going to be in any class with him."

Mrs. Giovanni stuck her nose in the air. "The same goes for my Joshua."

Dr. Dull paused a moment, then cleared his throat. "Perhaps we could all use this as a teaching moment. The boys are already here, so why not let them attend class and see how things go? If it eases your mind, I'll assume full liability should something happen."

Travis's mom and Mrs. Giovanni talked it over a minute with Dr. Dull before agreeing to let them stay.

"Now boys, how 'bout you go inside and take a seat?"

"Yes, sir," they said in unison and entered the classroom. Travis took a seat in the front and booted up his laptop while Giovanni sat in the back. "Asshole," he mouthed as he passed. Travis flipped him off, shooting him side-eye.

During the first class, they went over the syllabus and course policies. They were allowed two excused absences, one unexcused absence, and if they were more than ten minutes late, that counted as half an absence. Attendance and class participation were factored into their grade, and any altercations meant an automatic failure.

Dr. Dull took attendance and had them each tell the class something about themselves when he called their name.

"I hate stupid people and am only here because a moron and his friends decided to jump me at school," Travis said when he was called on.

Giovanni shot out of his chair. "Who ya calling a moron, fatso?"

Travis was out of his seat and heading for Giovanni when a burly guy in a red bandana stepped in front of him. "He's not worth it."

Travis wanted to kick Giovanni's punk ass but wanted to stay out of jail more, so he went back to his seat.

"Yeah. You'd better have walked away," Giovanni said.

Travis glared at him, and the lights flickered.

Calm down. He centered himself, and the lights returned to normal.

"Thank you, Buford, for defusing that situation. And Travis, you showed good restraint. Where'd you learn those breathing exercises?"

"A book on Zen Buddhism and meditation."

"Excellent. Meditation and having some form of spiritual practice are great ways to focus your mind and redirect your aggression. However, I'm disappointed in you and Joshua. Name-calling will not be tolerated in this class."

Travis nodded, and the class continued with them learning various breathing exercises and ways to de-escalate situations. The class closed with them doing trust falls. Travis's skin crawled at the thought of all those strangers touching him, but he endured it until Dr. Dull asked him to pair up with Giovanni.

"Hell no!"

Giovanni shot him a dirty look. "Not like I want to do them with you either. God knows I don't trust ya, and you'd prolly crush me anyways."

Oblivion whispered into Travis's ears, *"Don't let him besmirch you."*

With rage hotter than hell, Travis stared down Giovanni. "Disrespect me again, and I will lay you out and fill your mouth with your mother's menses."

"Both of you outside, now!" Dr. Dull led them by their arms. Once outside the classroom, he lit into them. "What is the matter with you? Joshua, why do you antagonize Travis so? And Travis . . . I don't even know where to begin with what you just said to him. By all rights, I should kick you out of class and call your probation officers."

"Don't!" they said in unison, glaring at the other.

"Why shouldn't I? You two have animosity that goes far beyond aggression issues."

Travis, lachrymose at the thought of dying in juvenile prison, graveled. "Please don't. We promise not to disrupt class again and do the trust falls."

"Yeah," Giovanni said.

Dr. Dull scratched his salt-and-pepper beard. "I'll make an exception in this case, only if you both agree to start therapy with me and complete an assignment for me."

"Anything," Travis said, and Giovanni agreed.

"I'll give it to you at the end of class, assuming you make it that long."

Travis nodded, and they returned to class and did the trust falls. Travis was tempted to let Giovanni fall on his ass but caught him at the last second. Giovanni's lithe frame fit in his arms almost too perfectly.

When class ended, Dr. Dull called them to his desk and told them their assignment was to learn as much as they could about each other before their first therapy session after class next Monday.

Shrugging, Travis said, "Easy. I still have your contact info, so we can do this online."

"No, it's too easy to create false personas online," Dr. Dull said. "I want you to do this face-to-face. You may go now, but I'm warning you. One more altercation and I will call the police. Is that understood?"

"Yes," they said.

"And if your parents ask, tell them I'll assume full responsibility should anything happen."

Giovanni requested a rideshare on his phone while Travis called a taxi. Travis turned to the other boy. "Hey, when do you wanna do this assignment?"

"I have community service most days from 9:00 am till 1:00 pm. You?"

"Six am till one pm most days, then nine am to five pm every other weekend. How's this Wednesday at three pm sound?"

"Fine."

They parted ways when Giovanni's rideshare arrived. Travis's taxi came a few minutes after Giovanni left, and he loathed the conversation he'd have with his parents.

When his father came home at eight o'clock that night, he told him the situation.

"Whelp, you made your bed, and now you have to lay in it. I'm sure your grandfather's trust will cover the cost of therapy, but we best not let your mother know about this, yeah?"

"Yeah," he said and went to bed. He had an early day; tomorrow was his first day of community service, and he was dreading being around more strangers so soon.

Five am came too early for Travis, but he ate a quick breakfast of Fruit Loops, then got ready for the day, dressing in basketball shorts, a Jordan jersey, and his favorite pair of beat-up Chuck Taylors. If he was going to be doing slave labor, then he'd be comfortable.

The SMART bus dropped him off half a mile from St. Michael's Episcopal Church, and he walked the rest of the way. He told the receptionist he was there for community service, and the middle-aged Black woman showed him to the kitchen entrance. "Joan will tell ya what needs to be done. Bless you."

"And you, too," he said, though he didn't mean it, and entered the kitchen. He was struck by the heat, but more so the sight of a tall white woman with fiery serpents for hair.

"Something wrong?" she said.

"Nothing. Just trying to figure out who you remind me of."

She cocked her head to the side, placing her hands around her face. "People tell me I look like Miley Cyrus all the time."

"Yeah, that's it. I'm Travis."

"So, you're the first newbie. I'm Joan," she said, handing him a hair net. "I'll start you off washing dishes, and once you've mastered that, I'll move you to dispensing soup."

She showed him the proper way to clean off dishes before washing them and then set him to work. It was monotonous, but it allowed his mind to wander back to the vision of Joan. As he worked, he caught glimpses of her scuttling about micromanaging everyone, but she looked normal. Maybe it was another side effect of Dr. Hu's treatment? He'd ask him next time he went up to the cabin.

Once Travis had worked his way through his stack of dishes, he was about to see what Joan wanted him to do next when a dark-skinned boy around his age plopped a stack of dirty dishes at his station. For the briefest of seconds, Travis could have sworn he saw a reptilian creature reminiscent of the Chupacabra movie he watched last night on SYFY. He blinked, and it was gone.

Two hours and many stacks of dishes later, Travis took a bathroom break, then resumed washing dishes until Joan told him to stop. "The next volunteer will be here in a bit, and I want you to train him, then go work the soup line. Understand?"

"Yeah," he said. *Hey, if it means I can slack off, I'm happy.*

At ten to nine, Giovanni showed up, and Travis groaned. *Of course, it'd be him.*

They glared at each other, but Travis, being the bigger man, trained Giovanni—or tried to.

"I'm not some idiot. I know how to wash dishes."

"Could have fooled me. Being a Giovanni, I'd expect you'd be pampered and have help for everything."

Giovanni flipped him off. "For your information, we only have a maid four days a week, and the rest of the time, I have to take care of things myself. You know what they say when you assume things."

Travis gave him an exasperated look. "Let's try to get through this day without killing each other."

Rolling his eyes and sighing, Giovanni agreed, and they continued with Giovanni washing while Travis dried and stacked. Joan showed up a while later and told them they made a good team.

"Don't say that," they said in unison.

Joan laughed. "Travis, come with me." She showed him to the front of the dining hall, where people were lined up awaiting their plates. The stations were organized assembly-line style, with soup being the last stop, and once all the food was on the plate, it was distributed to the people.

Joan placed her hand on his back, and he struggled not to cringe. "I have to warn you. Some people will try to get more than they're allotted, but you can't give it to them, understand?"

"Yeah."

He took his place next to the dark-skinned boy from before, who introduced himself as Dylan De Leon. Travis nodded at him and told him his name, then he got to work slinging tomato soup. He kept his eye on the clock, and as soon as it hit one o'clock, he had Joan sign his timesheet, and he was out of there.

The next two days passed without event, and at the end of his shift Wednesday, he was set to go home and murder M. Bison when Giovanni called to him.

"We're still on for today at 3:00 pm, right?"

I forgot. Scheisse! Ich bin ein dummkopf. "Yeah, why?" he said all smooth.

"Well, why don't you come over now? It doesn't make sense for you to go home and have a taxi take to you to my place, right?"

There was a twinkle in Giovanni's eyes and almost a pleading tone to his voice.

"Thanks, but I have things I need to do first. Like, wash the funk off me. And I suggest you do too because you're a bit malodorous."

"Huh?"

"You have major BO."

Giovanni's face went red. He discretely sniffed himself and made a sour face. "Dude, I reek."

Travis suppressed a laugh and went to get his timesheet signed, then left. The bus was only a few minutes late, and he made it home with plenty of time to shower, tinker with Cha, and curb stomp M. Bison. With a little over an hour before he was due at Giovanni's, he had second thoughts.

Why do we even need to meet up? We could do this asinine assignment online, and Dr. Dull would never know. I'll Skype him right—

"Kid, you're going, even if I have to hijack your body to do it."

As if you could.

"I been doing it for we—shit! I wasn't supposed to tell ya that."

What do you mean?

"Nothing."

The lights flickered, and a wind kicked up as realization dawned on Travis. *You've been body-jacking me, haven't you? And that's why I'm so tired all the time.*

"On a scale of one to ten, how pissed are you?"

Infinity plus one.

"Imma go."

How long has this been going on?

"Bro, calm down."

How long!

The overhead lights shattered, tripping the circuit breaker.

The screams of the twins and their babysitter broke through the haze of his fury; he used the breathing exercises Dr. Dull had taught them, and once he'd collected himself, he changed the fuse and cleaned up his room. Once the Wi-Fi was back on, he logged on to Skype to see if Giovanni was on.

"I get it. You're scared to be alone with him."

Do you want me to come in there and kick your ass? Because I will.

"Anything to keep you from seeing Giovanni, right?"

I'm not afraid of being alone with him.

"Then go over there already."

Done.

He called a taxi and told the babysitter he'd be gone an hour max.

~

The Giovannis' house was a mansion in a gated community, and the guard at the entrance side-eyed Travis upon hearing why he was there. "You're not the type JJ hangs with. How do you know him?"

"We attend Azure Plains Preparatory Academy together. Call him, and he'll confirm it."

"I'll do just that."

A few minutes later, Travis keyed in the passcode to the Giovannis' gate, walked up the driveway, and rang the doorbell.

Here goes nothing.

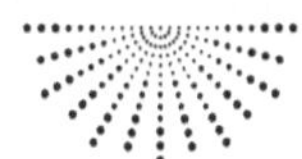

CHAPTER SEVENTEEN

JJ opened the door, smiling as he tried to tamp down his nervous energy. "Hey," he said, acting all suave, until his damp hair got in his face, ruining his façade.

Travis smirked. "Just got out of the shower, huh?"

JJ nodded, his cheeks warming from embarrassment. "Yeah. I kind of forgot the time. Lost in thought, ya know?"

"You use your right or left hand for that?"

It took him a second to get what Travis was implying, and he groaned. "Come inside before my nosy neighbors get the wrong idea about us."

Half-smiling, half-scowling, Travis said, "And we wouldn't want that. Or do we?"

JJ laughed and did his best Three Stooges impression. "Why I oughtta." He went to play slap Travis, who dodged and smacked JJ on the butt.

"Ouch!"

"Consider that the first of many to pay ya back. You gonna let me in or what?"

JJ tugged on his ear, lips pursed. "Umm, yeah. And . . . I'm sorry."

"You'll have to be more specific, considering you have years of atrocities for which to atone."

"For it all: the fight, bullying you, everything."

Travis gritted his teeth. "You expect me to grant you absolution because you've said you're sorry?"

JJ averted his eyes, heat creeping into his cheeks and ears as his anger and embarrassment soared. "That's how it works at church."

"Don't lie to me. I've been to confession; you must serve penance for your sins."

JJ's mouth hung agape. "You're Catholic?"

"I was an altar boy at St. Bart's until I gave up religion."

"I don't believe you."

Travis recited the Lord's Prayer and a Hail Mary, both in Latin.

"You seriously were an altar boy?"

"No, I memorized that for gits and shiggles." He reached out and grabbed JJ's pendent. "Hmm, St. Jude. Patron saint of lost causes."

JJ's heart fluttered at being so close to Travis. "G-good eye."

"Easy-peasy. We made rhymes to help us remember all the saints. St. Antony, we come to thee on bended knees; help us find our keys. St. Jude, if you pray to him, you're worm food. I've forgotten the rest."

JJ giggled.

"What's so funny?"

He looked at Travis and laughed again.

"Keep it up, mister chuckles, and see if you don't catch these hands again."

"I'm sorry, dude," he said between laughs, "but the thought of you in ceremonial vestments, carrying around a decanter is hilar AF."

They entered the foyer, and JJ could have sworn he heard someone say, "Big old . . ."

He stopped and turned back to Travis. "You say something?"

Travis said, "Yeah. A place this big, you could kill a guy, and no one would hear it."

"That was morbid."

"Spoiler alert: life is morbid. But I bet it makes for great parties. Not that I'd be into that type of thing, mind you."

Shrugging, JJ replied, "I guess, but sometimes I feel like Jay Gatsby."

"The getting-shot-to-death part of the parties?"

Giovanni laughed. "You know, you're kind of funny. In a dark, twisted way, I mean. But yeah, dude. Ev'rybody and they mama be tryna get up in the cut."

Travis stopped. "Don't do that."

"Do what?"

"Are you really that obtuse? Your attempt to build rapport with me by affecting African American Vernacular English is beyond repugnant."

"But I thought—"

"Because I'm a person of color, I talk like gutter tripe?"

"Dude, why you getting all butt-hurt?"

"One, I'm not your dude. Two, the only one getting butt-hurt around here will be you if you don't stop pissing me off."

JJ threw his hands up in frustration. "Jesus, Travis. All I did was try to talk on your level."

Though his industrial fan was cranked to the max, the temperature jumped, and JJ broke out in a sweat.

Travis took several deeps breaths and the temperature lowered.

Weird.

Travis's sunglasses slipped down his nose, and he was quick to push them back up. But not before JJ caught the briefest flash of red.

He was about to ask Travis about it when Travis cut him off. "You, like most people, are so beneath me you might as well not exist."

"And just when I was starting to like you, ya become a giant dick again."

Smirking and then laughing, Travis said, "How cute. You think your opinion of me matters."

JJ groaned, no longer caring about Travis's eyes. "Let's do Dr. Dull's assignment, and then you can go."

"Fine with me, Joshua."

He made a sour face. "I hate it when people call me that."

"I surmised as much. Let's go. The sooner we finish, the sooner I won't have to pretend to like you."

"You're such an asshole."

Travis half-smirked, half-laughed. "And proud of it."

JJ stormed off, shouting over his shoulder, "Come on, you insufferable douche master general."

Travis caught up to him. "Funny, I didn't think you knew any polysyllabic words, let alone how to use them correctly."

He rolled his eyes. "You're not the only one who can use big words. My room's up the stairs."

As Travis followed him, JJ explained that the floors were Italian marble, the staircases were lined with royal purple carpeting, and the works of the masters hung on the wall, which JJ told him weren't reproductions.

"I have the whole floor to myself. It's massive, right?" he said when they got to the top of the stairs.

"Actually, my wing at Grams' estate is bigger."

"I call BS. Who's this Grams, God?"

"Close. You'd know her better as Helena Ziglar-Aurum, widow of Marshall Aurum."

Folding his arms, JJ cocked his head to the side. "So, your grandmother is the richest person in the world?"

"Yep."

JJ's mouth hung agape. "You're serious, aren't you?"

Travis shrugged. "Yes. Her only daughter is Sarah Sophia Turner, née Aurum, my mother."

"So, you're mixed?"

He scowled. "The politically correct nomenclature is bi-racial, but yes."

"Jesus, dude. What are you doing slumming it around here?"

"Because Opa, in his infinite stupidity, set up a trust fund for me that stipulated I must attend a preparatory school or the equivalent."

"I mean, then why aren't you like at Choate or something?"

"Because Mother and Father had the final say on which school I attended and decided AP Prep was the most suitable candidate because of my habitual absences due to illnesses and surgeries."

JJ hung his head. "Helena Aurum really is your grandmother."

Travis rolled his eyes, sighing. "Your reaction is common. Most people don't believe me until I show them pictures of us."

"Right, but why aren't you living it up with her? I mean, couldn't she hire you the best tutors money could buy?"

"Trust me, after you and your hooligan friends accosted me, I tried to get Mother to let me live with—"

"Hold up. You're over here sounding like Draco Malfoy with all this 'Mother' business."

"You know what? You don't get to hear any more about me." He turned, but JJ grabbed his arm. "If you value your life, let me go."

"Hold up. I didn't mean to offend you. I was just trying to be funny. I'm sorry, okay?"

"You seem to be saying that a lot. But as I told you, they're mere words." He pulled his hand away.

JJ's frustration boiled over, and he unloaded on Travis. "For fuck's sake, can't you be nice to me for one second?"

"I'm only returning all the anguish you and your friends dealt to me over the years."

"But, what if we were to start over and try like being friends?"

Travis scoffed. "I don't need or want friends. All attachments are wastes of time and energy."

"You can't mean that. Everyone needs people in their life."

Travis ignored him and found his way to JJ's bedroom, stopping in the doorway.

"You're saying you don't care about anyone?"

"Let it go, Giovanni."

He folded his arms and shook his head. "Not until you answer my question."

"If it will hurry things, then aside from Grams and Jenny, a nurse who's taken care of me since I was a kid, I don't care about anyone. Familiarity breeds dependence and dependence upon anyone for anything is a weakness I will not abide."

"That's messed up."

"You say that like it matters what you think of me."

This dickwad. "Screw you. Let's get started already. Name, birthday, and family members."

"My full name is Travis Marshall Percy-Newton Turner, eldest son of Sarah Sophia and Sampson Eli Turner. My brother Robert 'Bobby' Seale Turner and sister Amber Kathleen-Cleaver Turner are twins and are a year-and-a-half younger than me. I was born on September 8, 2004, at 10:00 am. Your turn."

"What did you mean when you said all emotions are pointless? How can that be when emotions are responsible for music, art, literature, and video games?"

He pursed his lips, his expression pensive. "I meant that emotions are pointless because they cloud rational thought and prevent people from seeing the larger picture. Was that easy enough for you to understand?"

JJ glared. "Don't be a troll."

"I was asking per your previous comments."

He nodded. "Yeah, I understood all that, but come on, Travis. You mean to say you don't love anyone?"

"There are different types of love—familial, platonic, romantic, sexual. To which are you referring?"

JJ's face fell. There were so many things he wanted to ask Travis, but he didn't yet know how to express himself without sounding like a fool or giving away his feelings. He made his way over to his desk and removed a chocolate bar from it, munching on it as he thought. Finally, he said, "What about romance?"

"Didn't your mother tell you not to talk with your mouth full? As for that, it's a cosmic joke, an evolutionary trick of chemicals to compel the species to procreate, nothing more."

Wiping his mouth, JJ furrowed his brow, frowning. "Pardon me for saying this, but that's a load of crap. Why so serious?"

Travis laughed darkly. "The world is ten pounds of crap in a two-pound bag."

"Yeah, but friends, family, *lovers* . . . they make things a whole lot less shitty."

"You would think that. You're one of them."

JJ cocked his head to the side. "One of who?"

"First, that's, 'one of whom?'. Second, I mean the beautiful people."

"Hey, just cuz I'm totes cute doesn't mean I don't have problems."

Scoffing, Travis steepled his fingers. "And what pray tell could those be? You live in a mansion, have tons of friends, and look like a model."

"Shows what you know. For starters, I'm short, ginger, barely see my parents, and when they are home, they're either on their phones or constantly telling me to do better. I just wish . . ."

Travis looked over at JJ. "Go on."

"Nothing. It's not important. You gonna stand in the doorway or come in?"

"Nope. I'm liable to catch the Bubonic Plague or Streptococcus Necrotizing Fasciitis, aka flesh-eating disease."

"My room's not that bad, but I understand if you're scared."

Travis flipped him off and made his way to JJ's bed. "As I've told you before, that's Turner to you."

Letting out a sigh, JJ's exasperation mounted by the second. "Fine. Have you ever played Never Have I Ever?"

"Nope."

"It's a drinking game where people take turns making 'never have I ever' statements, and the others take a shot when it's something they've done. Understand?"

"I don't know about this. I've never drunken anything besides a few sips of champagne on New Year's."

JJ smiled. "I understand if you're too pussy to—"

"Get the alcohol!"

"Well, alright, alright, alright. I'll get the flavored vodka since it's your first time drinking and all."

"Go already," he said and tossed a throw pillow at JJ.

CHAPTER EIGHTEEN

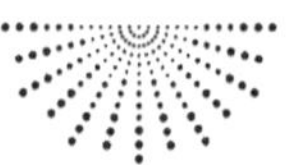

ravis took a swig of vodka, trying not to show how much it hurt going down, and passed the bottle to Giovanni as they reclined on his bed. "Never have I ever participated in a circle jerk."

Giovanni's face went red, and he reached for the bottle.

"Care to explain?"

"That wasn't part of the game."

Travis laughed. "Who's scared now?"

He faltered a moment before a resolute look came over his face. "Fine if I tell ya, then the rules of the game change."

"I'm listening," Travis said, not letting on how intrigued he was.

"We play Truth or Shots. We can ask each other any question, and you have to answer or take a shot. But for each question you skip, the number of shots you take increases until you answer a question."

Travis sized him up. "Where'd you come up with this game?"

"A couple of friends of mine invented it at summer camp a few years back."

"These wouldn't be the same friends you had a circle jerk with, perchance?"

He lowered his head, cheeks red, and muttered something under his breath.

"I didn't hear that."

"I said, yeah. My friend Sam snuck in some whiskey, and after a few shots, we decided to see who had the biggest dick. One thing led to another, and we jerked off together. No biggie. Lotsa guys do it."

"I wouldn't know, what with my perpetually being in the hospital and all."

They were quiet for a while until Giovanni said, "Why's your face like that?"

Travis reached for the bottle.

"Oh, come on. I told ya what me and my friends did."

Travis groaned. "One, that should be, 'My friends and I.' Two, it's none of your business."

Hanging his head, Giovanni let out a deep sigh. "Come on. If you tell me, we'll both have something on each other and be bonded for life."

I'm dying anyway, so why should it matter if I tell him?

"There was a fire when I was like two or three. I don't remember much of it, except when my heart stopped in the ER."

Giovanni leaned into him, their legs touching. "What happened?"

"I felt safe, like coming home. Then they pulled me back here, and that's when the hell started." Giovanni rubbed Travis's knee, and he flinched. "I don't need your sympathy. And that counts as two questions."

Giovanni moved closer, so their legs touched again, and Travis scooted away, leaving a six-inch gap between them. "Why do you keep invading my space?"

Reaching for the bottle, Giovanni's eyes had a glint to them as if he were hiding something.

"Question two: Why do you antagonize me so?" At Giovanni's bemused looked, Travis rephrased things. "Why do you bully me?"

The silence stretched out before them, so thick it was suffocating.

"If I tell you, it counts as two answers."

"One-and-a-half, and I'll take a shot."

"Deal."

He took the requisite shot, passed the two-thirds-full bottle to Giovanni, and leaned in.

"Can you take your sunglasses off? I want to look into your eyes when I say this."

Confused, Travis removed his Ray-Bans. "What's this about?"

"I," he began, his hands trembling and voice quavering. "Whoa, what's up with your eyes? One's red and the other's green."

"It's called heterochromia and . . ." Travis paused, weighing how much detail to give Giovanni. "It's a side effect of my genetic disorder."

The other boy's mouth went wide. "What type of disorder."

Travis scowled. "Don't change the subject. Why do you pick on me?"

Giovanni floundered before saying, "Because I like you and didn't know how to tell you, so I bullied you."

Travis didn't understand. "What do you mean you like me?"

Giovanni looked away, his face flushing red. "I want to be your . . . friend."

"That doesn't make sense."

Adam's apple bobbing as he gulped, lips quivering, Giovanni said. "At first, I was just following along with my friends."

"Perhaps you need some new friends."

He nodded. "I don't even like half of them, especially that epic-fail bag of douche Maxwell."

"Then why hang with them?"

"Because I don't want to be alone." He reached for the bottle and chugged it.

Travis took the bottle from him and downed a shot, so Giovanni wouldn't think him a lightweight. "People come and people go; we can only depend on ourselves."

"That easy for you to say. You have siblings and a grandmother that loves you to death. I have no one."

His comments sparked a war in Travis. On the one hand, he wanted to curse out Giovanni for presuming to know him and his home life. Alternatively, part of Travis wanted to comfort Giovanni. Maybe the alcohol was having more of an effect than he thought.

Instead of doing either, he said, "I still don't get why you picked on me if you wanted us to be friends. Not that I want to be your friend."

"It was the only way I could be around you without anyone getting suspicious."

"I don't understand. Why didn't you just walk up to me, apologize for being an absolute shithead, and then make amends for it?"

Hands shaking, Giovanni reached for the half-empty bottle. "Let's get back to the game. By my count, you owe me two answers."

"And you owe me three. Make it one answer and two shots, and I'll call it even and won't press you about why you want to be close to me."

"Fine. What did you mean when you said I look like a model?"

Travis grimaced. "Repeat this to anyone, and I'll rip off your balls and shove them up your ass."

Giovanni laughed. No need to be so cereal, bro. You have my word as a boy scout."

He took a shot. "I meant you're like totally handsome. Way more than I'll ever be."

"Oh." Giovanni's face fell, and there was a disappointed tone to his voice. "I mean . . . why don't you have plastic surgery?"

Through gritted teethed, Travis said, "This is after three skin grafts and four facial reconstructions."

"Don't bite my head off. For what it's worth, I don't think you're ugly."

Giovanni held his gaze, and Travis looked away. "My turn. Did you really sleep with all those girls like you've claimed?"

Giovanni looked everywhere but at Travis. "I-I've never had sex. Hell, outside of relatives, I've never kissed someone."

So, he's a virgin, too?

He looked at Giovanni, taking him in. He was shorter by several inches, built like a gymnast with a delicate air about him. However, what Travis zeroed in on was Giovanni's face. Such fine features, like a porcelain doll.

"Dude, you okay? You've been staring at me pretty hardco—"

Time froze as Travis leaned in to kiss Giovanni.

CHAPTER NINETEEN

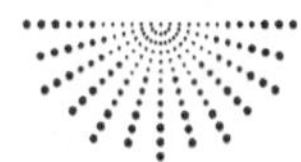

Travis was so close to Giovanni, he could smell the alcohol mixed with his minty breath. A few more millimeters, and their lips would touch. And then he stopped.

Travis pulled back and ran from the room as Giovanni called after him. In that moment, he wanted to be home more than anything. A tingle ran up his spine, and then liquid warmth enveloped him. When it passed, he was back in his room.

A wave of nausea hit him hard, and he rushed to the trash can and vomited. He cleaned himself up and washed the foul taste from his mouth, wondering what the hell just happened. He ran into the babysitter as he was coming out of the bathroom.

"When'd you get back?" she said with a concerned expression.

"Just now. I wasn't feeling too well, so I came home early."

"Okay. I'm here until five, so you can go back out if you want."

He told her he was good and went back to his room to think.

What the heck almost happened at Giovanni's?

"Bruh, you almost kissed my mans. Don't ya think you're on a first-name basis?"

Travis clenched his jaw, gritting his teeth in annoyance. *I didn't ask your advice, so do fornicate with a chainsaw.*

"Who you tryna fool? Ya likes him and wants to kiss him. Either accept that, or Imma make you go back there."

That's it! I'm coming in there.

~

When his mindscape materialized, Travis blasted Prometheus with a gust of cutting winds. Prometheus teleported behind him, catching Travis off guard with a kick to the head.

"Nigga, who you think ya finna beat with that pussy shit?" Prometheus followed up with a flurry of punches and kicks, overwhelming Travis.

"When did you get this strong?"

"Don't try and change the subject. You gon' stop acting a fool and admit ya likes JJ, or do I need to whoop that ass some more?"

The roar of blood filled Travis's ears, his rage and disgust building with each heartbeat. "I don't like Giovanni! How dare you interfere in my life like this."

The ground cracked, and white tentacles sprang up and gave Prometheus chase. He dodged them, then obliterated them with a wall of blue flames. *"Just for that, Imma take control of the old body."* He waved his hand, and chains bound Travis.

"Later, chump."

"You stay the hell away from Giovanni, or I'll . . ."

Prometheus vanished, leaving Travis alone with his thoughts. *How could I let him beat me like that? How long will he body-jack me this time? And what will he do? And why is he so insistent upon my socializing with Giovanni? I can puzzle that out later. I need to figure a way out of these chains.*

First, he blasted them with flames, but they didn't melt. Next, he formed diamond blades from the ground and used them to cut the chains. But every time he was on the verge of cutting himself free, the chains reformed. A pit of worry formed in his stomach as his anxiety skyrocketed. *What am I going to do?*

"Perhaps I could be of service?"

Travis recognized the voice immediately. Oblivion was floating above the edge of the plateau, a serene smile on his face. Only this close did Travis realize that Oblivion's teeth were made of bones and his skin, writhing souls. He fought back the urge to vomit. "W-w-what do you want?"

"To help."

"What's the catch?"

"Unlike the ignoramus whom you share your body with, my help doesn't always come at a cost. Tell me, have you heard the fable of The Frog and the Scorpion?"

Eying Oblivion, Travis shook his head. "Why?"

"A lesson. While there are several variations on this story, I prefer the frog and scorpion one the best. Once upon a time, a scorpion came upon a river and needed to cross it, so he asked a frog to carry him across.

"The frog replied, 'No. Surely you'll sting me.'

"The scorpion laughed. 'Then we'd both drown.'

"The frog agreed, and the scorpion hopped on his back. Halfway across the river, the scorpion stung the frog.

"'Why did you sting me?' asked the frog with his dying breath.

"The scorpion replied, 'It was in my nature.'"

"That's a stupid story. The scorpion could have waited until they'd crossed to sting the frog."

"True, but the moral of the story is that you must embrace your nature, whether that's your feelings for the Giovanni scion or your destiny. You will find no respite until you do."

"Right. Any tips on getting out of these chains?"

"I was under the impression you didn't want my help. Farewell."

"No. Don't. Damn it!"

Alone again, Travis's thoughts turned to freeing himself. This was his mind; he was the master of this domain. "Teleport," he told himself. Managing to move a yard but still bound, Travis prepared to teleport again when he had the sudden urge to try exploding the chains. With few options left to him, he fingered the links. "Explode," he said under his breath, but the chains remained. Next, he pictured the links exploding and, one-by-one, they did.

Once he was free, Travis intended to rip Prometheus a new one. But his plans changed when he heard a bird shrieking in the distance. Something told him to investigate it, and as he looked out over the plateau, the creeping greyness now coved two-thirds of the forest. The bird cried out again, more incessant this time as though its life depended on him finding it.

Each cry sparked the phantom of memory in Travis—men in Neo-Nazi outfits speaking German, the scent of gasoline, the taste of the chocolate, and the heat as flames enveloped him. Then there was only darkness.

The bird cried out again.

"I'm coming." He imagined himself flying, and he slowly hovered off the ground and followed the bird's cries. It took him a while to locate it, and what he found shocked him.

Before him was a brick wall floating in the air.

"Are you in there?"

The bird trilled, and Travis asked it to trill once for yes and twice for no.

"Yes," it trilled.

"Do you want me to free you?"

"Yes!"

"I don't know if I can, but I'll try."

He pictured the bricks exploding, as he'd done with the chain links. But the wall remained intact. Something in Travis told him destroying this wall was the key to everything. He tried again, focusing on the mortar. Centimeter by centimeter, he chipped away at the wall, but his head hurt like someone had taken a steamroller to it. When he'd removed enough mortar to pop out two bricks, a giant blackbird in chains stared back at him. Then a black light whooshed out of the wall into him, and with it, more memories and power.

However, before he could make sense of what happened, Prometheus showed up and resealed the wall.

Trave punched him. "What are you doing?"

"Making sure you don't go brain dead trying to free him before you're ready."

"Like hell you will."

They fought, and thanks to Travis's rage combined with the power-up from the wall, he trounced Prometheus and locked him away. But Travis knew that wouldn't hold him forever.

Once back in the physical world, Travis found himself somewhere he didn't recognize. Closing his eyes, he pictured home, but when he opened his eyes, he was at Woodward and Nine Mile Road, several miles from home. He checked his pockets and found a wad of twenties, which he used for the taxi ride home.

After sneaking in, he stashed the rest of the money in the loose floorboard where he used to hide his cutting supplies. Then he booted up his computer and scoured the internet for information on strengthening his mind.

When the babysitter left, he waited until his mother got off work to sneak to a local park he'd scoped out on Google Earth as a training spot. From his new memories, he'd learned he had dominion over all the elements and telekinesis, the latter of which he planned to train tonight.

Spotting a forty-ounce bottle laying in the grass a few meters away, he willed it to move. It wiggled a bit, but that could have been due to the wind blowing, so he tried again once it'd stopped.

Come on. Move!

The bottle exploded, and Travis nearly jumped out of his skin.

Let's try that again.

A dirty tennis ball lay three meters away by a trash can. *Come to me.* The ball wobbled. Then it rolled toward him, stopping at his feet. Travis yawned, rubbing his throbbing forehead. *That's enough for today.*

Settling into bed, he wondered if Oblivion was as bad as Prometheus led him to believe or if Prometheus was the real villain.

~

The rest of the week, Travis trained at the park every night and avoided Giovanni whenever possible until Friday when Giovanni cornered him in the kitchen at St. Michael's.

"What's up with you? And why'd you run away so fast?"

Swallowing back the lump of fear in his throat, Travis put on a brave face. "I don't know what you're talking about."

He went back to washing dishes, but Giovanni grabbed his arm. "Bull. You've been ghosting me all week," he said, dropping his voice to a whisper, "ever since our kiss."

"We did not kiss. And even if we did, which we didn't, it was because of the vodka."

Giovanni pouted. "Be that way, but we still need to complete that assignment for Dr. Dull before Monday."

"And like I told you before, we can do it online. I still have your contact information, and I assume you still have mine?"

Giovanni sighed. "When do you want to do this?"

Shrugging, Travis said, "How about tonight? Say five o'clock? Unless you have a party to throw or something."

"Nope. My ass is all yours," he said, and Travis laughed.

"What's so—oh!" Giovanni's face flushed. "I didn't mean it like that. Or did I?" he said, wiggling his brow.

"Giovanni, you're such a dork. Now scram before Joan gets on my back about not finishing these dishes before my shift is over." Travis said, swatting him on the butt, leaving a wet handprint on Giovanni's shorts.

"Thanks. Now people are gonna wonder why I have a handprint on my ass."

Travis snickered. "And that's my problem how?"

Shaking his head, Giovanni walked away, muttering obscenities under his breath. Travis's eyes followed him.

"I been knew you liked my mans, so why you fronting?" Prometheus said.

I'm not dealing with you today. Bye. Travis pictured chains enveloping Prometheus and then wall after wall surrounding him.

"Come on. No. Don't. You suck . . ."

Prometheus's voice faded, and Travis smiled. *That'll show him.*

CHAPTER TWENTY

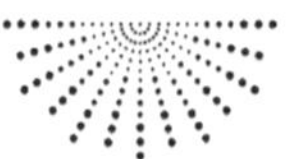

When JJ arrived home, he checked his phone and found a voice mail from his parents saying they'd be home next Tuesday, and they expected his room to be clean. Grumbling under his breath, he gathered trash bags and gloves and set to work. First, he picked up all the trash on his floor. Then he cleaned under his bed, cringing when he found a moldy slice of pizza and crusty socks. Once he'd gathered up all his dirty clothes and placed them in his hamper, he swept the floor and took the trash out. Then he showered.

Once he was clean, he called Brianna and Rachel to see what they were up to. Brianna was busy braiding hair while Rachel's phone went straight to voicemail. Henry was busy too, as were Lance, Mitchells, David, and Jason. Sighing, he told Alexa to play *I'm Just a Kid* by Simple Plan. He scream-sang along to the lyrics, feeling more alone than ever at that moment. JJ was halfway through his third listen when the alarm on his phone sounded.

Shit, I forgot all about my Google Hangout with Travis. He rushed around the room, trying to remember where he put his laptop. After finding it, he booted up and logged on.

~DaJoshFather has entered The Hangout~

It took a second for Travis's image to load, and when it did, he looked beat.

"Hey," JJ said, nibbling on a candy bar.

Travis yawned. "Cute username. DaJoshfather, like the God Father?

Smiling, JJ said, "Yeah. It's legit my fav movie. So, where do you wanna begin?

A pensive look came over Travis. "Your name, birthdate, and family history would be a good start."

JJ nodded. "My full name is Joshua." He cringed. "Joseph Giovanni and I was born April 1, 2003."

Eyes wide, Travis said, "You're almost two years older than me. How are we in the same grade?"

"I was held back twice. On purpose, mind you. I used to go to Choate, then I flunked all my classes to get my parent's attention. But all it earned me was a grounding. I did the same thing the next year, and they transferred me to AP Prep."

At Travis's confused look, JJ said, "What's wrong?"

"I don't get why you'd want to flunk two grades.

As soon as I'm old enough, I'll take the GED test and be done with school."

"Why do you hate school so much?"

Travis rolled his eyes. "Why do you think?"

JJ looked down. "Sorry."

Neither of them said anything for a while until Travis broke the silence. "What are your parents like?"

"Demanding. Always going on about how I must uphold the dignity and honor of our family and how my every action reflects upon them. Honestly, it's a load of horse shit. What about your parents?"

"Mother is an RN, and Father is an electrician with a local construction company. They work a lot, leaving me to look after the twins when they can't get a babysitter."

"I wish I had a brother or sister."

Travis laughed. "No, you don't. They're annoying brats, and I'd rather be an only child like you. Back to my parents. Mother, being from old money, is prim and proper, always hectoring me about 'dressing for success and my image. Father is stoic but has always stressed the importance of education and hard work. Even though I have a 3.666 GPA, he's always telling me I can do better. The truth is I learn more outside of school than I do inside it. Parents can be such . . ."

"Bastards?" JJ said, making a sour face as his resentment ratcheted up.

"I was going to say authoritarian Neanderthals, but that works. They act like because they're older, they know better. But I'm old enough to make decisions about my own body."

JJ raised his hands in the air. "Preach! Parents think they know everything, but they have no clue what we go through on the daily."

"Exactly. They wouldn't last thirty seconds as a kid today. I swear, they should require people to have a license before siring offspring."

"Amen," JJ said, and they laughed.

"You know," Travis said, smiling, "you don't completely suck, Giovanni."

"Thanks, and you're not half-bad yourself, Travis."

Scowling, Travis said, "That's Turner."

JJ rolled his eyes. "Don't you think we're closer than that, given our kiss?"

"One, we didn't kiss. Two, you must earn the right to use my first name."

And just when I was starting to like him, he goes and says that. "How about this: you can call me JJ if I can call you Travis?"

"No deal. It's either Joshua or Giovanni."

"Why?"

"Because JJ has tormented me for years."

"Huh? Wait. I get it. Then how about you call me Josh?"

"That's satisfactory. A glossy look came into Travis's eyes, and he froze as if in a trance before cracking a grin and saying, "You want to kick it at my crib tomorrow or what?"

"And the award for most schizo goes to you." He laughed.

Travis smiled wide. "I know I can be a real prick, but give me another chance?"

JJ didn't know what to make of Travis's mood shift. Should he accept the offer and hang with him or decline it? They both probably had enough info to satisfy Dr. Dull. And he was still pissed at Travis for getting them kicked out of anger management class. But the thought of being in Travis's actual room was too great a temptation.

"Imma need an answer soon."

Pushing aside his fears, JJ said, "Yeah. When?"

"Six PM?"

"Cool. Oh, can I have your cell number? In case my plans change."

They said goodbye, and JJ promised to text him later. For the rest of the day, he couldn't stop smiling. *Tomorrow, I'm gonna hang with Travis frelling Turner. But what if I spaz out, and he doesn't like me? What if this is all an elaborate prank to get revenge on me. What if I go over there and he tells me he hates me?*

He hyperventilated until he remembered the breathing exercises Dr. Dull had taught them. *Calm down. We're just going over there to hang. That's it. Maybe I should have a drink to chillax?*

He shook his head, thinking better of it, and spent the rest of the day on YouTube.

The next day, JJ spent hours agonizing over what to wear. He didn't want to dress too formally, but he didn't want to look like a slob either. He settled on a pair of khaki cargo shorts with a polo and Converses. Outfit decided, he attempted to tame the orange beast that was his hair. He was all set to begin the battle when he noticed he had a giant pimple on his nose.

Fuck! What am I gonna do?

He tried popping it, but it wasn't ready and swelled up, turning an angry reddish-purple. *Maybe Mom's concealer will work?*

Creeping up the stairs to the third floor, he entered his parents' room and searched his mother's side of the bathroom, finding several bottles of concealers. But which to use? He tested a bit of each on his hand until he found one that matched his skin tone. After applying it to his zit, he checked himself out in the mirror. It now looked like he had a huge bump/wart on his nose. "I'm hideous."

Screw it.

He put the concealers away, washed his nose, and got his hair presentable. When he was ready, JJ texted Travis.

"We still on to hang today?"

The message stayed on read for ten minutes before Travis replied, **"Yeah. See you in a bit."**

JJ requested a rideshare, and when it arrived, he piled in, heart in his throat.

Here we go.

CHAPTER TWENTY-ONE

Aiming his stick at a Wendy's wrapper, Travis stabbed it, placing it in his bag with the others. The sun was high in the clear sky, and the breeze from the cars rushing by was a welcome reprieve from the heat. He'd been at it since seven o'clock, arms and legs tired from walking the park. It was mind-numbing but easy work, and it gave him time to think about what happened last night.

He remembered talking with Giovanni—no, Josh—and then everything went fuzzy for a bit, and he found himself back in his mindscape, which could only mean one thing: Prometheus body-jacked him again. *Damn him and his—*

"Lunch break!" his supervisor called out. Everyone turned in their sticks and bags, then took their lunches from the cooler in the bed of the supervisor's truck. Travis ate his meal of ham and cheese sandwiches and a bottle of orange juice under the shade of a fir tree, then got back to work.

Two hours before quitting time, his phone vibrated. Thinking it was a voicemail from his parents or Grams, he opened it to find a text from Josh asking if they were still going to hang out at his place today.

Explain yourself!

"No need to shout, damn. And stop frontin' like you don't want to see him again."

That wasn't your decision to make.

"A little late for that now, bro. You gon' reply or what?"

Knowing you, you'd make me regardless of what I say. I should bury your ass under mental barriers.

"Chill, kid. Tell ya what. You hang with Joshy boy, and I'll leave you alone for the rest of the weekend."

Make it until Tuesday, and you have a deal.

"Monday afternoon, and I won't body-jack you for a week."

Done.

To ensure Prometheus didn't renege, Travis placed him behind several walls in his mind. He stared at the text for several minutes before replying.

At the end of his shift, he had his supervisor sign his timesheet. Then he called a taxi and hopped in the shower as soon as he got home. He was dressing when Josh rang the doorbell. He threw on a shirt and shorts and ran a comb through his hair, then checked himself out in the mirror.

"Coming," he said as the doorbell rang again. He opened the door as Josh rang it a third time. "Impatient are we? . . . ." He paused, taking in the smaller boy. "You look nice."

Josh smiled, a blush creeping up his neck. "Thanks. You look nice, too. You gonna let me in?"

Travis's cheeks heated. "Sorry. Welcome to Chez Turner. Shoes off at the door. Mother is anal about keeping the house clean. On your left are my brother and sister in their native environ. Bobby, Amber, say hi to Josh."

"Sup?" Bobby said, then turned back to the TV.

Amber looked up from her phone, gave a little wave, and giggled. "You got a girlfriend?"

Travis chuckled at Josh's panicked reaction. "Don't mind her. She's moved out of the boys-are-icky phase and wants to date every guy she sees. Come on."

He showed Josh to his room. "What do you want to do?"

Josh lingered in the doorway. "Travis, don't take this the wrong way, but you're not like a serial killer?"

"Please. It would take entirely too much time to find a target, learn their routine, find a place to terminate them, dispose of the body and all evidence, and craft an alibi."

Laughing, Josh said, "You've thought that through."

Travis shot him a dirty look. "I wonder why?"

Josh sighed. "Dude, I know I was an absolute shit to you for years, but we're never gonna be friends if you keep throwing that in my face."

"Speaking of faces, what's up with Mt. Everest on your nose?"

"Oh, screw you. It's not that bad."

Travis laughed. "I'm surprised that thing doesn't have its own orbit."

"Very funny. But on the real, why is your room so clean? And where are your electronics and video games?"

Travis hit the remote on his bedside desk. "Ask, and you shall receive."

The top of the dresser against the north wall opened, and an HD monitor, Xbox One X, and a horizontal computer tower raised from it.

"Dude, sweet. Where'd you buy that?"

"I built it myself. Granted, I had help from wiki articles and threads on Reddit."

"I love Reddit. What's your favorite sub? Mine's r/Gamingcirclejerk."

"Pervert."

Josh laughed. "Hey, it's not what you think. Besides, I'm too young to be a pervert. I'm a prevert."

"Right. Anyway, my favorite subs are r/Technology and r/Gaming. Speaking of games, you wanna get pwned in *Street Fighter II*?"

"You're on!"

Travis popped in the disk, and they settled on his bed for an epic Ken (Travis) and Ryu (Josh) battle until Travis announced he was tired of kicking Josh's ass.

"No fair," Josh said, sticking out his bottom lip. "That last match ended in a draw."

"Pouting doesn't suit you. What do you say to getting to know each other better—for Dr. Dull's assignment, I mean."

Josh lowered his head. "Right. Well, you already know I like videogames, But I'm also into comics, manga, anime, kaiju—"

"Hold up, you like kaiju movies?"

"Yeah, why?" Josh said in a huffy tone.

"Cool it. I just meant I like them too. Godzilla versus Space Godzilla is my favorite, you?"

"Mothra Versus Godzilla. You wouldn't happen to also like *Buffy, Farscape, Star Trek,* and *Star Wars*?"

"Yes to the latter, no to the former. I never even heard of *Farscape*."

Josh shook his head, smiling. "Oh, my sweet summer child, there is much I must show you."

"Right. Favorite movie?"

"You've prolly never heard of it. *Stand by Me*."

Travis stood there a moment in stunned silence. "What did you say?"

"*Stand by Me*, why?"

Travis clicked another button on his remote, and the drawers on the left side of the dresser opened, displaying his DVD collection. Riffling through them, he pulled out his copy of *Stand by Me* and showed it to Josh, who geeked out.

"This is some next-level shit right here. Who's your favorite character?"

Thinking a second, Travis walked back over to Josh and plopped next to him on the bed. "Gordie, because he's the closest to my personality."

"Yeah. I totes see that. Chris is my favorite, cause like him, I don't take crap from anyone. And I'm a fighter."

"I know."

"Hey!"

"Chill, I'm just messing with ya." Travis went to flick Josh's nose and hit his zit instead.

Josh held his face. "Ow."

"Shit, I didn't mean to do that. Are you okay? I'm sorry."

"I'll live," Josh said after a minute, "but that hurt like a bitch. Where were we?"

"Favorite characters."

"Right. What's your favorite scene?"

"The barf-o-rama scene."

Josh made a sour face. "I can't stand that whole sequence."

"Then what's yours, smartass?"

"You know that scene where Chris tells Gordie about how he wishes he could go somewhere no one knows him?"

"Yeah?"

Josh's eyes watered. "I feel like that all the time. I wish I could go somewhere far away and start over. But I can't. I'm just a stupid kid." Josh wiped at his tears, sniffling as his face and ears went red. "You prolly think I'm a pussy, right?"

Travis had three options here—he could ignore Josh's outburst and change the subject, make fun of him, like he'd done to Travis, or embrace him.

"I don't presume to know you or your homelife. Tell me about them."

"I'm basically a lonely rich kid. I can do and have anything I want, except what I want most. My parents' love. The only time they pay attention to me is when they're showing me off at parties and charity events. I'm like one of those teacup dogs women carry around in their purses."

Travis didn't know how to respond, so he changed the subject. "Tell me two things about yourself that no one knows."

Josh sniffled, and Travis handed him a box of tissues. He blew his nose and hacked up a loogie. "If I tell you this, you can't tell anyone."

"Agreed. It's mutually assured destruction."

Josh inhaled deeply. "I wet the bed until I was ten, and I'm g— never mind. I'm kind of a poet."

Travis noticed the slip but didn't question it. "I cut myself and have thought about killing myself."

Josh stared, wide-eyed, his mouth an o-shape. "Why would you ever think of, of doing that? Was I really that awful to you?"

"It wasn't just you. Your friends, my family, even random people on the street stop and stare or make comments about my face. Sometimes, it's too much to handle. So, I cut myself."

"God. Had I known, I—"

Travis balled his fists up, trying to control himself. "You'd what? Gone easy on me? I don't need your pity." Josh reached for his hand, and Travis flinched away. "Don't touch me!"

The lights flickered, and Travis took several calming breaths, centering himself. "Maybe you should go."

Josh shook his head. "I want you to know you can talk to me about stuff, okay? I know what it's like to want to not exist."

"How?"

"My parents didn't want me. I overheard them arguing about it once when I was five. The first poem I ever wrote was about them:

"I didn't ask to be born into a world full of negativity and hate because you couldn't wait to go home and masturbate. So, you stuck it in your date, filled her with your seed, and now I'm just another mouth to feed."

Neither of them said anything for a while until Travis hugged Josh. "What? You looked like you could use one."

"Thanks, I guess. I think I'm gonna head out."

"Okay. You want to hang out again sometime?"

Josh smiled. "Yeah. It's supposed to be in the nineties all next week, and I'm getting an above-ground pool installed. Thinking of throwing a pool party. Wanna come?"

Though part of Travis was leery of being around Josh's friends, a larger part of him wanted to learn more about this intriguing boy. "I'd like that. Call me with the details so I can work out transportation."

"Will do, Travis. Later."

Travis walked Josh to the door, and Josh went in for a hug while

Travis went for a fist bump. After an awkward moment, they settled on a one-arm hug that left a tingle in Travis's stomach.

"Travis gots a boyfriend," Bobby crowed from the couch.

"Do not."

"Do so," he said and stuck out his tongue.

"I'm done with this conversation," he said, walking to his room and shutting the door. He lay on his bed, the covers still warm from where Josh sat. Travis looked at his room, Sure, there weren't any clothes on the floor nor posters on the walls, and everything was labeled and in its place. But what was weird about that? He liked order – something he'd been lacking since he developed his powers.

Today was a close call and had he not controlled himself, he could have hurt Josh and his only shot at making a friend . . . or maybe more? Did he want that? Was that even possible?

What was he thinking? This was Joshua Giovanni he was talking about. No. It was best to keep things platonic, even if he had enjoyed their hugs.

His ringing phone broke his train of thought: It was Grams calling to ask him when he was coming to visit her.

"About that. See, what had happened was . . ." Without meaning to, he told her everything.

"Well, dear. Don't get mad, but I've known about your powers since they first appeared. I knew they wouldn't stay dormant forever."

"Why didn't you tell me about them?"

Objects around the room levitated and circled him.

"Your parents swore me to secrecy. They said I couldn't see you otherwise."

"They had no right."

"I know that. As for your feelings for Josh, don't overthink things. If you like him, so be it. I'll always love my caramel cowboy. I'll see what I can do about coming to visit you before summer's end. Bye, my special, special boy."

Travis hung up, cleaned up, and chilled until it was time for dinner. He washed up and then set the table while his parents removed the takeout containers from their bags. Stomach growling, he eyed the rotisserie chicken and reached for his plate. His mother smacked his hand and told him to bow his head while she said Grace. Though she couldn't see it, he rolled his eyes and waited for her to finish. Once she was done, he piled his plate with chicken, mashed potatoes, gravy, and biscuits.

"Save some for the rest of us, wide load," Bobby said. Travis kicked him under the table.

He hit me," Bobby whined to their mother.

She glared at Travis. "Apologize to your brother."

"But he—"

"I don't care. You're the eldest and are supposed to set an example for the twins."

Balling up his fists, Travis gave her a dirty look. "Why do you always let him get away with crap but—"

"Watch your language, unclench your fists, and apologize to your brother, or you can go hungry tonight."

"Not like he'll miss it," Bobby said, sticking his tongue out.

"Are you gonna let him get—"

"Travis, you have until the count of three to do like I asked. One . . ."

This isn't fair. He started it.

"Travis," Oblivion cooed, *"how long have you suffered his slings and arrows?"*

Years.

"And has he ever gotten in trouble for it?"

Almost never.

"And is that fair?"

Hell no.

"Right. If they aren't willing to punish him, then it's up to you."

Travis thought back to all the times his parents spanked and grounded him for things Bobby did routinely yet never was punished for. That ended now.

"Travis are you listening to me?" his mother said. "I'm up to two and a half."

You're gonna get a whooping," Bobby taunted.

Travis gritted his teeth, the sound of blood whooshing in his ears blocking out everything else. He rose from his chair, grabbed Bobby by his neck, and lifted him off the ground. Bobby flailed his arms and legs while their parents shouted at Travis to let him go. But he paid them no heed. He was done being their whipping boy.

"Let me go, psycho," Bobby said, clawing at Tavis's hand.

Travis smirked. "What's the matter? Scared?"

"Let him go right now!" his father shouted, making a move toward him. Tightening his grip, Travis raised Bobby higher, shrugging off his father's slap to his face. Being the one doling out pain felt good.

"I can't breathe," Bobby said, gasping, eyes rolling up in his head.

At those words, Travis released Bobby.

After checking on Bobby, his mother sent Travis to his room. A few minutes later, his father entered with a leather belt and gave him five smacks with it.

"You're grounded for three weeks, and I'll be calling your probation officer in the morning."

Once his father had removed all his electronics, he left, and Travis pondered things. Though his bottom stung a bit, he reminded himself that pain was an illusion. Had he gone too far? Perhaps, but Bobby got away with everything while he had to be the perfect son. And he was sick of it.

"Care to talk about what happened?" Oblivion said.

Not really.

"How did it feel? Being in control, making him pay for disrespecting you?"

Great. But also wrong . . . evil.

"Right, wrong, good, evil, these are merely words."

Of course, you'd say that. You're the devil.

"And what was it your Nietzsche said? 'The great periods of our lives occur when we gain the courage to rechristen what is bad about us as what is best.'"

Meaning I should embrace the darkness within me?

"That's one interpretation. Though, I was referring to your powers.

You deserve to live your life as you see fit, and you have the strength to do that."

But my parents—

"Are boils on the ass of creation. You are dying, so enjoy your remaining time."

Right.

He waited until the house stilled to sneak out to the park and train. Using his anger as fuel, he focused on creating fireballs of various sizes before mediating. Through the chatter of his mind, he heard the faint whispers of what he'd later learn were the minds of others. He blocked them out by raising his mental barriers and replayed the day's events. He came to a conclusion.

The world had better prepare itself because tomorrow was the start of a whole new Travis.

CHAPTER TWENTY-TWO

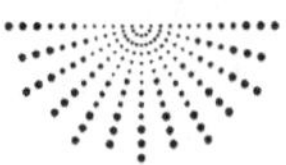

Travis mechanically washed and dried kitchenware, ignoring everyone around him as he stewed over last night's events. *Why do parents have to be such bastards? It's not as if I hurt Bobby. And besides, the brat deserved it.*

"Kid, we both know you're full of it. You could have killed him."

But I didn't.

"Still, you crossed a line."

As if I need a lecture from you, too. Bye. Travis pictured walls rising in his mind and locked Prometheus in a cage. Prometheus raged, but his voice faded until it was gone, leaving Travis to resume dish duty. When Josh arrived at nine o'clock, Travis switched to ladling oatmeal until breakfast ended at eleven, and they changed over to lunch. He was cleaning down the food stations in preparation for the lunch crowd when Josh joined him.

"Done with dishes?" he said, scowling.

"Yeah. BT dubs, what crawled up your vajayjay today?"

Suppressing the urge to roll his eyes, Travis told him what happened last night.

"Dude! Not cool."

Travis paused his scrubbing. "You say that as if my actions weren't warranted."

"But he's family, and blood's thicker than water."

"Actually, the phrase goes, 'the blood of the covenant of battle is thicker than the water of the womb.' Not that I'd expect you to know that."

"Hey, don't take your anger out on me. Remember what Dr. Dull taught us about finding constructive ways to channel our aggression."

Travis nodded. "Sorry. And speaking of the good doctor, we have class and therapy with him today."

Josh's mouth made an o-shape. "I legit forgot that was today. You think we have enough info for his assignment thingy?"

Shrugging, Travis said, "If we don't, we can bs our way through it."

"Right. Well, my pool should be delivered either today or tomorrow and once it's set up, I'll throw that pool party I mentioned. You still coming, right?"

"I'm grounded, remember?"

"So? YOLO, bro. Sneak out. What are they gonna do? Put ya on double secret probation?"

Travis laughed. "I love *Animal House*."

"Me too, and *Revenge of The Nerds* and *Scary Movie.*"

"Josh?"

"Yeah?"

"Did we just become best friends?"

"Yep."

They high-fived and chuckled.

"*Step Brothers* is hilarious," Travis said, smiling.

"I know, right? If you tell me you love anime, comics, and Disney movies, I'm gonna freak."

"Nope. But I do like comics, graphic novels, cheesy horror, sci-fi, and kung fu movies."

"You killed my master. Prepare to die," Josh said, moving his lips in an impression of a bad dub. Travis laughed but caught Joan shooting them dirty looks, so he told Josh they needed to get back to work. As they cleaned, they discussed their top ten favorite films. Josh mentioned *The Godfather,* which started a heated debate on what the best gangster movie was.

Shaking his head, Travis said, "You're crazy if you think *The Godfather* is better than *Scarface.*"

"And you're equally crazy if you think *The Untouchables* is better than *Casino.*"

Travis shook his head, laughing. "Fine, you got me there. But can we all agree *Goodfellas* is better than *Casino?*"

Josh chuckled, his cheeks red. "Dude, you're funny AF."

"I'm funny how?" Travis said, doing a wise guy impersonation, "I mean funny like I'm a clown? Do I amuse you?"

"LOL, bro. Now go home and get your effing shine box."

They spent the rest of their time quoting movies and goofing off until it was time for Josh to leave. Travis felt empty once Josh was gone, but he carried on with his duties until his shift ended. Instead of having Joan call him a taxi as his parents told him to, he walked a few blocks away from the church and tried Popping home, as he'd come to call teleporting. Picturing his room in his mind, he closed his eyes and heard a faint *pop.*

Opening his eyes, he found himself a block from home, dizzy but otherwise okay. With no electronics, he passed the time reading *Beyond Good and Evil* and *Thus spoke Zarathurstra* in the original German. In the past, he'd needed to stop to look up words in his German-to-English dictionary. But today, when he reached for the dictionary to look up terms he didn't know, they popped into his head as though they'd been there all along.

Perhaps this is a new ability. Or maybe I'm regaining my memories before The Fire.

In any event, as he read, he made notes about the Superman and morality. Were things inherently good and evil, or as Oblivion and Nietzsche suggested, were they subjective? And if the latter were true, then who decided what was good and evil? Society, the authorities, the majority, or the individual? Furthermore, what criteria would they use?

He didn't yet know the answers to these questions, But Travis knew if he were in charge, things would be different. But that would require more power than he currently had, which raised another question: could he be trusted not to abuse such power?

"Travis, your ride's here," the babysitter called to him. He gathered his stuff and left.

~

Dr. Dull had them do more breathing exercises and then asked each student to share a recent time they lost their tempers and how they'd dealt with it. It was mostly little things like people banging their thumb with a hammer while trying to hang up a picture, stubbing their toe or stepping on their kid's Legos, getting caught in traffic jams, etc. Then Travis recounted the incident with his brother, and the room went silent, all eyes on him.

Dr. Dull tutted. "Assaulting anyone, especially a family member, is unacceptable behavior, and I'm tempted to contact your probation officer."

"Mother already called her, and she'll be meeting with me this Wednesday," he replied matter-of-factly. Dr. Dull used this as a teaching moment and asked the class for better ways Travis could have dealt with his aggression. After five minutes of being the center of attention, Travis said, "Can we move on?"

Dr. Dull nodded, and they spent the rest of class roleplaying different scenarios and how to de-escalate them. When class ended, Travis was drained from interacting with everyone and longed to go home, but he had therapy to deal with.

Travis sat in the plush chair, kicked off his sneakers, and, sighing, activated the footrest.

"Long day?" Dr. Dull said.

"And then some."

"Travis, would you like to start the conversation?"

"If I must. Josh was born April 1, 2003, in Grosse Pointe Farms, Michigan. His mother and father are Lilith and Cain Giovanni, investment bankers with J.P. Morgan Chase, and are originally from Sicily,

Italy. His best friends are David Green and Jason Miller. He likes anime, manga, comics—"

Dr. Dull raised his hand. "While it's nice to know you've completed my assignment, don't you think we should discuss you assaulting your brother?"

Drumming his hands on the armrest in annoyance, he said, "What's there to discuss? He antagonized me, so I retaliated."

"Travis, have my lessons not been sinking in? We don't solve our problems with violence."

"Tell that to Hitler, Hirohito, and Stalin."

Dr. Dull steepled his fingers. "Meaning?"

"To quote Heinlein: Violence, naked force, has settled more issues in history than has any other factor, and the contrary opinion is wishful thinking at its best."

"Only because humans haven't evolved past their reptilian brains, but that's beside the point. Why did you think your actions were appropriate?"

"I'd like to know that, too," Josh said.

Travis stood, scowling, teeth bared, ready to rip out Josh's throat. "I don't need to explain my actions to anyone."

"God, you're so not who I thought you were. I can't believe you're the same guy who kissed me."

White-hot anger exploded in Travis's chest. *How dare he reveal something so private.* "We didn't kiss!" he lunged for Josh, knocking his chair over, and they tussled to the ground.

Dr. Dull separated them. "Joshua, please wait outside while I talk with Travis in private."

Josh wiped his busted lip. "Sure."

Once they were alone, Dr. Dull tried to engage Travis, but he remained silent.

"If you're not going to participate, then stop wasting my time. I'll let your judge know you are failing to cooperate, and—"

Travis spoke, barely above a whisper. "I thought I could trust him. I let him in, and he turned out to be like everyone else."

"How so?"

"First, we didn't kiss. I stopped before our lips touched. And the only reason I did that was because we were drinking vodka, and I felt sorry for him when he said he'd never been kissed. Is that clear?"

"I'm sensing major hostility here. Let me make this perfectly clear: anything you tell me in confidence stays here. Second, it's okay to be gay."

"I'm not gay. Not that there's anything wrong with that, but I like girls, too."

"Well, however you identify, know you are valid and worthy of love, dignity, and respect. Is Joshua the first male you've been attracted to?"

"First person, period."

"Okay, and why did you feel the need to attack him just now?"

"First, he had no right to share that information. Second, he was wrong; we didn't kiss!" The pictures on Dr. Dull walls rattled.

Dr. Dull clasped his hands. "Settle down and tell me what happened."

Travis went over the events of the day, and at the end, Dr. Dull asked him why he ran away.

"Because it was a mistake."

"Wanting to kiss him?"

"Everything. People come, people go, all attachments are pointless."

"And why do you think that?"

"I don't think that; I know it. Besides, what's the point of befriending Josh when . . ."

Dr. Dull offered him some tissues. "Take your time and tell me when you're ready."

Why am I even wasting my time here? I'm dying, so what's the point of anything?

"You look like you have something on your mind, son."

"I'm dying, okay? Happy now?"

Dr. Dull's water bottle sailed off his desk, clattering to the ground. "It would seem we have a bit of poltergeist activity. As to your dying, please explain."

Travis told him about his genetic disorder, and at the end of it, Dr. Dull nodded. "Confronting one's mortality is a lot for anyone to handle, let alone one as young as you. No wonder you're acting out. This doesn't excuse your actions, but I understand them, and you better now."

Dr. Dull's timer went off. "We only have thirty minutes left. If you'd like, we could pick this up next week or use the remainder of the hour to talk?"

"Next week's good for me. I just want to get home."

"Understood," he said and slipped him his business card. "If you need someone to talk to or vent, I'm here."

Travis stuck the card in his wallet and used Dr. Dull's cell to call a taxi home. On the way out, he locked eyes with Josh. "He's ready for you. Josh remained silent.

Travis held the gaze for three heartbeats before Josh turned and entered the office. Though he didn't want to admit it then, Travis could have spent eternity lost in those jade orbs.

CHAPTER TWENTY-THREE

*J*J slumped in his chair, slipped off his sandals, and wiggled his toes into the microfiber area rug.

"Care to tell me your recollection of events?"

"He came over, we did your assignment, and it got boring asking each other questions, so I suggested we play Never Have I Ever. That turned into Truth or Shots, and next thing I know, he's going in for a kiss. Then he backs away like I smacked him or something, and the kid's ghost."

"Hmm," Dr. Dull said when JJ had finished. "And what made you think it was a good idea to introduce alcohol into the mix?"

"I thought it would loosen him up, and we'd have a good time."

"Why was that important?"

He faltered, then managed, "I wanted him to like me."

Dr. Dull nibbled on his pen cap and scribbled on a legal pad. "It's important that people like you?"

"I don't know. I guess?"

"Which is it?"

"Yeah, okay. I want people to like me so that . . . so that I won't be alone."

Dr. Dull scribbled on his legal pad. "So, you don't have many friends?"

"Tons, but they only like me because of all my stuff and the parties I throw, and 'cause I'm funny. If they knew the real me, then they'd . . ."

"What?"

"Never mind."

"No, finish your thought."

"They'd hate me and wouldn't want me around."

"Okay, and who is the real you you're afraid they won't like?"

"I'm a geeky, dorky, spaz who likes DnD, sci-fi, and fantasy. And I'm . . ."

"Joshua, it's all right. You're in a safe space."

A serious look came over JJ. "You promise you won't repeat what I'm about to tell you to anyone, even my parents?"

Dr. Dull smiled. "Yes."

"I'm gay, and I'm so in love with Travis that it hurts."

Without meaning to, JJ revealed everything about how he'd bullied Travis to be close to him and how he'd been stalking him for months. Afterward, he felt lighter than air but scared shitless.

"What should I do?"

"That's up to you to decide. However, I will say this: if you hope to have a relationship with Travis, platonic or otherwise, then you must be honest with him."

"And what if he doesn't want to be with me?"

"That's a risk you must take. 'Tis better to have loved and lost than to have never loved at all."

"That's about as true as fat bitches loving salads."

"I'm not saying you must tell Travis about your feelings for him this instant, but you should consider doing it before you fall further for him, only to discover he's not interested."

"Yeah."

"And promise me you'll stop going by his house and watching him without his consent. I think we're done for today. If you'd like to continue one-on-one sessions with me, I have an open slot Mondays from 5-6PM?"

"I'd like that."

Dr. Dull added him to his schedule and gave him his business card.

On the ride home, JJ had much to think about. What was more important to him: honesty or losing the boy he loved? He didn't know how Travis felt about him, and after today, he wasn't even sure if he wanted to be with him. But some part of his heart still swelled with joy at the thought of them kissing. His busted lip, however, reminded him Travis was a threat, and there was no telling what he might do if he found out the truth. No, JJ would hold off confessing his feelings until he knew Travis's feelings for him.

When his uber pulled up at the entry to his house, he spotted Marianna talking with a delivery person in clipped Spanglish.

"It's okay, Marianna. I ordered the pool."

"The piscina is yours?"

"Si, Si. But you have to sign for it, firmar," he said, miming signing. She nodded and signed the tablet, and the delivery person unboxed the pool. When she was done, he emailed several pool companies to get quotes for setting it up and maintaining it. That done, he went inside to eat. Then he read comics until he fell asleep.

The next morning, he was awakened by his parents' homecoming. "You simply must breakfast with us," his mother said with a slight slur.

"I can't. I have to get ready for community service."

She pursed her lips. "Nonsense. You can do that another time. Shower, dress in your formal attire, and meet us in twenty minutes so we can have a family meal at the country club. And do something about that lip of yours."

JJ rolled his eyes. *Great, a day spent listening to them schmoozing people, then off to the junior members' lounge to hear an army of entitled brats complain about how their parents got them the 2016 Bugatti Chiron instead of the 2017. Fun.*

JJ washed, then put some concealer on his lip and reported for duty, sporting his tailor-made black Armani suit with matching Italian leather Oxfords. He rode shotgun while his mother lunged in the back, sprawled on the bench seat. As soon as he was in the car, his mother started in on him. "I noticed you ordered a pool. Why?"

"Well, Mom. It's the middle of summer, we're in a heatwave, and since you won't allow me to get AC installed, a pool is the next best thing." He sighed loudly.

His father glared at him. "Don't use that tone with your mother. We gave you that credit card, and we can take it away."

Whatever. It's not like you care about me anyways. "Yes, sir. Sorry, Mom."

"That's better," his father said, then proceeded to lecture him on all the networking and internships he'd miss out on this summer due to his 'silly' fight.

"If you ask me," his mother said, "they shouldn't allow his type at AP Prep."

JJ whipped around and gave his mom stink eye. "And what's that supposed to mean?"

Sighing, his father said, "Son, do we have to get into one of your social justice arguments? You know your mother meant his being poor, not his racial heritage."

Seeing his chance to one-up his father, JJ said, "Ha! Shows what you know. Travis's grandmother is Helena Aurum."

His mom laughed. "Dear, don't believe everything you're told. I've met Ms. Aurum, and there's no way that Turner boy comes from her stock."

He wanted to retort, but they'd arrived at the country club.

Breakfast dragged on. What time his parents weren't networking or on their phones, they spent grilling him on his plans to make up for this summer.

"I'll look up internships, extracurricular camps, and college courses to take when I get home."

"You do that," his dad said, taking a bite of his bagel and lox.

His mom finished her glass of champagne and ordered another. "I trust you've cleaned your room per our last discussion?"

He wanted to roll his eyes but knew that would only earn him another lecture, so he counted to ten mentally until the urge to cuss her out passed. "Yeah, Mom. And if you don't believe me, you can see it when we get home."

"We'll both examine your room," his dad sad. "Now, why don't you go mingle with the other kids?"

Nodding, he trudged to the junior members' lounge. Upon entering, all eyes turned to him.

"Looks like the jailbird escaped," Adolfo said, and the others joined him in laughing at JJ.

"Must be tough slumming it with the plebs," Kimiko said. "I'd rather kill myself than be stuck slinging soup all summer."

God, how he hated them. Adolfo and Kimiko ruled the junior members' lounge. Adolfo's father was a Spanish entrepreneur who'd invested in Google and Amazon early. Kimiko's father was a former yakuza boss—which Kimiko constantly reminded them of—who used his money to come to the US, where he started an import/export company that trafficked in gray market items.

JJ answered their stupid questions about whether he had a probation officer and if he'd dropped the soap.

If these are the future leaders of the free world, we're screwed. For the love of Kami, I'd rather be anywhere but here.

He was contemplating strangling Adolfo with his tie when a server came on the intercom system and told them JJ's parents needed him as they had to leave ASAP. Fear quickening his steps, he rushed back to the dining room, where his parents looked crestfallen.

"Dear," his mom began as she scribbled her signature on the bill, "we just received an emergency call from our people in Dubai. The deal we were working on fell through, and we have to leave immediately to begin renegotiations. Sorry."

Typical. They're not home one full day and are leaving again? Forcing a smile, he said, "No problem. We can spend time together when you get back."

"That's the spirit, Joshy," his dad said and hugged him, pulling away almost as soon as he'd embraced JJ. The ride back was full of their promises to make this up to him, but he ignored them, going through the motions as they said their goodbyes.

Once his parents were gone, he returned emails with the pool places and had a guy out that day. The tech filled the pool, put in chlorine tablets, and told him the process for maintaining the pool's pH and cleanliness.

"Can't I hire you to do all that?" he said, and the tech smiled, whipping out price charts. It wasn't his money, so JJ went with the platinum package, which included weekly cleanings and pH balancing. When the tech was done, he told JJ to give it a day for the chlorine to evenly mix into the water since the pool was so large. With that done, he called up his friends to organize the pool party. He told them not to invite anyone as he wanted it to be a small group, and he'd supply the food if they supplied the drinks. Jason said his older brother could score them beers and wine coolers for the girls.

While he'd promised Dr. Dull to go easy on the alcohol, what harm could a few drinks cause?

He was scrubbing dishes at St. Michael's when he caught Travis giving him weird looks. "Dude, what's your damage?" he shouted when it worked his last nerve.

"Nothing," Travis said, dumping a stack of dirty dishes on the counter.

"Then why do you keep side-eyeing me?"

"No need for dramatics. I was merely curious as to why you weren't here yesterday."

An ember of hope flared in JJ's heart. "Miss me, huh?" he said, quirking an eyebrow.

"Not hardly. Thanks to your bailing, I had to pull double duty. You're welcome."

"God, you're such an ass. Go already."

Travis shrugged and went back to the front, returning a few minutes later with more dishes. When JJ saw them, he went off. "There's no way I can wash all those before my shift ends."

"That's why Joan wants me to help you. I wash half, you do the other?"

Sighing, JJ nodded. "FYI, my lip's feeling better, no thanks to you."

Travis started washing a pan and mumbled something.

"What?"

"I said . . . I'm sorry."

JJ didn't say anything and continued drying his pan.

"You don't look half-bad. Your lip, I mean," Travis added hastily.

They worked in silence, and the whole time, JJ wondered what he saw in Travis. *He's such a jizz rag, but he did apologize. And it was totes wrong of me not to let them know I wasn't coming in. Maybe I should apologize?*

"I'm sorry for bailing on ya. My parents made me go with them to the country club and wouldn't take no for an answer. Then they ditched me to go back overseas for who knows how long."

"Right," Travis said, adjusting his Ray-bans. "You know parents are the worst. They treat us like objects instead of persons with our own personalities and ambitions."

JJ nodded. "Exactly. From the moment we're born, they tell us we're the future, and then they treat us like crap."

"Preach it!" Travis said, and they laughed.

Wiping sweat from his face, JJ continued, "I'm more than old enough to make decisions about my life, thank you very much, Mom and Dad. They give me all the responsibilities of being an adult with none of the rights and privileges. How's that fair?"

"It's not. Like you said, we're the future, yet now that our time has come, they won't step aside."

"Exactly! They had their shot and screwed up the world. Now they have the nerve to expect us to clean up their mess. Talk about entitled. The least we should get out of the deal is power." The more JJ talked, the angrier he got.

"A lion doesn't ask permission to roar," Travis said as he scrubbed a plate.

JJ looked at him sideways. "Huh?"

"Power cannot be given. It must be taken."

Smiling, JJ said, "*The Godfather III*?"

"Bingo. Our generation has limitless potential, and that scares the old guard. They're set in their ways, content with the status quo. If we want change, then we must crack the world asunder and remake it in our own image."

JJ looked at Travis, awed . . . and a bit scared if he was honest with himself. "Bro, you're eloquent AF. You should legit become a politician."

Travis frowned. "One, telling a person of color they're eloquent isn't a good look. Two, I have neither the time nor inclination to bother with that."

JJ covered his mouth with his hands. "Shit, man. I didn't mean to offend you. I just meant you speak well, and I could listen to you talk all day."

JJ's face flushed, and he wanted to crawl in a hole and die.

Travis laughed. "Josh, you are something else."

Looking up, JJ wondered what Travis meant. "Um, do you like me—I mean like talking with me?"

Scrunching up his face, Travis replied, "I don't not like talking with you."

It's a start, I guess.

JJ looked at the floor, mustering up his courage to form the words caught in his throat. "So, they finally delivered my pool and set it up. It'll be ready tomorrow. D-do you want to come to the party this Friday?" he said.

Travis looked at him for a second. "I'm grounded, remember?"

JJ's heart threatened to burst from disappointment. He wanted to fall into the center of the Earth. "Okay. I guess—"

"But I'll swing by if I can."

JJ smiled wide. "Look at you, breaking the rules."

"You're a bad influence on me."

"Oh, you just don't know," he said, wiggling his eyebrows.

Travis smiled wryly. "You're vexing but oh so intriguing, Joshua Joseph Giovanni."

He remembered my full name? Now I can die happy.

Before JJ could ask Travis what he meant by that, Joan told them it was almost time for them to leave. They still had a few dishes to go, but working together, they knocked them out and went to get their timesheets signed.

"Later," Josh said as they parted ways. Travis nodded and smiled, and a warmness filled JJ's chest.

~

After lying in bed awhile, JJ had called up the Squad and David and Jason; he put them on a conference call, and they set their squad goals for the day.

Since it was supposed to be in the high nineties that day, they would chillax in JJ's pool, listen to music, and catch up. Marianna had the day off, so they were on their own when it came to food. They settled on pizza from Little Caesars: one vegetarian pie for Rachel and Brianna, meat lovers for the men, and a cheese pizza for David. That settled, they ended the call to get ready.

JJ cleaned the house a bit, but the whole time his mind was on Travis. Would he come? And if he did, how would his friends react?

At a quarter to five, he slumped on the couch, sweat-drenched, red-faced, panting. Even with the industrial fans going and all the windows open, it felt like he was vacationing on the Sun. He was *so* tempted to use his credit card to have an AC unit installed. But he could already hear his parents lecturing him about wasting money. The way they acted, you'd have thought they were poor or something. Granted, they weren't Helena-Aurum rich, but then, most people weren't.

He still couldn't believe his Travis was heir to the Cadmus Fortune.

Hell, with that much dough, Travis could've had him iced 1,000 times over, but he didn't act like any of the rich kids JJ's parents forced him to network with.

And that was one of the reasons he liked Travis. JJ could be himself around Travis without worrying about being cool or bringing shame to the Giovanni name. There were no games with him. If Travis thought something was dumb or boring, he said so. None of the passive-aggressive gossip and backstabbing that was common with the kids at the country club or the functions his parents made him attend.

Brianna's squeaky voice coming over the intercom interrupted his thoughts. He checked his smartphone; they were twenty minutes early.

After buzzing them in, he led the girls to the guest room while he, Lance, David, Jason, and Henry changed into shorts. He couldn't help sneaking a peek at them and was happy that he wasn't the smallest in the room.

Once dressed, they marched to the pool, and Henry did a cannonball off the ladder, soaking the girls.

Rachel shot him a scathing look. "Boy, you know how long it's gon' take me to fix this?"

"Why'd ya come to a pool party if you didn't want to get wet?"

"I can't even . . . ooh!"

JJ got between them, which wasn't an easy feat, with Henry outweighing him by at least fifty pounds. "This is a drama-free zone. Henry, if you can't stop being a dick, then GTFO."

Henry raised his hands. "Who threw sand in your vag?"

He ignored the dis. "All I'm saying is stop being such a jerkass all the time."

Lance laughed. "Someone's on his period."

JJ cupped his nuts. "Both of you can suck it."

Henry's laughter died in his throat, and he glared at JJ. "We was joking. Damn, we haven't seen you all summer, and you acting hella petty."

"You can eat a bag of dicks. And FYI, I've been blowing up your cells, but you've been ignoring me. Or did you forget that?"

Jason stepped between JJ and Henry. "Jesus, guys. It ain't that serious."

David nodded. "Jason's right. Ya'll are acting like this is one of those dumb preteen dramas Asher and Shari watch. We're all friends here, so chillax."

Henry's face contorted like he'd eaten a mouthful of Sour Patch Kids. "He started it."

Brianna cut in. "Girls, you're both pretty. Now, are we gonna enjoy this pool or what?"

JJ looked from her to Henry, then stuck out his hand. "We cool?"

Hesitating a moment too long, Henry slapped palms with him. "We're cool."

He nodded, and a splash war commenced, the girls and Jason against the others. David sat out because his leg was still in a cast. And though Rachel complained about her hair, she got into the action.

A few hours passed, and they decided to grab dinner.

JJ snagged the keys to his father's jag and drove the three blocks to the pizza parlor. Usually, he hated any pizza that wasn't made by a fellow full-blooded Italian, but he'd make do for the sake of his friends.

At seven, Lance left, saying he had to clean his room. Henry followed soon after, excusing himself to work out, and David and Jason left shortly thereafter.

When it was only the three of them, the mood changed.

Brianna and Rachel kept shooting each other looks until finally, Rachel said she had to go water her neighbor's plants. No sooner had she gone than Brianna pounced on JJ, her lips crashing into his.

What the actual fuck?

He pulled away. She stared at him, mouth gaping, eyes like UFO's, confusion all over her face. "Don't you like me?"

"It's not you . . ."

"Then what? Is there another girl? Cuz I'll cut a bitch. For real, for real."

He hesitated a moment. Should he tell her the truth? Swallowing a lump in his throat, he said, "Another guy, actually."

She laughed, but when he didn't join in, she stopped. "You serious?"

He nodded.

"Who is he?"

"Travis Turner."

"Oh," she said, and that single syllable conveyed so much pain.

"Are you mad?"

"I'm so beyond mad, they have to invent a new word. How could you not tell me this?"

Fear and worry that she might out him to the others sprang up inside him. "I didn't know how."

"No, I mean, how could you think it would matter to me? You like guys? Big whoop."

He smiled. "We're cool?"

"Yup. Though your taste in guys sucks."

"Bitch," he said, and they shared a gut-busting laugh until they had tears rolling down their cheeks.

"Let's not tell the others just yet, okay?"

"Deal. And if Matthew or Henry give ya any crap, let me know, and I'll kick their ass. Real talk."

They hugged, and she apologized for kissing him. As he cleaned up the mess from the party, he couldn't help smiling. Things were awesome . . . so that could only mean they wouldn't last.

CHAPTER TWENTY-FOUR

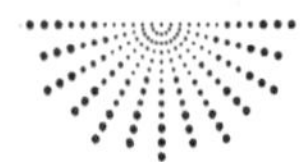

Travis's probation officer flipped through the file in her manilla folder and cleared her throat. "Since this is your first altercation, I'm considering giving ya a warning. But given the severity of your actions, I wouldn't be doing my job if I let you slide on hurting your brother."

While inside, he was scared shitless, Travis kept a cool demeanor, schooling his face into a blank slate. "What's the verdict?"

She eyed him sideways. "Depends on two things. Are you sorry for what you did?"

He wasn't but played along. "Yes, ma'am."

"And you won't do it again?"

In his most obsequious tone, he replied, "No, ma'am."

She nodded and put her folder into her beat-up leather attaché. "Here's what's going to happen. You start school in a few months, correct?"

He nodded.

"If you stay out of trouble until then, I'll let you off with a warning. But don't try me, kid."

She packed up and left, and Travis was ecstatic. *I'm not going to jail. I'm not going to jail. Whoot!*

His parents weren't as enthused with the news and told him if he stepped out of line once, they'd call the police and have his ass locked away. At first, this filled him with dread, but then he saw this for what it was: an empty threat. *If they could do that, they would have done so instead of calling my probation officer.*

He let them prattle on about curfews, cleaning his room, and taking care of the twins, while he nodded along, waiting for them to shut up. He got his reprieve when Grams called his mother's cell.

"Now is not a good time, Mother. No, you can't speak to him. Because he attacked Bobby, your other grandson. That's out of the question. You're rewarding his bad behavior. We were counting on that to tide us over during the winter slowdown. Fine! You can come next week."

Hair frazzled and cheeks red, his mother ended the called and turned back to Travis. "You. In your room. Now!"

"But it's not even five o'clock."

"Go."

He cursed her out in his head.

"What was that?" she said.

Schiesse. I projected my thoughts.

"Nothing, Mother."

"That's what I thought. Now scram."

That night, he ate his dinner in his room and had to do everyone's dishes before it was back to his room. He passed the time reading more of Nietzsche, wishing he were eighteen so he could move out and never deal with his so-called family again. To console himself, he imagined them dying in horrible accidents.

"Bro, you're all kinds of messed up," Prometheus said.

I don't recall asking you.

"Don't take it out on me. I'm just here to remind ya about your date with JJ."

It's not a date. And why are you so obsessed with my relationship with Josh?

"Meh. Shippers gon' ship? You going or what?"

Actually . . . yeah. It's hot than a mug, and a dip in the pool would feel fantastic.

"Right, and you liking JJ ain't got nothing to do with yo' decision at all."

Travis didn't reply and instead raised his mental barriers, drowning out Prometheus. In the still of the night, he closed his eyes and slowed his breaths, meditating, but the twins and their friends' laughter echoed through the house. He tried ignoring them, but it proved futile.

Around ten o'clock, the house settled down, but he waited another thirty minutes to make sure it was safe to leave. He dressed in shorts and put a change of clothes in his messenger bag. Then, picturing Josh in his mind, he focused on the house. After a few attempts, he Popped outside of the gate to Josh's house. He rang the bell, and Josh buzzed him in.

"You came!" Josh said. Then they exchanged an awkward greeting and headed for the pool.

"That thing's gargantuan," he said upon seeing the pool.

"Yeah. It took like four hours to fill it. Come on, the water's fine."

Travis hesitated a moment. Would Josh laugh at his scars or his blubber belly? Would he tell everyone what he looked like shirtless, and then they'd all make fun of the fat kid?

Would he—

"Come on," Josh said, pulling him toward the ladder of the pool.

I guess we're doing this.

He put down his bag, took off his shirt, and cannonballed into the pool. He came up sputtering. "God, that felt good."

Josh dove in after him, and they proceeded to have an epic splash fight. Travis only knew how to dog paddle, so he stuck to the shallow end. But this didn't stop him from grabbing Josh when he got close and tossing him into the deep end. They continued like this, splashing and laughing until they tired themselves out. Travis paddled by the ladder, resting his back against the rim of the pool as he caught his breath.

Josh swam up to him, huffing, cheeks rosy-red. Neither of them spoke, their shoulders rubbing against each other, the warmth a sharp contrast from the cool water. Travis looked up at the stars and felt both once at home and alienated in that moment.

"They're beautiful, huh?" Josh said, pointing to Polaris.

"Yeah. Who would have thought giant balls of gas millions of miles away could be so gorgeous?"

Josh chuckled and nudged Travis with his shoulder. "I mean, yeah, if you want to get all scientific about it. But ya know, stars are powerful things."

Laughing, Travis shook his head. "Don't tell me you believe in astrology?"

"How can't you? The evidence is all around us."

Travis went into a detailed explanation as to why astrology was a load of equestrian excreta. And when he was done, Josh shook his head, smiling. "There are more things in heaven and earth, Horatio, than are dreamt up in your science."

Travis splashed him. "Come off it. If it can't be analyzed, quantified, reproduced in a lab and independently verified, then it doesn't exist."

Josh gave him side-eye. "Dude, why so narrow-minded?"

Starting to get frustrated, Travis tried to keep his annoyance out of his voice. "I'm not narrow-minded. I'm a staunch materialist, which means I believe this is the only world that exists, and we get one shot at living life."

Turning to Travis, Josh's face bunched up in incredulity. "You don't believe in an afterlife, in God?"

"There's no afterlife. Once you die, it's game over."

"How can you say that when there's tons of evidence for a creator?"

Travis massaged his temples. "I don't want to get into a teleological argument with you."

"Why?" Josh stuck out his tongue. "Cause you'd lose?"

That smug, sanctimonious ass. "I know there's no afterlife because I've died before."

There, that'll shut him up.

Travis's triumphant mood lasted all of ten seconds when Josh said, "Right, you flatlined after The Fire. What was it like?"

"What?"

Cocky smile in place, Josh said, "You heard me."

Looking up at the star-dotted sky, he thought back to that time. "There were no pearly gates, tunnel of light, or fire and brimstone. As far as my eye could see, darkness enveloped me while I floated. It was the total silence I remember most. No breaths, thoughts, or heartbeats. Nothing."

"What happened next?" Josh asked, leaning into Travis.

"I floated until I felt a presence wrap me in liquid warmth. Then I came to."

"See, that was God," Josh said matter-of-factly.

Travis sighed, barely holding back his contempt. "Nope. It was just my synapses misfiring and my brain flooding with dopamine."

"Oh, give it a rest. Science can't explain everything. You lived because there's a higher purpose for you."

"Believe what you want. But the fault, dear Joshua, lies within us, not in our stars."

They talked a while longer about philosophy, metaphysics, and life. And though they seldom agreed, Travis enjoyed their debates. As they talked, Josh casually wrapped his arm around Travis's shoulder, pulling him closer until their sides touched.

While generally against people touching him, Travis ignored this as he didn't want to ruin a nice night. At one point, Josh ran his hand through Travis's hair, and he flinched away.

"I should go," he said, exiting the pool and gathering his bag. Josh called after him, but Travis kept going down the drive until Josh and the pool were out of sight. When he was a safe distance away, he Popped home. His swim clothes were still damp even after teleporting, so he set them in a chair to dry overnight and crawled into bed.

That was the first of Travis and Josh's nightly swim chats, and over the coming days, they debated everything from superheroes to epistemology. Travis didn't care about what they talked about. At night, when it was only them, he felt comfort and ease he'd never dreamed of having with anyone, let alone Joshua Giovanni. And he'd almost go as far as saying he liked the guy.

~

Before he knew it, Grams's limo arrived, and she crushed him in a hug. "I've missed you so, my caramel cowboy."

Travis's rolled his eyes but hugged her back. "I've missed you, too, Grams. How long are ya staying?"

Smiling, she said, "You got me for a whole week. Be a dear and help me with my luggage."

Travis hauled her bags to the basement, his euphoria not waning a bit at doing grunt work; honestly, her luggage weighed next to nothing to him, and he grabbed them in one go while Grams talked with his mother.

Given his condition, Grams decided they would go out to dinner that night and celebrate Travis's birthday early. They went to a steakhouse, and when they returned home, she surprised him with her homemade German chocolate cake and presents—$1,000 in cash, a sweater she'd knitted him, and a few games for his Xbox.

He hugged her tight. "Thanks, Grams!"

"Think nothing of it. But there's something I need to discuss with you later in private," she said in a somber tone. He nodded, and Bobby whined about how it wasn't fair he and Amber didn't get anything. Grams scowled, then went to her room, returning with a makeup kit and a cashmere dress for Amber and a Nintendo Switch with two games for Bobby.

"Thank your grandmother," his mother admonished them. They thanked her and went off to their rooms, leaving Travis to clean up the mess from cake and ice cream. He grimaced at his mother but carried out this chore without complaint since he didn't want Grams' stay to be marred by her and his mother getting into one of their legendary fights or risk him losing control of his powers.

When the dishes were done and put away, he went to Grams' room, where she was watching a rerun of *The Golden Girls*. She patted the mattress, and he sat.

"What did you want to talk to me about?"

She sighed, looking bone-weary. "I didn't want to bring this up in front of everyone, but I updated my will due to your disorder. As of yesterday, I'm leaving everything to your Cousin Austin."

"He's your great-nephew, right?"

"Yup. And should that doctor of yours find a cure, then I'll name you my sole heir as before." She hobbled over to her luggage and removed a box with a bow on it.

"What is it?" he said, insides squirming with anticipation.

She smiled. "Open it and find out."

He tore through the wrapping paper and whooted when he saw it was the newest model of iPhone. "These aren't due out until September."

"I pulled some strings and had them release one to me early. You have unlimited everything, and here's your new number," she said, handing him a sticky note. "Let's not tell your parents about this just yet, huh?"

He laughed and sat with Grams as she told him stories about what her life was like growing up in the 1940s. It was hard for him to picture life without video games or the internet. Around nine, Grams said she was tired and went to bed. Travis put his new phone in his pocket, and once in his room, he checked it out. Then he texted Josh.

who dis???

Travis, dummkopf.

Oh. New phone? Ya coming over?

Yeah and no. It's late, and I don't want to risk getting caught since Grams is here. Sorry.

Oh L

We can FaceTime if you want?

Abso-fucking-lutely, dude!!!

When Josh's face appeared, Travis filled him in on the dinner and his presents.

"Bro, I'm totes jelly. But why did you celebrate your birthday tonight if it's not for another three months?"

Travis went silent as he thought. *Should I tell him I'm dying? What if this changes things between us? What if he acts all patronizing? What if—*

"You still there?"

"Yeah. If I were to tell you something uber private, could you keep it a secret?"

"Totes!" Josh said a bit too eagerly for Travis's liking.

"I'm dy—never mind. Forget I said anything."

Josh chuckled, then sighed. "Travis, I promise not to tell anyone your secret, scout's honor."

"You were a boy scout?"

"For like three months, until I got sick of tying knots and camping in the woods on the hard ground. But don't change the subject."

Travis didn't say anything.

"You can trust me, I promise."

Taking a deep breath, Travis said, "I'm dying. That genetic disorder I told ya about is making my DNA unstable, causing my organs to shut down."

"There's gotta be a cure or something, right?" Josh said. His voice held a pleading tone, and he had a concerned expression. It brought a smile to Travis's face.

"I'm taking an experimental treatment that slows the effects, but there's no cure yet."

Josh went quiet. "How long before . . . you know?"

"A year—two if I'm lucky."

Smiling wide, eyes alight, Josh said, "Then I'm gonna make it my mission to pack as much fun into that time as I can."

Travis smiled, happy that Josh would suggest something so sweet when they barely knew each other. "I'd like that."

"Great, 'cause I wouldn't have taken no for an answer. Project Funnize commences once your Grams leaves. Later. I have a ton of planning to do."

Chuckling, Travis said, "Do you have to go this second?"

"No, why?"

"Because, Joshua, I'd like to talk some more."

"Somebody likes me. Admit it."

"You're such a dork."

"I know you are, but what am I?"

"About four feet of pale fugliness."

Josh flipped him off. "Ha, ha. FYI, I'm up to four-foot-nine now. And weren't you the one who called me a model?"

Cheeks flushing with heat, Travis replied, "That was the vodka talking."

Josh huffed. "Right. I supposed it was also the vodka that kissed me?"

"One, we almost kissed, and I was tipsy. Two, chill. I was just breaking your balls."

"It's hard to tell when you're joking and when you're being a dick."

"Look, maybe we should end things here."

"No. I wanna know why you almost kissed me. And what did you mean by I intrigue you?"

"I meant that I can figure out most people upon interacting with them, but you are a mystery to me. As for why I almost kissed you . . ."

"Yeah?"

"I don't know. I guess I was curious."

Josh didn't respond right away, but his panting let Travis know he was there. "You've never kissed anyone else?" he finally said.

"Nope."

"You ever been to a party?"

"No, why?"

"Then that's going to change, my man," Josh said and pumped his fist in the air.

Groaning, Travis said, "Not happening, captain. People suck."

"Dude, you're literally dying, so YOLO like a MOFO. Tell ya what, I'll ease you into it by having ya hang with my friends. Sound good?"

"I don't—"

"The only words I want to hear from you are yes and no. Do or do not. There is no try," he said, affecting a bad Yoda impersonation.

"Fine."

They hung up a bit later with plans to hang once Grams left. For the rest of the week, when Travis did his community service duty, he and Josh joked around, even getting into a splash fight once or twice while washing dishes.

Though Travis knew he was breaking all the rules he'd constructed to keep himself safe, he found his pulse quickening upon seeing Josh. And when he couldn't see Josh, they'd FaceTime or text late into the night, and he often fell asleep with a smile on his face.

When Grams left, she hugged and kissed him goodbye with a warning he'd better call her twice a week or she'd tan his hide. And knowing her, she'd do it, too.

He waited until after she left to tell his parents about the iPhone she'd gifted him. Bobby exploded. "It's not fair. He has two phones, and we only have one."

"He's not keeping it," his mother said.

He scowled. *How dare she try to take away a present from Grams!* "No."

His parents turned to him. "What was that?" his mother said, arms akimbo.

"You heard me. You're not taking it. You didn't give it to me."

"Be that as it may—" his father began.

"No!" Travis said, and the TV flickered off then on again. "Bobby has lost three phones this year. You can give that guttersnipe my old flip phone, but I'm keeping the iPhone."

Travis stood his ground until his parents relented. He deleted Josh's number from the flip phone and handed it to Bobby, who stuck out his tongue. He told them he'd be going over to Josh's house tomorrow, so they needed to find another babysitter. They called after him, but he walked away, smiling smugly.

~

After community service the next day, Travis rode in a rideshare with Josh to his house, and they set up for the gathering.

"What's everyone like?" he said as he filled a bowl with chips, placed a container of hummus and ranch dip on the coffee table, and put a case of pop in the refrigerator to chill.

Josh shrugged. "I mean, Lance's cool enough. Matt and Henry can be asses at times, and Brianna and Rachel are my sisters from other misters."

"Green and Miller won't be joining us?"

"No. Just the core group. You nervous?"

Travis crossed his arms and frowned. "I don't do nervous."

Josh came over and rubbed his shoulder. "Bro, relax."

Travis shirked away. "Remind me why I'm doing this again?"

"Practice for your first party. Besides, I wanna introduce you to my other friends."

"Cute. You think we're friends." Josh froze in place, and Travis laughed. "I'm joshing ya, Josh. The look on your face was price —ouch!"

Josh punched him in the arm. "Serves ya right."

"Punk. Imma get ya back," Travis said. Josh raced off, and the chase was on. He overcame Josh and, as punishment, gave him an atomic wedgy.

Josh adjusted his underwear. "Oh, it's on." He pounced on Travis, and they wrestled around on the ground, their bodies rolling over each other until Travis straddled Josh. Gasping for air, he leaned over the smaller boy. "Pinned ya."

Travis held his position, catching his breath and willing his erection to subside. From this perspective, Josh looked tiny and frail, and Travis had a sudden urge to kiss him. He leaned in close, but before their lips met, the doorbell sounded. They separated, and Travis adjusted himself while Josh answered the door.

That was close. I might have done something incredibly stupid.

But part of him hungered to know what kissing Josh felt like. For now, the part of him afraid of rejection won out, and he went to meet Josh's friends. Heaven help him.

CHAPTER TWENTY-FIVE

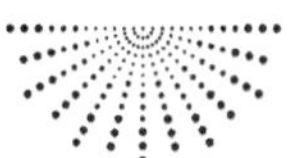

After Josh made introductions, they congregated in the living room to decide what they would do. Travis sat next to Josh on the loveseat, while Brianna and Rachel sat next to Matt and Henry on the sofa sectional. Lance opted to sit in the overstuffed chair by the big screen TV.

"I say we game," Matt said. Henry and Lance seconded the idea, and the girls sighed.

Brianna shook her head, her twisty braids whipping around her face. "Naw. We ain't spending all day inside watching you d-bags play your little games. All those in favor of us chilling in the pool, listening to music, and then getting our grub on say 'aye.'"

Rachel and Josh said, "aye," making Travis the deciding vote. He didn't mind doing either, but part of him was afraid to show them his burn scars.

"Kid, get over yourself and have some fun."

He caged Prometheus but decided to take his advice since with the heat index, it felt like it was 105.

"I say we chill in the pool."

Brianna whooped. "That's what I'm talking about. My mans." She stuck out her fist, and he dapped it. Now that he'd gotten a good look at her, he thought Brianna was cute with her coppery skin and mahogany eyes.

"You're biracial, right?" he asked her.

"Uh, yeah. I'm Afro-Latina, you?"

"Black and white. Mixed kids of the world unite!" he said, and they shared a laugh.

Josh cut him a dirty look. "Are we going swimming or what?"

Travis went with the guys to change in Josh's room while the girls changed in the guestroom. As they approached Josh's room, his heart was in his throat. Taking a calming breath, he squashed his nervousness down and put it in a box.

"Your room's way cleaner now," he said upon entering it.

"Yeah. My parents made me," he said, slipping off his shirt. The others followed suit, leaving Travis the only one in regular clothes. *Best get this over fast.*

He was sliding on his shorts when he felt someone staring at him. Turning, he found Henry and Lance gawking at him. "What?"

"Nothing," they said. He shrugged it off and went out to the pool while Josh got his Bluetooth speaker. Since Travis was the guest, he got first choice of song: he chose *Numb/Encore* by Linkin Park, featuring Jay-Z. As the song started, he bopped his head and locked eyes with Brianna, who was doing the same. He sang along, not caring what anyone thought. When the song ended, Brianna picked *Diamonds* by Rihanna, and this repeated with everyone choosing a song. Then Henry said he was bored and started a splash fight.

It was Travis and the girls against the others. And whenever Matt and Henry would gang up on someone, Travis sneaked up on them and dunked them. He couldn't remember a time he'd laughed as much. Then the mood turned when Henry and Matt sneaked up on Travis while he was dunking Josh and pulled down his shorts.

He turned, seeing red, thankful for his colored contacts. "What the hell?"

Henry held out his arms. "Chillax, dude. We were just playing."

"Do that again, and I will end you," Travis said, and a wind kicked up. Closing his eyes, he did 4-7-8 breath exercises. As his anger dissipated and Travis's breathing returned to normal, the wind stopped blowing. He dog paddled away from everyone, weighing whether he should leave.

Josh swam over. "You okay?"

"I'm fi—" A violent coughing fit racked him, and in between gasping for air, he told Josh to get his inhaler from his bag. Travis puffed on his inhaler twice. Able to breathe again, he took three gulps of air.

Josh placed his hand on Travis's shoulder. "You good?"

"Yeah," he said. It took him a few moments to recover, but he got back into the splash war.

Around two o'clock, everyone started getting hungry, so they got out of the pool and ate while watching YouTube videos on the 75-inch TV in the living room. Rachel left first, stating she had to work at her parents' Chinese fusion restaurant. Briana left a bit after Rachel because she had to watch her cousin's kids.

With the girls gone, Matt suggested they play *Halo*. But Travis countered they should play *Street Fighter*. Josh sided with him, and the tournament began. The only one to even come close to beating Travis was Josh, and they traded insults the whole time they played.

"Come on. Let's play *Halo*," Matt whined.

Lance concurred, and Henry added, "Yeah. This sucks,"

"Not as much as you," Travis quipped, not missing a beat as he hadouken'd Josh into oblivion.

"I'm outta here," Henry yelled.

"Me, too, JJ," Lance shot over his shoulder as he left.

Matt rolled his eyes as he got up. "Enjoy spending time with your boyfriend, ya knob gobbler."

Josh flipped them off, telling them to sit and spin. Travis and Josh continued playing in their own Travis and Josh world until David and Jason buzzed in.

Josh bumped fists and chests with them and introduced Travis, who shot them a death glare worthy of Thanos. "Hey."

David half-smiled, half-laughed. "You're the one our Joshykins has been spending all his time with, huh?"

Travis puffed out his chest, hands akimbo, chin raised. "What of it, Green?"

Josh looked from one to the other. "Cool it, guys. What say I cream the whole stinking lot of ya in *Halo*?"

Laughing, Jason ruffled Josh's hair. "Start it up already, shrimp."

Josh flashed Travis a smile. "We're playing teams. Travis is on mine."

"Go right ahead, squirt," Jason said. "He'll need all the help he can get."

The round started, and Jason ambushed Travis, getting in a head-shot as he turned a blind corner. "Ha, you suck."

"Not as much as your mom," Travis deadpanned.

David chuckled. "Damn, dude. You want some ointment for that burn."

Jason's face went red, and he lunged for Travis, but David held him back.

"Chillax. You'll get him back."

Jason cut Travis a dirty look but picked up his controller, and they played on; he and David scored ten kills to Josh and Travis's eight. Travis only got in one frag when David spawned right in front of him.

After a few more rounds, the score was tied at two.

Jason sneered at Travis. "Hey, ladies. You up for a little bet?"

"That depends," Josh said, looking frazzled and nervous. "What are the stakes?"

"Smart boy. If the Dave-meister and me win, then you two have to run down the driveway and back. Naked."

"No way," Travis said before Josh could reply.

Jason snickered. "It's okay. I understand if you're scared to show us your micro peen."

Travis narrowed his eyes. "Deal, cocksucker. But when we win, you have to be our slaves for the rest of the day."

Josh did a double-take. "You can't be serious. You can barely move without getting shot."

"Now, now, Joshykins," David said, flexing his biceps, "Travis is a big boy and can speak for himself. You're on. BTW, I like your style. You got balls, bro."

Jason cut in, "And we'll all see just how big they are when he loses."

Travis flipped him off, and the match commenced.

Josh played at top form, evidently having played hundreds of hours, but his skills weren't enough to overcome Travis's errors.

Jason and David cat-called and wolf-whistled at them as they undressed.

When they were down to their underwear, Josh turned to Travis. "We don't have to go through with this."

Travis thought a second. *I'm scared. Matt, Henry, and Josh were about the same size as me, but Green and Miller are almost four years older than me. Why if I do have microphallia?*

"I knew you'd chicken out," Jason said and clucked.

I'm not gonna let them think I'm a baby.

Travis shot him a stone-cold glare. "We made a bet, and a man keeps his word." He gathered up his clothes, not trusting the older boys.

Travis gave Josh a resolute look. "On the count of three. One. Two. Three."

Josh dropped his Superman boxers and ran down the driveway while Travis watched him transfixed. He snapped out of it, removed his tighty-whites, and ran after Josh, his twig and berries flopping around with each step.

"I can't believe you went through with this," Josh said as they reached the end of the driveway and doubled back.

Travis scowled. "One, I won't let them push me around."

"And two?"

"I got to see you naked." He punched Josh's arm and then took off, laughing.

"You're dead!" Josh shouted, laughing.

When they reached David and Jason, the older boys were screeching like howler monkeys, doubled over in laughter.

"And what's so funny, smart asses?" Josh said.

David flicked Josh's nose. "When we post this to the school's Snapchat account, everyone is gonna be LOL-ing so hard."

Travis stepped forward and got in David's space, his head barely reaching David's stomach. "Delete whatever pictures and video you took of us."

David jabbed his finger in Travis's chest. "Or what?"

Travis stared down David, his insides an army of angry bees trying to burrow their way out of him. Then he grabbed David's arm and twisted it behind his back. "Or I'll call the police, and when they find said material on your phone, you'll go down for production and possession of child pornography. Now, what are you going to do?" He twisted David's arm until he yelped.

"Alright, alright. You're stronger than you look."

Travis let him go and turned to Jason. "You, too."

"Jesus, bro. We were just messing around."

Travis had them unlock their phones, delete the images and videos, and then pass their phones to him so he could verify they'd followed through.

When that was done, only then did he finish dressing and go inside.

Once everyone was inside, David, Jason, and Josh got into an argument.

David puffed out his chest. "What the actual fuck? Turner's a psycho,"

"Maybe," Josh said, frowning, "but you were wrong as hell for recording us, and you know it."

Josh finished getting dressed and was about to tell David and Jason to leave when Jason grabbed his arm. "You're sticking up for Turner now?"

He yanked his arm free. "Yeah. Because, unlike some people, Travis likes me for me."

"What's that supposed to mean?" David said.

"Figure it out."

Meanwhile, Travis had gathered his things and announced he was leaving.

Josh's face fell. "Where ya going so soon?"

"I think I've had more than enough excitement for one day."

Travis was halfway down the drive when he paused and looked back at the house. He couldn't let things end like this, so before he had a chance to overthink things, he doubled back.

Josh's face lit up. "You came back?"

Rubbing the back of their head sheepishly, Travis said. "Yeah."

"When do you want to hang out again?" Josh said with a pleading look in his eyes.

"Depends. Will the dip shit twins be here?" he said, pointing to the older boys who were glaring daggers at them.

"We're leaving. Come on, David," Jason said and stormed out. David gave them a single grimace before joining him.

Travis let out a sigh of relief. "I thought they'd never leave."

Josh placed his hand on Travis's shoulder. "Hey, David and Jason aren't so bad once you get to know them."

He shrugged Josh's hand away. "I don't want to get to know them." Travis paused a beat, then said, "I want to get to know you." He hugged Josh.

Josh hugged Travis back, and they stayed like that, gazing into each other's eyes until Travis pulled away.

"I better be going. My taxi should be here in a few."

"Right." Josh's face fell. "See ya."

"Not if I see you first."

They both cracked up at this and started singing *The Ballad of Paladin* until Travis made for the door again.

"Later," Josh said. "And for the record, from what I've seen . . . you don't have anything to be ashamed of."

With a Cheshire cat grin, Josh waved goodbye, leaving Travis to think over what he'd said. Travis couldn't help feeling as though he'd won the lottery.

~

When Travis Popped home, he learned his parents took part of his birthday money to pay for a babysitter, and he was pissed, though not so much to risk another visit from his probation officer.

He remembered having a few old shoeboxes in his closet, and upon searching for them, he found one with over $12,000 in it. This made him think of that time Prometheus took over his body, and when he'd come to, he had a wad of cash in his pocket. Shrugging, he added the cash in the box with his money, put it all in a ziplock bag, and placed it inside the heating vent in his wall.

With that done, he called Grams and told her what his parents did. She told him she wasn't surprised and would set up a joint checking account for him first thing in the morning and email him the details. She also told him she'd give a piece of her mind to his mother. They talked a bit longer. Then he told her he had to go eat dinner.

After he'd cleaned the dishes, he read awhile, then FaceTime'd Josh.

"Hey."

"Hey yourself," Josh said. "Wanna hear a poem I wrote?"

"I do."

"It still needs some work, but—"

"Get to it."

"Ssh, you can't rush art," he said, clearing his throat. "I'm a Trekker who ships Lucifer/ Chloe Decker. I'm keen on all things Tolkien. A fiend for the lean, mean green fighting machines. I get wet for peeps with the X gene. I lose sleep playing games on Steam. I'm a sucker for characters who are more than they seem. I watch anime and Buffy slay. I play RPGs with glee. See, I'm a closet geek. What do ya think?"

"Two out of ten on artistry. Ten out of ten on the funny."

Josh stuck out his tongue. "Dick."

"Don't ask a question if you're not ready for the answer."

"Okay, smartass," Josh said, a serious expression coming over his face, "what did you mean by you want to get to know me?"

Travis sucked in his bottom lip. "That depends on the you in question."

"Come again?"

"I detest JJ but want to know more about Josh."

"But they're both me."

"Are they?"

Josh's brow furrowed, and his face scrunched up. "I mean . . . no. JJ is just an act, a role I play for my friends. But when I'm with you . . ."

"Go on."

"I can be my real self."

"And I like that version of you."

"I like you, too," Josh said. They talked long into the night about their plans for the rest of summer until Travis told him he had to go.

Josh sighed. "Parting is such sweet sorrow that I shall say goodnight till it be morrow."

Travis stifled a laugh. "Really. *Romeo & Juliet*?"

"Dude, don't be a moment spoiler."

"Fine, but just so you know, *Romeo & Juliet* was written as a satire of young love."

"Must you be so pedantic? See you tomorrow."

"Yeah. Later."

They ended the call, and Tavis couldn't help feeling sad like he was missing something.

"Or someone," Prometheus added. Travis ignored him and Popped to the park to train a while before bed.

That night he worked on the mental side of his abilities. One by one, he lowered his mental barriers; when the final one had been lowered, he was bombarded with a million voices in his head. There were too many, so he focused on one: Jenny. In his mind, he saw a blue ribbon form, and he followed it, over land and sky.

When the ribbon stopped, he was in Jenny's apartment, seeing things through her eyes. Agent Anderson was in bed with her.

It didn't take him long to figure out the score, and he exited. Only instead of coming back to his body, Travis was stuck in Jenny's mind, sensing everything she did.

To say he was repulsed was an understatement. Only when Jenny fell asleep was Travis able to exit her mind and return home. The experience left him drained and traumatized, so much he vowed to train all aspects of his powers every day, even if that meant pulling all-nighters. Once he slipped into bed, he fell right asleep. But his dreams were anything but pleasant.

~

Oblivion visited him, warning that Prometheus couldn't be trusted. Given all the crap Prometheus had pulled, Travis was inclined to believe Oblivion.

"Forget the Giovanni boy and focus on your training. You are close to breaking the other's mental blockade. And with its demise will come the power to save your life."

"How?"

"Have you done as I suggested and cleaved your emotions from yourself?"

"I've tried, but—"

"You've been preoccupied with Joshua."

"Yeah."

"Have you forgotten the rules that have well served you these many years? He will betray you like everyone you've ever let in. Search your mind; you know I speak true."

"Maybe you're right. Maybe I've imagined the looks of longing Josh gives me when he thinks I'm not looking."

"Yes, child. Harden your heart. Remember your words: people come into and out of our lives without predictability, so we can only depend on ourselves."

Oblivion's logic was sound, and he'd been honest with Travis from the start, but for the first time in his life, Travis listened to his heart. He liked Josh, and if that meant they'd only be friends, then he could live with it.

"No! I don't care what you say; Josh is my friend."

"Have it your way. I'm merely trying to spare you pain. Until we meet again, goodnight, sweet prince."

Oblivion vanished, and Travis woke up, lungs on fire as a coughing fit tore through him. He puffed on his inhaler but continued coughing. After three more puffs, he could breathe again, and he went back to sleep.

In the morning, he called Jenny to tell her about his coughing spells and to get more of his treatment as he was running low. He kept the call short as he had flashbacks to last night that made his skin crawl.

After he finished community service, she checked him over and said she wanted him to go to the hospital for a few tests. Three hours later, they diagnosed him with pneumonia, gave him some antibiotics, and told him to get plenty of rest and fluids.

Still, after taking the antibiotics for a few days, the coughing episodes continued. He shrugged it off, not wanting to bother Jenny or his parents. He kept his inhaler with him at all times and stocked up on over-the-counter cough suppressants, and carried on his training regimen. This helped some, but he'd taken to carrying a pack of tissues to cough into.

Soon enough, it was time for their next therapy session. Josh went first since he had to leave early for a charity event with his parents. As Travis waited, his thoughts turned to Josh. They had been trying to get their parents to agree to a sleepover, but they'd refused.

They were now entering the halfway point of summer vacation, and Travis's parents had started pushing back his curfew and making the twins go to bed earlier. Soon enough, school would start. But would he be alive?

CHAPTER TWENTY-SIX

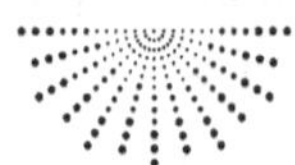

JJ slumped into the puffy overstuffed chair and got comfortable. Dr. Dull set a timer on his phone and got out his legal pad and JJ's folder.

"I'm ready whenever you are, Joshua."

Cringing, JJ started in about the latest almost-kiss with Travis when Dr. Dull interrupted him.

"While that's fascinating, how are *you* doing?"

JJ paused as he thought. "I guess I'm mad that Travis keeps—"

Dr. Dull tutted. "Stick to yourself."

JJ sighed. "This summer has been kinda hard on me."

"Why?"

"I haven't been able to hang with my friends like I usually do because of doing community service, and my parents have been gone, too. I just feel so . . ."

Dr. Dull gave him a reassuring look. "Complete your thought."

"Alone. And the only time I don't is when I'm with him."

Scribbling on his pad, Dr. Dull looked up. "Travis?"

"Yeah. When we're together, I can be myself and not worry about doing or saying something uncool or geeky."

"Right. But getting back to your earlier thought. Do you fear being alone?"

"I don't know, maybe?"

"And why's that?"

At first, JJ didn't know how to answer. Finally, he said, "I just want to belong, you know? Be with people who like the real me, who love me for me."

Pursing his lips, Dr. Dull wrote something on his pad. "What's your relationship with your parents like?"

"Nonexistent. They're gone most of the time, and I've basically raised myself since I was like ten."

"And when they are home?"

"When they're not ripping on me for embarrassing them, they're making me go to stupid charity events like tonight or forcing me to do extracurriculars. You know, I just wish for once I could talk with them and not have to worry about them criticizing me for every little thing I did or didn't do."

"And how does that make you feel?"

"Like I don't matter to them—scratch that. I know I don't matter to them."

JJ fought back his tears, but they came anyway. Dr. Dull handed him the box of tissues on his desk. "How do you know that?"

After he'd recomposed himself, JJ told him about a fight he'd overheard his parents having. His mother was sick of looking after "the snot-nosed brat," and his father told her, "I didn't want him either." Marianna started looking after him and the house soon after.

Sighing, Dr. Dull shook his head. "First, Joshua, I want to reiterate that you're worthy of love, dignity, and respect regardless of how your parents have treated you."

"Thanks, Doc. But it's hard not to feel like no one cares about me."

"That's understandable. Our relationships with our parents set the mold for all others. You seek love and validation from others because your parents never gave you that. But the truth is, no one can give you what you seek except yourself."

JJ cocked his head to the side, confused. "I don't understand."

"If you don't first love yourself, then you'll constantly search for it in others, accepting whatever scraps of affection and attention they throw your way."

JJ looked down, thinking about what Dr. Dull said. He recalled all the times he'd played the fool or went along with the crowd to be liked, how he'd said and done things he didn't want to, so he would belong. He wasn't being true to himself, and because of it, he'd hurt Travis more times than he could count. After getting to know him, JJ vowed that was the last thing he'd ever do again. At that moment, he decided he didn't want to be that person anymore.

"How do I fix things?"

"Know, it's not your job to fix things with your parents. You can open the lines of communications, but they must be receptive and take an active role. As for developing self-love, I suggest making friends with people who share your hobbies and accept you as you are. There's an LGBTQ+ community center in Ferndale that has a youth drop-in and other activities for people your age. I can give you the info if you'd like?"

JJ nodded, and Dr. Dull gave him a card that read, "Affirmations LGBTQ+ Community Center." He tucked the card into his wallet. "Can we talk about Travis now?"

Dr. Dull laughed. "You're incorrigible, but yes."

"So, Travis and I were play wrestling, right? When he pinned me and our eyes locked. I legit thought he'd kiss me, but then my friends buzzed in, and he rolled off me like I was The Toxic Avenger or something. I just don't get him."

"Has it ever occurred to you that you might be reading into things, and Travis might not know what he wants?"

"Why? Did he tell you that?"

"You know I'm not at liberty to discuss that. All I'm suggesting is you go slowly. First relationships are fraught with problems because you don't know what to expect. But in my experience, the relationships that last are all founded on a solid friendship. Have you told him you were stalking him?"

"No," he said, shaking his head, his cheeks flushing with embarrassment.

"Joshua, a relationship based on lies is like a house of cards. Eventually, it collapses. Tell him before things get too serious. The longer you put this off, the more it will hurt him. Travis—oh, dear. Our time's up. I think we've had a breakthrough here, though. Promise me you'll think about what I've told you."

"Sure, Doc," JJ said, but he didn't mean it. *Why does it matter I've stalked Travis? It's not like I still do it, so why should I tell him? He'd just blow up. Nope. What he doesn't know won't hurt him.*

As he passed Travis in the waiting room, they exchanged smiles and hashed out plans to hang out tomorrow. They bumped fists and promised to call each other later.

Travis watched Josh walk away, his skin still tingling from when their knuckles touched. He shook his head and went into Dr. Dull's office, shutting the door behind himself. Dr. Dull set the timer and got out Travis's file. "Anything happen since our last session that you want to discuss?"

"Grams visited, and we went out to dinner to celebrate my birthday early since I'm dying," he said, mumbling the last word.

"I didn't catch the last part."

"I said since I'm dying!"

The pictures on the walls rattled, and Travis admonished himself for losing control.

"And how does that make you feel?"

"Again, with this feelings crap. Don't you know how to ask anything else?"

Dr. Dull threw down his legal pad and stood. "Did that get your attention? Good. Session after session, I've sat here and listened to you bullshit me about how you don't care about anything or anyone. But that's all a front. Somewhere along the line, you got it into your head that emotions are a weakness. But they aren't; they're what make us humans."

"Actually, our superior mammalian brains capable of spatial awareness, toolmaking, logic, and self-awareness are what make us human."

"Why must you always reduce everything to materialism?"

"Because science is the only proven method to determine reality."

"And what about emotions? What about love?"

"A trick of brain chemistry."

"Then why is it every time I bring up your feelings for Joshua, you shut down?"

"I do not!"

Dr. Dull's massive, cherrywood desk sailed forward, pinning him against the wall.

Fick mich!

He pulled the desk off Dr. Dull and apologized.

"How did you move my desk so easily? It weighs close to 300 pounds. And how did it move in the first place?"

Agent Anderson said not to let anyone know about my powers, or they could cause trouble for us. Schiesse. What am I going to do now? I can't exactly lie. Can I trust him? I mean, he's never told me anything about his sessions with Josh, and Josh has never mentioned anything I said in my session, so—

"Travis, are you going to tell me what's going on, or do I need to call the police?"

He groaned, massaging his forehead. "I have powers." He gave Dr. Dull a synopsis of events without mentioning Prometheus or Oblivion since he didn't want to be committed.

Dr. Dull stood in stunned silence, open-mouthed like a fish. After he regained himself, he said, "So, the poltergeist activity from before was . . . you?"

"Yeah. My abilities are tied to my emotions, so when I lose control, things go flying or explode."

He nodded. "Then emotions aren't just a weakness to you. They're a liability. No wonder you've been reluctant to accept your feelings for Joshua. You're afraid of losing control and hurting him?"

"More or less."

With shaky hands, Dr. Dull pulled a bottle from his desk, took two big gulps, and put it back in his desk. "Perhaps if you stopped suppressing your emotions and dealt with them in a healthy way, you wouldn't lose control like this."

Travis scoffed. "When did you become an expert on super-powered humans?"

Dr. Dull scratched his chin. "I'm not. But it stands to reason if emotions trigger your powers, then learning to express them constructively could help you master them."

Travis couldn't fault his logic and thought back to Oblivion's advice to separate his emotions from himself. He'd hit Google when he got home.

"Anything else you want to discuss?" Dr. Dull asked, voice quivering. "We still have twenty minutes."

"Josh introduced me to his friends."

"How'd that go?"

"Amicable, mostly, but I wanted to rip Henry and Matt a new one when they pantsed me."

"That's a normal reaction. And have you sorted through your feelings for Joshua yet?"

"No."

"Why?"

"What's the point? I'm dying, and it's not like he'd want to be with me anyway."

"Travis, catastrophizing serves us no good. Everything is possible, but that doesn't mean it will happen. Talk to Joshua. And worst-case scenario, you'll stop being friends."

"What if I'm not willing to take that risk?"

"I—we'll have to take this up next time. Promise me you'll at least consider telling him how you feel."

"I will."

Travis waited until he was a few blocks from Dr. Dull's office to bring up his location on Google Earth then map the route from there to his house. Pictures in mind, he Popped home, only off by two blocks this time, a bit tired but otherwise fine.

After browsing online for a while, he got bored and went to work on his robot Cha. He'd gotten it to do the cha-cha slide and was now working on making it do the nae nae. He'd put in the last line of code and was about to hit execute when Josh called him. It was close to midnight, and he sounded drunk. "I hate my parents!" he scream-cried and proceeded to tell Travis about his horrible night.

He'd hadn't wanted to go to the stupid party, but his parents insisted he attend. Then they forced him to play the good son and mingle with the other teens there. An hour in, and he'd started sneaking glasses of champagne, and when his parents found out, they had a blowup and went home.

"I'm never, ever gonna be good enough for them. I'm sorry I'm not perfect. I just wish they loved me. Nobody does."

"That's not true. Your friends—"

"They don't care about me. No one does. No one would miss me if died."

"I would," Travis said. And he meant it with all his heart and soul.

"You would?"

"Yeah. Now go to bed, and when you're not so drunk, we'll talk all about your crappy parents."

"Imma hold ya to that, mister," he said, slurring his words.

"Night, Josh."

They ended the call, and, after training, Travis went to bed so happy, he was still smiling when he woke up four hours later.

CHAPTER TWENTY-SEVEN

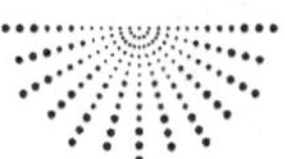

When Josh showed up at St. Michael's the next day, he had a sickly pallor and bloodshot eyes.

"You look horrible," Travis said as Josh slipped on an apron and hairnet.

"Thanks," he said, his words dripping with sarcasm. "I feel a million times worse."

Josh rubbed his forehead and got to work scrubbing pans while Travis mopped the floors. Travis tried engaging Josh throughout the day, but he waved him off, saying they'd talk about it later. The day passed without event, and as they were getting their timesheets signed, Josh asked him if he still wanted to hang.

"Can't," he said. "My parents are going out of town for a romantic weekend, so I'm stuck watching the twins."

"That sucks a bag of dicks."

"Yeah," Travis said, then smiled. "But they did say you could sleep over."

"Finally." Josh pumped his fists in the air, whooping. "I thought they'd never agree to it."

Travis laughed at Josh's enthusiasm. "I know, right? But they only agreed because Jenny said she'd check in on us periodically."

"Meh. I can live with that. So, I'll swing by my place, get my stuff, and head to your house at like three-ish?"

Travis nodded, and they bumped fists.

~

Travis straightened his comforter and pillows for the millionth time, double-checked they were stocked on junk food and pop, and went over his itinerary for the night. He'd planned their activities down to the nanosecond and didn't want anything to ruin his first sleepover. He was a ball of nervous energy but tried to act cool so no one, especially Josh, didn't catch on to how much this meant to him.

At a quarter to three, Bobby stuck his head into Travis's room. "Getting ready for your boyfriend?"

"Shut up!" he said, hurling a pillow at Bobby, who went whining to their mother. She stormed into the room, all done up, and told him to leave Bobby alone or he could forget about his sleepover with Josh. Suppressing the urge to curse her out, he nodded and told her it wouldn't happen again.

"Did you add our cell numbers and the hotel number to your phone?" she said as she and his father prepared to leave.

He nodded.

"And what do you do if there's an emergency?"

"Call Jenny, and if severe enough, call 9-1-1."

"Good. We'll be back Sunday night, and I expect this house to be in one piece when we return. Understand?"

He rolled his eyes and sighed. "Yes, Mother."

"Behave yourselves, or you're grounded," his dad said.

After their parents left, the twins asked if they could have some friends over. He agreed with the caveats that their friends had to leave before dinner at six, and they had to clean up any messes they made. They agreed, and with that settled, he finished preparing for Josh's arrival.

Josh showed up a little after 3:30 PM with bags in tow. He'd brought several of his Xbox One games and controllers along with DVDs and enough clothes to last a week.

"Let's get this party started," he said, dropping his bags in the corner of Travis's room. Travis whipped out his itinerary and was going over it when Josh interrupted him.

"Hold up, dude. All that sounds nice, but let's just do whatever."

Not wanting to disappoint Josh, he nodded. "What do you wanna do?"

"We could talk?"

And they did. Travis and Josh reclined on his bed, bitching about parents—how unfair, hypocritical, illogical, and outright crazy they and their rules could be. Afterward, Travis felt refreshed and said as much to Josh, who said he did too.

"Maybe we should do this on the regular? We could call it our bitch fests?" Josh said, causing Travis to laugh. They bumped fists, agreeing they would.

Travis fixed Josh with a pensive look. "You going to tell me what your call last night was about?"

"Nothing much to tell. It'd been a while since I'd drank that much, and I guess I overdid it."

"And what was that stuff about no one caring about you?"

Josh faltered a bit before saying, "It's just . . . I wish my parents loved me half as much as yours love you."

"You can have them."

"Hey," Josh said, shoving Travis, "that's no way to talk about them."

"You live with them for almost thirteen years, then tell me what ya think. Anyway, I meant what I said. I would miss you."

Josh smiled. "And I you."

As they lay there in silence, staring at each other, Travis felt like he'd found a kindred spirit in Josh. Sure, they weren't in the same group at school or socioeconomic sphere. But when they were together, it was nothing short of magic.

"What ya thinking about?" Josh said.

Travis licked his bottom lip. "You."

"Only good things, I hope?"

"But of course."

Josh's cheeks reddened. "You're not like other people, ya know? When I'm with you, I'm free, like I can fly."

After hearing that, it was Travis's turn to blush. "Thanks. That's the sweetest thing anyone has ever said to me."

Josh's fingers brushed Travis's. "And I mean it one hundo."

Travis pulled away. "What say we game a bit? *Halo*?"

"Sure."

They were starting their third round when Bobby stuck his head in to say he was hungry. But when he saw what they were playing, he asked if he and his friends could join.

"Get lost," Travis shouted at him.

"No, it's okay," Josh said, smiling wide. Travis grumbled at Bobby hogging his time with Josh but went along with it. Travis reset the game and paired his Xbox One with Josh's controllers, and the five of them played. They wrecked Travis, but he slowly got the hang of the game and started winning a round here and there.

Around the time his hands got sore, everyone complained they were starving, so he used some of the money (his money) his parents left him to order pizza. After everyone had eaten, he told the twins' friends it was time for them to leave.

"Why can't our friends sleep over, too?" Amber whined, her face done up like a clown.

Bobby puffed out his chest. "Yeah?"

"Because I cleared my sleepover with Mom and Dad beforehand. Besides, you've spent the whole day with them."

"That's not fair," they wailed. Travis made the necessary calls, and within the hour, parents arrived. Then he made the twins take a bath and put them to bed. When they were finally asleep, he plopped on the couch.

Josh sat next to him. "Are they always like that?"

"Yeah. But now that the terrible twins are asleep, what do you wanna do?"

Josh suggested they pop on the SYFY Channel. They did and

proceeded to watch a movie about a giant alligator fighting a giant python. They laughed at the cheesy dialogue and ripped on the awful acting and special effects.

"Dude," Josh said in between laughs, "worst movie ever. And they made two sequels? Come on."

Travis laughed, his cheeks hurting from all the smiling he'd been doing. "Exactly. And don't get me started on all those Sharknado movies. Who thinks up this crap?"

"A room full of white dudes."

"Truth." Travis laughed, then looked at the time. Since he'd be watching the twins all weekend, he'd taken Saturday and Sunday off from community service. But it was after Midnight, and he still had to train once Josh fell asleep.

"You getting tired?"

"Kind of," Josh replied.

"We could listen to music with headphones if you want?"

Josh shook his head. "I can do you one better. I brought my MacBook Pro and AirPods. We can share them."

"Cool."

After setting up an air mattress for Josh, they brushed their teeth and dressed for bed in tees and undies.

"What's your Wi-Fi password?" Josh asked as he booted up his laptop. Travis told him, and Josh logged into his Spotify premium account. Josh put one AirPod in his left ear, and Travis had the other in his right ear.

As soon as the song started, Travis recognized it as *Stand by Me* by Ben. E. King.

"I freaking love this song," he said, drumming his fingers on his leg to the beat.

Josh nodded. "Me, too. Sometimes I listen to it and imagine who inspired this song, ya know?"

Travis didn't, but he agreed anyway.

"Like I just want someone to love and who loves me as much as the inspiration for this song. It's stupid, right?"

"Not at all. Everybody wants to be loved." *But could Josh ever want me to be that person? Could I ever let him?*

"That reminds me of a song . . ." Josh put on *You Are Loved* by Josh Groban. It was a bit saccharine for Travis's taste, but he found himself humming along to it.

When the song ended, he commandeered Josh's laptop. "My turn." He put on *My plague* by Slipknot and sang along, not missing a word even when Josh paused it.

"Wasn't this in the first *Resident Evil* movie?"

"I know why—yeah, it was."

"You know this song by heart, huh?"

"Yeah. I have phonographic memory, so I hear something once and can remember it in perfect detail."

"Show me."

Travis agreed, and Josh hit the randomizer on his dashboard, and after each song would play, Travis sang it back to him in his bass tone while Josh pulled up the lyrics.

"That's amazeballs." Josh smiled wide, showing off his teeth. "I'd kill for that ability."

If he thinks that cool, he'd go into conniptions if he ever found out about my powers. Should I tell him about them? No. Agent Anderson said the fewer people who knew about them, the better.

"You okay?" Josh said, shaking Travis's leg.

"I'm good."

"You sure? You went away for a second."

Travis waved him off and faked a yawn. "I'm just tired, I guess."

"No wonder," Josh said, "it's after 1:00 AM. Let's call it a night, yeah?"

"Yeah."

Travis gave him his AirPod and rolled over. He was about to drift off when Josh asked him if he was still awake.

"What do you want?"

"Can I sleep up there with you?"

Travis paused in thought. *The air mattress isn't the comfiest, but why didn't he ask to sleep on the couch? Could Josh feel the way I feel about him?*

"Well, can I?"

"Yeah. But if I wake up with my pants around my ankles, you're dead."

Josh flipped him off. "You won't be molested. Or will you?"

Groaning, Travis tossed a pillow at him, and a pillow fight ensued until they were both out of breath. They looked at each other and broke out in giggles. When they'd settled down, Josh took the right side of the bed, and Travis turned away from him.

After he was sure Josh was asleep, Travis sneaked away to train. But the whole time, his mind was on Josh.

"Told ya you liked him."

Screw you. He caged Pro and resumed training. He levitated several tennis balls a few meters off the ground and started the stopwatch app on his phone. He held them afloat as long as he could, then checked the timer: three minutes.

Next, he trained his elemental powers, seeing how far his wall of flames could reach before he lost control of it. He did the same with earth, liquifying the ground and sending waves of it outward. Using his phone's tape measure app, he found that the lengths for each were 250m and 100m.

For air and water, he focused on creating tornadoes of each. He stepped 50m away, then hit record. Using the angle of the shadow each cast, he worked out the height of the waternado as 33m and the tornado as 40m.

That done, he switched to the mental side of his abilities. After lowering his mental barriers, Travis again focused on one mind: Josh. A magenta ribbon appeared, and he traced it back to his house through his mind's eye.

Once there, he slipped into Josh's mind and discovered he was dreaming. He and Travis were at the Michigan State Fair, riding a Ferris wheel, cotton candy in hand as they laughed. There was something so wholesome about it that brought a smile to Travis's face. He exited Josh's dream and returned to his body; he Popped home, drained, and slipped into bed next to Josh, nodding off almost instantly.

When Travis awoke the next morning, Josh was cuddled up on his back, snoozing away. While he was of the mind to shove him off, he would be a liar if he didn't admit it felt nice. But his bladder needed emptying.

When he came back, Josh was up and sporting morning wood. Face flushed, he rushed to the bathroom. "Nothing like the first piss of the day, huh?"

"Yeah," he said and told Josh how'd he'd discovered him that morning.

"I'm sorry. It won't happen again."

"Chill. It was no biggie. Just don't make a habit of it," he said, smiling.

"Right."

After they exchanged a few awkward words, Tavis told Josh he better shower before the twins used up all the hot water. While Josh was doing that, he started breakfast. And when Josh and the twins arrived in the kitchen, he served them bacon, scrambled eggs, sausages, pancakes, and French toast.

Josh patted his belly, then burped. "That was awesome sauce."

"Good, because you're doing the dishes."

He stuck out his tongue. "Meanie."

When Travis hopped in the shower, the water was cold, so he had to heat it up with his fire abilities. He was scared he'd burn down the house when he accidentally lit the shower curtain on fire. But once he extinguished the fire with the showerhead, he relaxed, and everything went smoothly.

Afterward, he checked in with his parents, who told him since he'd stayed out of trouble thus far, they might go away more often.

More unpaid babysitting? Nope!

He kept those thoughts to himself and asked if Josh could stay over again and emphasized his being older. His mother refused it but said she might consider letting him stay another time. Hopes dashed, he told them to enjoy the rest of their weekend and ended the call.

He broke the news to Josh, who was equally dejected.

"If you need back up, I'm only a text or FaceTime away."

"Right."

They spent the rest of the day gaming and listening to music, each complaining how the other's taste sucked. Josh favored Pop and EDM, while Travis preferred Death Metal and Alternative.

"Can't we listen to something where the people aren't screaming or talking about death and destruction?" Josh all but whined.

"How 'bout Motown?"

"Never heard of it."

Travis did a double-take. "You've lived in Michigan practically your whole life and have never heard of Motown?"

"I mean, I know a few songs like *My Girl* or *Dancing in the Street*. But that's it."

Travis shook his head and commenced Josh's musical education, starting with the queen herself, Aretha. Then Martha Reeves and The Vandellas, Dianna Ross and the Supremes, and the other girl groups. Then they moved on to The Temptations, The Four Tops, Marvin Gaye, Stevie Wonder, and countless others.

"Where'd you learn all this?" Josh asked hours later as they ate leftover pizza for lunch.

"Some of it's from old movies I've watched, but a lot of the songs I learned from an online college class I took last summer on the historical and cultural development of rock."

Josh asked him for the information, so his parents would get off his back about extracurriculars for a while. All too soon, six o'clock arrived, and Josh had to leave. He promised to text him later.

To pass the time, Travis worked on Cha and a few side projects in his lab, checking on the twins every half hour before putting them to bed at eight. Once he was sure they were down for the night, he Popped to the park and trained. He tried to anyway, but his thoughts kept returning to Josh. He'd had fun on their sleepover and wanted to do more. But there was always a ticking clock at the back of his mind, reminding him his time was running out.

He shook his head, removed a pack of tennis balls from his messenger bag, and centered himself. He set a few tennis balls a meter away and focused on moving them, pushing aside all his thoughts and emotions. His world narrowed to him and the balls. He visualized them moving. One wabbled, then shot toward him, colliding with his Timbs. The others followed a few seconds later.

"Yes!" he cheered. Then he levitated them, succeeding in raising them a few centimeters before a coughing fit hit him. After five minutes of hacking up what felt like a lung, he decided to move on. He placed tennis balls at intervals of a meter and Popped to them and back. He kept training until exhaustion blurred his vision.

Popping home, he checked on the twins, then went to bed.

He woke up to two texts and a missed call from Josh. He texted him and apologized, saying he'd lost track of time in his lab. Apology accepted, Josh asked if he, Rachel, Brianna, David, and Jason could hang at his house. Travis begrudgingly agreed and told him to bring his Xbox One X and extra controllers.

When Josh and his friends arrived at noon, Amber followed Brianna and Rachel around, asking them tips about makeup and hair, while Bobby declared he was hanging with the men.

They congregated in Travis's room and fired up *Halo*. At first, it was every man for himself, then they split into teams, with one of them sitting out the round and joining in the next. This worked well until Bobby whined how it wasn't fair that he had to sit out because he was "way better" than Travis.

"Everyone has sat out at least one match, so shut up," Travis said, taking the controller from him so he could start his round.

"Imma tell Mom and get you in trouble."

"Go right ahead. Now out."

"But that's not fair."

"Spoiler Alert: life isn't fair."

Travis locked the door after Bobby left, and they played on.

"Don't you think that was a bit harsh?" Josh said.

Travis turned a corner, getting a lucky headshot on Jason's avatar. "Nope. The entitled brat is always pulling crap like this."

"Still."

David caught Travis with a plasma grenade. "The David's with Turner on this one, JJ. My brother Asher is the fucking worst, always going into my room and taking my shit. Put a lock on my door, and he picked it. So, the David popped him one, and he stopped."

Jason ducked behind a wall, tossing a plasma grenade. "Naw. I say Turner went too far. Is he an annoying shit? Yeah. But he's your bro, ya know?"

Travis rolled his eyes. "Whatever."

They switched teams, he and David against Josh and Jason. Things were going well until Brianna knocked on the door with Bobby in tow, crying crocodile tears. He'd fabricated a story about how the older boys were bullying him and wouldn't let him play. Travis explained the situation.

"Well, let him play."

The nerve of her. She doesn't know me, yet here she is, acting like my mom.

The fire inside him begged for release. The air in the room got heavy. People fanned themselves as they broke into a sweat. *Center*, he told himself, putting his anger in a box and locking it away in his mind.

"He can stay, but if he acts up, I'm sending him to his room."

Crisis averted, Travis tossed his controller to Bobby, and they played until four o'clock when Travis kicked out Josh and his friends, stating he didn't think his parents would appreciate coming home to a house full of strangers. He did tell them to swing by another time, though.

Shortly after, he started dinner, a frozen lasagna, which finished cooking just as his parents returned.

"Travis had a buncha people over, and they were mean to me," Bobby said, starting with the fake tears again.

Travis cut him off, explaining exactly what happened.

His mother tutted. "You won't play with your brother but will with strangers? That's not right."

"They're not strangers. I know Josh, Jason, and David from school. And I've hung out with Brianna and Rachel before at Josh's."

"I like them," Amber, said showing off her toothy smile. "They taught me lots about hair and makeup."

His mother made a sour face. "For future reference, you aren't allowed more than two friends over at a time when your father and I aren't here, understood?"

"Yes."

"And be nicer to your brother."

"You got yourself some friends, huh?" his father said, eyeing him.

"Yeah."

"They the ones you've been running off with all summer?"

"It's mainly been Josh, but yeah."

"Without you around, we've been pressed to find babysitters. I wanna see your face around here more, ya hear?"

"Yes, sir," he said and went to set the table.

Despite the facade he put up, Travis didn't know everything. But he did know one thing. His parents were crazy if they thought they could keep him from hanging with Josh.

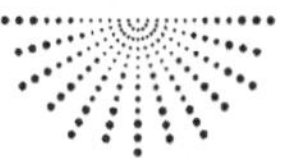

CHAPTER TWENTY-EIGHT

As summer rolled along, JJ and Travis became inseparable, having sleepovers at each other's houses every other weekend. And on days like today, when Travis had to babysit the twins, he brought them with him to JJ's house. David was chilling against the side of the pool while Asher and Bobby ran wild. Meanwhile, David's sister Shari and Amber were busy watching makeup tutorials on YouTube.

JJ exited the pool to grab a pop, and Bobby and Asher pulled down his shorts, laughing as they ran away.

"You're dead when I catch you!" JJ said as he hoisted up his shorts. Running after the pair, he'd almost caught them when they split up.

Screw them. It's too hot for this shit.

He got a can of Mountain Dew from the cooler and chugged it, burping when he'd finished it.

"Still wish you weren't an only child?" Travis said, smirking.

"Yeah," David said, laughing as he scratched under his cast.

JJ's heart skipped a beat. "Dudes, you scared the crap outta me. And no offense, Travis, but Bobby's peak r/EntitledKids material. And with Asher around, they're frelling monsters."

David chuckled. "Hey, Asher isn't that bad. It's Bobby that's the real monster."

Travis shook his head, laughing. "Dude, tell me something I don't know." He turned to JJ and whispered, "There's something I need to tell you."

JJ's heart went aflutter. Could this be the moment Travis declared his undying love for him, and they kissed and more?

"Earth to Josh," he said, waving his hand in front of JJ's face. "You listening?"

Cheeks flushing, he said, "Sorry, I zoned out for a minute."

Looking annoyed, Travis sighed, then sucked in his bottom lip. "I asked if you were busy later."

"Nope. What's so important?"

"I'd rather not say." He cut his eyes toward David. Then he slapped JJ on the ass and ran away. He gave chase, and when he caught Travis, he tackled him. They rolled on the grass, each trying to pin the other until Travis tapped out.

Puffing twice on his inhaler, he sighed and placed his arm around JJ's shoulder. "You're quick for a shrimp."

"Oh, you can screw right off. You're only four inches taller than me," he said and play-hit Travis, starting a shoving match that turned into them wrestling on the ground again. JJ laughed until he felt Travis's erection against his, and Travis bolted for the pool.

After that, David and his siblings left, followed by everyone else, until JJ was alone. He cleaned up the chip bags and pop cans, then read comics and manga awhile before pulling up *Two Peas in a Pod*, one of his all-time favorite online gay love stories. He'd read it like a million times. It was your typical story about best friends who are secretly in love with each other but damn if it didn't always hit him right in the feels.

Around five o'clock, his stomach growled, so he heated up some of his mother's famous lasagna. She'd made it as a peace offering for her and his father not being home like they said they would. They had to fly out to Singapore for another big deal, two days after returning from Dubai.

He could literally count on one hand the times he'd seen his parents that year. He got that they needed to make money to keep up their lifestyle, but he'd rather they lived in a modest neighborhood like Travis's if it meant seeing them more often. He'd told them as much on several occasions, only to have them laugh him off. He didn't understand it. What good was it to gain the world but lose your soul in the process?

This was too deep for him to figure out on an empty stomach.

After eating, he cleaning his dishes, then hopped on social media to see what his friends had been up to. Their posts were mostly pictures of them doing shoots or smoking weed. God, what he wouldn't give to get high. While he was browsing and liking posts, he got a DM from Drew Long, a friend of a friend, asking him when his End of Summer Party would be. He'd forgotten all about that. Honestly, he had no interest in hanging with anyone besides Travis and the Squad, so he told him to spread the word there wouldn't be a party this year.

 Next, he set up a group chat with the Squad, and they decided to hang together sans Travis the next day since they were all free. Afterward, he texted Travis to let him know he'd be busy tomorrow.

Travis's reply was: **OK**

U mad?

No

What did ya wanna talk to me about?

Forget it.

K 

Later

JJ tried texting him again, but his messages stayed on read, so he went back to reading.

～

JJ belted out the lyrics to *Welcome to the Black Parade*, strumming his air guitar with gusto. When the song ended, everyone gathered in his room laughed.

Lance popped out his prosthetic eye and rubbed the hole where it used to be. "Dude, what's up with you today? Your spaz level is off the chart."

JJ glared, wondering why he bothered. "Nothing, I'm just being myself is all."

Lance blew on his eye and then popped it back in place. "Well, you're at an eleven, and Imma need ya to bring it down to a seven."

JJ ground his teeth, clenching his jaws. "If you don't want to be here, then leave."

Rachel looked up from her phone, frowning. "Hey now, we've barely seen you all summer, and you're being douchey AF."

JJ chewed on his bottom lip before saying, "Excuse me for not being the life of the party all the time. You know, I have feelings, too."

Matt looked at him sideways. "Jesus, JJ, what crawled up your vag and died?"

Rachel and Brianna shot Matt dirty looks.

JJ shook his head. "I'll tell ya what my problem is. I'm sick of people riding my dick so they can partake in my booze and hospitality."

Mouth agape, Henry did a double-take. "Who are you, and what did you do with our JJ?"

"Don't mind him. He's just extra salty that he can't hang with his boyfriend," Jason said from the doorway.

JJ glared as Jason and David entered the room and sat on the beanbags situated around his bed. "Go screw yourself with a rusty hacksaw."

Jason laughed and flipped him off. "What? It's true. We barely see ya anymore, and when we do, you're always texting or calling Turner."

"Has it occurred to you that I like hanging with him more than y'all?"

David shook his head. "You don't mean that, and you know it."

Brianna cleared her throat. "Really? Cuz I'm starting to wonder that myself."

Chomping his gum, Jason smacked his lips and then blew a bubble. "He's been acting different ever since he and Turner started hanging. If ya ask me, he's been replaced like in that movie with them pod people."

"*Invasion of the Body Snatchers*," JJ said, scowling. "And FYI, I'm just being myself. Something Travis likes."

Henry flexed his arms, his two-sizes-too-small shirt straining against his muscles. "Jesus. The way you keep bringing up Travis, it's like you're in love with the kid or something."

"I am not!"

"No need to shout," Lance said, eyeing him hard. "Bro, there's a party tonight, and you're going with us. Unless you'd rather spend time with your precious Travis?"

Frell me. If I don't go, they might start to suspect Travis and I are more than friends. Are we? Never mind.

"Alright, cum guzzler. I call your bluff. I'll go with ya."

Lance smiled. "My man."

"On one condition: Travis comes with."

Everyone, save the girls, groaned.

"What? He's my friend, too, and he's never been to a party."

A mischievous glint came into Matt's eyes. "Then let's get him fucked up."

Right," everyone but JJ said.

JJ tugged on his ear. "I don't know about this. The kid drank vodka once max, and I don't want him getting too wasted. Ya feel me?"

Matt scoffed. "Stop being a pussy. Besides, that's all the more reason to get him hammered."

JJ gave several reasons why that wasn't a good idea until Henry cut in. "What you scared he'll hook up with a girl . . . or another guy?"

"Fuck you!"

JJ called Travis and told him about the party, but he declined. "Come on," JJ begged, "you've never been to one, and I'll be there."

"Even if I wanted to go, I have to watch my siblings."

"Dude, they're plenty old enough to be by themselves. My parents left me home all the time, beginning when I was ten. Plus, your mom's working a double shift, and your dad won't be home till tomorrow afternoon. Plenty of time for you to go and be back without them ever knowing."

"What if Bobby and Amber tell on me?"

"You'll get grounded, big whoop."

"All right, I'll go."

"Yes!"

He told Travis to be at his house at nine o'clock sharp and to wear something besides his standard hoodie/tees and sweatpants/basketball shorts. Travis grunted and ended the call.

For the rest of the night, JJ and his friends listened to music, which they voted JJ couldn't choose since he was acting all extra. Then they played video games and laughed as they told stories about old times. But JJ couldn't shake the feeling something bad was going to happen at the party.

At eight o'clock, he brought out the vodka, and they each had a couple shots as they waited for Travis to arrive.

At ten to nine, Travis called, saying he'd was walking up JJ's driveway. When JJ saw him, he could hardly contain himself. Travis had parted his hair down the middle, gelled it, and was wearing a beige polo with matching khakis and Hush Puppy shoes.

"You look good," he said, trying not to let on how turned on he was right then.

Travis laughed. "Yeah, Mother got me this outfit last Christmas. Though, why she still insists I attend church is beyond me. Jason, David, good evening."

When he got to Brianna and Rachel, he bent and kissed their hands. JJ swooned, wanting to be them hella bad. "Ya Goddamn phony."

Travis laughed and threw his arm around JJ's shoulder. "Someone's totes jelly."

"As if," he said and then whispered to Travis if he'd been browsing urbandictionary.com again. "Fo' shizzle my gnizzle frizzle."

At this, everyone laughed, save Jason, who was sending Travis death glares. JJ would have to talk to him about that later, but right now, he was too busy enjoying Travis's company to care. He offered Travis a drink, but he declined, saying he would have something at the party.

"Who'll all be there?" Travis asked.

JJ ticked off names, but Travis stared at him with a vacant expression. "Aside from you guys, I won't know anyone there."

Brianna wrapped her arm around Travis's waist, and he flinched, but only JJ was perceptive enough to notice it.

"My mans, the point of a party is to get wriggity, wriggity wrecked. And besides, I met all these assholes, no offense, at one of JJ's parties. So maybe you'll meet some folks, too. Who knows, you might get lucky before the night's over."

Blushing, Travis nonchalantly wiggled out of Brianna's grip, and everyone laughed at him.

"I think Travis is a virgin," Matt said and laughed that foghorn laugh of his.

Travis folded his arms, inclining his head. "What's the matter, Mitchells? 'Fraid someone will get to me before you?"

Matt stared at him, grimacing, and then burst out laughing. "Good one, kid. But ya keep that shit up, and Imma get medieval on that ass."

They bullshitted around a while longer until Jason announced he'd received a text from the host of the party saying it was time for them to head out. Jason requested an Uber SUV, and JJ requested an Uber black, and they split the fare.

"You're good for your portion, right?" he said to Travis as he entered the BMW Series 5.

"Yeah. Don't go leaving me alone, okay?"

"Keep saying stuff like that, and you'll make me think you like me."

Travis socked him in the arm, and they were off.

When they arrived, JJ tried to stick close to Travis, but inevitably, some friend pulled him away to catch up. As the night wore on, he lost track of Travis. He felt guilty at first but thought, *Hey, he has to learn to fend for himself some time, right?*

CHAPTER TWENTY-NINE

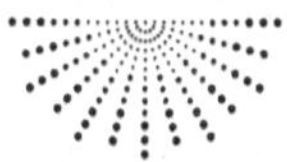

Travis glared at Josh's retreating form.

That moronic, maladjusted midget. He said he wouldn't leave me alone, and there he goes, off for who knows how long this time.

"Travis, why are you mopping?"

He about jumped out his skin at Oblivion's words. *What do you want?*

"Merely to remind you of the ticking clock. You only have a short while left, yes?"

Yeah, so?

"So, forget Josh and have some fun. There are plenty of drinks and mates of either sex from which to choose."

Technically, that should be 'of either gender.' However, gender is a socially constructed spectrum—

"Are you going to lecture me on the finer points of political correctness, or are you going to, as the kids say, do it up big?"

Travis smiled. *You're right. Screw Josh.*

He made his way through the crowd to the table where drinks were laid out, and picking one at random, he downed it and winced, then downed another.

"Slow down, dude. You're gonna hurl."

He turned at the sound of the mellifluous voice, ready to tear the speaker a new one when he was struck by her all-black garb.

"You don't look like the type to be at a place like this," he said, giving her a once over. He took in her combat boots, corset, leather micro-mini, fishnet stockings on her arms and legs, and lipstick.

She flashed him a wry smile. "Usually, I wouldn't be caught dead in a den of such idiocy, but my cousin convinced me to tag along with her, then bailed on me."

"Same. My soon-to-be ex-friend said he wouldn't leave me and has spent the whole night blowing me off to hang with his other friends."

She pursed her pouty lips, shaking her head. "That's a violation of rule one of the friend code. Leave no friend behind."

He chuckled. "I know, right? I'm Travis, by the way." He stuck out his hand, and she shook it.

"My legal name's Ashley, but I go by Raven. Aren't you going to ask me why I'm wearing all black?"

"If I were to guess, it's to symbolize the omnipresence of death and how we're all hurtling toward the great abyss."

Her mouth hung open, and then she snickered. "I didn't take you for a goth."

"I abhor labels. But if you press me on my philosophical underpinnings, then, while I empathize with the Goth ethos, I'm more an anti-natalist, Nietzschean Nihilist, with shades of Secular Humanism."

Raven gave him a half-smile. "In other words, kids suck, and everything's pointless, but we should try to make the best of things while we're here?"

"Basically. Want to sit and talk about it?"

She sipped her drink, her pale-faced scrunched up. "It beats standing around listening to this shite."

Travis snagged another drink, and they made their way to the couch, which, given the number of people at the party, he was surprised to find empty.

After discussing Nietzsche's concept of the Uber Mensch, during which Travis bragged about reading *Beyond Good and Evil* in the original German, they moved on to the purgatory that was middle school.

"I can't wait until I'm old enough to drop out. The whole education system is just a racket to indoctrinate us into becoming brainless worker drones for the capitalist machine," Raven said, pausing to vape, her sandy-blonde hair falling in her face.

"True, though learning itself is a worthy endeavor that we should strive to continue all our lives, short as they may be." He took a sip of his drink and made a sour face as the next song started. "Whoever chose the music has awful taste."

"I know, right? I've been trying to hack into the Spotify station all night, but no luck."

Travis racked his mind, trying to remember whose house this was.

Nolan, something. James? Johnson? Graham? That's it!

He told her to input Nolan's name, but that wasn't it. Next, they tried, "NolanRulez." Nope. Then they tried, "NalonRulez!"

"I'm in," she said. "Now let's play something that doesn't make me nauseous."

She selected *Disposable Teens* by Marilyn Manson, an oldie but goodie, and they bopped their heads, singing along.

Raven laughed, her hazel eyes sparkling. "Didn't take you for a Manson fan."

"If it's angry, anti-establishment, and has a good beat, I like it."

She smiled and stood. "Shall we show these sheeple how it's done?"

Travis looked from her to the dance floor. "I guess— "

He barely had time to down his drink as she pulled him to the dancefloor, her body mashing into his as he tried not to make a fool of himself. She held him close and said, "Relax." He relaxed his shoulders, calming the ball of nerves in his chest, and got into it, gyrating along with her.

When the song ended, all eyes were on them, but he didn't care. Travis had her cue up *Beautiful People* and shared a smile with Raven as they danced. Raven's body ground against him as he stood there in shock. It felt good, but he couldn't help thinking he was betraying

Josh. But Josh had abandoned him, so he went with it and ground his crotch into hers; his head bobbed to the baseline as she grabbed his ass, pulling him closer.

When the song ended, he wiped the sweat from his brow and tried to catch his breath. "That was fun."

"Yeah," she said, then looked down and giggled. He followed her gaze and wanted to die.

He tried laughing it off, commenting it was due to her sensuality. Raven smiled and queued up another song when a blond boy with cornrows stepped onto the dancefloor and shouted to get everyone's attention. "Yeah, let's listen to something not on the school-shooter playlist."

He put on a slow song, and when Raven tried to change it, she told Travis someone had changed the password. His face fell as disappointment washed over him. "So much for that."

"We can still dance, even if the music's crap."

Why not?

Taking her hand, he wrapped his other arm around her waist, and she did the same, her breath warm against his skin.

"I like you," she said, then kissed him full on the lips.

Part of him felt he should stop this, but the larger, drunker part of him said, "Fuck it," and he kissed her back.

Raven's lips were smoother and softer than he'd expected, and she wasn't shy about taking charge, grabbing his hands and placing them on her breasts.

He was edging his way down her back when he heard a familiar voice.

"What the actual fuck?" Josh yelled, storming up to them and grabbing Travis's arm.

"What's your problem?" Travis said, slurring his words.

"You. Me. Outside. Now!"

He looked to Raven, who shrugged.

"Be right back," he said, then followed Josh behind the house, where a few people were smoking a joint.

"What the fuck is wrong with you?" Josh said when they were a safe distance away from the others.

Travis scrunched up his face, confused. "I was having a little fun like you told me to."

"You call making out and feeling-up that girl a little fun?"

Face warming with rage, Travis raised his voice. "Why are you getting mad? You left me alone after you said you wouldn't."

"I can't believe you right now."

"What? Jealous much?"

Josh grunted. "You're so full of shit right now."

People were starting to shoot them looks, and Travis had about reached his drama limit for the night. "Maybe you shouldn't have abandoned me."

Josh threw his hands up in the air. "I can't even with you right now. You put on this big act like your heart's made of stone, but I know the truth."

He got in Josh's face, their noses touching. "And what's that, Giovanni?"

"Your heart's made of glass, and you're so scared of it getting broken, you push everyone away."

"Since when did you care so much about whom I kiss?"

Josh shoved him. "That should've been me!"

Their gaze met. There was longing in Josh's eyes, but Travis couldn't deal with that right now. He ran back inside, exchanged numbers with Raven, asked Nolan to call him a taxi, then went outside to wait for it, ignoring Josh, who kept shooting him hurt looks.

When the taxi arrived, he got in over Josh's pleas for him to stay.

He got as far as his $20 would take him and then Popped home once the taxi was out of sight.

After fixing Bobby and Amber grilled cheese sandwiches and tomato soup, he stood in front of the mirror, staring at his reflection.

Joshua-fucking-Giovanni likes me romantically? That's impossible? I'm not as handsome as him, and I could stand to lose a pound or twenty. And if Josh likes me, then why has he bullied me for so many years?

No, this has to be a sick joke.

After eating, he trained, focusing on his pyrokinetic abilities until his vision blurred. Still keyed up, he sat on the scorched ground and meditated. Try as he might, Travis couldn't get Josh's words out of his head, so he called it quits. He crawled into bed, hoping things would make sense in the morning.

Travis woke up to five voicemails and ten texts from Josh, all saying some variation of, "I'm sorry. Can we just be friends and pretend last night never happened?"

However, it did happen, and now Travis didn't know what to do.

Over the next week, Travis ignored Josh at community service and didn't return his calls or texts. He would have continued avoiding Josh had Dr. Dull not called him on his bullshit.

Josh gave him an anemic smile as they passed each other in Dr. Dull's waiting room. "Hey, stranger."

"Hey yourself. Um, I'm—"

Before Travis could finish his sentence, Dr. Dull called him into his office. He started with his usual question about if anything interesting had happened since their last session.

Against his better judgment, Travis told him about the party and Josh's revelation. "What should I do?"

Dr. Dull steepled his fingers and sighed. "That's not up to me. However, if you're asking my advice, I'd say to look inward and ask yourself how you truly feel about Joshua. And if you don't want to be more than friends with him, tell him and let the chips fall where they may."

"But what if I don't know how I feel about him?"

"Then tell him that and ask that he respect your boundaries until you've come to a decision. First loves can be tough. But if you do want to be more than friends with him, I'll be here to give you the advice I wish I had when I was younger."

"Right."

They talked about the upcoming school year, and Travis told him he didn't see the point as he probably wouldn't finish the year anyway.

"You know, the mind is a powerful thing, and research has shown that our thoughts influence our bodies at the quantum level. If you think positively, things will turn out all right for you."

"As Grams would say, wish in one hand, shit in the other, and see which one fills up first."

"Give it a try. What have you got to lose?"

He grunted and grabbed his messenger bag. He passed Josh in the waiting room, then stopped. "Give me some time to sort things out, please?"

Josh hung his head. "Okay."

He hugged Josh, his embrace lingering a little longer than was accustomed of friends, and they parted ways.

Travis stared at his phone, typed out, **U wanna hang?** and then deleted it for the fifth time in a row.

What do you say to someone who's basically admitted they love you when you don't know if they're telling the truth?

He shook his head and turned his phone off, channel-surfing until he landed on a cheesy fantasy movie. As he watched, he couldn't help thinking if Josh were there, he'd be cracking wise about the cheap costumes and bad CGI effects.

Damn it. Why can't I stop thinking about him?

After flipping through the stations and finding nothing good on, he turned off the TV and Popped to the park where he trained for a while. Every time he closed his eyes, he saw Josh's hurt look.

"Admit it. You miss him, Prometheus said.

I don't need crap from you today.

"Not my fault Josh has you all twisted up in the game."

He does not.

"Keep telling yourself that, and maybe you'll believe it. I don't care what you feel for dude. Just admit you feel something for him and go see him, so I don't have to listen to ya wangst all day."

When I want your opinion, I'll ask.

Raising his mental shields, Travis pushed Prometheus to the back of his mind and focused on levitating himself. He made it a few centimeters off the ground before he lost his concentration and crashed to the ground with a *thud*. Rubbing his butt, he tried again but only lasted thirty seconds before thoughts of Josh intruded again.

He cursed Josh and himself for being in this situation and returned home, only to find his parents screaming at each other about the budget, which his mother had blown by buying $60 worth of lottery tickets.

Nope.

Popping back to the park, he walked around aimlessly until he found himself in Josh's neighborhood. Whether accidentally or intentionally, he couldn't say.

Sucking in a lungful of air, he walked past the security station, his heart pounding as he neared Josh's house.

"What are you doing here?" Josh said when he opened the door.

"The sperm and egg donor are on the rag, so you get the pleasure of my company. Ya gonna let me in or stand there looking all shook?"

"Why don't you go hang with Raven since you like her so much?"

"You're acting childish. It's not even that serious."

Josh's face went red. "Then, you go around kissing everybody?"

"Nope. She was my first kiss."

"Why are you even here? Go kiss her."

"I miss your shrimpy, red-headed ass." He pulled Josh into a hug, and they stayed that way until Josh pulled away, clearing his throat.

"I guess we should go inside, huh? FYI, I'm still legit pissed at you."

Blushing, Travis smiled. "Yeah. *Mortal Kombat*?"

"You read my mind. Prepare for total pwnage."

"In your dreams!" Travis shoved him and ran off giggling.

Josh chased him, pinning Travis against the wall in the foyer. "Caught ya."

"Let ya."

Staring into Josh's eyes, Travis had the urge to kiss him but pushed it away. He didn't want to mess up things again.

"Come on." He pantsed Josh and ran away as Josh hurled death threats at his back.

Once in Josh's room, they kicked off their shoes and settled next to each other on beanbags. He gasped when Josh's knee touched his.

"Sorry." Josh scooted away, turned on the game, and they played several rounds. Travis didn't miss the tension between them. Perhaps if he had more time, he could fix things, but now the best he could hope for was an amicable detente.

As the hours passed, Josh tried to make small talk and crack a few jokes, but it all seemed forced.

"Can we not pretend there isn't an issue between us?"

Josh paused the game. "Meaning what?"

"We're mad at each other, and acting as though we're just friends isn't working, is it? We're both scared of offending the other, so we're pussyfooting around the issue. But that's only making things worse, right?"

"Right, so what do we do?" Josh said, scratching the back of his neck.

"Damn if I know. But I guess I'll start by apologizing for kissing and grinding up on Raven."

"Apology accepted if you accept my apology for bailing on you once we got to the party?"

"Done. But why were you mad?"

Josh rolled his eyes, sighing. "Duh, I'm gay, and I like like you."

It took Travis a minute to process things. "Then when you said that should have been you, you weren't joking?"

"Nope. And I totes want to kiss you now."

"Would you settle for a cuddle?"

In reply, Josh hugged Travis and then pulled away. "I don't feel like playing, but you can still if you want?"

Travis reset the game for one player and played a few rounds until Josh got behind him, wrapping his arms around Travis's back, resting his head against Travis's shoulder.

"Comfy?"

"Mhmm," Josh all but cooed.

Travis found it hard to concentrate on the game with Josh so close, and part of him wanted to tell him to let go of him. But a small and growing part of him reveled in the contact. As all good things must, the cuddle-fest ended when Travis's mother called him.

"Where are you?"

On the fly, he said, "I'm working in my lab. Why?"

"Dinner's ready. It's Hamburger Helper Lasagna."

"I'll be there in a minute."

He told Josh goodbye but promised to call him later.

After dinner, he called Josh, and they talked about what they were going to do for the rest of summer vacation.

"I want to spend it with you if you let me," Josh said, his voice trembling.

"I'd like that, assuming I don't have to share you with the douche-bag brigade."

"David and Jason aren't that bad."

"David's okay, but Jason's is such a cocksucker. No offense."

"I don't get the hate between you guys."

"Something about him trips my bullshit detector, and I don't trust him."

"You'll have to learn to share me."

"If I must. Night, Josh. And . . . I'm glad we hung out today."

"Me, too."

Over the next several days, any time Travis wasn't stuck at home or doing community service, he was at Josh's house. There were a few more setbacks when Josh tried kissing him. He declined, as he was still convinced this was an elaborate joke. Josh would get mad and stop returning his calls and texts for a while. Travis would apologize, and things would be all right for a while.

One day, near the end of June, things changed.

Travis and Josh were lounging around in shorts and tees, sweating rolling off them as they tried to beat the heat. Travis fanned himself, but it did little good. "Remind me again why your parents don't have AC?"

Josh pushed his hair out of his eyes. "They say it's an unnecessary expense."

"Well, I'm dying over here." Travis removed his shorts and shirt, sighing. "That's better." He caught Josh's gaze and half-smiled. "See something ya like?"

Smiling, Josh wrapped his arm around Travis and pulled him close.

Travis let out a little coo. "Hey, I'm honored you told me. About your being gay, I mean."

Josh gazed into Travis's eyes. "Yeah. Do ya want to listen to some music?"

"Yeah."

Josh hit shuffle, and *Crash and Burn* by Savage Garden played. Travis had heard the song a few times before when he snooped around Josh's favorites list, but today the song took on a new meaning.

As the last verse of the song played, he looked at Josh and smiled. "You know, it wasn't until just now that I realized something."

"What?"

"I want a friend like in that song. Someone who will be there for me through the good and the bad."

Josh trembled, his bottom lip quivering. "I want to be that friend, more than anything if you'll let me."

Is Josh being honest? There's one way to find out.

"Do you remember when I wanted to talk to you about something?"

"Vaguely, why?"

"Get dressed and follow me outside." Josh shot him a confused look but complied. With each second that passed, Travis doubted himself more. But he had to do this.

"What's so impor – "

Travis tossed a fireball from hand to hand before extinguishing it. "Surprise!" he said, looking down. "I have powers."

CHAPTER THIRTY

Josh gawked at Travis, transfixed before his face broke into a wide grin. "Dude, sweet! What else can you do?"

"You're not . . . scared?"

"Fuck no. I'm totes jelly. How long have you had powers? Does anyone else know? Have you been tracking the progression of them? If not, can I? I'll need a photography drome, a camera, and—"

"Slow down. You don't need to buy all that crap."

Josh lowered his head. "Oh. I'm not trying to buy your friendship, ya know?"

"That's not what I was implying. I just meant that I can build most of that stuff for a fraction of the cost."

Josh smiled. "So, I can help you train?"

"I don't think that'd be a good idea since your presence would distract me."

The truth was Travis wasn't worried about that. Instead, he feared losing control and hurting Josh. But he kept that thought to himself, not wanting to ponder what it meant just yet. Travis answered Josh's questions each in turn.

"So, there's a government agency dedicated to tracking and capturing peeps with superpowers? I'm legit shook. I thought stuff like that only existed in comics. What's it like having powers?" Josh said, leaning in close.

"You wouldn't want them."

"Oh, come on. Who wouldn't like teleporting, super strength, healing, psychic abilities, and elemental control? I give both nuts for that."

Anger flared up in Travis. "You don't get it. From the moment my powers manifested, I've felt like I live in a world of sandcastles. On the surface is the illusion of stability. But one mistake, and it all comes tumbling down. It takes constant control, and I wouldn't wish this on anyone."

Josh stared at him. "Then that weird wind at the bus stop, the times the temperature's jumped, and when I saw your eyes change color, were all you losing control?"

Travis nodded. "Daily meditation and training have helped me rein in my abilities, but it's still a work-in-progress."

"Could you like blow something up for me?"

Travis thought for a second. Should he accept Josh's request, it could serve to bond them. Yet if he lost control, he could destroy other things, or worse, hurt Josh. Swallowing the lump in his throat, he made his decision. "I don't know about this."

Josh stuck out his bottom lip. "Please?"

Seeing the pleading look, Travis caved. "Okay, but I better do it out here."

Josh hugged him. "Sweet! I'll be right back." He returned with an ugly lamp. "Here. Wreck the shit outta this."

"Why the animosity?"

"Mom's had it for years and gives it more attention than me."

"Understood."

Josh set the lamp on the ground, and Travis told him to stand back. Then he focused on it, opening the box in his mind containing his anger, and let it loose. *Boom.* The lamp shattered, and Josh whooped. Travis went to lock away his emotions, but they slipped his reins, and he set the manicured lawn ablaze.

"Go get a fire extinguisher," he yelled to Josh while he tried containing the fire. Reaching out his hand, he commanded it to stop, but the flames continued spreading. Closing his eyes, he tried again, this time more forceful. *Return!*

Heat licked at his ankles as the fire washed over and into him. As though sentient, he felt the flames resist his attempts to cage them.

No. I am your master. Return! And then it was done. A loud *thud* drew his attention. Josh had dropped the fire extinguisher and was staring at him with a terrified expression. Neither of them said anything at first, and Travis wondered if Josh thought him a monster.

Josh broke the silence with a loud, "Holy shit! That was epic. But my parents are gonna kill me when they see the lawn."

Travis laughed. "Seriously, that's your only concern?"

Josh nodded. "You're amazeballs with awesome sauce on the side." After he'd finished geeking out, Josh called his lawn care company to schedule an emergency appointment. The cover story he gave them was they'd been playing with fireworks when one of them accidentally set the lawn on fire.

Travis side-eyed Josh, impressed and worried about the ease with which he'd come up with that lie. He filed this away, and they went inside, where Josh badgered him until he agreed to demonstrate his telepathic abilities.

Happy now?

"*I'm euphoric AF!*"

Don't shout like that.

"*Sorry. Say you haven't been reading my thoughts without my permission, though?*"

I'd never do such a thing. It goes against my ethos.

"*Okay. Just checking.*"

Travis closed his connection with Josh, but not before he got the impression Josh was hiding something from him. Shrugging it off, he suggested they have a kung fu movie marathon, starting with *The Five Deadly Venoms*. They laughed at the badly dubbed movies, imitating moves and having a great time until Travis had another coughing fit that left him gasping for air.

"You okay?" Josh asked him when it had passed.

"No. Scar tissue has formed in my lungs, causing my cough. My lung capacity's down to 80 percent. Eventually, I won't be able to breathe at all if my lungs don't fill up with fluid first."

Josh placed his hand on Travis's knee. "You're pretty sick, huh?"

"Yeah, but let's get back to the movie."

At five o'clock, Travis's mother called him home for dinner.

"Promise you won't tell anyone about my powers."

"Deal."

"Or about the other thing. And promise me you won't treat me any differently."

In response, Josh hugged him. "I promise. And I meant it when I said I was here for ya."

Smiling, Travis nodded and Popped home.

After Josh got his lawn fixed, he and Travis began talking more, often from dusk to dawn, prompting Travis's parents to ask Josh over for dinner. Travis stalled them as long as he could, but that didn't work forever. On the last Friday in June, Josh came over for dinner.

Travis pulled at his tie, the collar of his shirt like a vice, cutting into his throat. He straightened his jacket, the buttons threatening to pop off any second.

The things I do for Josh. Note to self: lose weight.

He gave himself a final appraisal in the mirror. He even tried taming the monstrosity that passed for his hair with a wet comb but only made things worse.

"Travis, dinner. Now!" His mother's bellicose tone told him he'd better make an appearance post-haste if he didn't want to be double-grounded. Halfway to the dining room, he received a text from Josh.

I'm here.

He strode past his mother, ignoring her question about where he was going. Opening the door, Travis reached up to fix his hair, but Josh smoothed the offending strands. "That's better, yeah?"

Travis's breath went out of him upon seeing Josh. His hair was slicked back with gel, reminding Travis of old gangster movies.

Though Josh's suit hung off him in places, he looked fresh from the runway.

"Thanks," he managed to say. "You look nice."

Josh snickered, his toothy smile making Travis's stomach flutter. "This old thing? Mother makes me wear it for black-tie events." He laughed. "Ya got me sounding like you now."

Travis wiggled his eyebrows and lean in. "I could think of worse things."

Josh pulled at his tie, his cheeks and ears reddening.

"Son, are you going to continue acting like we're not here, or are you going to introduce us to your friend?"

Travis looked at his father, on the verge of rolling his eyes, but thought better of it. Clearing his throat, he said, "Mother, Father, I'd like you meet Joshua Joseph Giovanni, alias JJ, alias Josh."

His father stood and extended his hand. "What should we call ya, son?"

Josh, hand trembling, bottom lip quivering, stuttered out, "Josh will be fine, sir."

His father's mitt of a hand encased Josh's, clamping down.

Don't show any fear.

"Right."

Josh locked eyes with Travis' father, continuing the shake until his dad released his red hand.

"Your parents are Lilith and Cain Giovanni, correct?" his mom said, her lips turned up in the beginnings of a coy smile.

Josh sat, massaging his hand. "Yes, ma'am. They've been away on business a while now. Otherwise, I'm sure they would have loved meeting you."

Arching a contoured eyebrow, his mom made a sour face. "Am I to understand you've been without adult supervision for prolonged periods this summer?"

Josh wrapped his arms around himself. "More or less."

She harrumphed. "Travis, we'll discuss this matter later. Now, Josh, what have you've been doing that has turned my son into a virtual stranger in his own home?" She interlaced her fingers, looking down her nose at Josh, who was squirming in his seat as though he had worms.

Relax, she's only busting your balks to get a rise out of ya. Don't react, and she'll move on.

"You know this how?"

Been reading her mind.

Josh stared at him, his expression blank. *"I thought you didn't read people's minds?"*

I don't. But she's broadcasting them, so I'm taking advantage of the situation.

His mother pursed her lips. "Why do I get the feeling you two are having a conversation we're not privy to?"

"Oh, Mother, you're being paranoid. To answer your question, we've spent this summer doing the usual things—gaming, ripping on bad sci-fi and horror movies, watching YouTube videos, listening to music, and plotting the overthrow of the status quo. You know, typical stuff."

"Really? Because I heard from a reliable source that you two—my, that's the timer. The roast's done. We'll continue this when I get back."

"What does she know?!"

Travis rubbed his right temple. *You have any idea how painful it is when you scream your thoughts at me like that?*

"Sorry, but—"

But nothing. Chillax and let me handle it.

"Okay."

Bobby shot them a puzzled look. "Why do you guys keep shooting each other looks like that?"

"Brother dear, you're, as they say, straight trippin'."

"Naw," Bobby said, running his hand through his finger-wave curls, "you have powers."

His father pounded on the table. "I will not have that mess in my house."

Everyone at the table stared at him.

"There's no such thing as superpowers, and Travis most definitely doesn't have any." He uncorked the bottle of wine in the center of the table and filled his glass, slopping some in the process and hastily mopped it up.

Travis smiled.

However, his moment of celebration ended when his mother returned to the table with the roast. She took one look at his father and turned to Travis. "What did you do?"

"Why do you assume I'm at fault? 'Twas Robert who set Father off by mentioning something about my having powers and . . ."

She nearly dropped the roast, recovering in time to place it on the table. Then she sat, the color draining from her face. "Robert, don't scare your father and I with such nonsense. Getting back to the topic of our earlier discussion. Is it true you two are . . . lovers?"

"No, Mother. We aren't partners. Would there be a problem if we were?"

"I suppose not. But I heard from a friend of a friend that you two had a lovers' quarrel. So, I was curious if you were, you know?"

"Mother, if you're asking about my orientation, then no, I'm not gay. As for Josh, it isn't my place to say. Satisfied?"

His mother wiped her chin. "I see. Well . . . know you can talk to your father and I about anything."

"Right." He believed them about as much as he believed in god.

Travis's father brought up the subject of their relationship again, but Travis shrugged him off.

"Mr. Turner," Josh said, between bites of the pot roast, "Travis told me you were in the military."

"Yup, I was in the Army Corps of Engineers for eighteen years. Woulda been twenty if it hadn't had been for The Fire."

"Right. Uh, what did you do exactly, if you don't mind me asking?"

"Not at all, son. Nice to see *somebody* take an interest. I mostly helped design and construct hydroelectric dams and other infrastructure. It was hard work, and I spent many a long day trying to cut through red tape. That's why I like civilian work. Nowhere near the hassle."

Travis looked at his father and Josh, dumbstruck. He'd wanted them to get along, but here his father was divulging information to Josh he'd never told Travis.

His father looked at him askew. "Awful quiet over there, Travis. Got anything to say?"

"Only that this is the first I'm hearing of all this, Father."

"Anyway," he said, ignoring Travis, "Josh, you given any thought to what course pathway you want to take for ninth grade?"

"I mean, that's still a whole 'nother year off."

"True, but it'll be here before you know it."

His mother cleared her throat. "Travis, what are you taking?"

"Probably the STEM track, most likely either one of the sciences or something in IT."

Smiling, Josh placed his knee against Travis's. "Cool. Why those, though?"

Shrugging, Travis said, "I've always been fascinated by science. I love computers and electronics and taking apart things to see how they work. Why not get paid to do that?"

"Gotcha."

"Son," his mother began, "that sounds like a good plan b, but perhaps you should think of something more practical like law or medicine, or maybe become an electrician like your father."

Gritting his teeth and fighting back the urge to scream, Travis exhaled through his nose, counting to ten in his head. "Mother, I'm old enough to decide for myself what I'll do with my life."

She forced a smile. "My parents may have left you that trust fund, but that doesn't mean you can do whatever you want."

"This has nothing to do with Opa's trust fund or Grams naming me heir to the Cadmus Fortune and the Aurum Estate."

"I just don't want you to make a mistake that'll ruin your life."

"It's my life to do with as I please."

Travis's father slammed his fist down on the table, knocking over his wine glass. "Apologize to your mother right now, and if you keep showing your ass, you and Josh won't be hanging out anymore."

Travis clenched his fists.

"You unclench your hands this instant," his dad barked

"Or what?" Travis stood from his seat. "You'll beat my ass again? Like I care."

The pictures on the wall rattled. The wind outside picked up, blowing tree branches against the windows and sides of the house.

"Are you okay?" Josh asked.

He counted to ten in his head, pulling back his power and locking his emotions in their boxes. "I'm tired, and I'm going to bed. You coming, Josh?"

"Hold it right there," his dad said. "If you think you can disrespect your mother and I like that, you got another thing coming. Josh, it was nice meeting you, but it's time for you to go home since Travis is acting all hard-headed."

Josh looked at Travis. *"Do you want me to go or stay?"*

Go. I'll see you later.

"Later," Josh said and requested a rideshare.

Once Josh left, Travis's parents sent him to his room and grounded him for a week. Not that it stopped him from sneaking out to see Josh and train, but it was still an inconvenience.

Over the coming days, Travis scavenged the junkyard for parts for their photography drone, while Josh ordered the camera and parts he couldn't find. And by the time he was off punishment, the photography drone was ready.

To ensure Josh's safety, Travis had him stay a minimum of 100 meters away while he trained. Together, they tracked his progress in the hopes it might help another metahuman.

June gave way to July.

Travis was preparing to head to Josh's for their weekly bitch fest when Grams called him.

"Do my ears deceive me, or is that really you, my caramel cowboy?"

"Sorry I haven't called in a while. I've been busy."

"This wouldn't have anything to do with a certain Joshua Giovanni?"

"Hmm, could be."

"You know, Josh's mother tells me you're all he talks about these days."

Travis smiled, a warmness starting in his stomach and spreading to his whole body.

"Do you like him?"

"I, uh . . . um . . ."

She laughed. "Cat got your tongue?"

"It's just . . . I've never liked anyone before, much less loved someone."

"Ah, so it is love."

"I mean, I don't know. I like being around him when it's just us. But I don't know if I'd go as far as saying I love him."

"Matters of the heart can be quite confusing. It took me six months to catch on that your grandfather liked me. He used to pick fights with me and tease me something fierce before I hauled off and cold-cocked him."

He couldn't help laughing. "Grams, you're a straight-up original gangster."

"Thanks, I think. Tell me about this boy that has my grandbaby all twitterpated."

"Well . . ."

And, without meaning to, he gushed about Josh for twenty minutes straight, even telling her about their naked run up his driveway.

"Dear, this is just my two cents, but it sounds like you're rather smitten with him."

"Yeah, I think I am."

"Then tell him."

"But I'm scared. What if he doesn't like me, and I lose my only friend?"

"I'll let you in on a little secret: those we care about the most have the power to hurt us the most. Lord knows that's true of your mother."

"Then why bother with it?"

"Because nothing in this world compares to the joy of being with those you love."

"But what if I get hurt?"

She chuckled. "Boy, if I let fear stop me from doing things, I'd never leave the house. Sure, you might get hurt . . . or you might find the love of your life. But you won't know unless you take a leap of faith."

"That's a leap into faith. But how do I know this isn't a giant joke, and when I tell him how I feel, he won't laugh at me?"

"You don't, but could you live with yourself if you never told him?"

"No, but I'm afraid."

"Listen to me, my sweet boy. Inside us all is the ember of a hero, a phoenix waiting to rise from the ashes of our fears. Tell him and let whatever happens happen."

"Okay."

They talked a bit longer. Then Travis ended the call with a promise to call her tomorrow.

When he materialized at Josh's house, the older boy was on his laptop and quickly closed it.

"Did I catch you watching porn?"

"Ha, ha, and no. I read my porn, thank you very much."

"Ah, a refined pervert. You use your left or your right?"

Josh's face went red. "Dude, are you seriously asking me about my jerkoff habits?"

"Yep. BTW, I use my left."

"Me too," he said, flustered.

Travis's words caught in his throat, but he pushed through his nervousness. "Maybe we could give each other a helping hand sometime?"

Josh licked his lips. "I'm down if you are?"

Heart aflutter, Travis squeaked out, "How about tomorrow?"

"Okay."

That decided, they watched YouTube videos on Josh's laptop until they got tired.

Travis Popped home and allowed himself to think a thought he'd been scared to admit: *I love Joshua Giovanni.*

CHAPTER THIRTY-ONE

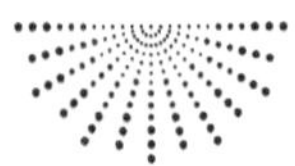

JJ checked the printouts of his favorite stroke stories, straightened the towels on his bed, and fiddled with the bottle of K-Y Jelly on his nightstand. His insides were abuzz at the thought of Travis's touch. But he was also conflicted.

What if I do something wrong? What if this is a setup, and once I drop my guard, he'll take pictures of my junk and post them to the school's WhatsApp account? What if we do this, and he decides he doesn't want to be friends anymore? What if he was joking and freaks out when he sees all this? What if—

"Ah!" he said when Travis's voice came over the intercom. JJ told him he'd be right out. With a long sigh, he gave his bed a final glance.

They exchanged their typical greeting of "Sup," bumped fists, and one-arm hugged. JJ shot him furtive looks as they sat on the couch and vegged out to YouTube videos.

"Something the matter?" Travis said, looking a bit squirrelly.

JJ had two options: tell him nothing was wrong or ask if they were going to jerk it together. Swallowing the lump in his throat, JJ tugged at his right ear.

"You ready to be the masters of our domains?" he said, forcing a smile.

Travis paused, staring at him. "I mean if you want to? It's cool with me."

It was an out, but when would JJ get another chance like this? "It's cool with me if you don't want to. If you're scared, I get it."

"Nonsense. Let's go."

Upon entering JJ's room, they kicked off their shoes, chose a story, dropped their shorts, and got to it. JJ sneaked peeks at Travis, longing to touch him. A few minutes passed before Travis huffed and asked to borrow JJ's laptop so he could watch porn on it.

"Sure," he said, his voice husky. JJ stopped reading and watched Travis load an MFM scene and spread out on the bed, propping himself up with pillows. While JJ was no stranger to gay porn, he'd never seen bi porn before and was curious.

Edging closer to get a better look, he rested his knee against Travis's. "Those guys are totes hot and hella hung."

"Yeah. The girl isn't too bad-looking either. Pass the lube."

When their hands touched for the briefest of moments, it took JJ's breath away. He watched a second, mesmerized by the hypnotic movements of Travis's hand, the urge to touch him growing. Soon, all thoughts of the porn left him and, more scared than any time in his life, he grabbed Travis's erection.

Travis froze, looked at JJ wide-eyed, and leaped from the bed.

"Hold up," JJ called to him as Travis dressed, but it did no good. As soon as Travis was clothed, he teleported away.

JJ tried texting and calling Travis, but they went unanswered. For the next several days, Travis ignored JJ and refused his invites to hang. JJ's worry ate him, and he didn't eat or sleep much, which Dr. Dull brought up at their session.

"I think I fucked things up with Travis," he said and explained the situation.

Dr. Dull tutted at him. "I know it's hard dealing with your feelings, pun unintended, but it is paramount that you have the other's affirmative consent before engaging in any sexual activity. You broke Travis's boundaries and trust by not asking his permission. Don't do that again, with him or any of your other partners. Understand?"

JJ's stomach roiled at the thought of violating Travis like that. He would apologize to him and do whatever it took to make it up to him.

They spent the rest of their session going over what was and wasn't affirmative consent, and JJ left with several book recommendations on the topic. Once home, he kicked Operation Romeo into high gear. Seeing as how Travis might not be around to see his prom, JJ had decided to throw him a prom for two, and he had been looking at prom boards on Pinterest for inspiration. He made a list of everything he'd need and ordered them. Then he set about contacting their principal, Mr. Malo, who was sympathetic to his cause.

As the days passed, JJ finalized the setlist, got his tux and their boutonnieres (white roses), and researched promposals. Unlike himself, he suspected Travis wouldn't be into a huge public display, so he'd have to be lowkey about things.

The Fourth of July came and went without a word from Travis, so JJ decided he'd have to restart things. He cornered Travis in the kitchen at St. Michael's, blocking him from washing dishes until he agreed to talk with him. Huffing, Travis nodded and told JJ he could come over to his house after his shift ended.

JJ smiled. "Thanks. And so sorry for . . . you know. Won't happen again."

A panicked look came over Travis's face. "Yeah. Ask next time."

Hope swelled in JJ's chest. "There will be a next time?"

Travis smirked. "Maybe. If you're a good boy."

"Ass," JJ said and moved aside.

JJ had asked Travis to teleport them to Travis's house and was regretting it as he hurled into the trash can. Once it passed and he'd washed out his mouth, and Travis had cleaned out the trash can, they sat on his bed.

"About what happened," JJ began, "I'm sorry for not getting your permission. It was wrong of me."

Travis stared at him hard. "Good. Honestly, I liked what you did."

"Then why'd you leave and freeze me out?"

"Generally, I don't like to be touched, especially not somewhere that intimate. It was a shock, so I ran before my powers got the better of me."

"How do you mean?"

Sighing and face going red, Travis said, "Ever since . . . I've been having nocturnal emissions about us doing more stuff."

Smiling, JJ patted Travis's leg. "Ain't nothing wrong with that, dude."

"You don't get it. When I explode, I explode. I've caught my bedding on fire twice and now sleep with a fire extinguisher."

Realization dawned on JJ. "You've been avoiding me this whole time cause you're afraid of us going further and hurting me?"

Travis nodded. "I've been meditating more and abstaining from onanism until I can get a handle on things."

"That's rough. I doubt I could go a day without spanking it."

"Now do you understand why I had to cut contact with you?"

"Look, we don't have to mess around. We can just chill and play video games like before."

Travis growled. "It's not that simple. Every time I see you, I want to . . . never mind."

JJ wanted to press Travis on what he was about to say but let it slide. They gamed until Travis's parents arrived home and told JJ he had to leave.

"Want me to teleport you home?"

No. I'll take an Uber.

With the end of summer fast approaching, he got on Group Chat with the Squad and told them to spread the news he wasn't throwing another party for a while. Henry, Lance, and Matt were a bit butthurt, but Brianna and Rachel understood once he told them why later. They demanded to help him plan and set up the prom for two.

The trio met up every day after JJ got home from Travis's, and by the end of July, everything was ready. And not a moment too late since Travis's condition worsened, requiring him to use oxygen at night to ease the strain on his lungs and heart. His cough was near-constant now, and JJ worried they didn't have much time left. It saddened him to think of never seeing Travis's smirk or hearing him laugh again as they watched kaiju movies.

A week before school started, JJ convinced Travis to let him blindfold him and ride with him in a Lyft. He was cryptic, only telling him to wear a suit, preferably a tux.

"Is this really necessary?" Travis asked as they rode along.

"Yes," JJ said, slapping at Travis's hand as he reached for the blindfold. "We're almost there."

"Meanie."

"You'll thank me later. I promise."

"We'll see about that."

The car arrived in front of AP Prep. JJ helped Travis out and guided him to the gym, where they'd set everything up. "You can take your blindfold off."

Travis looked around, his eyes wide, a smile splitting his face. "What's all this?"

JJ hugged him tight. "Welcome to Prom."

CHAPTER THIRTY-TWO

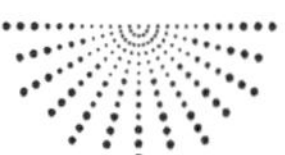

Travis couldn't help smiling as he took in the gym. White and yellow fairy lights lined the north wall, accompanied by silver and gold streamers on the western wall. On the eastern wall were tables with punch and finger foods and silver and gold balloons that had "Prom 2017" on them. And against the south wall was a huge banner with, 'An Enchanted Evening,' printed large across it.

"You did this all for me?"

Josh smiled, his ears going red. "I had help from Brianna, Rachel, David, and Jason. But yeah." He reached into a bag, pulled out a white rose, and affixed it to Travis's lapel. Then he pressed a few buttons on the remote he'd pulled from his pocket. A strobe light turned on, bathing them in rainbow-colored lights.

"Someone went all out," Travis said, enjoying every second of it.

"When it comes to you, there's no expense I wouldn't spare," Josh said, leaning in.

When Josh's cologne hit Travis, he couldn't help sighing, content to stay like that forever.

"Shall we?" Josh said, cuing up the music.

They danced the night away to songs by Rihanna, Darude, Drake, The Weekend, Future, and other hits of the day, along with oldies by

Savage Garden, The Backstreet Boys, N*Sync, and other boy bands. Josh had also added some of Travis's favorites, and they moshed, limbs flailing as they moved to the music.

"Whew!" Travis said, plopping down on the bleachers and wiping sweat from his forehead as *My Plague* by Slipknot finished.

Josh handed him more napkins. "You okay?"

He nodded. "Just need a second to catch my breath."

Josh paused the music and got him a glass of punch.

"Thanks," Travis said, taking a sip and pausing. "You spiked the punch?"

"Of course; it's prom law." Josh laughed. "Don't worry, I only put like one-third of a fifth of vodka. So, having fun?"

Travis didn't have to think before he answered, "Fuck yeah!"

Josh whooped. "My man. You ready?" He held out his hand, looking like a puppy waiting for a treat. Finishing his drink, Travis rose, and Josh restarted the music.

As the night progressed, the music changed from high-energy pop and EDM to slower R&B music.

"May I have this dance?" Josh asked, slurring his words a bit as *Beautiful Soul* by Jesse McCartney started. Shrugging, Travis agreed, but he wasn't prepared when Josh came in close and wrapped his arms around Travis. He began a dramatic lip-sync that was the most adorable thing Travis had ever seen.

When the song transitioned to *Stand by Me,* they paused and smiled. He wrapped his arms around Josh, pulling him closer for a slow dance. The heat of Josh's body against his filled Travis's head with butterflies, and he longed to kiss the older boy, yet he still wasn't sure whether Josh returned his feelings or if this was a prank.

The song ended and transitioned to what he'd later learn was *Yours to Hold* by Skillet. As it played, Travis thought over his feelings for Josh, seeing him anew. Hands tremoring, Travis lifted Josh's head, leaning in close. Josh's breath blew warm against his skin.

He found want in Josh's jade eyes. Travis traced his thumb across Josh's lips.

"Please," Josh begged, his lips quivering.

Though Travis wanted nothing more than to kiss Josh, he couldn't bring himself to close the distance between them. Then he remembered Grams' words to him:

"Inside us all is the ember of a hero, a phoenix waiting to rise from the ashes of our fear."

He held Josh's gaze for what felt like forever. Then he pressed his lips against Josh's, kissing him long and hard, only stopping when the fairy lights blew out from the burst of energy pouring off him.

"Took ya long enough," Josh said, hitting him on the arm before pulling him for a slower, gentler kiss. Travis melted into Josh's embrace, reveling in the comfort and joy he found there. He didn't know what the future held for them with school starting next week and his symptoms worsening, but that day, he learned an important lesson: bravery isn't the absence of fear. It's facing what terrifies you head-on. Because on the other side of fear is hope, is love.

Between kisses, they planned how they'd spend every second possible together before school started, neither of them daring to mention Travis's health. That could wait for another day.

The next morning found Travis, Josh, David, Jason, Rachel, and Brianna cleaning up the gym.

"So," Jason began, "you ever gonna tell me who the lucky lady was? 'Cause I bet money this was a panty-dropper."

Josh shot Travis a dreamy look. "Who says it was a girl?"

"LOL, funny, JJ," he replied, shaking his head.

"Dude, I'm gay and in love with Travis."

Jason stopped and looked from Josh to Travis and back. Then he laughed. "Good one, JJ."

Travis rolled his eyes. "Miller, Josh isn't joking. And . . ." He paused, conflicted over whether to say his next word. After two heartbeats, he said, "I love him, too."

Jason's jaw dropped. "Dude, you two are together for real?"

"Yep," they said, smiling.

Jason faltered. "I never would have guessed. When did this bromance happen?"

"Well . . ." Josh explained the events of the summer, leaving out the bits about Travis's powers.

David congratulated them and told Jason to pick his mouth up off the floor.

"You knew?" he said, raising his voice.

Brianna, hands akimbo, shook her head. "We been knew. What took y'all so long?"

An argument broke out over who knew what and when.

Travis put a stop to it by shouting, "Everyone shut up! It doesn't matter who knew first. You all know now."

"Yeah," Josh said, reaching out for Travis's hand. "And I'd appreciate it if you let us decide who else to tell."

Travis agreed, not so much caring who knew about them but more so for t solidarity. They resumed cleaning and finished by noon, grabbed lunch at Leo's Coney Island on Woodward, then dropped Travis and Josh off at Josh's house.

"What now?" Josh said once they were alone.

"We make the most of our time."

"Yeah," Josh said, placing butterfly kisses on Travis's lips.

Travis pulled away. "Josh?"

"Yeah?" he said, looking concerned.

"No matter what happens. I'm glad to have met you. You've given my life meaning."

Before Josh could reply, Travis pulled him in for another deep kiss.

They pulled apart, gasping for air. "I could get used to this," Josh said with a big dopey smile.

"Me, too."

Travis and Josh staggered along Josh's driveway, laughing in between kisses. Every night since Josh's prom for two, they'd met up to talk, drink, and make out. Tonight, they might have overdone it. Travis held up Josh, taking a deep whiff of his hair, as he keyed in the gate code. He couldn't help himself and pinned Josh against the gate, kissing him as he copped a feel on Josh's ass.

"We should stop," Josh said, pulling away.

"You're no fun," Travis whined before he pulled him in for another kiss.

Josh moaned into his mouth but broke the kiss. "Much as I'd like to spend all night doing this, tomorrow's the first day of eighth grade."

"Right. Night."

Travis hugged him tight and Popped to the park to train.

The next morning, Travis slumped in his seat on the bus, nursing a migraine that could down a rhino. He attempted to drift off when Josh asked him to sit with him and his friends. He shrugged and complied, noticing the stares everyone gave him as they passed. Sliding in by the window, he gave Henry, Lance, Mitchells, David, and Jason an anemic, "Hey."

Mitchells looked at him sideways. "Since when does Turner sit with us?"

Josh cut him a dirty look. "Since he and I became friends over the summer."

Mitchell's face scrunched up. "Right. You guys had to do community service cause of the fight last year."

Josh nodded. "Speaking of which, what's your schedule like?"

Travis brought up his calendar app. "Homework from 3:30PM-5:00PM, community service from 5:00PPM-8:00PM except on Mondays when I have Dr. Dull's class and therapy. You?"

"About the same. Hey, we should do our homework together, so we finish faster."

"Right. and we should volunteer at the same places, so we can carpool." *By which I mean teleport.*

They carried on making plans until Mitchells cut in. "It's cool you guys are friends and all, but what about the Squad?"

Josh looked from Mitchells to Travis. "I mean, I guess we can all do our homework together." *"And we can hang out alone before bed?"*

I have to train, but that's workable.

With that solved, they chatted along with Josh trying to include Travis in the conversation, but he was content listening to podcasts on his phone. In no time, the bus arrived at school, and they piled out, heading for the gym to get their schedules and locker assignments. As Travis entered the gym, he smiled, remembering the night he and Josh kissed for the first time.

After getting their schedules, they compared, and by some miracle or abomination of the scheduling gods, he and Josh were in all their classes together and had the same lunch period.

Josh whooted. "Sweet! I'll go check with the Squad."

As Josh walked away, Travis felt a pang of jealousy, knowing there were things they would never share. Before his emotions got the better of him, he stuffed them in their boxes, locked them away, and took three deep breaths to center himself.

Josh returned, telling him they all shared three classes together— Math, English, and Science. Josh said he'd create a group chat on What's App, then showed Travis how to create an account. With that done, they went to their first class: History.

Travis's headache intensified as the day progressed, and the only other time he'd felt like this was when his powers first activated. Acting on his hunch, he raised his mental barriers. His headache dulled to a small throb at the back of his mind. He'd been so busy with Josh the past week that he hadn't trained at all. He had to be more diligent; he couldn't afford a slip-up.

Everything was fine until lunch. Travis had become accustomed to kissing and touching Josh for hours on end, and now he was fiending for a hit of his ginger teddy bear. At the end of their last class before lunch, he hauled Josh to the nearest restroom and pulled him into the handicap stall.

"What the—mmmmmm," Josh moaned as Travis kissed him, running his hands over his body. They stayed like that, lips smashing into each other as they copped a feel. It was only when the tardy chime sounded that they pulled apart.

Josh, panting, wiping the spittle from his lips. "That was an epic win."

Travis took a puff from his inhaler. "Yeah, but I shouldn't have done that. Anyone could have seen us or walked in on us."

Josh flashed his cocky smile. "We'll just have to be extra careful, right?"

Travis socked Josh's arm playfully. "Yeah. You go out first. Then I'll follow in a bit."

Lunch was interesting. Again, Josh tried involving Travis in the conversation, but he wasn't into it and chose instead to do their History reading assignment.

"You were a real conversationalist back there," Josh said.

"I know the Squad means a lot to you, but we don't have anything in common."

"You have me in common."

Travis sighed. "For your sake, I'll try being more gregarious."

"That's all I'm asking."

When Travis arrived home from community service on Wednesday, his mother told him his probation officer left a message that she wanted to meet with him Friday after school. A pit of dread formed in his stomach. He'd completely forgotten about her.

He popped his dinner in the microwave, and when he'd finished eating, he told his mother he was going for a walk. In actuality, he was going to train. After sleeping in and almost missing the bus twice already, he decided it was better to train before he visited Josh at night.

The night air was cool against his skin when he Popped to the park, but that was to be expected as they were moving into September; Monday was Labor Day, and soon enough, it would be his birthday. Grams had said she would fly in to spend the weekend with him, and Josh had been hinting at a special present for him. Travis had told him he needn't give him some lavish gift, that their being together was gift enough.

He put the drone in stationery mode, and it hovered 30 meters above him, recording him. Tonight, he worked on manipulating earth and water, combining them to make mud. Then he focused on transmogrifying the mud into metal.

He levitated the mudballs around himself, imagining them turning into ball bearings. One by one, they turned from brown to grey, grape-sized globes of metal. Buoyed with joy, he next pictured them elongating into arrowheads. Once they had formed, he flung them into a nearby tree with a telekinetic blast. Though crude in their design, they penetrated the tree trunk.

Yawning, he sat and meditated, picturing a pinprick of light. Next, he imagined the point of light expanding outward, filling his whole body. The air pressed on him, but he continued until the point of light was as big as the Sun. Then he squashed it down into himself.

His body shook as the energy inside him fought to get out. Taking a deep breath, Travis visualized the energy flowing to his hand. Outstretching his right arm, a wave of liquid warmth flooded it. He willed the energy to form a ball. He opened his eyes, and a tennis ball-sized orb of blue energy was cradled in his palm. He held it until he got light-headed and snuffed it out. Travis decided he'd done enough for the day and Popped home to finish his homework. After he finished, he watched YouTube videos until it was time to get ready for bed. Once he was sure his parents were asleep, he Popped to Josh's.

"Hey," Josh said, stifling a yawn as he curled up with Benji, his plush Bengal Tiger.

Travis kissed him on the forehead. "You look adorable, ya know that?"

Josh laughed him off, and they talked about their day, but the mood changed when Travis brought up the impending meeting with his probation officer.

Josh crawled into Travis's lap, running his hands through his hair. "You scared?"

"A little, but if they send me away, I can always teleport back here anytime I want."

Josh planted a kiss on his lips. "Me likey."

"Me, too. But I just wish I could go back in time and stop myself from making that mistake, ya know?"

Josh nodded. "If I could, I'd go back and make it so I never bullied ya and instead befriended you sooner, so we could have gotten together way before now."

Laughing, Travis said, "Stop it. You're gonna give me diabetes with all this sweetness."

"It's true. I feel like such a douche canoe for the way I treated you."

Travis rested his head on Josh's shoulder. "But that's in the past. And now you're stuck with me. Du bist mein Ein und Alles."

"Huh?"

"It means, 'you are my one and all,' in German."

"Oh. Back at cha. And ya know I love you, right?"

Travis gave him a ghost of a kiss. "Yes, and I love you too. Nothing you do or say will ever change that."

"Promise?"

"I swear," he said, then broke into *I Swear* by All 4 One.

When he was done, Josh cuddled him close. "You're my cinnamon bun."

Travis agreed, running his hands through Josh's hair, breathing deeply of his natural scent, feeling at home in his arms.

CHAPTER THIRTY-THREE

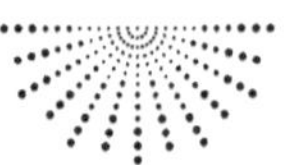

Travis stared across the desk at his probation officer while she leafed through his file; she made the occasional tsk as she jotted down things in an indecipherable script. As the seconds ticked away on the old-school clock on the wall, the pit of anxiety and dread in his stomach grew larger.

Ten minutes had passed, allowing his mind to conjure up worst-case scenarios, such as his death in juvenile prison or having to kill someone and never seeing Josh again.

He jumped when she finally spoke.

"It seems you've kept out of trouble since our last visit. Your parents told me you've been on your best behavior, aside from talking back to them a few times. How are your classes going?"

"Well. Josh, the Squad, and I usually do our homework together so we can help each other out (*not that I need help*). I've continued doing community service after school; I have my timesheets if you'd like to see them?"

He reached into his messenger bag for them, but she waved him off. "That won't be necessary. By all accounts, you've done well, so I'll recommend the judge add more hours of community service to your sentence instead of sending you to juvy. Keep up the good work, and I'll check in with you in a few weeks to see how you're doing."

With that, she dismissed him, and his father drove him to school. He'd missed the first two periods, but Josh told him he could borrow his notes. The day was uneventful, and with Labor Day Weekend upon them, they rushed home, did their homework in record time, and chillaxed in the pool, spooning each other.

"You doing anything Monday?" Josh said, nuzzling Travis's neck.

Travis sighed. "I have to go to the cabin for tests this weekend and won't be back till Monday afternoon."

Josh pulled away from him with a hurt look. "But I thought we were going to spend all weekend together?"

"I know, and I'm sorry," he said, pulling Josh close and kissing his neck.

Josh pouted. "Promise you'll sneak away to see me when you can?"

"Of course, mein Lieber."

They stayed in the pool until it got too cold for them. Then they gamed until Travis's parents called and said he had to come home. They kissed goodbye, and Travis Popped home.

Yawning as Jenny took his vitals, Travis wanted to get the tests done.

"Left or right arm?" Jenny asked as she prepared to draw several blood samples. Out of habit, he flung his left arm out, inadvertently unleashing a telekinetic blast, causing her to fall.

"Are you okay? I'm sorry! I didn't mean to do that," he shouted as he helped her up. Dusting herself off and gathering her equipment, she said she had a bit of a sore ass but would be fine. She drew his blood. Then she told him Agent Anderson wanted to speak with him in private. Shrugging, he went to see Agent Anderson, who was in the study going over a stack of files when he entered.

"Hey!" Agent Anderson said as he rushed to hide the files. "How's it hanging?"

"Cut the crap and tell me why you wanted this meeting."

He frowned. "Has anyone ever told you how much of a dick you can be?"

"Get to the point, Mr. Anderson."

"Hey now. Mr. Anderson's my father. Call me Tommy. Anyway, you know how your abilities have been growing? Well, my boss's boss predicted this as well and has given an extraction team the green light to capture you by any means necessary."

Travis shook with fear. "I thought you'd been feeding them false data?"

"I have, but they're on to me."

"Why do they want me so bad anyway?"

"Because you're Subject Prometheus, the holy grail of Metahumans. You were the first and, thus far, most powerful subject the DMRC has ever encountered. Thus, they've made your recapture their top priority."

"Subject Prometheus?" Travis mumbled. He had a flash of memory; he was two or three and had wandered away from his parents and into an alley where the men from his dreams offered him a Three Musketeers candy bar. He smelled gas. Then only pain as they set him ablaze.

Agent Anderson shook him. "Travis, are you listening to me? After experimenting on you for several years, you escaped, killing many in the process. No one save for Dr. Hu and the few others who survived Day Zero knows exactly what happened."

Putting aside that he had no memories of these events, he said, "Why are you telling me all this?"

"So you're prepared to do what's right when the time comes. If you fight them, people you care about are going to get hurt."

Rage welled up, threatening to pop the lock on its box in his mind. "In other words, you want me to go gently into that good night. I don't think so!"

Agent Anderson grabbed Travis's shoulder, shaking him. "This isn't about your fucking ego. Think of Jenny. Think of Josh."

Travis fought back the urge to roast him alive. "With all due respect, keep their names out your mouth, or we're going to have a problem."

"Hey, if they get hurt, it's on you."

Travis didn't bother replying. He Popped outside and trained harder than ever, only stopping when he passed out. He vowed to do so the next day and the next so he'd be ready for the DMRC. He didn't care what happened to him. But if anyone hurt Jenny or Josh, no force in the universe would stop him from tearing them apart.

Travis was curled up in bed, spooning Josh, as they enjoyed the last minutes of Sunday night together. It'd taken more effort than he'd expected to Pop to Josh's house from Dr. Hu's cabin, and he didn't feel like making the return trip, so he texted Jenny to let her know he was at Josh's, and she needn't get up early to drive him home. He spent the morning at Josh's, too, before Popping home to feast on leftover grilled hot dogs, brats, and hamburgers.

Between school, community service, homework, and training, Travis was asleep most days as soon as he crawled into bed with Josh. He slept so soundly that Josh had to dump cold water on him to wake him up, and they had a few close calls where Josh's mother or father had almost walked in on them, prompting Travis to set multiple alarms on his phone.

By Friday, they'd fallen into a rhythm: Travis would sleep with Josh, get up at 5:00 AM, train till 6:30 AM, be home by 7:00 AM, shower, and have breakfast. Then he was off to school. And after homework and community service, he and Josh would chill. He then went home until his parents went to bed, trained again, and slept at Josh's.

Their system was foolproof but not Josh-proof.

The night before his birthday, Travis and Josh were in bed, enjoying a bit of mutual masturbation.

"Mmm, that's nice," Travis began, "but stop for a second."

Josh whimpered. "Babe, you tryna give me blue balls?"

"Well," Travis said between kisses, "I thought we could try something new."

Travis pulled Josh into his lap, kissing him full on the lips. An explosion of sensations washed over him as he worked his way down Josh's neck, moaning as he struggled to control his powers.

So many new feelings, all happening at once, overwhelmed him as he rolled Josh onto his back.

"What are you—oh!" He caught on and ground himself into Travis. "God, this feels so . . ." He trailed off in a moan.

As Travis edged closer to the precipice, doubt and fear crept into his mind. *Am I doing this right? Does Josh like it? Does he like me, or does he think I'm a pervert, a sex fiend?*

"OH, GOD!" he scream-moaned. How Travis managed to not explode anything when he climaxed, he credited to a combination of his training and luck.

Afterward, as Josh handed him tissues to clean up, Travis looked at him sheepishly while fumbling to get his underwear dry. "How'd you like that?" he said, in what he hoped was a debonair tone.

"I'd be lying if I said I didn't want to do it again, like right now. Ha."

Josh liked it?

"But next time, I should be on top. No offense, but ya damn near crushed me."

All the energy went out of Travis, and the post-coital bliss he had been experiencing was gone. In its place was only rage. He didn't bother finishing getting dressed. Without a word, he Popped home.

How could I have been so stupid to think he liked me? I'm a freak, and that's all I'll ever be. I've been such a fool. I've broken all my rules. And for what? I should have never let him in. I shared something precious with him, bared my soul, and he thinks it was a joke?

Objects in his room levitated and whirled around as the storm inside Travis spiraled out of control.

"Travis, calm down. You're better than this," Oblivion said.

Shut up! You don't know how much this hurts.

"On the contrary, I know what it means to be betrayed by those

closest to you. But I've come to remind you of your rules. What was it again? Rule three: crying solves nothing. Rule four—"

Rule Four: All attachments are pointless. I should have never gotten involved with Joshua-fucking-Giovanni.

"Yes. Now use those emotions for good. Go to that lake you like and train."

Over Prometheus's objections, Travis listened to Oblivion.

He dressed, then Popped to Harrison Lake.

The regular fishers were nowhere in sight, which suited him fine as he took out his hurt and frustration on the trees. He hammered his fists into their trunks, leaving softball-sized dents, but that wasn't enough for him. He ripped them from their roots, set them ablaze, and watched them turn to dust. Yet this did nothing to abate his anger.

Oblivion whispered to him, *"Stop holding back. Let it all out."*

And he did.

The ground quaked and broke apart as power poured from him. Hopping into the lake, he vaporized the water with the intensity of the bluish-white flame that rushed from him. The wind moaned into his ears, whipping around him until it formed a tornado that sucked up the remaining water in the lake.

Travis didn't care about getting in trouble, didn't care about giving the DMRC an excuse to move up their timetable for capturing him, didn't care about the physical pain he was in. His emotional pain outweighed all that.

"Yes, that's it. You were born for this. You are my vessel, destined to bring on The End of Everything. Josh and everyone else are but worms beneath your feet, not worthy to lick the excrement from betwixt your buttocks. Long have I waited for this day. You are the one I've—"

"Travis, stop this," Josh said.

"What are you doing here?" he shouted over the wind and the roar of the thunder in his ears.

"You looked hella mad so . . . I knew you'd come here."

"How do you know that?"

Josh looked away. "You told me."

"I didn't. So how do you know I come here when I'm uber angry?"

Josh faltered, stumbling over his words before saying, "I've been watching you for months."

Bile rose in Travis's throat. "Before or after we started hanging out?"

Josh didn't reply.

"It was before?!" Travis shouted.

He nodded.

Travis's emotions swirled inside him, repulsion and betrayal warring for control of him. "You've been stalking me!"

"Travis, please? Let me explain."

"Shut up!" Travis formed a fireball and aimed it at Josh while Oblivion laughed, egging him on.

A wave of nausea wracked him at the thought Josh had been lying to him this whole time. Was he a joke to him? A bet? It didn't matter. They were done.

"Please, babe. I give me a chance to—"

"I said shut up." The fireball in his hand grew in size and intensity, casting the area in a white glow.

"Don't listen to him. He will only hurt you again. You opened your heart to him, and he betrayed you. He deserves to be punished."

Prometheus cut off Oblivion. *"Don't listen to him, kid. I know you're pissed. But icing Josh would be the dumbest thing you could do."*

He ignored Prometheus and focused on Josh. How could he have been so stupid? Was he a real person to Josh or just his creepy obsession?

"Babe, stop, please! I love you."

At Josh's words, Travis's emotions slipped from their reins, and his powers went crazy in an eruption of black light. At the back of his mind, he heard chains breaking and the screech of the blackbird.

~

In the next instance, he was reliving the moments leading up to the men setting him on fire. Only this time when the match ignited him, the memory continued, and he watched as Prometheus took control of their body and tore the men apart, drawing the attention of soldiers. A protracted fight ensued in which they were shot, the sting of the bullets hot and throbbing. Eventually, the soldiers captured them and took them to a holding facility where the DMRC began their experiments.

Every step of the way, they used the promise of his going home to his parents to win his compliance, even going so far as to bring his mother into the lab. But they never let him go until he broke free.

The memories came in a jumble of faces and sensory information and emotions, but he made out a younger Dr. Hu and a giant spider. The latter, Prometheus rode as they laid waste to the lab. But their freedom was short-lived, for soldiers doused them with a purple liquid that burned them like nothing he'd ever experienced. Catatonic from the pain, he almost missed Prometheus receding into the depths of their mind.

When Travis exited the black ball of light, he knew three things: the true origins of his burns, everything that happened to him and the powers that came along with those lost memories, and that his parents didn't care about him.

He Popped home, ignoring Josh's calls for him to wait.

His parents had sown the sparks, and now they'd reap the inferno.

CHAPTER THIRTY-FOUR

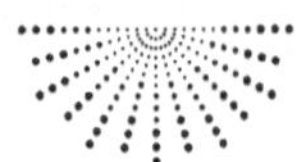

JJ looked at the spot Travis had been seconds before, too stunned to speak. While he'd seen him train, he had no idea Travis was capable of such feats, and he was equally awed and terrified. He didn't like the look of malice on Travis's face when he teleported away. Though he didn't think Travis had meant to, he'd broadcasted his thoughts, and JJ knew nothing good would come of this. He drove to Travis's neighborhood and was shocked at what he found there.

Putting the car in park, he rushed over to where Travis was slamming his parents against their brick house with telekinetic blasts. "Stop. This isn't you."

Travis turned, eyes like hot coals. "This doesn't concern you." He flung his hand, and a wave of flames slashed JJ's arm, knocking him on his ass.

He grabbed his arm, groaning as pain shot up it. "Fuck!"

Travis's hardened expression softened a moment. Then he turned back to his parents, white fireballs aglow in each hand.

Not thinking of his own safety, JJ got between them. "Don't do this. They're your parents."

"Step aside, or you can join them." He made to attack JJ when two

Black Hawk helicopters circled overhead. Soldiers repelled from ropes and surrounded them.

"Everyone on the ground now!"

JJ did as they said, but Travis readied to unleash fireballs on them. They opened fire, riddling his body with bullets.

"No!" JJ screamed. Travis staggered a bit, closed his eyes, and the helicopters exploded. He laughed, then disappeared, leaving behind a pool of blood. JJ was in full panic mode. Travis had hurt him, but he was still concerned about him.

Everything happened at lightning speed after that. He called 9-1-1 and waited for them to arrive. Meanwhile, the soldiers still on their feet searched the area, going door-to-door. Then they ordered everyone to stay inside.

Once the ambulance arrived, the EMTs wanted to treat his burns, but he told them to treat Travis's parents first. Next, he went to check on the twins. Then he called their emergency contact, Jenny Adams. She arrived with a man who introduced himself as Agent Anderson.

He explained everything that happened, and their faces went white.

Agent Anderson whistled. "I knew he was powerful, but what you're describing is on a whole 'nother level."

"Sweetie, let's clean up that burn of yours," Jenny said.

She had him run his arm under cold water for a few minutes, and she put some of Travis's burn ointment on it and dressed the area in gauze. "That should hold you for a bit, but you really should get that looked at ASAP."

"Kinda hard with World War III going on."

Agent Anderson cut in. "So, remind me again, what set off Travis?

JJ's cheeks warmed. "We were being intimate, and afterward, I made a crack about his weight."

"Talk about overreactions," Agent Anderson said.

Jenny swatted his arm. "He's a teenager, and this is his first relationship. Of course, he overacted. Though, that doesn't justify his actions.

Agent Anderson's phone buzzed, and he went into the kitchen to answer it. He came back grim-faced. He explained that his bosses had told him since he was supposed to be Travis's handler and had failed to secure him for the extraction team, he was off the case. Furthermore, when they found Travis, they would terminate him on sight and collect his body for study.

JJ's stomach flipped. "They can't do that, can they?"

"Kid, we're talking about the United States Government. They can do whatever the fuck they want."

On that somber note, JJ excused himself to get some air. Soldiers were still milling about, so he flagged one over and asked him if he could head home yet. After radioing his superiors, the soldier told JJ he could go but warned him to head straight there.

Once JJ got home, he sent up Google alerts for any news stories about injured boys matching Travis's descriptions. Then he sat and thought. Could he continue being with Travis, knowing he was capable of such violence? He didn't know, and that scared him.

CHAPTER THIRTY-FIVE

Travis reveled in causing his parents pain, but it was only a fraction of what he'd endured at the hands of the DMRC. And he would have continued punishing them had Josh not intervened when he did. The moment he saw Josh, Travis's rage bloomed anew.

He'd lashed out at Josh, fully intending to maim if not kill him. But he paused when Josh screamed out. Sure, he was well past furious, but part of Travis still loved Josh. He went to comfort him when agents from the DMRC arrived and opened fire on him. He'd never forget the searing pain as their bullets tore through him.

Vision darkening around the edges, head spinning and woozy, he tried Popping to Grams'. Instead, Travis found himself in a desert filled with pueblo caves, the arid wind blowing against his face as he swayed on his feet. Spotting a sign, he learned he was in The Mesa Verde National Park.

What am I doing here?

"The answers you seek can be found north of here," boomed a new voice in his head.

Who are you?

"I'm the power of your body, and in time, you'll meet the power of your mind and spirit. You must master each of us."

How do I know I'm not going crazy? Travis sucked in a breath, wincing as pain radiated up his arms and chest.

"Time grows short, young one. If you are to survive, then do exactly as I say."

Body, as he dubbed the voice, guided Travis through the process of removing the bullets via telekinesis by first focusing on the pain. Then, Body had him visualize the bullets and shoot them out of himself.

"I can't do this," he said through gritted teeth, fighting back the pain and losing.

"Yes, you can!"

Biting the inside of his cheek, Travis dug down deep. With a loud scream, he expelled the bullets and passed out. When he came to, night had fallen.

Where to now? he asked Body, wrapping his arms around himself to keep warm. It guided him to a group of pueblo caves a mile north of where he'd passed out, and when he arrived, a bright white light surrounded him, lifting him upward.

When it passed, he was in a massive cave filled with technology he'd never seen before.

"Welcome home," Body said.

He fainted.

Blinking, his vision cleared, revealing two entities above him; they were talking in a language that sounded like a blend of Japanese, Mandarin, and birdsong. They had flamingo limbs, ostrich necks, and peregrine claws on their outstretched hands.

Their luminescent eyes—the smaller one had purple, while the other had amber—popped against their obsidian-black skin. Travis backed away, summoning a fireball in each hand.

Their lipless mouths formed into something akin to a smile, showing off their serpentine fangs.

"Another step, and I'll deep-fry ya."

They looked at him, their almond-shaped eyes reminding him of an eagle's. The larger one spoke in the weird language, and when Travis didn't react, it waved him over to a machine.

He stiffened, drawing back his arms.

"Wait! Maybe we should do like my mans says and follow him," Prometheus said.

One, how do we know we can trust them? Two, how do you know that's a male?

"I mean, they could have murked us while we was passed out, right?"

True. But I still don't trust them.

"I feel ya. But don't you think it's highly sus we was led all the ways here just to be killed?"

That remains to be seen.

"Whadda we got to lose?"

Our viscera and genitalia.

"Boy, you play too much."

Okay. But if we wake up in an ice-filled tub missing a kidney, it's on you.

Travis stood in front of the machine it pointed at and examined it. It had a console with a square panel and what looked like a microphone. He touched the panel, and the cave came alive with action. Machines beeped and whirled, lights flashed . . . and then, dead silence.

He stood in awe at the sight before him, wondering if he'd stumbled upon a clandestine military base, when indecipherable symbols ran across the monitors lining the walls of the cave. He struggled to comprehend how such a massive compound could exist without people discovering it and how it fit in the mountainside when it was several times wider than the mountain itself.

The creatures approached, speaking rapidly, but he couldn't understand them and made to attack.

"Hold up. Maybe you should go Professor X on them before making with the violence?"

His frustrated expression must have told them he didn't understand them, for they stopped speaking and burst into tears.

The smaller one approached, placed its hand on his face, and uttered a series of chirps. Travis flinched away.

What are you? he asked it.

It paused and then looked up at him, its eyes boring into him. *"Ta (|tah|) Bi (|bee|) Tanna (|Tahn| |nah|) wo(|whoa|) Baha (|bah| |ha|)."*

I don't understand.

It let out a forlorn cry, and the image of a woman cradling a baby flashed into Travis's mind.

You're my mother?

"Ahi(|ah| ' |he|)! Baha." She pointed to the taller one. *"Tochi (|toe| |chee| ')."*

He followed her seven-fingered hand. *Father?*

She nodded.

This isn't happening. I must be having a psychotic break or something.

"Freak out later, dip shit. I wanna hear what else she gots to say."

You're enjoying this, aren't you?

"Like a crackhead sparking up after three days."

He pointed to himself. "Travis."

She shook her and warbled.

He pointed at her. "You?"

"Ta Bi Luscinia (|Looh| ' |sigh| |knee| |uh|)."

"You're name's Luscinia?"

She nodded, pointing to herself, and then to the machine next to him. Grabbing the microphone-like device, she said, "Na (|nah|) wo Esu (|a| ' |sue|)."

He took the device from her and said, "Hi," causing the monitor attached to the machine to turn on and flash a checkmark.

The taller creature came over and pantomimed writing, then pointed to his throat.

"Okay." He recited the English alphabet, then, after conferring with Luscinia, added pronunciations for each consonant and vowel combination.

He pointed at the taller one. "What's his name?"

"Co'laf (|koh| ' |loff|)," he said in a deep voice.

Luscinia pointed to the microphone, and for the next few hours, Travis, in a daze, helped them create a translation dictionary. The process involved their showing pictures of items and his naming them in English. Several times he didn't know what an item was, or they didn't have a word for it in their language, so they had to rely on telepathy to show each other what they meant.

At the end of the process, they had a rudimentary understanding of each other's language. He learned their language was called Na'iva (|Nah| |ee| |vuh|), which meant 'speak to the wind.' Travis, being the tone-def misfit he was, couldn't produce the notes necessary to speak traditional Na'iva, so instead, they taught him Na'el (|nah|' |el|), rock voice, a dialect of Na'iva that wasn't tonal.

Travis dove into learning their language. Anything to keep his mind off this being real. He would have continued in this illusion had his stomach not growled. "Got anything to eat?" At their confused looks, he corrected, "Sorry. Urebatnomo (|ooh| |ray| |bot|' |noh| |moh) ka (|kah|)?"

Luscinia showed him to a machine at the edge of the cave. She explained it was a molecular printer that could create almost anything with the right program. She keyed in a few commands, and while he waited for it to finish, Travis asked her about the cave's power source. According to her, everything was powered by a set of solar-powered fusion generators.

"So, this cave has been here this whole time?"

She nodded. "Waiting for you . . . we have been."

"Isn't that a little stupid? I mean, what if someone discovered this place before me?"

Her face scrunched up in confusion, so he repeated what he said telepathically.

"The cave is invisible to all except those of our lineage."

In other words, it has biometric security? Then that means I'm. . .

The molecular printer beeped before he had a chance to complete his thought. It extruded sohan (|soh|' |hän|) 'seed soup,' an oatmeal-like paste into a bowl along with an aquamarine liquid called miqua (|me| |kwa|) or 'life and energy' into a cube-shaped pottery cup.

He sipped the sohan, more like gruel, and downed the liquid, which was flavorless. Soon after, he felt sleepy and nodded off.

An alarm woke him. He was in a machine, the door disjointed from its hinges, Luscinia looking at him concerned.

"You drugged me!"

Springing from the machine, he grabbed her by the throat and tossed her aside, readying an energy lash when Co'laf blocked his path.

"She harm no mean. Back our son we want."

"Explain."

And so he did.

Luscinia and Co'laf were aliens called Torins (|tore| |inns|), which meant 'flame people' or 'energy people,' from a now-destroyed planet named Aves (|eh|' |vis|). Torins were living stars, energy beings that had evolved from creatures similar to the birds on Earth. Luscinia was an intergalactically-renowned scientist and inventor, and she'd created the devices that built the cave and spared their lives.

"What happened?"

Rather than tell him, Co'laf showed him using telepathy.

Torins had been celebrating something. Travis's birth. Then other aliens that looked like giant cats attacked, killing many, and set off a machine that created a series of supermassive black holes that wiped out Aves and most of its galaxy.

Luscinia and Co'laf transferred their minds into computers, becoming the corporeal holograms before him, while their son was . . . bonded with Travis.

When the vision ended, Travis had a ton of questions. "What was that machine you put me in?"

"Defuse you from our son it was to," Luscinia began, "but

malfunctioned the technology did, merging your . . . DNA. Permanently fused are you."

"Nope. Not real. Not real," he repeated, his chest heaving as he hyperventilated. The edges of his vision darkened, and the room spun. "This isn't happening," he screamed.

Aliens weren't real. None of this was. He was crazy; he had to be. This was all some hallucination, and any second now, he'd wake up in a psych ward.

Travis clung to this thought because otherwise, he'd have to face the truth that the pillars upon which he'd built his life were a lie. Energy arced off him as his breathing sped up until he passed out.

CHAPTER THIRTY-SIX

"I think you broke him. The name's Pro, by the way. Come on over here so I can see where I get my shit from."

Co'laf indulged him, letting Pro examine him, then box with him.

"A natural you are but moves yours sloppy be. Start your training, in the morning we must. Last of Torins you are and bad name us giving you can't."

Pro smiled, not believing what he was hearing. All this time, he'd been trapped in Travis's head, thinking he was an alternate personality. Come to find out he was a damn alien? This was like one of those whack-ass sci-fi movies Travis watched; the only things missing were the bad acting and lame CGI.

Then again, he'd always felt like he and Travis were two separate people, so maybe this explained why? Bet that! But if he was stuck with Travis forever, then at least he could be the one in charge of their body.

"Right. Why don't we start right now?"

Co'laf laughed and went over the basics of Ramu'i (|rah| |moo|' |ee|), 'circle.'

The rules of Ramu'i were simple: players decided on the diameter of the circle, then who would be inside it. The Adota (|ah| |doh| |tah|) 'defender,' and the Ivata (|ee| |vah| |tah|), 'attacker,' who would try to knock the Adota outside the circle. The Ivata could use any attack they wanted, save fatal ones. The Adota was free to move however they wanted, provided they stayed within the bounds of the circle. Ramu'i was meant to train your reflexes in preparation to learn Fae'li (|fay| |lee), |, 'the fist that protects,' a martial art only taught to members of the Torin royal family.

"Hold up, I'm an alien prince for real real? Not for play play?"

"Yes, but worthy of this knowledge yourself, you must prove."

I'm starting to think Travis was right about this being a hallucination. But let's roll with it.

"How?"

"In Ramu'i, defeating me must you.

"What?"

"Sorry, Circle."

Pro wiped his nose, chuckling. "A'ight. Let's go, Pops."

Co'laf laughed.

"I say something funny?"

He nodded. "' A'ight' in Na'iva meaning something akin to your 'butt monkey.'"

"Meh. Who's going first?"

Co'laf elected to be the Adota, explaining that while you were allowed to move inside the circle, the best players moved as little as possible and thus were called Ado (|ah| |doh|) no (|noh|) Isha (|ee| |shaw|), 'the stone-footed.'

Co'laf etched a two-meter-wide circle in the red dirt with his claw. "Eki (|ay|' |key|) shyoma (|show| |ma|) 'Ready'?"

"Yeah," Pro said, rushing him. Co'laf turned to the side at the last second, holding his feet in place as he twisted at the waist.

"Ukahya(|oo| |kah| |he—yah||) fa(|fah|) jani (|jah| |knee|)"

Pro cocked his head to the side. "Not hungry enough?"

"Not fast enough." Co'laf corrected.

Pro redoubled his efforts, trying to fake out Co'laf at the last second, but he was always one step ahead of him.

"Screw it." He blasted Co'laf with a telekinetic wave, knocking him out of the circle.

"Woot! Mess with the best, get wrecked."

After dusting himself off, Co'laf asked Pro to be the Adota. He popped his neck, cracked his knuckles, and smirked. "I'm ready whenever you are."

No sooner had he got in the circle than Co'laf Popped behind him, sweeping Pro's legs out from under him. He hit the ground with a *boom* that echoed through the cave.

"Ouch," he groaned, rubbing his butt.

Co'laf laughed. "We stopping can."

"Like hell." Pro got up and tried again, lasting a few seconds longer this time.

Over the next hour, he tried and failed to beat Co'laf again. Bruised, limbs aching, and eyes heavy with sleep, he vowed to beat Co'laf after some rest.

He took off his pants, using them as a pillow, and curled up on the floor of the cave.

He had almost drifted off when Luscinia called him over.

She showed him to the uren (|ooh| |ren|) khau (|cow|), 'the sleep pod'; it was a grey, egg-shaped container, and as he climbed inside, she handed him a blanket and pillow. The blanket was blood-red, embroidered with a golden Na'iva pictograph that looked like two infinity symbols making an x-shape. The pillow was also red, inscribed with more Na'iva symbols that he couldn't make out, save for the same x-shape symbol, which was at the beginning and end of the pillow.

"What are those?"

"Your baby blanket and pillow," she said.

He wiped his eyes. "And those symbols?"

"The names of your ancestors going back to the first emperor of Aves, whom we named you after."

He pulled at her sarong. "Ma, what's my name?"

She made the bird song from before. "It's ancient Na'iva and means 'the strength that endures; the power that overcomes all obstacles.'"

He stared up at her, eyes wide with wonder, grinning big. "So . . . I'm a prince?"

"Yes. Lie down, and the story of the Four Princes tell you your Tochi will."

Pro gathered the pillow and blanket and lay in the sleep pod as Co'laf started the story.

~

Long ago, there were four princes who never agreed on anything. Their kingdoms had been at odds since the death of their Great-great grandfather, the first emperor of Aves.

However, everything changed when then the Nekoshin (|nay| |koh| |shin|) Empire attacked. Though no match for the princes' technology, the Nekoshin forces overwhelmed them.

As Corvidae (|kor| |vee| |day|), Emperor of Earth Kingdom, Fifth of his Name slept, Gato (|gah| toe|), the Crusher of Souls, ripped his heart out and devoured it. One-by-one, Accipitridae (|ahk| |sip| |eh| |tree| |day|) of Wind Kingdom, Aethopyga (|eh| |thoh| |pie| |gah|) of Flame Kingdom, and Aptenodytes (|ahp| |ten| |oh|' |die| |tees|) of Ice Kingdom fell prey to Gato.

All seemed lost.

Then, above the great wailing, rose the voice of Prince Talon (|teh| |lon|) of Earth Kingdom. "Who is like Corvidae?"

"No one!" his people replied, and they took up the fight, driving back Gato and his men.

Inspired by their cousin, Bubo (|boo| |boh| of the Flame, Studur (|stew| |door|) of the Wind, and Adeliea(|ad| |eh| |lee| |eh|) of the Ice joined the fight.

For a time, they had Gato on the run, but they could not overcome their old rivalries and soon turned their forces on each other. In the chaos that followed, Gato and his men wiped out half of the princes' forces, leaving alive those too injured to fight.

The princes were all that stood between Gato and the destruction of their people.

Nevertheless, they fought. Not because they hoped to win, but because it's what their fathers would have done, what the Emperor would have done.

Those who witnessed that battle speak of it in reverent, hushed tones. For on that day, four boys stood against ten thousand.

They combined their powers—impaling some with shards of ice, exploding others, and raining down great balls of molten rocks on the rest. Only Gato remained, but the princes were too exhausted to continue. "Surrender, and I'll spare your lives," he said.

But they refused and as one spoke. "In bright of day or black of night, we are the sons of light. For all those who've come before us and have yet to come, no matter evil's might, we shall stand . . . and fight!"

A black-light radiated from the princes as they fused. With one burst of their golden flames, Gato fell dead.

The princes separated, and below them lay items of incredible power. Talon received the Hammer of Storms; to Studur, the Razor-Whip of Invisibility; to Bubo, the Sword of Inferno; and to Adeliea, the Lance of Freezing.

Their fathers' voices issued from the weapons and congratulated the princes. The kings told them they would always protect them as long as their weapons never fell into evil hands. They gathered the items and returned home, vowing never to let their differences separate them again.

~

"Cool story, Dad." Pro yawned. "So, I'm related to the princes in the story?"

He told Pro that Luscinia was a descendant of Princes Talon and Adeliea, and he from Princes Studur and Bubo. And that after nearly 25,000 years, Pro's birthed marked the reunification of the royal bloodlines.

"Nice. Sleepy now. Talk more later."

Pro curled into the fetal position and drifted off. The lights in the cave dimmed, bathing him in soft yellow light as music played. He couldn't make out the words, but the melody reminded him of Brahm's Lullaby. Co'laf covered him up, kissing his forehead. "Sleep well, Tanna (|tahn| |nuh| 'my darling' (used when referring to children)). Much to learn, having you.

CHAPTER THIRTY-SEVEN

ravis floated in a white void, unaware of even his heartbeat. Time held no meaning to him as he drifted along until a black light filled the void, enveloping him.

"Despair not, young one."

He startled. "You're the one who guided me to the, the . . ."

"And now I will guide you out of here."

The black light took the shape of a great golden-brown eagle, wings spread wide.

"What's the point? I don't even know who or what I am."

"The circumstances of your birth matter not. You are who you choose to be."

"And what if I want this z sci-fi movie to end?"

"I only open the door. What comes after is up to you. You always have a choice. Stay here and cede control of your body to the other."

"Or?"

"Follow me and retake your birthright."

Travis thought long and hard. *Is any of this real? Have these last months been all in my head? No, that can be right because then Josh and I . . . No! I know that was real. So then, this is real?*

But what about Oblivion and the prophecy? Or those . . . aliens?

"Your time grows short, young one."

Travis came to a decision. "It doesn't matter who or what I am. I decide my destiny!"

"Of course." Body landed, letting him climb aboard, and took off.

~

Time passed. How much, Travis didn't know.

"I think this is . . ."

A slit in the white void opened, and sunlight sparkled off the clear waters that ran through the verdant forests of his inner mindscape.

"What now?"

"Free us."

With an eardrum-shattering cry, Body disappeared in a plume of golden light, knocking Travis on his ass. He dusted himself off and tugged on Prometheus's psychic leash.

"Get that weak shit outta here."

Rubbing his ass, Travis got off the ground. Liquid ran down his nose; wiping it, he found blood. Pulling the mental leash again, Prometheus knocked Travis on his ass that time and each time afterward, his strength ebbing with each attempt until he gave up.

You better hope I never get out of here because when I do, your ass is mine.

"Shut up."

A prisoner in his own body, Travis raged, uprooting trees until he tired himself out. With nothing better to do, he surveyed the area. More flora had grown since he'd last been there if that was even possible. And the encroaching grayness now bisected the land.

Once he got the lay of the land, Travis set off in search of the blackbird, scouring the waters and forest until, at last, he came upon the wall where the chained bird was. Only the wall was gone. In its place was a black stone well, the cover of which was etched with a strange X-shaped symbol.

"You found me."

"Who are you?"

"The power of your spirit."

"But you couldn't talk before."

"I always could, but you couldn't understand me until now."

"How do I get out of here?"

"Free me, and you'll free yourself."

"How?"

"Unite me with the power of your mind and body."

"And how do I do that?"

"You have to figure that out on your own."

"That's great."

He melted the well cover, smashed it with his fists, even blew it up, but every time, it reformed instantly. Since he didn't know how long he'd be there, Travis created a few creature comforts, starting with a puffy chair, then advanced to making his Psyche Sanctorum, a castle that would house his most private thoughts and memories, so they could never be used against him.

Reclined in his puffy chair, Travis replayed the happier memories of him and Josh. But try as he might, Travis couldn't help thinking of Josh's face twisting in anguish when his wave of fire blasted hit him. The image filled the monitors, Josh's screams echoing off the walls.

"I'm sorry," he repeated until the monitors went dark. Travis was jolted from his seat when a shockwave rippled through the Psyche Sanctorum. *"Little pig, little pig, let me in."*

A close-up of Oblivion appeared on a monitor in front of Travis, and he shuddered upon seeing Oblivion.

"What do you want?"

"To talk. By the way, I like the castle. Though, the tower is a bit gauche if you ask me."

"Well, Martha, I didn't. So, sit and spin."

"We have much to discuss."

Travis leaned in. "Such as?"

"A way out."

"Go on."

"Why don't you come out so we can talk man-to-man?"

"I don't know if that's a good idea. Bad things happen when I listen to you. Not to mention you lied to me."

"I mean you no harm. And I didn't lie to you. While your powers may be from those aliens, I'm responsible for them reactivating. So, it technically wasn't a lie."

Travis glowered at him. "Why should I believe you?"

"Because I'm the only one who's never lied to you."

What a load of horse sh—

"Think about it. Your family, your Jenny, your Josh, all lied to you."

"But Grams—"

"Knew about your powers and what the government did to you, yet never said anything about them until they reactivated."

"Still—"

"That's lying by omission. I, on the other hand, have always been upfront about my intentions."

"But you're evil incarnate."

"I don't deny that. There is no good without evil, no light without dark, no creation without destruction."

Travis didn't know what to believe. On the one hand, Oblivion did try to kill him during their first meeting, and he *had* lied to him about the origins of his powers. But he'd been nice ever since.

"I thought you wanted to help me find a way out of here? Instead, you're spouting metaphysical mumbo-jumbo."

"I'm getting to that, but first, we must attend to other matters."

Travis folded his arms, reclining back in his puffy chair, his patience wearing thin.

"Tell me, had you not been attacked and discovered this cave, would you have killed your parents?"

"Yes," he said without hesitation.

Oblivion smiled. *"That's all I needed to know. Do you know how evil begins?"*

"Is that a koan?"

"In a roundabout way. You see, evil begins not with the act but the thought that precipitates it. But this thought isn't enough. To be truly

evil, you must consciously choose to act on said thought. And you did both."

"I'm not evil. They deserved to suffer."

"You'll get no disagreements from me."

Travis exited the Psyche Sanctorum.

"Glad to see you decided to join me."

"I figured since we're having this heart-to-heart, we might as well do it face-to-face."

"Good. Walk with me. As I was saying, your parents deserved everything you dished out to them and more. In fact, the whole world should be taken to task for how it's treated you."

Travis nodded, his lips quirking up in a smile. "Yeah. Their crimes have gone unpunished long enough."

"And with me by your side, you could do that."

"I don't know. I want them to pay, but I want to do it with my own power."

Oblivion clapped him on the back. *"Fair enough. Question: have you've heard the fable of The Lion and the Mouse?"*

Travis shook his head.

"Well, it goes something like this: one day, a mouse comes upon a lion, and the lion says he'll eat the mouse. The mouse begs for its life in return for helping the lion. The lion laughs but frees the mouse. A while later, a hunter captures the lion. And who should come upon him but the mouse? Though small, the mouse works its way through the hunter's net, freeing the lion. And the moral of the story is that we all need help sometimes."

Travis shook his head. "Sounds like the lion got lucky."

Oblivion's laughter echoed in Travis's mind. *"Good answer. Now about getting you out of here?"*

Travis stumbled, catching himself. "What's the price?"

"Free of charge."

"Why so generous?"

"You still don't trust me. Good, you shouldn't because everyone is a potential enemy."

"Rule Five. How did you know?"

"Like I've told you, I've been watching you from the moment you were born."

"I get the whole prophecy dealio, but why me?"

"You're a very special boy."

"Yeah, I'd rather be normal."

"As the Bard of Avon said, 'Be not afraid of greatness.'"

"Let's get back to how you're going to get me out of here."

"It's all business with you. Grab my hand, and you'll have the power you need. But before you do, a bit of advice?"

"Yes?"

"The longer you deny who and what you are, the longer your training will take."

Travis thought that over. While it was sound advice, could he trust Oblivion? Then again, with this powerup, he could regain control of his body and see Josh again. But what if Oblivion was lying? Only one way to find out.

He grabbed Oblivion's hand.

CHAPTER THIRTY-EIGHT

JJ itched at his bandage. Though it'd been two weeks, he still hadn't heard from Travis, and he was starting to think the other boy didn't care about him. He settled into the puffy chair in Dr. Dull's office and toed off his shoes.

"How are you this week?" he asked.

"Good, I guess. Travis hasn't called or text, and he's pissing me off."

Dr. Dull nodded. "I heard what he did to his parents. Did he do that to your arm, too?"

JJ looked away and mumbled no.

"Joshua, you can tell me anything."

JJ gritted his teeth. "I said no, okay! Like I told you last time, I burned myself cooking fried chicken."

"Well, I want you to know that abuse in any form isn't love, and you don't deserve to be treated badly. How's school going?"

"Fine. I just wish he'd let me know he was okay. I mean, I'm pissed at what he did but more so that he hasn't bothered even texting me. I thought I meant more to him."

Nibbling on his pen cap, Dr. Dull mmhmm'd. "Joshua, perhaps you should use Travis's absence as a break and work on yourself. Go out, meet new people and explore. Have you visited Affirmations like I've suggested?

JJ tugged his ear. "No."

"Why?"

"I don't know. I've planned to. But every time, I get halfway there and turn back."

"It's okay to be scared, but we can't let our fears rule us. Perhaps you could take off community service one day a week and go there instead?"

JJ nodded, and they agreed he'd try going there this Friday for their youth drop-in. They spent the rest of his session talking about how things were going with his parents. While they'd been home more lately, they spent most of their time going to charity events and dinner parties, forcing him to come so he could network. It took all his willpower not to go off on them, but he'd managed to stay calm using the techniques Dr. Dull had taught them.

As the week rolled along, JJ's nerves ratcheted up, and when Friday came, he was a hot mess. He'd thought about bailing, but Dr. Dull called to check up on him, and they talked briefly about his fears.

"Joshua, you don't have anything to fear. Just go there, and if after ten minutes you don't like, you can go home."

He agreed and set out for the bus stop.

Palms wet, JJ asked the woman at the reception desk where the youth drop-in was located. She smiled and told him it was located in the basement and gave him directions.

When he entered the room, there were kids with multicolor hair, some with tattoos and piercing, others wore pride flag pins or stickers.

"Welcome!" a tall guy a few years older said. He introduced himself as Cody and asked him to sign in. Afterward, they went around the room introducing themselves, some giving their pronouns. When it was his turn, JJ faltered before saying, "Hi. I'm JJ, he/him, I'm gay and like anime, video games, and writing poetry."

They welcomed him and Nicky, a girl wearing a trans pride pin and an electric pink mohawk, waved him over. She asked him where he was from, and they chatted a bit before Cody called them to order.

"JJ, you're in luck. Today we'll be screening *Fullmetal Alchemist: Conqueror of Shamballa.*"

While Cody set up the DVD player and projector, JJ and the others got snacks from the café and picked a seat. He chose to sit next to Nicky and Ryan, who identified as lesbian and had a tattoo of "beauty" and "beast" on her arms.

They settled in, and the movie started. He'd seen it before and spent the time chatting with the girls. It was nice being able to be so open about himself and his likes. They asked him about his poetry, and he blushed, saying he wasn't that good. They told him about a monthly open mic night and writing group the center hosted and told him he should try out some of his poems.

"Maybe," he mumbled.

Afterward, Cody thanked everyone for coming out and came over to JJ. "Hey, I'm glad you made it tonight. A group of us usually hits up White Castle or Coney Island. You wanna come with? You can ride with me."

Cody flashed his brilliant smile, and JJ swooned. "I—"

His phone played his parents' ringtone, and when he answered it, his father demanded to know where he was.

"With friends."

"Well, come home. Your mother and I are throwing a dinner party, and guests will be arriving shortly."

"Okay," he said, but what he really wanted to say was, "Fuck you."

He ended the call. "Another time," he told Cody."

Cody smiled again. "I'll hold ya to that.

JJ came back the next week and the week after that, but he kept blowing off Cody's invites to eat. Part of him liked the older teen, and if JJ were being honest, he thought Cody was hot with his scruffy goatee and bedhead blue hair.

He did take them up on the open mic night and had been working on a poem all month, but now that the night had arrived, he was scared shitless.

"Ugh." He threw up in the toilet, then washed his mouth out. Cody rushed over. "Dude, are you okay? You look pale—well paler than usual."

"Nerves," he said, and dry heaved.

"Hang tight," Cody said, leaving and returning with a bottle of Vernors and saltines from the café.

JJ thanked him, and once his stomach settled, he went over his poem again. As he read the last line, they called his name. With sweat-slicked shaky hands, he took the mic and introduced himself. "I'm JJ, and this poem's entitled, 'Seen.'

"From my red-orange hair and skin so fair to my eyes so green, I am a human being and demand to be seen. Look up from your screens and see me . . . all of me. I'm more than the sum of my parts; I'm a lover of the arts, a gamer, a mischief-maker, heartbreaker, faker, no bs taker, a prankster, but no court jester. I may be short but have the heart of a lion. I don't mean to be mean, but I'm done crying, done trying to be who I'm not, done hiding who I am; I'm a gay teen. Whether you accept that or not, I'm a human being and deserve to be seen."

When he was done, the crowd went silent. Then they burst into applause. JJ reveled in the moment, basking in the knowledge something he wrote affected so many people. Nicky and Ryan came over and congratulated him.

"See, that wasn't so hard," Cody said, ruffling up JJ's hair.

Ryan nodded. "You slayed the house down, dude."

JJ's cheeks warmed. "It wasn't that good, and I should've added more imagery."

They told him he was crazy and made him promise to read more of his poetry at the next open mic night. He reluctantly agreed but declined their invitation to grab dinner.

"Come on, JJ," Cody begged.

"Naw. I have to go home and get started on my next piece. I wouldn't want to disappoint my fans."

Cody ruffled his hair again. "Okay, but you're coming with us next time."

JJ laughed him off and walked toward the bus stop. On the ride home, he couldn't stop smiling, and he couldn't remember a time he was happier. Maybe he didn't need Travis as much as he thought?

CHAPTER THIRTY-NINE

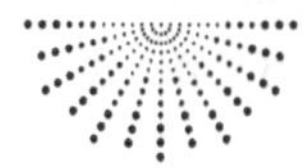

*P*ower surged through Travis, and when he yanked on Prometheus's psychic leash, he appeared. Wasting no time, Travis locked him in a cage. Prometheus rattled the bars. *"Let me out, or that ass is grass."*

"Not a chance. But don't worry. You'll have company soon enough." He flipped off Prometheus and resumed control of his body, coming face-to-face with Co'laf.

"Tanna, you are neg'gi (|neg|' |ghee| okay)?"

"I'm fine," he said, shrugging off Co'laf's hand. "And I'm not your son."

Co'laf froze, his lipless face contorting into a look of disgust. "You're the pagu (|pah||goo|)."

"The what?"

"The . . . vessel."

"Fuck you."

Co'laf and Luscinia argued in Na'iva, and to Travis's annoyance, he only understood one out of ten words. Luscinia told him the gist was Co'laf refused to accept Travis as his son while she'd argued he was every bit their child since he shared Prometheus's DNA. The argument broke out again anew, and Travis had had enough.

He locked onto Grams' mind and Popped to her. But when he materialized, he was still in the cave.

"What's going on?"

An alarm sounded, drawing Co'laf's and Luscinia's attention.

"Uki(|ooh| |key|| go/leave) jani (no)."

"And why the hell can't I leave?"

"Sleeping, while you—well, you the other — were, night of last, tests I ran. Dying you are," Luscinia said.

"No shit, and I'd like to spend my remaining time with my grandmother."

Co'laf huffed.

"There a problem?"

"Jani."

"Good, then undo whatever's keeping me here." Travis stalked toward the cave entrance.

Luscinia shouted after him. "Wait! You did have to don't ."

Travis stopped at the edge of the cave's opening, looked over his shoulder at her, and arched an eyebrow. "Go on."

She explained his healing factor, though immature, was keeping him alive for the time being. As energy beings, Torins were walking fusion generators. And it was this energy that fueled their abilities.

They could channel power from their cores (basically a battery) to accelerate the healing process, allowing them to recover from wounds normally fatal to other species like humans.

But in Travis's case, his core hadn't reached its full potential yet. Thus, his healing factor and abilities weren't as strong as they could be. But were he to tap into his full potential, he'd be healed completely.

Stupid brain, giving me false hope like this. But what if it's true? Then Josh and I could . . . Meh, let's go with it.

"Why didn't you say so before? How do I do that?"

"Do'un (|doh| |oon|)," she said. Training.

"Then what are we waiting for?"

Co'laf butted in. "A commoner in fae'li, I refuse to be training."

Luscinia's eyes glowed brightly. "Then shall I."

Co'laf scoffed, folded his arms, and turned away while she reviewed the rules of Circle with him.

While they trained, Travis got flashes of Pro's memories and used them to outmaneuver her. They trained, swapping places every twenty minutes or so, until Travis, covered in sweat, vision blurred, gasping for breath, collapsed. He stood on shaky legs, then vomited tarry, black bile.

She hovered around him. "Tanna, long enough at it we've been. Uren (|oo| |rin|), rest."

"I'll sleep when I'm dead."

Co'laf laughed. "Your tahi (|tah||he|) be having such strange wordings."

"When I want your opinion, I'll take my chodar (|chi-yo ||dahr|), 'dick,' out your mouth."

Co'laf charged him and grabbed his shoulders, his talons digging into Travis's skin.

He headbutted Co'laf, blasted him with fire, and Popped behind him, kneeing him in the back. Then he kicked him in the side of his head.

Co'laf turned, blasted him with a gale-force wind, knocking Travis off balance. He slammed into the ground. Then Co'laf encased him in an earthen cage.

He exploded the cage, sending shards of molten rocks at Co'laf.

Travis stood on jelly legs, then collapsed.

Too weak to continue, he curled into a ball and passed out.

He awoke to the sounds of Co'laf pounding on the crystalline ball which now enveloped him.

That's new.

Blasting the crystalline ball apart, he grabbed two shards and Popped behind Co'laf. He drove the shards into Co'laf's shoulders, laughing at his screams.

"I win."

Co'laf pulled the shards through his shoulders and looked down at them. "Underestimating you, being I. But still unworthy of fae'li learning are you."

"Let's make a deal. I beat you in Circle, and you teach me fae'li."

"Ahi!"

Travis elected to be the Adota, and Co'laf nodded, going on the attack. He threw everything at Travis, even going as far as liquefying the ground, forcing him to hover in the air.

Co'laf smirked. "Uwaro (|ooh| |wha| |row|). You lose."

"Actually, a circle has three dimensions, and if you notice, I'm still within the boundaries."

"Right he is," Luscinia said and gave a twenty-minute lecture on multidimensional geometry. And by the end of it, Co'laf conceded Travis was right. However, Travis didn't know if it was worth the headache he had.

According to her, there was an infinite number of dimensions parallel to the standard eleven dimensions humans knew about. Moreover, she and others had postulated that given enough energy and focus, a Torin could teleport to these parallel dimensions.

After eating more sohan and miqua, Travis set out to train more, but Luscinia stopped him. "Rest no. The Torin creation myth, to you, I will tell.

Though he'd rather train, Travis bedded down for the night, thoughts of Josh, Grams, Jenny, and his parents running through his head as he listened to The Tale of the Two Brothers.

In the beginning, there was the void, and all was still. Then came the great schism. From the void arose a cataclysmic explosion that created two brothers. The first was Lukarus (|loo| |car| |us|), Lord of Light and Love. And the second was Kamori (|kah| |more| |ee|), the Lord of Darkness and Fear.

The brothers stared across the event horizon from whence they came and charged forth to do battle. They were evenly matched, so a new contest was designed.

Lukarus pulled a rib from his body, and from the wound, blood poured forth, creating all the stars in the sky. From his rib, he formed the planets and breathed life into them, thus creating the Torins.

Kamori saw what his brother had done and was jealous. From his chest, he pulled out his heart and flung it into the cosmos. Thus, evil entered the universe.

Torins believed the first emperor was imbued with his powers by Lukarus and that children from his bloodline would grow stronger with every generation until a child was born with power that rivaled even Lukarus's. This child would lead them into a new age of peace and prosperity.

They also believed Kamori would sire a child that would herald the end of all creation, and the fate of the universe would be decided in a titanic battle between the child of light and the child of darkness.

As he drifted off, Travis wondered if he was a child of light or darkness and if Josh would ever forgive him for hurting him.

Travis went through the forms for fae'li, trying to keep the moves straight, but he kept thinking about Josh and what he'd done to him. Luscinia watched him, shaking her head. Two weeks had passed since entering the cave, and every day had been the same. They began with Fae'li training, followed by Torin cultural and history lessons, then it was time for language lessons. Travis taught them English while they taught him Na'iva and Na'el. With practice, Travis mastered conjugation and vocab lessons but struggled with syntax. Co'laf, despite his gruff exterior, took an interest in English lessons and was slowly getting the hang of grammar and syntax. Though, he commanded to see Prometheus at every opportunity.

"Urawo!" Luscinia said. "Me, you watch." She spread her legs so they were shoulder-width apart, her feet at forty-five-degree angles, then went through the motions for him.

Co'laf looked on, snickering under his breath.

Travis swore he'd prove that smug bastard wrong. Drumming his fingers on his aching thigh, *X gon Give it to Ya* by DMX played in his head. Bobbing his head along to the beat, he began the taka (|tah| |kah|), form', again. This time, his movements were more fluid, coming without thought as he sang under his breath. He practiced until his limbs were too sore to lift under the weight of 2g, twice Earth's gravity.

"Better getting, you are," she said.

"Humph. How long before my core matures?"

"Hard to say."

"Then increase the gravity to 3g."

"But – "

"Do it." He turned, addressing Co'laf. "If you find something funny, why don't you say it to my face?"

Co'laf's eyes glowed. "A challenge, is that ?"

"Yeah, unless you're scared?"

"I'sau (|ee| |sow|)!"

Travis chuckled at the Torin curse word. "Giraida ka (|ghee| |rye| |duh| |kah|), 'you mad'?" he retorted.

Co'laf materialized behind Travis, piercing his arms with ice blades, then swept him off his feet. Travis struggled to recover, gasping for breath, sweat cascading down his face, stinging his eyes. Co'laf stood over him, laughing. "Yield."

"Never." The ground rumbled as black energy arced off Travis's body. His hair flickered from black to silver, and his eyes turned red as the sound of screams filled his ears.

He jumped up, and the fight was on. Popping behind Co'laf, he caught him with a right hook to the jaw. Co'laf spun around from the force of the blow. Travis followed up with an energy blast to Co'laf's back.

"Stop," Luscinia shouted, but Travis ignored her, continuing to pommel Co'laf until he collapsed.

~

He woke up in a cramped room lit up by white lights. Upon closer inspection, the lights were plasma beams similar to lightning bolts. One shot toward him, and he covered himself, wincing at the thought of the pain. When it struck him, it left him feeling better than he ever had. He relaxed, letting the device do whatever its job was.

He'd drifted off just as an alarm sounded, and the device deactivated. He grumbled as the door opened, revealing Luscinia.

"Quite the scare you gave us," she said.

"I wanna stay in longer."

She shook her head. "a toy the Pueri(|pure| |ee|)'khau isn't."

"The what?" he said, rubbing his eyes.

"Star Chamber. It's meant to increase your abilities by feeding energy directly to your core."

"Oh. How's Co'laf? Not that I care." Travis exited the Star Chamber and cued up dinner in the molecular printer. While he waited, Luscinia told him Co'laf was fine but still mad at him. Though he wouldn't say so explicitly, she'd deduced he was scared of Travis.

"Serves him right."

He ate and then meditated.

Within his Psyche Sanctorum, he visited Pro, who let loose several curses in English and Na'iva. Ignoring him for the moment, Travis visited the well and discovered several cracks in its cover. Golden light shone through the cracks, and he made out the blackbird, its wings free, but its feet and body still bound in chains.

"You did good, Boss."

"Any pointers on freeing the rest of you?"

"To thine own self be true."

"Meh. On that note, I bid you adieu."

Travis conjured his puffy chair and lowered his mental barriers. First, he searched out Josh, curious to know how he was doing. Shame and repulsion rose up in him at the thought of his hurting Josh. Even if he'd been stalking him, Travis had no right to attack him like that.

When Josh came into sight, his arm was bandaged, and he had bags under his eyes like he hadn't slept in weeks. He was on his bed playing Call Of Duty with David and Jason, but he kept catching his phone.

"Travis, where are you?"

I'm—

Josh looked up, and Travis stopped himself mid-thought. No, he couldn't face Josh yet.

Next, he focused on Grams. She was in her rocker knitting a sweat with a big "T" on it, praying.

"God, if you bring my sweet boy home safe, I'll donate half my fortune to charity."

The scene was too much for him to take. The thought of never seeing her or Josh again cut him deeper than Co'laf's ice blades. Centering himself, Travis decided to check in on his other (?) parents. His mother and father were both in leg and arm casts, while his father wore a neck brace. They were in the same hospital room connected to morphine drips. Though part of him regretted what he'd done to them, Travis still burned with rage at what they allowed the DMRC to do to him.

When he checked on Jenny, he was shocked to find her looking after the twins, who were crying for their parents.

"Hush, now," she said, rocking Amber as she sobbed.

"Damn it, Travis! What were you thinking? If you ever come back, your ass will be under the jail."

At that moment, a thought struck Travis, *This is all my fault. Maybe I shouldn't come back.*

Shaking his head, he raised his mental barriers and set to work, adding a dungeon and torture chamber to the Psyche Sanctorum. Next, he entered the holding cell and focused on the boxes containing his emotions. He sat there for the longest time, but nothing happened, so he gave up and tried the next day and the next until, at last, he'd done it.

In the holding cell were five birds, each a different color. He queried them each in turn and learned Wrath was a fiery-red cardinal, Despair was a blue jay, Pride was a green parrot, Love/Hope was a pink flamingo, Body was a Bald Eagle, and Mind was a grey-brown great horned owl.

With his emotions partitioned from him, Travis had super focus and calm, enabling him to train longer and harder. Yet, despite all his gains, he still hadn't freed Spirit or realized his core's full potential, so he tried a new tactic.

"Boss, you don't want to do this," Mind said as Travis strapped him to the torture rack.

"But I do."

It screamed.

Much later, after Travis had pressed, drawn and quartered, beheaded, and ripped Mind limb from limb, he was at a loss for what to do next.

"Have you tried flaying him, then dousing him with vinegar?" Oblivion whispered to him.

"Good idea."

Mind screamed when Travis tore the skin from his body. *"Boss, doing this won't get you any closer to mastering me."*

He threw a bucket of vinegar on it. "Bored now."

When Travis passed him, Prometheus spoke up. *"You one sick mofo."*

"I try."

"I can help you."

Travis scoffed. "I don't need or want your help."

"Oh, but you'll listen to the freaking devil?"

"Oblivion has been straight with me from the start. Unlike some people."

"I kept those memories hidden for a good reason."

"This conversation's over."

"I get it. You're scared to let me out 'cause ya know I'd whoop that ass."

"Nice try. But that's not going to work."

Travis had been in the cave (called Magova, |ma| |goh| |vuh|) going on a month now and had graduated to sparring with Luscinia and Co'laf simultaneously. Travis dodged Luscinia's nekli (||nay| |clee|), 'fist blade,' blocking it with his own curved wrist blade. He hooked it with his, pulling her close, and jabbed her shoulder with his left nekli.

Co'laf blocked the attack and dropped under Travis's guard. He made to stab him in the gut, but Travis backflipped in the air, blasting them with ice spears as he tumbled over. Landing, he knocked them off balance with a gust of wind, then surrounded them in a pool of lava.

"Urawo," Co'laf said, making a "T" with his hands.

Travis groaned. "I was just warming up."

"We know," Luscinia said. "Tanni (|tahn|' |knee| 'my darling'; used when referring to your significant other) and I have been discussing it, and we feel you've outgrown us."

"Can't you just increase the gravity?"

"Five times your planet's gravity, you're up to," she said, shooting Co'laf a pensive look. "Moreover, much more results, I feel you won't get. Therefore, the next phase of your training, we want you to begin."

Travis cracked his knuckles. "Which is?"

"Far more intense than us, foes and challenges the hologram-trainer can generate."

"When do you want me to begin?"

"In the morning," Co'laf said, eyeing Travis. "But speak with our son first, we want to."

"Our other son," she added, shooting Co'laf a dirty look.

Inclining his head, Travis eyed them sideways. "What do I get out of this deal?"

Co'laf huffed and crossed his arms. "Stronger you'll become. Isn't that enough?"

"No. If I agree to this, Luscinia must show me how to use and program the machines."

Co'laf inclined his head. "Done."

"Then tomorrow, you'll speak with him."

"Time for your Torin cultural lesson," Co'laf said. He pointed to the square cushions on the ground floor. Travis sat, folding his legs in his lap, and listened to the story of Pueriel (|pure |ee| |el|), the Golden Child.

~

Long ago, when the world was new and Torins still worshiped the old gods, a plague befell them. The chief consulted the mages, and they said to offer the gods a sacrifice.

They did, but the plague continued and struck the chief's son, Yahiko (|yah| |he| |koh|, 'Summer Child'). He beseeched whoever would listen to save his child. At once, a golden figure appeared.

"I am Lukarus, God of Light and Love. I will save your people on two conditions. Worship me and pay me tribute on this day every cycle. As for your son, I will save him, but he will have a cursed life. As long as he draws breath, he will never know rest from the works of my brother. Do you accept?"

"Yes, my lord!" The chief fell to his knees and kissed Lukarus's flaming feet.

"Then as it is spoken, so it is done." In a flash, he was gone, and the plague ended. The chief's son took the name Pueriel, 'Starchild,' and forever was a champion of good.

~

"Interesting story, but doesn't Pueriel also mean light of heaven and God's fire?" Travis asked, juggling fireballs casually.

"Yes, and if you studied your vocabulary more, you'd know the meaning of words in Na'iva is context-sensitive."

"Normally, I'd love learning about languages, but I have more important things to worry about."

"Hi wo Peuriel, 'Pueriel's Day,' is the most sacred of Torin holidays, and you'd do well to remember that. Speaking of which, it falls on the . . . 31st day of the tenth month of your calendar."

"That's—"

"Travis, if you can hear me, come home. Everyone's worried sick about you."

Josh?

"Thank God. Where are? Why haven't you been answering me?"

I'll explain later. Hey. Um. Do you forgive me for . . . you know?
"We can talk about that later. Come home."
"Travis, you paying attention?" Co'laf said.

He explained the situation to them and asked to leave. Co'laf forbid him, which Luscinia agreed with. Travis plowed ahead, vowing he'd let them speak to Pro whenever they wanted if they let him spend the day with Josh. After a long back and forth, they agreed.

CHAPTER FORTY

JJ slipped off his Nikes, groaning when a jolt of pain raced up his arm. He grabbed it, hoping that would help. The pain passed, but it hadn't gone unnoticed.

Dr. Dull asked him, "Are you finally going to tell me what happened?"

Dr. Dull had been asking him what really happened for weeks now, and JJ was tired of hiding the truth. He stumbled over his words, mustering up the courage to speak.

"Joshua, relax. You know anything you tell me is confidential."

JJ looked at his feet. "Travis did it."

Nodding, Dr. Dull said, "Tell me about it when you're ready."

The thought of it still struck him with fear. The look of pure hatred in Travis's eyes as he flung the wave of flames haunted JJ's dreams. "He found out I'd been stalking him and . . ."

Dr. Dull handed him a box of tissues, and JJ wiped his eyes. When he'd gathered himself, he told Dr. Dull everything. When he'd finished, JJ didn't know how to feel.

"Let me start by saying you were very brave for sharing this with me. Second, it wasn't your fault, and you shouldn't blame yourself."

"But if I hadn't stalked him—"

"Let me stop you right there. Yes, you shouldn't have done that. But That doesn't excuse Travis's actions. Powers or not, he crossed a line, and you'd be within your rights to never talk to him again."

"But I still love him!"

Sighing, Dr. Dull pinched the bridge of his nose. "I get that, but sometimes love isn't enough. Can you accept he might harm you again?"

He had to think about this a bit. Given what he'd seen, Travis could kill him a hundred times over. But love conquers all, right?

"I want to make it work between us, but I'm scared of him. What should I do?"

"I advise against rekindling your relationship. But knowing teenagers, you'll do what you want regardless of what I say."

JJ leaned forward in his seat. "So?"

"If you and Travis are to be together, then you must set clear boundaries and stick to them. And above all else, go slow. It will take time to rebuild trust. As for your fears, there're well warranted. I suggest you let him explain his actions before making a decision."

"Right," he said, and they spent the rest of their session talking about how things were going with his parents and school.

In the weeks that followed, JJ tried contacting Travis, but he'd been met with silence until a few days before Halloween.

Currently, JJ was attending Sunday service. He couldn't stop squirming in his seat, his insides buzzing with excitement—and fear. Mass was a blur; all he could think about was seeing Travis. Just thinking of him filled JJ with equal parts excitement, nervousness, and terror, prompting a boner.

Jason, who'd rode with him, nudged him. "Come on, ya perv. Time for Communion," he whispered, shaking his head and laughing with his eyes.

JJ placed his hymnal over his crotch and made his way to the altar, where Father O'Keefe gave him a knowing look. He exited the church before he went full-blush mode and died of embarrassment.

On the ride to his house, Jason ripped into him good. "Dude, how ya gonna pop a boner in God's house? Even a man-hoe like me knows that's a no-go, bro."

"Like you haven't done things a million times worse?"

"Nothing that sacrilegious."

JJ laughed. "And since when did you become so sesquipedalian?"

"What did ya call me?"

"It means someone who uses long words. Travis taught me it since dude is like a walking thesaurus/dictionary combo."

"Oh, good word to know. And FYI, while you've been up Turner's butt, I've been studying for the ACT and SAT. Your arm heal yet?"

JJ hesitated a second, wondering whether he should come clean. Taking in a deep breath, he said, "I told ya. It was a fireworks accident."

Jason shook his head. "Dude, why ya lying to me?"

"I'm not."

Jason ruffled his hair. "Are so. You always lick your bottom lip when ya lie. And you said it was from frying chicken. So . . .?"

Heat flashed in JJ's face. "I'll explain everything when we get to my house."

And he did.

"Bro," Jason said, veins popping on his forehead, "that's all kinds of fucked up. How could you still want to be with Travis after that?"

Looking down, JJ said, "I haven't decided yet whether to get back with him. I told my therapist about the situation, and he agrees I should at least hear him out."

Jason shook his head. "Still, dude, if he ever hurts you again, I'll kick his ass. Powers showers."

"Thanks, man."

Jason ruffled JJ's hair again. "Why'd ya wait so long to tell me?"

"I was afraid you'd do something stupid."

"Too late, Squirt," he said, wrapping JJ in a bear hug, careful of his arm. Then he gave JJ a noogie.

JJ laughed and wiggled out of Jason's grasp. "Watch the merchandise, Miller."

This led to a pillow fight that turned into a wrestling match.

"I win, bitch."

JJ rolled his eyes. "You only out-weigh me by like 100 pounds."

Jason lifted his shirt and rubbed his abs. "All solid muscle."

"You're such a fuckboy."

"And proud of it. Ya know you're gorgeous, right?"

JJ's world went upside down.

"You like . . . like me?"

"Yeah. You used to be an annoying little shit. Then you got hit with the puberty stick and . . ." Jason trailed his hand down JJ's chest, and JJ flinched.

"Stop it."

"Why? I'm hot, you're hot, so drop that zero and get with all of this."

"You may be cuter and have more muscles than him, but Travis has something you don't."

"What?"

"My love."

"JJ, I'm not asking to marry ya, just hookup. He's a total psycho and—"

"Who's a psycho?"

JJ couldn't believe the sight before him. What was left of Travis's clothes hung off his toned body.

"Damn, son. You got jacked," Jason said, open-mouthed.

"Josh, I need to speak to you. Privately."

"Yeah. Jason, you should go. And promise you won't tell anyone about his powers or that he's back."

Mouth hanging open, eyes wide, Jason nodded. "Yeah, we'll finish our conversation later."

As he passed Travis, he stopped and made a sour face. "Dude, you reek."

"That tends to happen when you don't have access to a shower."

Jason fanned the air as he left.

Once alone, Travis turned to JJ. "Mind telling me what I walked in on?"

"No offense, but Jason was right. You stink."

After Travis had thoroughly showered and raided the fridge, they settled on JJ's bed.

"I missed you," JJ said, running his hand up Travis's stomach.

"And I, you."

He pulled JJ close, kissing him long and hard, his hands kneading JJ's butt.

It felt so good, JJ couldn't help moaning, but Travis put a stop to things.

"What's wrong?" JJ said when he pulled away.

"Mind telling me why you told Miller about my powers?" he said, raising his voice.

"Calm down. He won't tell anyone."

"What was that conversation I walked in on?"

JJ looked down. "He sort of . . . came on to me."

"I'll kill him."

He grabbed Travis's hand. "Don't. You'll only get yourself in more trouble." Looking into Travis's eyes, JJ saw anger, but more importantly, love. And if Travis could forgive him for what he did, then JJ could forgive Travis for what he did. All doubts about their relationship left in that moment. "Besides, I told him I wasn't interested. I'm with you."

Travis's scowl softened into a smile. "Good."

Travis kissed him, then pulled JJ onto the bed, snuggling him close.

"I've missed your scent. Tanni was—"

He cut himself off and kissed the back of JJ's neck.

He turned around, facing Travis. "What did you say?"

"I didn't say anything."

"Uh-huh. You said, 'tanni wa' or something."

Travis didn't say anything for a long moment and then broke the silence with, "Tanni wa (|wah|) Pueri i ga (|gah|) Tawo (|tah| |whoa|) Da'keisai (|dah|' |kay| |sigh|). It means you are the light of my universe."

"That's beautiful. What language is that?"

"It's not important. Being here with you is all that matters."

JJ smiled and kissed him, his hands running up Travis's flanks, reveling in the sensations and comfort that came from being with him.

Travis moaned into JJ's mouth, reached for his belt, and JJ jerked back.

"Something wrong?" Travis said, looking confused.

"Yeah," JJ said, scooting away from him. "I think we should hold off on that stuff till we figure out our relationship status. For starters . . . why'd you burn me?"

Travis's eyes roved JJ's arm, where the purple burn scars popped against his pale skin. "I'm sorry. I never meant to hurt you."

With fear in his heart, JJ said, "Then why did you?"

"I felt betrayed and disgusted that you'd been lying to me all this time, invading my privacy. And when you touched me, I was repulsed and felt violated. And above everything else, I was angry that I'd trusted you. So I lashed out."

JJ didn't reply for a while as he processed things. "Do you regret doing it?"

"Do you regret stalking me?"

"Y—" JJ stopped himself. He and Dr. Dull had discussed setting healthy boundaries, and right now, Travis was trying to gaslight him. "We're talking about you and can discuss my actions later."

Travis pursed his lips. "Yes, I regret my actions. I've had a lot of time to reflect on things and know it was wrong to use my powers on you regardless of how angry I felt."

Pursing his lips, JJ voiced some of his concerns. "Putting aside your anger issues, you put your parents in the hospital, broke probation, and the government's after you. How are we gonna be together with all that?"

"I'm a teleporter. As for that other stuff, we can figure it out later. But tell me. Do you regret your actions?"

JJ smiled. "Yeah. I regret stalking you, bullying you, and not telling you my true feelings sooner. Dr. Dull said if we're gonna make this relationship work, we need to rebuild trust in each other. I'm willing to give us a second chance if you are. Though I don't know how it'll all work out with you in Gitmo."

A quiver of terror shot through JJ as he awaited Travis's response.

"Let me worry about that, okay?" he said, smiling wide.

They shared a hug, snuggled close. Travis wrapped JJ in his arms, and they lay like that, with JJ as the little spoon, until they fell asleep.

∾

JJ woke before Travis, untangled their limbs, careful not to wake him, and grabbed his phone to call Agent Anderson.

"It's me."

"There a reason you're calling me out of the blue?"

"Promise you won't freak."

Agent Anderson yawned. "Depends. Is Travis back or something?" He laughed.

"Yeah, he's sleeping in my bed right now."

"Are you joking?"

"Nope. Tell Jenny, too."

He ended the call, drained his bladder, then crawled back in bed with Travis and drifted off.

∾

"Open up! Police," demanded a gruff voice over the intercom. JJ bolted up in bed.

301

"What's going on?" Travis said, yawning and stretching his limbs.

"Police," he mouthed, then hit the intercom. "I'll be right out."

He booked it to the front door, his pulse racing.

"How can I help you, officers?"

The clean-shaven officer, hands on his hips, glared at JJ. "We got a report a wanted person was in the area, so we're conducting a door-to-door search. Mind letting us inside?"

Travis, the cops are here. Hide!

"Fuck my life. What am I gonna do?"

"Go right a—"

"That won't be necessary."

JJ looked around the officer, and Agent Anderson was striding up the driveway with Jenny in tow, clutching her medical bag.

"Who might you be?" the officer said, grimacing and sticking out his chest, hands-on-hips.

Agent Anderson flashed his badge. "This case is under my jurisdiction."

The officer looked at him and half-smiled, half-laughed. "Really? Which alphabet-soup outfit did you say you were with?"

"I didn't. Step aside."

"Or what?" The cop got in Agent Anderson's face, poking him in the chest while the other officers looked on, their hands hovering above their weapons.

"Or I'll call Madame President Paxton herself and have your ass in Gitmo so fast you won't know what happened."

They stared each other down before the cop said, "You make that with your 3-D printer? Let's see what the Captain has to say about you." He took Agent Anderson's badge and walked away. JJ looked at the retreating cop, his heart in his throat as the seconds ticked away.

The cop came back grimacing. "All right guys. Let's pack it in and let Mr. Anderson handle things."

On his way out, the cop brushed past Agent Anderson, bumping him hard.

Agent Anderson scoffed. "The nerve of some people. You believe that guy?" He did an impression of a pig.

He and Jenny entered the house, and their first question was, "Where's Travis?"

"One second."

It's safe to come out.

Seconds later, Travis appeared, clutching his head.

JJ rushed to his side. "What's wrong?"

"Too many voices in my head."

The lights flickered, the house shaking from the gale-force winds that had kicked up.

"Jenny, can't you do something?" JJ shouted over the thunderclaps.

She fished around in her bag, quickly producing a needle and a bottle of some medication. JJ and Agent Anderson held Travis down while she administered it. Windows broke as the storm outside intensified. Travis thrashed, then stilled, and all was quiet.

JJ stayed behind to clean up the broken glass while they carried Travis to the guest room so Jenny could examine him.

"How is he?" he said when he saw her a while later.

"He's resting. His pulse and blood pressure are low but steady, and from the look of his eyes, he's severely dehydrated."

"What happens next?"

"I'll get a few items from the hospital and start him on IV fluids. Then get several doses of his treatment from Dr. Hu. For now, let him rest. When are your parents due back?"

"Not till the end of the month, but they've returned early before."

Then we'll have to be on our toes, won't we?" She smiled.

He checked on Travis every hour or so until he awoke on the third day, acting as though nothing happened.

Jenny wanted Travis to go to the hospital so they could do a comprehensive workup, but he refused. At JJ's insistence, Travis agreed to check in a few times a week and have Jenny examine him and supply him with his treatment and other goodies so he could continue training. What this training was, or where it took place, he never let on much to JJ's annoyance, which he repeatedly voiced to Travis to no avail.

The night before Travis left, they spent the whole night cuddling. When JJ awoke the next morning, Travis was gone, taking a part of JJ with him. Jason denied calling the police, but JJ had his suspicions.

CHAPTER FORTY-ONE

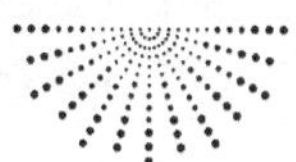

Inside Travis's mindscape, he and Prometheus faced off. Travis Popped behind Prometheus and, tongue hanging out of his mouth, blasted him into the ground with flames.

Prometheus rose, dusted himself off, and liquefied the ground, trapping Travis.

Travis formed his earthen prison into diamond armor and daggers and gave chase. Prometheus dodged his attacks, conjuring diamond daggers of his own, and they squared off.

Travis's blades clashed against Prometheus's, leaving a chip in each. Then they retreated and attacked again, repeating this pattern until their weapons were reduced to diamond dust.

"Yield," Travis said through gasping breaths.

"Nah, kid. Looks to me you're gassed AF. Give up."

Travis wiped his face. "One last battle. We hold nothing back."

"I'm game if you take off that armor."

Travis removed his armor, and they got into fae'li sparring stances, each raising one arm and grabbing the other's wrists while placing one foot forward, so their ankles touched.

They counted down, and on one – i'tochi (|ee|' |toe| |chee|), Prometheus tossed Travis over his shoulder. Righting himself in midair, Travis blasted him in the face with a blue energy beam, then kneed him in the groin. Prometheus's body hit the plateau with a *thud*.

Then he Popped above Travis and stomped him into the ground.

"Mess with the best, get wrecked." He did a victory dance while flipping off Travis until the ground around Travis exploded and shards of rock-turned-metal sliced through Prometheus.

"Nigga, that hurt."

Travis formed one of the metal shards into a Bowie Knife and Popped behind Prometheus. He cut him from ass to shoulders. Then he ripped out his spine. Prometheus clunked to the ground.

Travis smirked. "I win. And I told you not to use that word."

He stomped on Prometheus's limbs, then shattered his ribs.

"Enjoy."

~

Back in his body, Travis shook off the effects of being locked in his head. Following Travis's return to the Magova, Prometheus wanted out all the time. At Oblivion's suggestion, he and Prometheus would battle, and whoever won got control of their body. This meant Travis spent hours, sometimes days trapped in his mind, only let out to visit Josh.

He used this time well, practicing their mental abilities. He could now pinpoint minds and block thoughts at will, an unintended consequence of which was an increase of the range he could pick up thoughts and Pop.

He stood, working the kinks out of his back and legs, then took three steps and passed out, waking up in the Star Chamber. An alarm beeped, and the machine powered down.

His thoughts were fuzzy and jumbled together, as though he hadn't slept in a while. His brain was on fire. Luscinia and Co'laf helped him stand.

"What's wrong with me?" he said, fighting to stay on his feet as waves of nausea hit him. They looked at each other. She gave a command to the CPU, causing three-dimensional images to appear overhead.

"The picture on the left is of a human," Luscinia began, "and the one on the right is of a Torin. Note the smaller organs and circulatory systems," she said, and the hologram zoomed in to show the delicate blood vessels.

"This is due to our kahu'ki (|kah| |who|' |key|), our cores."

"You mentioned that before."

"Yes. It provides us with most of our energy, enabling us to go long periods with little to no food, water, or oxygen." She tapped Travis's chest. "Due to your human nervous system interfering with your Torin circuitry—the system that allows energy to flow anywhere it's needed —your core has become unstable."

Travis swallowed the lump of dread in his throat. "What does that mean?"

She rubbed his face. "Tanna, it means if you keep pushing yourself, your core will explode, obliterating most of this hemisphere."

"What about my fainting?"

"Your circuitry has been overloading your nervous system, causing the latter to shut down."

"Is there any way for you to stabilize my core?"

"Were you fully Torin."

Rage and fear bubbled up inside him until rage won out. "But I'm not! What are my options?"

"You can continue training, on the off chance your core stabilizes once your powers mature and risk killing millions if it explodes, or you can go home and spend your remaining time with loved ones."

Travis didn't have to think about it.

He would train.

First stop was the hologram trainer.

A jungle took shape, and he dashed off toward where he saw move-ment. *Smack* went his feet when they connected with the chest of the first of three opponents. Before the body hit the floor, Travis pivoted, decapitating the next with a well-placed energy blade.

The final Torin went airborne. Travis gave chase, levitating and blowing a hole through its chest. He landed, fists pumping in the air.

"Travis wins; flawless victory," he said and continued celebrating.

He plowed through the next level using a tree as a giant baseball bat and got to level five before his combination of luck, dirty tricks, and raw skill wasn't enough.

"This is bullshit," he said after his opponent knocked him down for the fifth time in less than a minute.

"You're holding back. Don't," Oblivion whispered to him.

Chest heaving with each breath, pulse quickening, Travis's vision tunneled until all he saw were the opponents before him. In a frenzy, he tore them apart, leaving a pile of bloody limbs and organs.

"Beginning next level," the computer said. Reprograming it in English had been one of his greatest achievements to date.

"Targets will increase to eight; gravity will increase to 5g. Be safe, Travis," said the computer.

When the gravity took effect, Travis fell to his knees, his chest feeling as though it would explode from the pressure.

He stood, only for his legs to give out, sending him face-first into the ground. His enemies circled him, blasting him with fire, electricity, and ice attacks. Travis Popped a few meters away to buy himself some time while he thought.

"If ya need some help, why don't you ask your bro Pro?"

I don't need your help or anyone else's. Now shut up, you motherfucking ass-licking cunt.

"Whoa, you just cussed me out in fluent Na'iva."

Travis paused and smiled. "I did, didn't I? Cool."

He severed the connection by placing Prometheus behind several mental barriers and turned back to the fight at hand. If he couldn't walk, then he'd levitate. This proved more difficult than he thought, so he resorted to lightning attacks to move them into position for his coup de grace.

Once they were in place, he skewered them with metal spikes formed from the ground, then electrocuted, burned, and froze them for good measure.

"Level complete. Would you like to continue?"

"No."

After the trainer powered down, Travis limped over to Co'laf and flopped on the ground. "I know you hate me, and the feeling's mutual. But if I die, so does your son."

"Point taken. Go on."

"Show me how to master my powers, and I promise to find a way to separate your son from my body."

"You can do that?"

"Between Luscinia and I, we should have it figured out soon enough."

"I'll agree on the condition I can speak with my son every day."

"Ahi."

That was how Travis brought Co'laf to his side. They trained for five or six hours a day under increasing gravity, only stopping so Travis could eat, meditate, and check-in with Josh, Grams, and Jenny. Then it was off to the hologram-trainer, followed by eight hours of sleep, though he only slept because Luscinia disabled the gravity amplifier and hologram trainer.

From Jenny, he learned his parents were now out of the hospital but were restricted to bed rest for the next several months until their various fractures and breaks had healed. As for the twins, Grams had elected to stay with them at their house until their parents recovered; she'd also cover their bills.

"I understand why you did what you did," she'd said when he visited her. "But you took the lives of those men and very well could have killed your parents."

"It wasn't that bad," he'd said, brushing her off.

"Listen to me." She grabbed his arm. "You can't go around abusing your powers. You were given them for a reason."

"But they—"

"I don't care what they did or didn't do. You have an obligation to help those who can't help themselves, to be a champion of good. Please, listen to the better angels of your nature."

He'd hadn't wanted to acknowledge her at first, but when Josh echoed the same sentiments, Travis was forced to accept his actions weren't as justified as he thought.

"Dude," Josh had said, "you killed people. That's villain territory."

"I acted in self-defense."

"Bull shit! You could have teleported away."

"I . . ." *Josh is right. I could have Popped to Grams or anywhere else. But I chose to kill those soldiers, and the truth is I enjoyed it.*

"Well, what do you have to say for yourself?"

Travis hung his head. "I lost my temper and allowed my emotions to dictate my actions, and now several people are dead because of it. I understand if you don't want to be with me anymore." He turned away and prepared to Pop back to the Magova when Josh stopped him.

"Travis, I love you. But you have to promise me right now you'll do your best never to harm me or anyone else with your powers, regardless of how mad you get."

"What if I have to defend myself from the DMRC or others?"

"Can't you knock them out instead of killing them?"

"Yeah."

"Then do that."

"Okay," Travis had said, but he wasn't sure he could keep that promise.

"No, no, no!" Co'laf barked through gritted fangs. "All wrong. Your abilities, your urus (|er| |us|) come from here." He pointed to his chest. "Not here." He slapped the side of Travis's head.

Massaging his head, Travis glared at him. "I'm doing the best I can."

"Urawo ka, you want to stop?"

Travis shook his head.

"Then this time, do it right. Urus aren't . . . tools. Extensions of you, a part of you they are. Again."

Co'laf had been trying to teach him how to draw energy from the surrounding environment, but each time Travis got it wrong, either drawing too much at once and overloading his core or too little, so he passed out from the effort.

He planted his bare feet in the red dirt and focused on pulling the energy from it. Picturing water washing over his feet, he smiled at the energy's caress, willing it higher. But not too fast. Modulating his breathing, on each inhale, he pulled a bit more energy, then paused with each exhale. Sweat beaded down his face, clouding his vision, but he continued until the energy made it to his chest.

He smiled, but it wasn't time to celebrate just yet. Raising his arms, he visualized the waves of energy spreading to his hands.

"Good, Tanna, ju—"

"Sshh!" Luscinia hissed.

Travis closed his eyes, imagining the energy turning into a ball as he waved his arms in a circular motion. Legs shaking, he pushed through the exhaustion that threatened to overtake him until his hands warmed, and Co'laf clapped.

"Well done. Took you long enough."

Travis opened his eyes, and a ball of green energy floated in the air next to him. He smiled and did a victory dance.

"Now uz (|ooze|) it, absorb it, and try again."

Travis repeated the exercise until he was too tired to continue. He plopped beside Co'loaf on the cushions as he explained more about Torin abilities. According to him, their powers were partially sentient, and every Torin had to win their affinity before they could unlock their true potential. This sounded like one of Josh's anime shows, but given what Travis had experienced already with Body and Mind, he figured it was worth listening to.

"Every Torin must go through the vidashi(|vee| |dah|' |she|), the battle between life and death, before their powers fully awaken."

"Then why don't we start this thing already?"

"No Torin knows the day or hour of their vidashi. Like a bolt of lightning, it comes upon them without warning, testing everything they know about themself and their powers. Fail, and you die."

Travis stared at him slack-jawed. "And it's the only way to master my powers and awaken my full potential?"

He nodded. "That was the point of all these lessons. So much time has been lost. I fear you won't be ready."

"Right," Travis said, drinking his miqua.
"Now you realize why I'm so hard on you?"
Travis nodded.

Toward the end of December, Travis's fainting spells grew worse, lasting an hour or more.

Josh asked him about it one day, but he brushed it off as tiredness. He hated lying to him, but he didn't want Josh to worry.

The night before Josh's parents were due back for New Years', Travis held him in his arms for the longest time, inhaling his scent. He didn't know why, but he had a gut feeling he wouldn't see Josh again for a while. As Josh nodded off, Travis looked at him and smiled, thanking whatever gods may be for such an awesome boyfriend.

He watched Josh sleep, planting butterfly kisses on his lips until he couldn't keep his eyes open. He scrawled out a letter and placed it under Josh's pillow. Then Popped to the Magova and rested.

CHAPTER FORTY-TWO

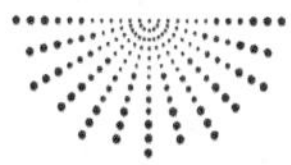

"Computer, increase gravity to 15g." Travis gritted his teeth and took one step. Then another. And another.

He broke into a run, then flipped in the air. A wave of flames rose under him, and he rode it out, then flipped back into the air. As his feet hit the ground, he called the flames to him and whipped them like a lasso.

Pausing, soaking in sweat, chest heaving, he sprinted forward. Shaping the flames into blades, he cut the air. Every atom of his body ached, yet he continued.

He brought his hands up to his chest, then pushed them outward, sending a wave of flames forth. Popping in front of the flames, he stretched out his right hand, and a torrent of water blasted the flames back as he pushed all his will into the stream.

His eyelids felt like a ton of lead, and his knees shook as he strained to hold the conflagration at bay. Normally, this wouldn't have been a challenge, but he was running on fumes. His legs threatened to give out, knees wobbling and feet slipping as the wave of fire advanced on him.

The scent of singed flesh filled his nostrils, thighs, and upper body seconds from being engulfed in flames. But Travis refused to give up.

He dug his feet deeper into the red dirt and fought through the pain, determined to succeed this time. Centimeter by centimeter, he battled back the blaze.

Closing his eyes, he dug deep, finding nothing. The fire advanced on him, burning his arms. *No. I can't give up, won't give up!* Pushing past his pain and exhaustion, Travis pictured the well opening, and new strength poured forth. At last, the water overcame the flames.

"Congratulations, young one. You've mastered me," Body whispered to him.

He smirked and laughed, limping to the Star Chamber. He got halfway there before he collapsed. Luscinia shook her head while Co'laf did a slow clap. Together they helped him the rest of the way.

After healing, he practiced the mental side of his powers: expanding the reach of his telepathy. In his mind's eye, he saw thousands of strings, but he ignored those, pushing past Earth to the farthest reaches of space when a voice popped into his head.

"Help me."

He saw a vivid image, and it was as though he were standing there.

In the next instance, Travis was on a new world. The creature before him was a humanoid lizard, and leopard-men were attacking her. *Nekoshins?*

There were only five of them, but if he didn't act soon, the lizard-woman would die.

He called forth energy whips and attacked, incapacitating the first and sweeping the legs out of the second.

With the element of surprise gone, the others attacked him at once, surrounding him. He tried accessing more energy, but it wouldn't come. Then ten more Nekoshins appeared. Travis fought as hard as he could, but they deflected his attacks as if they were nothing.

Through blurred vision, he crawled toward them, impotent as they took turns with the lizard-woman, her screams forever etched into his brain.

"I swear, you will pay!" he screamed.

They blasted him and laughed. The final insult came when, after breaking all his bones, they pissed on him, chanting, "Delbon (|del| |bhan|)."

He later learned this meant 'weakling' in Gatonese (|gah| |toh| |knees|), the primary language of the Nekoshin Empire.

Right before they delivered the death blow, Travis gathered enough power and Popped back to the Magova.

Luscinia gasped at his wounds and rushed him to the Star Chamber.

Travis opened his eyes and groaned, but the throbbing in his head wouldn't let up. Sirens sounded. The Star Chamber opened, and he crawled out. The rancid scent of the Nekoshins' urine still clung to him, and he retched. Luscinia and Co'laf tried taking him back to the Star Chamber, but he refused their help.

"Computer, priority code Alpha 173. Password: Necro Paladin." The computer acknowledged his request, and the gravity increased to 100g. Veins popped out from his skin, throbbing with each beat of his heart. As he inched forward, his skin fell off in places, but he didn't care.

He had to be stronger, whatever it took, to defeat those creatures. He took a few steps, and an explosive pain in his chest shot through him. Travis fell to the ground, shaking, and light poured from his chest. He vomited black bile, electricity arcing off of him.

The pain in his chest soared to new limits, each breath sending a million stabs of pain through his lungs. The world spun, and all Travis could hear was the blood swishing in his ears.

Then nothing.

Travis exploded, wiping out the Magova and everything in it.

However, since he'd depleted most of his energy in his fight with the Nekoshins, the explosion wasn't as powerful as Luscinia predicted, killing only Travis.

Travis woke in a golden room, feeling better than he ever had. "Where am I?"

"You are in the void between life and death," several voices said in unison.

Turning, he saw the personifications of his emotions, Prometheus, Mind Body and Spirit, and to his horror, Oblivion.

He took a defensive stance, one hand raised while the other protected his chest. "Why am I here? Am I dead?"

"That depends. You may choose to move on and become one with the cosmic Godhead, and in doing so, learn the secrets of the multiverse. Or you may go back," Spirit said.

"No!" Travis screamed, and the room shook.

Oblivion put up his hand. *"Calm yourself, child, and listen. Have I not been helping you these past weeks?"*

"Yeah," Travis said, taking a few calming breaths.

"Don't you trust me?"

"I guess."

Oblivion chuckled. *"You're as cautious as ever. I wish to discuss Joshua."*

"Don't listen to him," Prometheus and the others yelled.

Travis Ignored them, his head feeling funny. "What of him?"

"I want to make a deal. Join me, and I'll heal you."

Travis looked up at him, meeting his dead eyes. "What type of deal?"

Spirit cut in, *"You can't trust him."*

"Fulfill the prophecy, and you can have Joshua to yourself."

Could it be that easy? Against his better judgment, Travis pressed onward. "What happens to everyone else?"

Oblivion shrugged. *"Them? They die. But what's a few billion lives weighed against enteral happiness?"*

"No!"

Prometheus got in Travis's face. *"I swear to God, if you listen to him, Imma rip ya a new one."*

"Pay him no heed. We can workshop the terms of this deal later. Say yes, and we can get Armageddon started within the hour."

Vision blurring, Travis shook his head. "My answer now and always will be no."

Steepling his hands, Oblivion groaned. *"This is how you repay my kindness?"*

He roared, transforming into a giant, seven-headed red dragon. Oblivion pummeled him repeatedly, but Travis refused to stay down. He was broken, yet the others shouted at him, *"You got this. Keep fighting. When things seem their darkest, there's always hope."*

Oblivion advanced him, murder in his eyes. *"You can't defeat me. I am evil given flesh. I existed before creation and will exist long after your universe draws its last breath. Yield."*

He sank his tentacles sinking into Travis. The familiar cold sensation washed over him, and he was tired: tired of fighting, tired of life, tired of everything.

"Help me," he pleaded to them.

"Tell us, who are you?"

"Now's not the time for twenty questions."

The coldness spread further, and he struggled to keep his eyes open. *Where am I again, and why are they yelling at me?*

"Kid," Prometheus began, *"this is serious. What's your name?*

He struggled to find the words. "Travis Turner, son of Sampson and Sarah Tuner."

"No," they shouted, "that is your name. *Who are you? Say it now!"*

Travis tried to think, but his mind was fuzzy.

He wanted to give in, but Mind, Body, and the others wouldn't let him. And they were right. Travis had come too far, been through too much to give up now. *"Think boy. All your life, what have you done?"*

"I've stood out, always been different. I've tried to be better than everyone else, so their picking on me wouldn't get to me."

"No. Go deeper. Why haven't you killed yourself, even though you've thought about it more times than you can count?"

Travis shook off the mental fog. "Because they would win, and my pride won't allow that."

"Why?" they said, urgency seeping into their tone.

"I'm better than that, better than them. I've been fighting all my life to make a place for myself. And I'll be damned if anyone takes that away from me."

"Who are you? Speak it now before all is lost."

"I'm thirteen years old. How the hell am I supposed to know who I am?"

"Think, Boss," Body said. *"Forget everything that's happened. Who are you when no one's looking?"*

"I don't know. Why does this matter?"

Pain shot through Travis, and his arms disappeared.

"Time's almost up," they shouted. *"Who are you? Say it now, or all is lost!"*

"I am the sum of all those who've come before me. All their sacrifices, all their hopes, led to my being born. And I won't let their sacrifices be in vain."

Oblivion chuckled. "What are you prattling on about? "You can't win. Surrender."

Travis rose on shaky legs, his toes having disappeared. "I will fight you with everything I am. All my hate. All my doubt. All my pain. Everything!

"Not because it's easy, not because it'll win me glory or accolades, but because it's the right thing to do."

Travis remembered Jenny's, Josh's, and Grams' words about being a hero and doing right, and Luscinia's telling him what his name meant in Na'iva. In that moment, he knew the answer to their question.

"I am a warrior, champion of the innocent, punisher of evil. My name is . . . Phoenix!"

Golden light washed over him, and before him, Mind punched him in the arm. *"Took you long enough. Now let's kick his ass."*

He, Body, and the rest of the rainbow-colored birds surrounded Travis, and energy beams shot into Travis. He raised his hand, issuing forth a golden flame.

Oblivion screamed. *"You'll pay for this!"* He disappeared in a cloud of white flames, and one by one, the others congratulated Travis on completing the vidashi.

"What now?" he asked.

"You absorb us and awaken your true power," Mind said. And he did, saving Spirit for last.

"Farewell, old friend."

"You've done well. Yet, great tribulations lie ahead. When things seem hopeless, remember you are the power that endures, the strength that overcomes all obstacles. Remember who you are, and we'll never fail you. Farewell, Prince Phoenix."

Travis nodded, smiling. *I like the sound of that.*

In the instant Travis absorbed Spirit, he connected with countless people throughout the multiverse, his strength becoming theirs and theirs his. All across the world, the ground trembled and cracked, long-dormant volcanoes erupted, and tidal waves inundated cities. The heavens themselves broke open as the Magova and everything in it reformed.

Travis's tomb became the womb of his rebirth, his palingenesis. His wounds instantly healed, and untold power radiated from him. Luscinia and Co'laf looked on, shock and awe all over their faces.

"Tanna, are you okay?" Luscinia asked him.

"Ahi," he said, nodding at her. "I've completed vidashi."

Co'laf gave him the once over and did a slow clap. Luscinia's scans confirmed his core was not only stable but three times its previous size.

Travis felt a million times better, but his ego was still bruised from his defeat at the hands of the Nekoshins, and he would rectify that matter immediately.

Cracking his knuckles, he Popped back to the Nekoshins.

May God have mercy on their souls because he wouldn't.

Riding high on the power coursing through him, Travis paid the Nekoshins a visit. The soldiers burst into laughter when they saw him. His hatred boiled over, and when he struck, white tentacles bursting from him, and he tore apart two of the ten.

The rest fled, but he wouldn't allow that. He gave in to the hunger for blood, and at once, he heard Oblivion whisper in his ears to let go. He did.

His hands turned into disfigured claws, and his teeth became like daggers. Sprouting more tentacles, he decimated his enemies. Their limbs strewn around him, Travis wallowed in the carnage. His spine tingled as their blood met his tongue. Enthralled, he ripped out their hearts, devouring them whole.

"More!" he said as his hunger mounted. He ripped another in half, laughing as its blood washed over him. It felt divine and tasted even better.

However, he hungered for something more.

For what, he didn't know.

As if waking from a dream, Travis saw what was left of the Nekoshins and vomited. Images of what he'd done flooded him, and he retched until there was nothing left.

How could I have done this? No. It wasn't me. It was Prometheus. This is all his fault. Damn him and his alien abilities. I never asked for this. Get out of my body!

Unspeakable pain coursed through him, body ripping asunder atom-by-atom. He looked down and saw he now had four arms and legs where two had been. A jolt of pain shot through him. When it passed, Prometheus stood before him, identical to Travis save for his red hair, green eyes, and lack of burn scars.

They glowered at each other. Then Travis dashed forward. He landed a kick to the head and followed up with a left jab to the gut. Prometheus Popped behind Travis, blasting him with a wall of flames.

Travis didn't even feel it, and they squared off again, the wind blowing hair in their eyes. Blow-for-blow, they were evenly matched until Travis gave in to his blood lust again. He sprouted fangs and talons, then came the tentacles, thick as tree trunks.

Prometheus dodged, but he was now no match for Travis. He covered his face when a battle-axe appeared on the ground; taking hold, he swung it as Travis charged him.

When it connected with Travis's tentacles, an explosion hurtled them through the air.

Travis laughed and sent more tentacles, skewering Prometheus in place. His body went limp.

Travis formed an energy blade and struck, but before he made contact, a portal opened, and two green monsters stepped through and captured him in a net of purple energy. He fought, but in the end, they dragged him through the portal.

~

"Hey," JJ said to Cody as he signed in for the youth drop. He could hardly believe two months had passed since Travis had vanished without a word. At first, he'd cried himself to sleep, and his grades tanked. Then he frequented Affirmations more often and found being around other LGBTQ+ teens like himself helped take the edge off things.

They'd play games, watch movies, and once a week, he presented his poems at their writing group. He'd learned a lot about writing and expressing himself from them.

Tonight, they were making stained-glass pride flags. He laughed at Nicky as they tried to spell supercalifragilisticexpialidocious. They were big on Marry Poppins ever since Cody screened the movie a week back.

Slowly, JJ was learning to live without Travis, and though he missed him at times, he was starting to like himself more with each day. Dr. Dull had told him to use this time to find himself and explore. And that's what he's doing.

"Hey, JJ. A group of us are going to Leo's Coney Island. Wanna come with?" Cody asked, showing off his flawless teeth.

"Yeah," JJ said without hesitation, shocking Cody. Over these past weeks, JJ was slowly learning he didn't need Travis or anyone else to be happy. So wherever Travis had gone off to, it wasn't JJ's problem. He'd continue focusing on himself. Because, to paraphrase the words of Gloria Gaynor, "He will survive."

They clowned around as they ate, laughing and telling inside jokes. And when Cody asked for his number, JJ gave it to him without second thoughts. They made plans to hang, and JJ was excited for the first time since Travis bailed on him.

CHAPTER FORTY-THREE

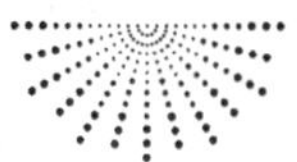

Travis found himself in a desert with volcanos in the distance when they exited the portal. His survival instincts kicked in, and he tried Popping back to Earth but only managed to free himself from the net. He caught the monsters off guard, skewering them with his tentacles, and dined on their flesh and souls, inhaling the white balls of light into his mouth.

All of his senses heightened, and he smelled something good up ahead and took off in a run, tearing through chimera, manticores, and other creatures that stood in his path. He continued until he found himself in a tropical jungle full of iridescent plants and strange beings that looked like rejects from a bad SYFY movie.

They carried swords and spears that had glowing runes on them and were dressed in armor with monstrous faces on them, alive and contorting in pain. They advanced on him, and he attacked, ripping them apart, savoring the taste of their blood and feasting on their souls.

He tore through them until someone said, "That will be enough of that."

Red eyes aglow, Travis turned toward the voice. A man with lavender hair in a ponytail with makeup on held a lone white rose in one hand. He sent Travis a condescending look.

Dessert. Travis unleashed his tentacles on the interloper. The man raised an earthen shield and dodged. Travis's tentacles struck the shield, crumbling it. The man laughed, wagging his beringed finger. Then he blew on the rose. A vine grew with enormous thorns, and he fired them off like bullets.

Travis waved his hand, and the thorns rebounded, impaling those who hadn't the sense to get out of the way. His opponent hissed, then slammed his hand into the ground. Roots sprang up, encasing Travis as the man disappeared in a cloak of shadows.

He reappeared with a bracelet covered in gems and precious stones etched with runes like those on the creatures' weapons. He wiped some of the white blood from his wounds onto it, and the bracelet glowed red.

He placed it on Travis, and Travis stilled, his mind clearing and the blood lust leaving as the bracelet took effect.

"Where am I, who are you, and why am I imprisoned?"

"Child, you killed several of my vassals, but we'll speak of repayment later. I am Lord Abraxas (|uh |bracks| |us|), King of Rose. And were it not for me, you'd be condemned to the life of the strigori (|stree| |gore| |ee|), mindless animals that live only to kill."

That's nice," Travis said and torched his way out of the cage.

"That's not possible. The bracelet should have bound your demonic powers. Unless . . ."

"What?"

"Nothing, boy. Come with me. There is much you must learn."

"I don't think so." Travis formed a sword of flames and leveled it at Lord Abraxas.

The king frowned and began chanting at a rapid pace. When he was done, he'd knocked out Travis and imprisoned him in a cage of brambles.

∼

Travis awoke with a headache in the bramble cage.

"You're up. Welcome to The Palace of Desires."

324

"Where the hell is that?"

"There is much you must discuss, boy."

"The name's Travis Turner."

He Popped out of the cage and blasted Lord Abraxas with every-thing he had, but the Calvin Klein model wannabe flicked his wrist, and pain shot through Travis's body.

"What did you do to me?"

"A simple spell that you will learn in due course. However, consider this your first lesson. When you aim for the king, don't miss."

He flicked his wrist, and another wave of pain shook Travis.

"Welcome to Pandemonium. Do try not to let that tongue of yours get you killed."

Lord Abraxas strolled away, leaving Travis writing in the air.

And thus, we've reached The End of this chapter in Travis's tale . . . but his story is far from over.

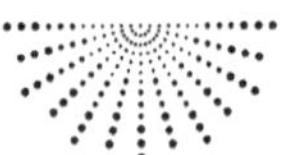

*P*ro fell to the ground and said, "Fuck me," when he saw more Nekoshins had arrived and were out for his blood. He closed his eyes and tried to Pop home but passed out instead.

"Come on, wake up."

He opened his eyes, finding himself on a bed next to an eight-armed bipedal dog creature in a high-tech hospital.

"Is the neural-com operational?"

"Yeah. So what do you think he is?"

"Hard to say. He looks almost Torin, but they went extinct ages ago."

"Well, whatever he is, he's awake. Prep him for his first fight."

Pro turned his head and found a gelatin creature in front of him that reminded him of Cookie Monster. It turned, opening its mouth, but the sounds came out like the badly dubbed Kung Fu movies Travis and Josh loved so much.

"Alright, newbie, listen up. The furballs did a number on ya, and the cost to fix ya up wasn't cheap. Until further notice, you'll be working off your debt to the boss as his newest prizefighter. Drink this."

He handed Pro a cup of green liquid the consistency of molasses. It burned going down, but afterward, he felt wide-awake.

"Yeah, Mido (|me| |doh|) packs a punch. Just be careful you don't get addicted to the stuff."

He nodded and followed Gelatin Man, who explained how things worked. All fighters were charged room, board, and any expenses incurred fixing them up. If they won, they got a cut of the prize money.

"Now you can bet on yourself. Long as you don't get greedy. The fastest way out of here is to go pro and get your debt — out by a —"

"What was that?"

"Never mind. We're here. Good luck."

Pro looked out at the audience, and his jaw dropped. Creatures he never imagined stared back at him. Some had hundreds of eyes, while others were covered in rainbow-colored hair. What stopped him cold was the giant rodent he was to fight. The thing looked like a gerbil, only it was green and stood thirty feet tall.

No sweat. I got this.

Then it fired lasers from its massive eyes.

"Crap."

"Don't worry, newbie. Stick and move, and you'll be fine." Gelatin Man said from the safety of the stadium's force field.

"Creatures and creat-ettes, put your appendages in the air, if you have them, and give a welcome to the newest fighter out of Flan's stable. From parts unknown, making his first, and maybe only appearance in the Slaughterhouse. Give it up for the one, the only, Catatonic Kid."

The crowd roared and stood, or floated in some cases, from their seats, and the match began. The Giga Gerbil roared as the force field holding it turned off, and it bolted for Pro. He popped behind the behemoth and sent a wall of flames, but the Giga Gerbil shrugged it off and roared. Then it blasted him into the corner with its eye lasers.

Pro dusted himself off, marveling as his wounds healed instantly. "Well, ain't you a big one? Boss up, bitch."

The beast galloped forward, its four huge legs *booming* as it ran. Pro waited until the last possible second to sidestep it.

It hurtled past him, losing its balance, and crashed.

Seeing his chance, Pro hopped on its back, wrapping energy whips around its neck. The Giga Gerbil bucked him, but he held on, imitating a bull rider to the cheers of the crowd. But it shook and rolled on its back, trapping him.

"Folks, it looks like Betty's claimed another victim," the announcer said.

The crowd booed until Pro burst through the Giga Gerbil's chest. He called forth his axe, and with one swing of it, a blade of golden energy severed the Giga Gerbil's head.

The axe disappeared, and Pro, covered in green blood, soaked in the cheers.

"Good job. They love ya. Keep this up, and you'll be out of here in no time. Now go wash up; you stink. And pro tip: you can't use that axe of yours unless the rules say, or you'll be dis—la—ied."

"What?"

"Neural-com must be on the fritz again. Never mind," Gelatin Man said and showed him to his cell and explained how the sanitation units worked. Pro waved his hand over the washing station, causing a stream of pink liquid to come out. After he lathered up, the liquid turned into a gel, then hardened and fell off, leaving him clean.

A few minutes later, Gelatin Man appeared and showed him to the cafeteria. The entrees came in as many colors and forms as they were stars in the sky—soups, sandwiches, casseroles, wraps, and what he suspected were giant maggots. The only thing he dared eat were bluish drumsticks, which he piled high on his plate and dug in.

"Mmm, mini-gitauros (|ghee| |tour| |ohs|). Nice choice." Gelatin Man sat beside him, snagging a drumstick off his plate.

"What?" Pro asked, drumstick halfway to his mouth.

"Sorry. That thing you fought? Those are its smaller cousins. We breed em for food. Where ya from?"

"Don't suppose ya heard of Earth?"

"What crap name is that for a planet? Now Drac'con (|drack|

|khan|), there's a name for a planet. Homeworld of the Hebin (|hay| |been|), by the way. Dirty fighters they are. Smelly, too, but so would I if 'n I lived on a dust ball."

"Are you done?"

"Sheesh, newbie. I was just tryna school ya, but I can take a hint."

Pro sighed and finished off dinner. He didn't care if he was eating gerbils; it tasted delicious, and he went for seconds and thirds.

Then he wondered, *Should I try Popping to Earth?* Ultimately, he decided to wait until he had a bit more control. He didn't want to mess around and teleport into the middle of space.

Speaking of control . . . he wondered how that psycho Travis was doing. The next time they met, Pro was legit wrecking his shit.

IT GETS BETTER

If you or someone you know is thinking of harming themselves, know you matter, it gets better, and that help is available.

thetrevorproject.org and itgetsbetter.org are suicide crisis sites geared towards LGBTQ+ youths.

suicidepreventionlifeline.org and 1-800-273-8255 are general suicide crisis resources within the US.

A list of suicide crisis hotlines by country: https://en.wikipedia.org/wiki/List_of_suicide_crisis_lines

ACKNOWLEDGMENTS

First and foremost, I want to thank Charlie Knight, my amazing editor; without their insightful guidance, this book wouldn't be half of what it is today.

Second, I would like to thank The Mad Hatters, my first writing group at Affirmations. Without their encouragement I would have never pursued writing this book.

Third, I want to shoutout Mychelle Martin of the Auburn Hills Writer's Group, whose kind words and advice gave me the resolve to keep going with this project when I lost faith in myself.

Fourth, I want to thank my cover designer Rocko Sigolon for listening to me ramble about my WIP and translating that verbal diarrhea into an awesome cover.

Last, I want to thank you, the reader for taking a chance on me. I hope you've enjoyed this book, and that it has left you better for reading it.

AFTERWORD

Now that you've read this book, I hope you've enjoyed it. I'd be grateful if you reviewed it and joined my mailing list at tyeronejohnson.com/mailinglist

ABOUT THE AUTHOR

An elder millennial, Tyerone Johnson was raised on a steady diet of anime, comics, video games, sci-fi, fantasy, and horror movies. He lives in suburban Detroit, where he writes about complex queer people of color who save the world with panache.

When not writing, he enjoys listening to music, watching random videos on YouTube, drawing badly 😂, reading, gaming, and using the Oxford comma.

He can be reached at his website: tyeronejohnson.com, on Facebook (@TMJohnsonAuthor) and facebook.com/TMJohnsonAuthor), or on Twitter (@silentbutcuddly)